SAFE
CRACKER

SAFE
CRACKER

A GRANTCHESTER "DUKE" DUCAINE THRILLER

JESSE DeROY

**UNION
SQUARE
& CO.**

NEW YORK

**UNION
SQUARE
&CO.**

NEW YORK

UNION SQUARE & CO. and the distinctive Union Square & Co. logo
are trademarks of Sterling Publishing Co., Inc.

Union Square & Co., LLC, is a subsidiary of Sterling Publishing Co., Inc.

Text © 2024 Ezekiel Boone, Inc.

ISBN 978-1-4549-5559-7
ISBN 978-1-4549-5560-3 (e-book)

Library of Congress Control Number is available upon request.

For information about custom editions, special sales, and premium purchases,
please contact specialsales@unionsquareandco.com.

Printed in Canada

2 4 6 8 10 9 7 5 3 1

unionsquareandco.com

Cover design by Faceout Studio, Tim Green
Interior design by Kevin Ullrich
Cover image by: PixelSnap/Shutterstock.com

For Teo.
Love You.

1

THE FIRST TIME I KILLED A MAN, I was eleven years old.

My sister and I had been raised by a thief to be thieves ourselves. Maybe if our mom had lived, things would have been different. But she didn't, and they weren't. Our dad brought us up as if he'd won Wimbledon and his mission was to mold his children into the greatest tennis players of all time. Except, instead of spending our childhood with rackets in our hands, it was lockpicks and Glocks.

And it worked.

By the time I was eleven, I could crack safes, bypass alarms, plan a heist, shoot equally well with both hands, and hold my own in a fight against a grown man. Ginny, who was fifteen months older, could do the same. But better.

The job we were on was a total milk run from start to finish: no guards, an outdated security system, and a safe you could have opened by breathing on it. It was really a one-person job, but part of Dad's training regime was to bring us along when he could. He had every reason to expect it would be a clean heist. The fixer was an old friend who was in a bind, and even though Dad hadn't seen him in probably two decades, they'd been close once. Dad thought he could trust him.

He was wrong.

We were in southern Portugal, near the border with Spain, which doesn't really matter, except that it was far from Los Angeles, where we lived when we weren't working or on vacation. Everything had been arranged from a distance, and it's possible that the friend didn't know that Ginny and I even existed, but we were supposed to meet him with the statue we'd stolen at an old seaside fort. A simple exchange: he gave Dad a flat-rate fee, Dad gave him the statue—it was small, neatly packed away in a foam-lined, hard-sided travel case—and the friend pocketed whatever the difference was between what he was paying Dad and what the person who had commissioned the job in the first place was offering.

Ginny and Dad were waiting on a low stone wall. I was messing around on the rocks. I don't remember what I was doing—I was eleven, so it was probably something dumb—but I was out of sight.

When I scrambled back up, I saw a very pale man holding a pistol on Dad and Ginny. I knew that Dad had an automatic in a shoulder holster, but it was under his zippered jacket. Ginny was carrying a SIG Sauer holstered in the small of her back. Their hands were up and empty. Dad's old friend had clearly gotten the drop on them. Easy to do when you thought you could trust somebody.

I was in the man's blind spot. I saw my dad's eyes flicker to me and then back to his old friend's face.

The sun was out, but the wind came cold off the water. I was wearing a light jacket that didn't do much to keep me warm, even with the Kevlar vest underneath, but I had a little five-shot snub-nosed revolver in my pocket. I took it out. I was at a twenty-degree angle behind the man, enough so that I could shoot him in the back without worrying about hitting my sister or Dad. I raised the pistol slowly.

When we weren't working, Dad had us practice shooting five or six times a week, two hundred rounds with each hand. I'd probably fired a quarter million rounds in training by then. I was a natural righty, but at twenty-five yards, I could shoot a two-inch grouping with either my left or right hand. Even though the revolver I was holding was made for close-up work, this would be like shooting fish in a barrel. Except it wasn't a fish.

It was a man.

And while I was standing there, trying to get myself to shoot a man from behind, he fired first, two quick shots into my dad's chest.

His gun flicked up.

I recognized what was happening even before I processed it: Mozambique drill. Two to the body, one to the head.

I'd done it thousands of times on the range in close-quarters firearms combat training. The Mozambique drill—or "failure drill" depending on who's teaching it—was a natural response to body armor or to the fact that it was possible to shoot somebody in the body twice and still manage to miss anything vital. Two quick shots to the chest to slow your opponent for a beat—center mass, the easiest target—and buy yourself the chance to aim properly for the much smaller and more difficult—and final—shot to the head. One, two, and then three, done.

And I saw the man shoot my dad one, two, and in that short window of time before three, I understood what was about to happen, and that I had no choice if I wanted to stop him from killing my father.

I shot the man in the back of the head before he got a third shot off.

He went down hard. I ran past him, trying not to look at the dark, wet cave in his skull. Ginny was already kneeling over my dad by the time I got there.

He was gasping and clawing at his chest. Ginny pushed his hands aside and unzipped his jacket so she could work the straps on his bulletproof vest.

"You're good," she said, a note of relief in her voice. "The vest did its job. Neither bullet went through."

"Ribs," he said, still trying to catch his breath. "I'm okay. Deal with your brother."

Ginny looked up at me. She shook her head. "Stop crying, Duke. It's done. Dad's fine. Get over it and grow up. We don't have time for you to be a baby."

I wiped at my eyes and my nose with my sleeve. Ginny held out her hand and I gave her the revolver. She climbed down to the rocks, scrambled over to the water's edge, and threw the pistol as far as she could into the ocean.

Dad, in obvious pain, slowly pushed himself up with one arm until he was in a sitting position. His other arm was clamped across his ribs.

"Next time," he said to me, "don't hesitate."

He knew I hadn't wanted to pull the trigger.

And he knew there'd be a next time.

2

I WAS ON MY WAY to break open a safe when the phone rang.

Blocked number.

Back when I was a full-time criminal, a blocked caller ID wouldn't have stopped me from picking up, but since I've gone on the narrow, one of my rules is that I don't answer calls unless it's a phone call I'm expecting.

People in Los Angeles like their blocked numbers the same way criminals do. But none of my friends would have blocked their number, and I figured if somebody was trying to reach me about a job—a *legal* job—and I didn't pick up, they'd leave a voicemail.

Rule number one for my new life: stay clean.

I used to have a lot of rules when I stole for a living, except I thought of them more like guidelines. Ginny, who was a bit more classical to my jazz, used to make fun of me for my improvisations, even when they worked out. As an adult, she'd become exactly the thief our dad had trained us to be: think through every possible angle before the job, make a plan, stick to the plan. The rules were the rules, and you kept with them no matter what your gut was telling you.

I should have stuck to the rules.

Maybe if I had, my dad wouldn't be in a federal prison and Ginny wouldn't be in a coma. Just dumb, bullshit luck that other than a bullet scar, I walked away clean.

Since then, I've been trying to stay out of trouble, even if it felt unnatural to earn money without stealing; I'd been raised to be a criminal. But I'd been an honest-to-god civilian for close to two years now. Legit work only. I was still opening safes, but I was doing it for people who *wanted* them open. Mostly simple lockout jobs. Mom-and-pop stores when they forgot the combo, showing up for home-owners when they discovered a long-forgotten safe behind the walls during a renovation, a few installations, and, when I could get it, consulting work for businesses that wanted to stop people like me from breaking in. It was piecemeal, and it was a grind.

Whoever said crime doesn't pay never worked a day job, because if you do it right, crime pays really, really well.

Working straight meant I had to take what I could get, however, which was why I was on my way to open a safe—a standard, totally un-felonious estate job—even though it was a Saturday afternoon, and even though my surfboard was in the back of my truck and the waves were solid while still being small enough that I could handle them.

But Saturday meant I could charge my emergency hours rate, and I desperately needed the money. And by desperately, I mean *desperately*. As in, if I didn't have at least twelve hundred bucks by the end of the day I was going to get a harsh lesson courtesy of my bookie, Paulie Lashes. Aunt Paulie. My father's sister.

I looked at the phone again. Maybe it was Paulie calling. *She* always called from a blocked number. Maybe she was calling to tell me I could have an extension. But I doubted it.

You'd think Paulie would go easy on me *because* she's my aunt, but she's made it clear to me that her being my aunt is precisely the reason she can't go easy on me. I'd had dinner with her last Sunday, and that had been three weeks in a row that I hadn't been able to come up with the full vig. She explained what would happen if I missed it again this week.

"You know how it is," she said, spearing a piece of chicken on her fork. "If it looks like I'm letting you off the hook, people will think I'm going soft and try to take advantage of me. But this way, people will say, 'Did you hear what she did to Duke when he didn't pay? And he's her *nephew*! Can you imagine what she'll do to somebody who *isn't* related to her?'"

She passed me the bottle of wine, a sauvignon blanc that paired well with the meal, and said, "It's bad enough being a woman in this business. If I get a reputation as a softy, I'm done. I need people staying awake at night, sweating about getting me every last dollar I'm owed. But I'm serious, if you want to wipe the books, I've got a job for you that will more than—"

"No. I'm done. Ginny—"

"Enough, Duke," she said, cutting me off. "Ginny will recover, or she won't. What's done is done. Move on."

"I have," I said. "I'm out."

Paulie took a sip of her wine and considered me. "How long are you going to punish yourself, Duke?"

"As long as it takes," I said.

Paulie nodded. "Okay. I can't say I agree with you, but you're not a kid anymore. You want to quit, you can quit. But if you miss another payment, I'm going to have to make an example out of you. Reputation is everything, and like I said, it's worse because I'm a woman. Sorry, Duke, but pay up, or I'll have my guys *start* with your thumbs."

Honestly, it was a pleasant dinner except for the interlude where she was threatening me with bodily harm.

But as much as I didn't want any of her goons working me over, she had a point, particularly about the difficulty of being a woman in her position. My aunt had her finger in a lot of pies. She wasn't just my bookie. That was more of a side business. Mostly, she was known as a shot caller, a fixer, and a fence, and keeping up her reputation meant everything. Except she already had enough of a reputation that most of the criminals on the West Coast were afraid of her, and the ones who weren't afraid of her just hadn't met her yet.

Some of the stories about her are urban legend territory—she did not personally dangle Michael Caputo off the roof of the Staples Center by his ankles and then drop him because he was five dollars short on a three-thousand-dollar debt—but I do know for a fact that the rumors about Teressa Farro are true because I was in the helicopter when that infamous incident happened.

And I can confirm that when Donny the Bear tried to screw over Paulie for her commission from setting up the Montgomery job, Donny's hands were found in a dumpster in Sacramento.

Donny's head was found in a gym locker in Cleveland.

There are twenty-four hundred miles between Cleveland and Sacramento, but as far as I know, none of Donny's other body parts showed up in between the two cities.

I looked at the phone as it kept ringing.

Maybe it was Paulie. Maybe it wasn't.

But assuming it was Paulie, she *could* have just been calling to invite me over for dinner—she takes her role as an aunt as seriously as she takes her job as a bookie—but then again, there was the whole "late on my payment three weeks in a row and working on four" thing. I didn't want to answer a phone call from Paulie until I had money in my hand, and I was just around the corner from my client's house. With my weekend rates, I'd make enough to buy me another seven days of grace before Paulie's goons broke my thumbs.

Probably. Hopefully.

I liked my thumbs.

I wondered if I could surf with broken thumbs.

I stuffed the phone into my pocket and let the call go to voicemail. Maybe it was just somebody calling me about another safe they couldn't get open.

3

THE CLIENT WAS STANDING in the driveway of his deceased father's house, leaning against his sleek, low-slung convertible and tapping his immaculately loafered foot. I hadn't even gotten out of my truck, and I already wanted to punch him. He was wearing starched dress pants and a collared polo shirt that was a size too small to hide the paunch starting to gather around his waist. He pointedly looked at his watch, as if him tapping his foot wasn't enough for me to know he was annoyed I was late.

"Sorry," I said. "Traffic."

I was lying.

I was late because Meg had offered to take me to lunch. She'd originally been my sister's friend, but since Ginny's accident, Meg had pretty much become my best friend. Meg was generally badass: she was my hand-to-hand combat coach, taught surfing a few mornings a week even though she was good enough to have gone pro, and worked the rest of the time as a sort of fixer and unofficial private investigator. Meg was like the other, mostly legal side of the same coin as me and Ginny. I wasn't in the position to turn down a free meal, but lunch with Meg was always worth making time for, because despite our friendship, we had an on-again, off-again romance; I was half in love with her.

I closed the door of my truck as the client gave it a skeptical look.

Fair enough. My Taco—a Toyota Tacoma—had nearly two hundred thousand miles on it. It was still running strong, but it had a lot of rust and even more dents and dings, most of which had come with the car, but a few of which were my fault. I drove it hard, on-road and off-, and it was perfect for what I used it for: hauling tools when I was working, carrying surfboards and camping gear when I wasn't. Even if I could have afforded a nice car with fewer miles on the odometer, it wouldn't have suited my new life as an honest citizen. I needed a work truck, and more importantly, I liked being able to get out of LA sometimes; surfing trips to Baja meant a certain amount of rutted dirt roads and driving on sand. I didn't have to worry about babying my truck.

The client sighed. "I've already spent nearly two grand on three different locksmiths, and they all said to call . . . you."

"Well, yeah. Your assistant told me the safe's a Henshaw 40. Most locksmiths aren't going to be able to open it at all, and even if they could, they'd trash it in the process. That safe is worth a lot of money if you decide to sell it."

"Not as much as the collection inside," he said smugly. "I've already got a buyer lined up for both. But it's time sensitive. How long is this going to take? I've got better things to do with my Saturday." He shook his head, not even bothering to pretend that he was more upset about his father's death than about the inconvenience of having to wait for me to open the safe.

What a dick.

I glanced at his car. It was a McLaren. It looked like a rocket ship and easily cost him as much as a three-bedroom house in Omaha, Nebraska. He was one of those white guys who might have been athletic once upon a time but had gotten rich enough that nobody bothered to point out that his best days were behind him. His hair was combed like it was running scared, and he kept conspicuously glancing at his Rolex. I recognized the model: it was a gold Sky-Dweller with an oyster bracelet and white dial. I'd stolen a Sky-Dweller during a heist in Japan when I was a teenager. As far as high-end watches went, it wasn't a supernova, but it was still worth more than my truck would have been even if it had been brand-new. I'd sold my Sky-Dweller—along with practically everything else I had of value—just to get my gambling debts to the point where I could *almost* manage the weekly vig. The only things I had left to sell were my tools and my kidneys.

"Come on, I'll show it to you," he said curtly, turning without waiting to see if I was ready to follow him.

He took me in through the four-car garage, past a Lexus, a Mercedes, and a Honda minivan. The fourth spot was empty. At least my client's father had been a little more subtle with his wealth. Not that those three cars were shabby, but even in Los Angeles, driving around in a three hundred and fifty thousand dollar McLaren made you look like a douchebag.

There was a separate room at the back of the garage. A workshop. About half the size of the garage, which meant it was still big. The workshop was immaculate, with a place for everything and everything in its place, but I could smell the faintest hint of sawdust and gun oil.

Which was why I was there.

According to my client's assistant, his late father had been a gun collector. High-end stuff. You'd be surprised at how much people were willing to pay for a shotgun. And he'd kept that gun collection in a Henshaw 40.

The safe was bigger than some New York City hotel rooms. No way to fit something like that through a doorway. They would have had to bring it in and then build the workshop around it.

They were hard to notice, but there were tool marks on the corner of the door. No locksmith would be dumb enough to think you could just pry open a Henshaw 40 without damaging it. Clearly my client had given a go at opening the safe himself. Found a crowbar and a hammer in his dad's workshop, decided it couldn't be that hard. One of those masters of the universe kind of guys who thinks he's capable of anything. If somebody like me, driving my crap-box truck could crack a safe, how hard could it possibly be?

He might as well have been trying to open the safe with a marshmallow.

4

I STOOD IN FRONT OF THE SAFE. It probably looked like I was studying the Henshaw 40, but I wasn't. I was staring at a small hole in the drywall to the side of the safe. The kind of hole that might be left behind by a thumbtack.

Which almost certainly meant the old man had just kept the combination on a slip of paper thumbtacked to the wall. Spend a fortune on the safe, leave the combo right out where anybody can see it. Shockingly common. It must have fallen off the wall at some point.

"So?" the client said. "How long? Like I said, I've already wasted close to two thousand dollars on you locksmiths."

"That's your problem right there," I said.

"What?"

"You hired locksmiths. I'm not a locksmith."

He looked at me like he'd just found a dead fish in the back seat of his McLaren. "What the hell do you mean you're not a locksmith?"

"A locksmith cuts keys, unlocks your car if you accidentally lock yourself out, and maybe, if they are good, can open a decent safe, the kind you buy to protect documents, or small amounts of cash, or some hunting rifles. But like I said, none of them are going to be able to open a Henshaw 40. Not without rendering it inoperable. A dermatologist is still a doctor, but you don't call one for a heart transplant."

I leaned in and knocked on the door of the safe. Then I spun the dial and leaned in even more, pretending like I was listening for something. "I'm not a locksmith. I'm a safecracker. Bring a locksmith in if you want, but you'll *still* end up calling me and paying me because none of those other locksmiths can unlock this safe."

"And you can?"

"Yep," I said. "But it's a weekend, so my rate is time and a half." I'd already quoted his assistant double my normal rate, which was *already* double the normal rate of most locksmiths, because, hey, it was a Saturday. If it weren't for the whole thing with my aunt threatening to have one of her goons teach me a lesson, I could have been out surfing with Meg.

The client looked irate. "Time and a half? Give me a break."

I couldn't help myself. "Time and a half. Plus tax."

He gave me the entitled rich guy look at the "plus tax" line, and said, "I'll pay cash for a discount."

Which was fine with me. It might make me a poor citizen to avoid paying taxes, but cash is king when you've got to pay a bookie. A check meant depositing it into my bank account—adding to the hefty balance of thirty-eight dollars and change currently in there—and then having to wait until Monday or Tuesday for the money to clear. Cash was immediate. The one concession Paulie made to our relationship was that she gave me a serious break on the points, but even after liquidating everything I had to try to get my debt to a manageable level without going back to stealing, I still had to come up with cash every week just to keep treading water.

I felt my phone buzz in my pocket, ringing again. Instead of pulling it out, I looked down at my hands and wriggled my thumbs.

I really didn't want to have one of Paulie's goons break my thumbs.

Forget working or even surfing, how the heck was I supposed to go the bathroom with two broken thumbs?

"Fine," I said. "Cash and we'll skip the tax. But I'm not cutting my rate." I had my pride.

"I call any other locksmith in town, and they're a quarter the price," he said, almost sputtering.

"True," I said cheerfully, "but you've already called every locksmith in town. They don't charge as much as I do, but then again, you're already out two grand and that doesn't seem to have gotten you anywhere."

"How long?"

"I could do it in five minutes if it wasn't a gun safe and you didn't care if I trashed it," I said. "But this safe is worth a lot of money if you want to sell it. Way more than you'll pay to have it opened without destroying it. Not that it matters anyway, because it *is* a gun safe. In my experience, that usually means there are things inside that might react poorly to the more invasive ways of getting in. So even if you didn't care about selling it, we'd be looking at more like four, four and a half, minimum. Probably more."

"Hours?" He puffed up like a little dog in front of a big bone.

"That's correct. Hours," I agreed. Did he think I was quoting him weeks? "At time and a half. But hey, you're paying cash, so there's no tax." I tried to keep a blank face.

For a second, I thought he was going to tell me to leave, and I panicked, because I really did need the money. And my thumbs.

I blurted out, "Are you a gambling man?"

He positively lit up at the question. I figured he would. He had the kind of avarice and entitlement that made him believe he was naturally lucky. He assumed that as a matter of course he'd win whatever bet I was about to propose.

"What's the bet?"

"That it takes me less than three hours. Three hours at my Saturday rate—let's call it fifteen hundred dollars even. And we're still talking cash. I'm betting it takes me less than three hours to open the safe. You're betting it takes me longer than three hours. No matter how long it takes, you pay fifteen hundred. If I win, I come out ahead, and if you win, you save however much I would have billed for the overage."

I could see the dumb look of greed in his eyes as he did the math and thought about how long the locksmiths who'd already tried had worked on the safe. The look got brighter as he figured out how to tilt the odds even more in his favor: "If you can't open it, I pay nothing?"

"Deal."

We shook on it, and he left. I was pretty sure when he walked out of the room he was grinning.

I sure as hell was.

5

IT TOOK ME SEVENTEEN SECONDS to open the safe.

I'm good at what I do. Maybe the best. I'd lied through my teeth to the client: three hours was a ridiculous amount of time. I'd figured it would take me five minutes, maybe ten minutes if one of the locksmiths who had tried earlier had jammed anything up, but nobody, and I mean nobody, is "crack a Henshaw 40 safe in seventeen seconds" good. To open any kind of UL-RSC-rated safe in seventeen seconds without explosives or other violent means is impossible, but sometimes a little luck—like finding the combination written down on a slip of paper—goes a long way.

For the past few years, I'd been in short supply of the good kind of luck. The only luck I'd had was the kind that has the Steelers' kicker doinking the football off the goalpost on three separate extra point attempts in the same game. If he'd made just one of those tries last week, I'd have covered the spread.

But you can't win if you don't gamble. Sometimes luck is on your side, and sometimes, even when it's not, you can manufacture your own luck.

The room was well organized, but packed full. Aside from the safe, there was a workbench with gunsmithing tools, handloading equipment for ammunition, firearm cleaning supplies, a vise, and other assorted tools. The other two walls were lined with shelves stocked with rubber tote bins and toolboxes, a mix of woodworking equipment and a few other esoteric things I didn't recognize but that looked expensive and mechanical. The client's father was serious about his guns. Or, he had been. The workshop had that feel like somebody hadn't used it in a long time, and I wondered if the old man had gone quick or if he'd been sick for a while.

Either way, somebody had been keeping it clean, dusting and straightening. And I assumed it was that person who'd accidentally knocked the slip of paper with the combination off the wall.

As soon as the client left, I dropped down to my belly. Sure enough, there was a scrap of paper about the size of a fortune cookie slip under one of the shelving units. I fished it out, stood back up, looked at the combination, and then opened the safe. Seventeen seconds of work for fifteen hundred dollars. It was positively criminal.

I was just dusting myself off when the client came walking back into the room. He had already started speaking but cut himself off when he saw the open safe. He looked at me blankly, and then blurted out, "I'm not paying."

"We had a deal," I said.

"Bullshit. That was too quick. I'm not paying."

"Okay," I said. I closed the door to the safe and locked it. "Good luck."

I walked past him and was already in the driveway by the time he caught up with me.

"Sorry," he said. "I overreacted. Come back in and open it up again."

I shrugged. "Cash first."

He hemmed and hawed and sputtered for a few seconds, but his heart wasn't in it. "Fine," he said. "Wait in the library. I'll get the cash."

The library had a pair of leather couches, one of those old-world globe things that opened to be a bar, and a professional-quality billiards table already racked up for a game of nine-ball.

I leaned against the pool table and twiddled my thumbs. Twelve hundred dollars of the cash would go to Paulie to buy me another week's worth of breathing room from her goons, and three hundred dollars would go in my wallet. Maybe I'd see if Meg wanted to get dinner somewhere fancy. And I'd still start tomorrow with some walking-around money. Even if I didn't get to go surfing, all in all, it was a good Saturday afternoon. For the first time in a long time, I was ahead.

The client came in and counted out the money in hundred-dollar bills on the rail of the pool table.

I looked at the cash. I looked at the client. I looked at the pool table. I looked at the cash again. It was a nice stake to work with, and I already knew he was a gambling man.

"You play?" I asked.

6

I GOT INTO MY TRUCK, clenched the steering wheel, and screamed. Then I screamed again.

My phone rang. Blocked number. Again.

I closed my eyes and tried meditative breathing. It did not make me feel any more peaceful about the idea of Paulie having my thumbs broken. Or any happier about having had the money in my unbroken and fully functional hands and then gambling it away.

I opened my eyes and started the truck. My phone rang once again, but this time, I answered it. "Come on, Paulie. I've got until tonight," I said. "I'll have the money."

"Is this Grantchester Ducaine?"

Huh. It was not, in fact, my aunt. Which gave me some concern. Did that mean she'd already sent her muscle after me? Technically, I had until midnight to pay this week's interest on my debt, but it was quite possible Paulie had set the dogs on me early in order to teach me a lesson.

Paulie was big on lessons.

I pulled out of the driveway.

"Duke," I said.

"Pardon me?"

"I go by Duke."

"Of course." A pause. "I've got a job for you."

It was a man on the other end. It was hard to pin an age on him based just on his voice, but he sounded serious. Official.

I knew what that meant. He was either a cop or a fed.

"Not interested," I said, and then I hung up.

There weren't a lot of upsides to working with the police. They took forever to run invoices through the system, they spent the entire time on a job looking over my shoulder, and then when I was done, they always tried to figure out a way to arrest me for some job I'd pulled in the past. Feds were worse than cops. And cheaper too.

My rule might have been to take any legal job that came my way, but working with law enforcement left me feeling conflicted for other reasons as well.

Like my dad.

Besides, it wasn't like the government paid cash, and by the time I did get paid, I'd be lucky if I only had a pair of broken thumbs.

The phone rang again, but I didn't even bother with it. I just dumped my cell in the center console and pulled out of the driveway.

It was only when I was already on the highway that I realized I was being followed.

7

THEY WEREN'T TRYING TO BE SUBTLE. It was a big, black American SUV with tinted windows. It was unmarked, but after the phone call, I didn't need a car like that to have writing on it for me to know it was government issue.

There was a part of me that wanted to try to lose them, but even for me that seemed like a dumb idea. Aside from the fact that my truck was broken down and slow with brakes that were a fifty-fifty proposition at highway speeds, these guys clearly knew who I was and how to find me. If they could find me at a job on a Saturday afternoon, they could find me at home. Losing them now just meant they'd show up again later, likely in a foul mood. Not that feds were ever in a good mood. Plus, there was no guarantee they wouldn't show up at a more inconvenient time. And while they clearly weren't local cops—I had enough issues with the LAPD, thank you—I was pretty sure that running from Uncle Sam would cause me more trouble than even I could get out of.

The phone rang yet again, and I answered it for a second time.

"Fifteen minutes," he said. "Give me fifteen minutes."

"Not good timing," I said. "I'm a little pressed for time." Which was true. I wasn't sure how I was going to hustle up the money to pay Paulie this week's vig, and I didn't have a lot of time to figure it out.

"I'll pay you. Just to talk."

The car immediately behind me changed lanes, and the SUV pulled in behind me. I could see a hard-looking white dude in his early thirties driving. The man on the phone was in the passenger seat. He was Black and looked mid-forties, and he was wearing a jacket and tie and a pair of sunglasses. He tipped his sunglasses at me as I looked at him in the mirror.

"Cash?"

"Sure," he said. "How about a thousand bucks?"

The lord taketh, the lord giveth. And Duke asketh for more.

"Fifteen hundred," I said.

He laughed. "A hundred dollars a minute. Fine."

"Next exit, follow me for a few blocks. The Market House. It's on the left."

I took the exit, keeping it nice and slow and signaling my turn in plenty of time. As long as I was going to let them follow me, I figured I might as well make it easy.

I had to make a left turn through traffic to get into the parking lot of the Market House, and I waited a minute with my turn signal on until the timing was right. There was a good gap I could have turned through, but I waited an extra beat, making it impossible for them to ride my tail into the lot. I saw the driver of the SUV say something that I assumed was not complimentary.

It was juvenile, but it would buy me a minute or two inside before they came in. Enough for what I was hoping for.

I backed into a spot—an old habit that had served me well on more than one occasion when I'd needed to make a hasty exit—and then hesitated. I might not have pulled a job in nearly two years, but that didn't mean that my past wouldn't come back to haunt me. I had a Glock 19 chambered with 9mm rounds under my seat, but also, my possession of the pistol was only kind of sort of mostly legal.

I left the pistol under the seat and went inside.

I hadn't been to the Market House since early summer, but as I'd hoped, Mimi was working her regular shift.

She saw me and greeted me with her usual enthusiasm.

"You owe me money, you piece of shit," she said. She stabbed an empty bottle of beer toward me like it was a knife. Thankfully, she was behind the bar. Otherwise, she might have used a real knife. She was feisty like that.

During a break with me and Meg last year, Mimi and I had dated off and on for a few months. Mostly off. It had ended because I borrowed fifty dollars and never paid her back. Also, I accidentally slept with her sister after a night of drinking. The accidentally was on my part; her sister was deliberate about it. They were identical twins with an extremely complicated and unhealthy relationship. Something to do with something one of them had done in high school that had escalated. My dad was a single dad and a career criminal who brought me and Ginny up to follow in his footsteps, but Mimi's family made mine look like the Brady Bunch in comparison.

"You and everybody else. Listen, I need a favor."

"I hope you eat broken glass and die on a toilet full of blood, Duke."

"That's a reasonable response," I said, "but I'm going to have two suits following me in here in a few seconds. Feds."

"FBI?" She grimaced.

"I don't know. Some kind or another. They're paying me good money just to meet with them, and I'll pay you back as soon as we're done. In the meantime, can you get a few pictures of them for me?"

"You're an asshole," she said.

"True, but these are feds. Puts us on the same team, doesn't it?"

She gave me something that passed for a smile, which I took as a willingness to help me out. Honestly, we weren't a bad couple except for the part where we fought all the time. And the thing with Miranda.

Again, though, not my fault. Not exactly. By the time I'd figured out it was Mimi's sister, things were well underway. I don't think anybody could have blamed me for soldiering on. Well, other than Mimi. She definitely blamed me.

"You mind bringing a beer over? I want to get seated so I can see them come in."

She shook her head, but there was a real smile now and a twinkle in her eyes. Just because she threatened to stab me didn't mean the chemistry was gone. I'm a decent-enough-looking guy: a shade under six feet, dark hair with sun-bleached highlights from surfing, and I train hard to keep in shape. Mixed martial arts, yoga, running, mostly focusing on functional strength. According to Mimi, I "fill out a pair of jeans nicely." Mostly, though, I like to think it's my natural charm.

I was just lowering myself into my chair when the pair of feds came in. They looked the part. Shiny suits, cheap ties, the bulge under their arms. They were both unremarkable. If I'd had to describe them to a sketch artist, I would have bored myself to death.

I'd taken the outside chair on my side of the table. My back was against the wall, one of those rules that had been drilled into me by my dad. The Black guy saw me immediately. He stopped to say something to Mimi, and then they came over.

The two of them sat down, and the Black guy said, "Mr. Ducaine—"

"Duke. Like I said on the phone. I go by Duke."

"Sorry. Duke."

"My dad was a fan of John Wayne." That usually got at least a weak laugh, and every once in a while, somebody would take it way too seriously and try to convince me that, no, the nickname "Duke" was because of my last name, not because of John Wayne. I mean, seriously?

The Black guy smiled with his lips closed, but the white guy didn't seem to get the joke. Blank stare from across the table. The white guy looked at the Black guy and then back at me again.

I tried, "John Wayne? The Duke?"

The white dude didn't know what I was talking about. He was a decade younger than the other guy, close to my age, so maybe that was it.

The other guy said, "I'm Baker. This is my partner, Cleary."

"Let me guess," I said. "You've got a job for me."

Mimi came over carrying three beers. A local microbrew hefeweizen for me and two Coors Lights for them. She put the bottles on the table and then waited, hovering.

Cleary looked at her, irked. "What?"

"Twenty-six," she said.

"Twenty-six what?"

"Dollars."

Baker laughed lightly. Evidently, he was the charming one of the two. "How about we start a tab. We might be here for a bit."

"How about you pay right now?" Mimi said. "I don't know you, but if you're stupid enough to drink with Duke, I don't trust you to run a tab. Cash on the barrel."

There was just the thinnest sliver of hesitation before Baker laughed and pulled out his wallet, and in that sliver, I saw something hard and dangerous on his face.

Sharp teeth, ready to bite.

8

"FIFTEEN HUNDRED DOLLARS," I SAID.

"While I have my wallet out, do you want me to show you my ID?"

I laughed. "You guys might as well be wearing windbreakers. You're either FBI or the other guys."

Baker shook his head. "We're not FBI."

Mimi was back at the bar. The stereo was playing early Springsteen, and there were barely ten other people in the Market House, so we had all the privacy we could want.

Baker counted out thirty fifty-dollar bills and handed them over. It was the second time today I'd earned salvation, and this time I was determined not to gamble it away. I resisted the urge to make the bills disappear in a flashy fashion and simply shoved the money into my pocket.

"That buys you fifteen minutes," I said, "but I can already tell you I'm not interested."

"But you're here, talking."

"No. *You're* here talking. I'm here, taking the United States government's money and drinking a beer that you paid for. Like I've already said—twice now, I believe—I'm not interested. Not sure how you're missing that. But thanks for the cash."

The white guy, Cleary, leaned forward, grabbing the edge of the table, his face twisting into a snarl. "Listen, you—"

Baker touched Cleary's forearm. It was instant. The attack dog called off.

"It's a quick job. Three days max, including travel. And we're offering twenty thousand dollars," Baker said, "on top of the fifteen hundred I just paid you."

I stood up. "Gentlemen, thank you, but I am *definitely* not interested."

Twenty thousand dollars would solve almost all my problems. I could pay off the bulk of my gambling debt to Paulie, I could . . . well, that would eat up pretty much the whole twenty grand, plus the fifteen hundred he'd already given me, with maybe just enough left over for a visit to a taco truck. Still, it would mean that for the first time in a while I wasn't playing catch-up. I could get ahead of the curve a bit. Give me a chance to make some good decisions.

But twenty thousand dollars was also the biggest, reddest, flashing warning sign of all time. A klaxon might as well have been blaring in my ear. There was no government job on earth that was going to pay me twenty thousand dollars for three days' work. If I wanted to go on the wrong side of the law again, I could find a dozen jobs in that price range before breakfast, but the government liked to be righteous about everything, *especially* their rate of pay. If they were offering that much, it had to be something extremely dangerous, and that didn't sound appealing. I'd had my fill of exciting jobs, and it was only through incredible luck—maybe the only good luck I'd had in my entire life—that I wasn't in prison with my dad. Or dead.

Or that I didn't end up like Ginny.

There was a reason I'd gone mostly straight.

"I know what you're thinking," Baker said. "No way we'd offer that much money unless it was something dangerous."

"Reading my mind."

"No, Duke, I'm telling you, this is the safest job you'll ever do. Like wrapping yourself in bubble wrap and falling onto a mattress. In, out, twenty grand for less than seventy-two hours of your time. It's risk free, but it requires discretion. The kind of discretion that doesn't come with paperwork."

"We'll pay in cash," Cleary said.

"Really?" I said. "Is that what no paperwork means?"

The tension in Cleary's neck made me wonder how long it would be until this guy gave himself a coronary. Or until he decided to beat me to death. For whatever reason, he'd taken an intense dislike to me.

Maybe it was because I'm an asshole.

Baker gave me that smile of his. There was no hint of the shiny danger I'd seen a few minutes ago. I wondered if I had imagined it.

"How about you hear me out," Baker said. "I paid you for fifteen minutes of your time, and unless you want to give me the money back, you still owe me at least ten minutes. You might as well finish your beer. Plus, twenty thousand dollars is just my opening offer. I have room to negotiate."

God help me, I sat back down.

9

"FOR OBVIOUS REASONS, I'm not going to tell you what's in the safe," Baker said, "but here's a picture. Can you open it?"

He took a sheet of paper out of the inside pocket of his suit coat. I caught a flash of gunmetal and a ballistic nylon holster under his arm. He unfolded the paper and put it in front of me. I looked at the photograph printed on the paper.

"Is this the actual safe and location?"

"No. Different location. But it's installed in a similar fashion, with open access to the front, both sides, and the top, and it's the exact same model of safe."

It was an American Castle Galaxy Nine. They ran more than a half million dollars retail. Except you couldn't buy them retail. This was not the kind of safe you kept in the back of a mom-and-pop convenience store or in some suburban business park. This was the kind of safe that you bought if you absolutely, positively didn't want somebody getting at whatever it was that you wanted locked away.

I pretended to think for a second, staring at the paper. When I looked up, I said, "I'm guessing you already know what kind of a safe this is, and you understand that it's not the sort of tin can that just anybody can open. If it was, you would've used one of your own boys."

Cleary poked the picture with one of his fingers. "Can *you* open it or not? We're in a hurry. Quit wasting our time."

I noticed a little dirt under his nails. I wanted to bend his finger back until it broke.

"Quit wasting *your* time? You're the ones who wanted to talk to me."

Baker took a sip of his beer and then said, "So?"

"Can I open it?" Given the two suits in front of me, I was betting that this steel box wasn't full of just jewelry.

"Yeah," Cleary said. "Can you pop it open?"

"You don't just 'pop' open an American Castle Galaxy Nine," I said. "There are maybe twenty safecrackers in the world who could open one. And none of them work for the government. Probably fewer than twenty. Shirlene Van can do it for sure, and I know Tomaz Brug has done it, and Ginny . . ." I stopped for a second. I hadn't meant to say Ginny's name.

I could see Cleary stewing. He looked like a little kid about to throw a tantrum because he'd been told that the restaurant was out of ginger ale. But Baker. He looked like a man who knew where the good booze was kept.

I continued, "Look, most safes aren't designed to keep people like me out. They're designed to keep, well, people like *you* out. People who don't know what they're doing. Or burglars, or snoopy kids, or your wife, or your maid, or your father-in-law. People keep cash or jewelry in them, they keep financial documents, guns, homemade porn. I mean, even with cell phones and the internet, you wouldn't believe the amount of homemade porn people keep in safes. But you buy a safe for a few thousand dollars, you aren't keeping *me* out. You aren't keeping any halfway decent safecracker out. All you can hope for is to slow a professional down. Sometimes for a few minutes, sometimes for a few hours."

I tapped the piece of paper. "This safe is different. This is going to keep almost anybody out. But not me. Opening a Galaxy Nine is like creating a painting that's going to hang in a museum. You're not hiring a safecracker for a job like this. You're hiring an artist. And to answer your question, yeah, I can open it."

"But?" Baker was relaxed in his chair. He took a long pull of his beer.

"But twenty grand gives me pause. Heck, even the fifteen hundred you gave me just to talk with you is a warning sign. It means you're not telling me something. Sure, you need an artist to do this, and the list of people who can open one is darn short, but it's still an hourly rate kind of job. Artists tend not to have security clearances and government jobs. But even with my normal rates, which are way above standard locksmith rates, at most, you're talking three or four thousand dollars, maybe five at a stretch. You've clearly done your homework, and you've got to know that coming in and offering me twenty thousand dollars makes me hesitate. Even with a day of travel on either side plus expenses on top of that, the amount of money is . . ."

"Sorry," Baker said. "I should tell you the full parameters. It's not just about opening it. Has to be nondestructive entry. No drilling. No explosives."

"Again, doable. And it would take longer, but only a couple of hours," I said. "The math for an opening offer of twenty grand still isn't there." I crossed my arms. "And to be clear, I sat back down because you said you've got room to negotiate. So, sweeten the offer and then tell me, what's the catch?"

Baker smirked but had that charming twinkle in his eye again. "Thirty grand. But you need to do it so that nobody knows we've ever been there."

"You want me to open a Galaxy Nine, close it up again, and leave no trace?"

"Correct."

"Oh. In that case," I said, "no."

Cleary frowned. "No, what?"

"No, I can't open it and then close it back up so that nobody knows I was ever in there."

Baker nodded. "You'll have a ten-hour window. Can you do it in ten hours?"

"I can't do it in ten million hours," I said. "Nobody can. Don't get me wrong. That money would go a long way for me right now, but to open and close a Galaxy Nine without anybody knowing you did it? That's impossible. I can't do that. Not for twenty thousand dollars."

"I'm already at thirty thousand," Baker said.

"Fine. I can't do it for thirty thousand dollars."

I was absolutely bluffing. I was gambling I could get him to go up.

BAKER KNEW I WAS BLUFFING, because he asked, "You can't do it because it's impossible, or you *won't* do it for thirty grand?"

I didn't say anything, and he took a sip of his beer before continuing. "I thought you were the man who can unlock anything," Baker said. "That's the reputation you've got. The thing you did in Albuquerque three years ago? In and out in sixteen minutes. Our guys said it should have taken you at least six hours, and that the way you did it was technically impossible."

I couldn't stop myself from grinning. It *was* technically impossible, but that was just a technicality. "I've never been to Albuquerque," I lied.

"And the all-nighter you pulled for the LAPD last year?"

That one I was proud of. I had gone legit by then, so I needed the money, but that was a job I would have done for free. I'm not normally a friend of the police, but the guy they were after was into kiddie porn. "Took them six months to get around to paying me for that job, and they *still* haven't wiped out the parking tickets."

"They call you 'The Man Who Can Walk through Walls.'"

I didn't say anything. The actual nickname was "The Ghost Who Walks through Walls." I had another nickname too: "The Duke of Pain." I'd earned that one after I started tracking down the men who'd hurt Ginny. I wasn't finished with that task, though. I'd hit a dead end. Literally. But there were still at least two more people that I needed to find and even things up with: the fixer who'd lined up the job, and the person who had commissioned it in the first place. I had the name for the first, Janus, but no location. For the other, the client, the person who had made the decision that it was cheaper to try to kill me and Ginny than to pay us, I had nothing.

Sooner or later though, I'd figure it out. If I could track down the fixer, Janus, I could make him give me the name of the client.

And then I'd kill them both.

11

BAKER MUST HAVE SEEN that he was going somewhere dangerous, because he offered his soft, fake smile again. The smile that said "buy what I'm selling."

Baker said, "If anybody can do it, it's Grantchester Ducaine."

I didn't bother correcting him on the name thing again. The truth was I *could* get in and out of an American Castle Galaxy Nine without leaving a trace. And I could do it in less than ten hours.

The problem was that Galaxy Nines were airtight and pressurized with argon gas. As soon as the seal was breached, the pressure sensor went off. Triggering the pressure sensor sent an alert out via a cell signal. That wasn't a big deal—you could easily block a cell signal and erase the call history—but the safe also had a counter that logged all openings. Any kind of pressure breach added a number to the hard count, and there was no way to reset the counter without destroying it. As soon as the pressure dropped, whomever it was who owned the safe would know somebody had been in there.

Plus, anybody who owned a Galaxy Nine likely had other security precautions. And I wasn't dumb. If it was imperative that I get in and out without a trace, there would be serious blowback if I screwed up.

It wasn't worth it. Which is what I told them.

"Money talks, but there isn't enough money to drown out the voice in my head saying this is a bad idea," I said. I clearly was not averse to taking a gamble, but this was a colossally bad idea. Which hadn't stopped me before, but this payoff wasn't worth the risk.

"I can offer you something more than money."

"A coupon for free frozen yogurt?"

Cleary was obviously impatient, but Baker seemed to be enjoying himself. He tapped the table with his finger and said, "Time served."

"What?"

But I knew what he was talking about.

Time served for my dad. He was less than two years into an eight-to-twelve at a federal prison. And the only reason he was there was because after I screwed up, while I was still in the hospital, he'd been rushing to get to me and Ginny. It was just a fluke that he'd gotten pinched, the wrong place at the wrong time, but that didn't make him a free man. And it was on me.

Baker's offer changed the equation. A bet I wouldn't make at two-to-one or three-to-one odds was suddenly showing up at forty to one. Hard to resist.

"Time served," I said. "And he's out today, by the end of the day."

"Time served," Baker countered, "and he's out the minute you finish the job and get home. You can pick him up yourself on the way back from the airport."

I squinted. I didn't like the sound of an airport, but it was probably better for me to be working somewhere other than my own backyard. "Fine," I said, "but double what you're offering. Sixty grand. I'll take the twenty you opened with now, like a down payment. The rest when we're done. Plus expenses. I'll need to get a bunch of equipment. Some of it's kind of esoteric. Probably another ten grand or so for that."

"Deal," Baker said. He reached into his jacket again and took out a thick envelope. "Here's the twenty."

That made me nervous as hell. Why hadn't he argued or said he needed to check with his boss? He offered up my dad's release and then agreed to sixty thousand like it was nothing. I had the feeling that I could have asked for six *hundred* thousand and he wouldn't have blinked.

"Start writing a list of what you need," Cleary said. "Forget expenses. We'll take care of getting everything. You're wheels up in four hours."

"Wait, what?"

"That's part of what we're paying you for," Baker said. "We've got a tight window. If you'll pardon the phrase, time is of the essence. I hope you have a valid passport," Baker said. He reached into his pocket yet again—I was starting to wonder what else he was carrying in there—and put a printed boarding pass on top of the envelope of cash. It was for a flight out of LAX, booked for Grantchester Ducaine. Business class.

Switzerland.

I had mixed feelings about the country. I was seventeen and Ginny was almost nineteen the first time we went to Switzerland. Dad had been working a job in Liechtenstein and he'd dropped us off in Zurich to steal a diamond necklace as a sort of test of our training. Ginny and I made a stupid bet with each other over who could snatch the jewels the fastest. We'd gone back together a few times after that, a mix of work and vacation, and we'd both liked the country. But my last trip to Switzerland had been solo and all business: I went to Bern to kill one of the men who'd hurt my sister. That's when the trail had gone cold.

"You know I've got a phone," I said. "I don't need an actual paper ticket."

"Sorry, but you do need a paper ticket. One of the conditions is that you aren't bringing your phone. I suppose you could have gotten your boarding pass at the airport, but hey, I had a printer." He gave me his charming smile again. "We're flying separately from you, but Cleary will meet you at the airport when you land. We drive from there."

Neither the fact that they'd already bought me a business class ticket—and, thoughtfully, printed it out—nor the smile reassured me. I felt my phone buzz and risked a glance over at the bar. Mimi winked. She'd sent me the photos she'd taken of Baker and Cleary.

I said, "Where are we going after Switzerland? Driving distance from Zurich, obviously, but do I need to pack a parka, or should I plan for sun and sand? And is it just the safe, or am I going to need to deal with anything else? Can I assume you'll have some basic tools on-site, or should I bring everything?"

"You aren't going to bring anything," Baker said. "It's not just your phone. You're leaving *everything* behind except for your passport. Like Cleary said, if you need it, we'll get it for you. Everything. Including a parka. Or a swimsuit. In and out without a trace. You're traveling light. No tools, no gear. Get on the plane with nothing but what you're wearing, your ticket, and your passport. Leave your phone at home. Buy a paperback at the airport if you want something to do on the plane. Everything you bring with you other than your passport gets thrown in the trash as soon as you land."

"How am I supposed to buy a paperback if all I'm carrying is my passport and ticket?"

Baker laughed—it seemed genuine, this time—and said, "Pay cash." He took out his wallet, snagged another fifty-dollar bill, and put it on top of the envelope with the twenty thousand. That made a total of $21,550 dollars in cash so far. At this rate, I could retire soon.

"And here," Baker continued, handing over a business card that was blank except for a phone number. "Use this number if you need to reach me in the meantime. Now give us your list and we'll make sure it happens."

I shrugged. I preferred working with my own tools but trying to get safecracking and lockpicking gear through airport security was always a hassle. I didn't like the idea of leaving my phone behind or working with somebody else's tools, but for a legal, government job paying me sixty thousand dollars and my dad's freedom, I'd fly barefoot and naked.

"Tell me what you've got to have," Cleary said. "I'll make sure it's ready for you when we land. And don't forget anything. If it's not on the list, you aren't going to have it. We're not going to be able to just run out to Home Depot and pick up a spare of something."

I picked up the envelope full of cash with the fifty-dollar bill on top. I had to resist opening the envelope and counting the money right there at the table.

It must have shown on my face because Cleary scowled at me. "It's all there."

"Don't worry. I trust you."

We all knew that was a lie.

I started making my list.

12

THE CLOCK WAS TICKING when I left my apartment. I'd spent thirty minutes going over my list with Cleary, and then gone directly home. Aside from grabbing my passport—I kept it in an old dial lock Top Shelter wall safe that I'd salvaged off a job a few years ago—I had a few errands to take care of.

I called my dad on the way to Ginny's care home.

If I just wanted to chat with my dad about the weather, I could do that during visiting hours or when he called me, but there were other ways to get in touch with him that were outside the purview of the Department of Justice's Bureau of Prisons. Plus, the utter bullshit required to talk on the phone with an incarcerated person is staggering. Aside from the predatory pricing of private companies charging fees that would make Aunt Paulie blush—frankly, it used to be much worse in state and federal institutions, but it's still part of the baked-in cruelty of city and county jails—there was always a scarcity of phones, limited availability, and the assumption that everything you said was monitored. Of course, like everywhere else, cell phones had become ubiquitous in prison. Unauthorized contraband, but ubiquitous, nonetheless.

I was pulling into the care home parking lot when he called me back.

"I'm headed out of town. Three days. Four, max, with travel," I said. "I'll be black." Unreachable.

I could hear men yelling in the background. Nothing portentous, just the sound of a soccer game in the yard. They had a rigorously organized soccer league that ran quarterly and was in the middle of the playoffs. I had twenty dollars riding on one of the teams.

"You're working?"

"Not like that," I said. "It's a government job."

"What a waste," he said.

"Do we really have to relitigate this?"

There was a sudden burst of noise on his end. Cheering. A goal. Neither one of us spoke for a few seconds.

Finally, without apologizing, Dad said, "What's the job?"

I told him. He asked a few questions about the American Castle Galaxy Nine, but Ginny and I had long outpaced him in technical abilities, and he didn't have much to offer. And when I told him that part of the deal was that they were offering him early release, he grunted.

"This goes against everything I ever taught you. If it sounds too good to be true, it usually is. What's in the safe that they're willing to dangle releasing me from prison as part of the deal?"

A small, orange hatchback pulled into the staff portion of the care home's parking lot. A man dressed in nursing scrubs got out and walked into the care home. I didn't recognize him. He must have been new.

"It doesn't matter," I said. "I'm just there to open it for them. It's straight contract work."

"I didn't raise you and Ginny to—"

"Yeah, well," I said, cutting him off, trying to ignore the scorn and disappointment in his voice. "Ginny's *here* because of me, and you're *there* because of me, and . . ."

He was quiet for a bit. Then he said, "You're with Ginny?"

"In the parking lot. About to go in. I wanted to see her before I left. Then a quick stop to see Paulie, and from there to the airport."

"Paulie told me that you've been late on your payments."

That one sentence was loaded with a lot of meaning. He knew what I'd gone through to clear my original debt. The job I'd convinced Ginny to pull with me—bypassing our dad and working with a fixer we didn't know—to try to dig myself out without Dad knowing, and then how I'd more or less had to sell everything I owned after the debacle that ensued. And he knew that after nearly six months of being almost smart, I'd started betting again. The money I owed now was nothing compared to what I'd had on the books two years ago, but the difference now was that I had nothing left to sell. Twenty thousand dollars might as well have been twenty million. Except that Baker had shown up and offered me a "get out of jail free" card. Literally.

"I've got it under control." I had the money to pay off Paulie in my pocket. A fresh start. I'd be out from under the debt, and I'd do it differently this time. I wouldn't make another bet. I'd make good decisions. I'd swallow the drudgery of opening cut-rate safes, rekeying locks, and installing alarm systems. I wasn't too proud to do honest work.

He started to say something, but a buzzer went off in the background. He said, "I've got to go, kiddo. Good decisions, okay? And give Ginny a kiss for me."

GINNY LOOKED LIKE SHE WAS SLEEPING. She always looked like she was sleeping.

Because it was a long-term care facility, it was significantly more peaceful than the intensive care and the step-down units at the hospital. Her autonomic nervous system still worked fine, and her swallow reflex kept her airway clear, which meant she was able to breathe on her own. The whiteboard on the wall showed that the nurse had just finished with an hourly check. Even though she didn't need to be monitored every second of the day, an entire army of people tended to Ginny on a regimented basis: toilet care, regular vital checks, cleaning her, moving her to prevent bedsores, feeding her, physical therapy to limit muscular atrophy. Paulie insisted that Ginny also get a haircut and a manicure every few weeks as well, something my sister had liked before she was injured; Paulie wanted to make sure Ginny was treated like an actual person who might wake up one day, not just as a patient.

Not that she could tell the difference, but I'd tried to make Ginny's room at the facility feel like it was *her* room. I'd replaced the generic watercolor of a sailboat on the wall with an original painting from Ginny's apartment that she'd bought in Barcelona and hung two others that I knew she liked. I filled her dresser and closet with the clothes from Ginny's own dresser and closet and insisted that the staff use her clothing, so she wasn't only wearing a hospital gown all the time. Sometimes I brought her a cup of coffee and just left it on the table next to her with the lid off, thinking that maybe she could smell it. And in the same way, when I visited, I talked to her, asked her questions as if she could answer, told her stories as if she was listening.

I wanted to make sure she knew she wasn't alone.

Like I was.

14

SHE WAS MY SISTER, and my partner in crime, but she had also been my best friend, and I was hers. It had been that way from the beginning. It sounds corny, but it was true. Almost all the pictures of us from when we were kids were of the two of us *together*. We just *got* each other. And I don't know if that would have changed if Mom hadn't been killed by a drunk driver, but after it happened, when I was seven, Ginny and I turned in toward each other. We both made real friends as we got older, but as kids, there wasn't a lot of space in our lives for people who weren't part of our family.

For better or worse.

After I killed the man in Portugal, Dad decided we should take what he called a sabbatical. We holed up in Salamanca, Spain, for a few weeks until his ribs healed, and then we just traveled for fun for about six months. He kept up with our training and schooling—he hired tutors wherever we went so that we could get a proper education, though some of the tutors he hired specialized in less savory matters than geometry and grammar—but mostly, he said, it was just a chance for us to see the world. A well-earned vacation.

We never talked about what had happened at the stone fort by the ocean. The wet cavern of the man's head.

I turned twelve partway through our travels, and at some point, a few weeks after my birthday, there was a day where I was just feeling sulky and tired, and I didn't want to go do whatever it was Dad had planned that day.

I'm not sure what it was he had lined up, and I'm not even sure exactly where we were. Somewhere in North Africa. Marrakesh or Tunis or Algiers. Dad didn't try to get me to tell him what was bothering me, but even if he had, I was either too young to understand, or too young to explain it to him.

I think I convinced myself that it was simply that I missed my mom.

She went into her marriage with her eyes open, but even though she took the Ducaine name, she wasn't interested in the family business. After she died, Dad did his best. Ginny and I both knew we were lucky to have him, but he had to be our dad *and* train us to follow in his footsteps at the same time. He needed us to be able to operate ruthlessly when necessary. I might have only been eleven when I killed the man who was supposed to be Dad's friend, but it wasn't like I'd made a choice. I'd done the only thing I could do.

From Dad's perspective, there was nothing to think about, nothing to linger on, nothing to talk about: if I hadn't shot the man, he'd have killed my dad, then Ginny, then me. What was the point in dwelling on it? The only thing I'd done wrong was hesitate.

Our dad knew who he was, and he knew who Ginny and I were going to be. He wasn't concerned with making sure we had conventional childhoods so much as making sure we could take care of ourselves as adults. His dad had done the same thing for him, and then, when my grandfather was no longer available, Helen MacDonald had taken over his training. It was the family business. The only difference with me and Ginny was that we started much younger than Dad had. We had to, Dad said, if we were going to be better than anybody who came before us. I don't think it even occurred to him the damage that could cause.

Maybe if my mom hadn't been killed, it would have been different, because she wasn't worried about anything other than being our mom. Just our mom. Although, sometimes, I felt like I only ever knew her as a collection of stories that Ginny and my dad told me, fragments, feelings, photographs.

But it had been a long time since my mom died, and months since I'd shot the man in Portugal, so I don't think Dad or Ginny— or I—understood why I was in such a petulant mood that day.

I didn't have to explain anything to Ginny, though. She just told Dad to go out and do whatever it was he had planned without us, and then she made me put on my swimsuit and dragged me down to the hotel pool.

I don't remember anything else about the hotel—we were traveling in high style, and the opulence of our accommodations tended to blend together—but the pool was surrounded by lush gardens: olive trees, some of which were supposed to be half a millennium old, and lemon trees, orange trees, and fig trees, with rosebushes and cacti and a general sense of order among the wildness. The pool itself was wide, low, and long. An older man was swimming laps with a lazy rhythm, but otherwise, it was just the two of us in the water.

We could hear the soft buzz of conversation and clinking silverware from the brunch buffet around the corner, and the *pok, pok, pok* of people playing tennis on the clay courts to the side.

Ginny faced me, took my hands, and said, "Crisscross, applesauce. One, two, three."

We submerged, blowing out air until we sank to the bottom of the pool together, sitting cross-legged. I had my eyes closed, and I felt Ginny squeeze my hands. I opened my eyes and looked at her. She was staring back at me. She had a funny smile on her face. The kind you get when you're trying not to cry, and I could see a thin stream of bubbles coming from the corner of her mouth.

She squeezed my hands again.

I squeezed back.

I couldn't have put it into words. Not then. Not for a long time. But I understood it. She was trying to tell me that she knew, that she felt it, too, but that I didn't have to worry. She was trying to tell me that as long as the two of us had each other, we'd make it. She was trying to tell me that she'd stay underwater with me for however long it took; even if it meant she had to drown, she'd never let me go.

Twenty months of Ginny in a hospital bed. Three different surgeries and enough time for the broken bones to heal, but the real question, the one the doctors couldn't answer, was what would be there when—and I kept trying to convince myself it was *when* instead of *if*—she opened her eyes again?

It was like being underwater all over again. I couldn't let go, but I knew I owed it to Ginny to try to surface.

Or, maybe, if I stayed down there long enough, I'd learn to breathe underwater.

15

I SAT IN MY TRUCK FOR A MINUTE gathering my thoughts. I sent Meg a quick text telling her I'd be gone for a few days; when I got back, I said, I wanted to take her to dinner. Then I texted Jameel, my upstairs neighbor—he was a college friend of Ginny's who knew about our real lives, and I was tight with him and his daughters—and asked him to check my mail. I got a heart emoji back from Meg and a thumbs-up from Jameel.

From there, the traffic gods smiled on me. There was just enough time for a quick stop at Paulie's to pay my debt, which was good, because if I'd skipped town without paying—even for a job, even if I came back with double—it would cost me more than my thumbs.

Paulie kept her offices on two floors above Charlie's, a pool hall and bar she owned and had named after my uncle Charles, who was quite the nine-ball player in his spare time. Charlie's was upscale, but it was also a straight-up bar and pool hall. No funny business. Despite Paulie's business dealings, Charlie's had a strict no-betting policy in place.

Something I could have used a few hours earlier when I thought I could hustle my client. Sigh.

If you tried playing a game of pool at Charlie's for anything other than a round of drinks or cared more about your football team winning than pride allowed, you'd be shown the door. Uncle Charles knew how Paulie made money, but she kept him at arm's length from it. He went to Charlie's several days a week to play in a league or shoot a game with a friend. He was good. Even I wasn't dumb enough to try to bet Uncle Charles. Friendly wager or not, he'd make you eat your teeth. But he stayed downstairs. Paulie's offices were off-limits.

He was a good egg, but that being said, I wouldn't choose to get between Uncle Charles and whatever it was he needed to do to keep Paulie safe. He was as close as you can get to being a civilian while marrying into the Ducaine family, but he was no pushover.

Uncle Charles wasn't there, so I went up the back stairs without delay and knocked on the door. There was a standard speakeasy grille on Paulie's office door. Exactly what you'd expect: the metal slot slid back, one of her cadre of tough guys gave you the once-over before slamming the cover closed again, and then and only then, were you given access to Paulie's lair. All unnecessary given that there was a camera on the corner by the ceiling, but my aunt liked her theatrics.

Except that, this time, while I was waiting for the grille to open so that somebody could eyeball me from inside, the door swung open, and a mountain yanked me inside. Before I had a chance to do anything, I was sitting on my ass holding my hand to my jaw. It felt like a cartoon anvil had been swung into the side of my face.

"Goddamnit, Rick," I said. "What was that for?" I gave an exploratory poke with my tongue. Thankfully, it didn't feel like he'd broken any of my teeth.

"You're late," the mountain said. His voice was much higher than you'd expect from somebody so spectacularly large. He looked like somebody had stuffed a dozen duffel bags full of golf balls and then cobbled the duffel bags into a threatening giant. Which made him both look and sound like a Muppet. Which was somehow even more threatening.

He said, "Paulie wanted me to give you a little tune-up before I rip your thumbs off." Rick hauled back his leg to give me a kick, but I was already moving by then.

It was undignified, a sort of butt-scooting crab walk, but I was out of the way before he swung through. Good thing, too, because his foot was about the size of a cinder block.

"I am *not* late," I insisted, as I continued to scuttle farther into the room.

I probably should have been heading out instead of deeper in, but Rick was blocking the door. I made my way behind a deep, brass-buttoned leather couch and then got into a squat so I could peek over the back. "And you're supposed to *break* my thumbs, you moron, not rip them off."

He hesitated. "I don't know. I'm pretty sure she said break them *off*, not just break them." A smile lit his face. "We can split the difference. I'll rip one thumb off, but I'll just break the other one. You can choose which is which. How's that sound?"

"Honestly?" I watched him close the door. The lock snapped shut. It wouldn't stop me, but it would slow me down enough that he'd catch me before I could get out of the room. "Having any of my thumbs ripped off still sounds pretty lousy."

Rick shrugged. "How about you just come over here and get it over with? I ate a big lunch. I don't want to have to chase you around. It's a small room. I'm going to catch you sooner or later." He frowned, a thought suddenly coming into his thick skull. "Why'd you come here? I mean, we would have found you, but you don't usually make things this easy."

"I've got the money," I said. I pulled out the cash I was carrying and showed it to him. "*All* of it. Not just the vig. Go tell Paulie."

To his credit, Rick looked relieved. He didn't actually like the violence part of the job, but he was six foot eight and nearly four hundred pounds. His size was usually enough to get people to pay up well before he had to get physical. Beside which, Paulie paid her help well, treated them right, offered health and dental, a Christmas bonus, and three weeks' paid vacation. It was a sweet gig aside from occasionally needing to rip the thumbs off deadbeats like me.

"Okay," he said. "Let me talk to her."

"Thanks."

He considered me, and then said, "So you know, Duke, if you run, I'm going to take it real personal. I might not stop at just the thumbs."

16

I COOLED MY HEELS while he went up the stairs. Even though Rick still had about eight inches and two hundred pounds on me, he was slow. I could take him as long as I fought dirty. Which is the only way to fight. Since things had gone south with Ginny and Dad, I'd been training even harder than normal as a way of coping. Meg had me sparring with the pros at the gym, and I was more than holding my own; I was running about two hundred and ten pounds of muscle. But fighting Rick wouldn't be pretty, and it would just piss off Paulie. If she thought she had to make an example of me now, it would be a lot worse if I hospitalized one of her goons.

Thankfully, when he came back down the stairs a few minutes later, Rick had a big, dumb smile on his face, and instead of going for my thumbs, he ushered me into Paulie's office.

Inside, Paulie was sitting on the edge of her desk watching the televisions. There were six TVs on the walls, most of them in a quad configuration, showing four games at once. She liked keeping her eyes on the action. She looked like she normally looked: hair cut into a neat bob, wearing a pair of colorful Dansko clogs—the same kind you saw nurses wearing—black pants, a cream-colored blouse. Her only jewelry was a wedding ring and a pair of tasteful gold hoop earrings. In other words, she looked like a middle-aged mom who also worked a moderately successful corporate job instead of what she was, which was the most connected shot caller, bookie, and fence of stolen goods on the western seaboard. If you wanted to do any kind of a big job in the territory, you needed her blessing.

Frankly, if she hadn't been my aunt, I would have been terrified of her.

As it was . . .

"Come on over, you dumb shit," she said. "I hear you've got my money."

Meekly, I went over and submitted myself to a kiss on the cheek. It was the same cheek that Rick had slugged, and it still felt tender.

She sized me up. "How's my favorite nephew?"

"Why the hell did Rick think he was supposed to rip my thumbs off?"

"Because I told him he was supposed to rip your thumbs off," Paulie said.

I could hear my voice squeak. "What?"

"You were late again. You've been late three weeks in a row, and this was the fourth week. Time to lose your thumbs."

"Break my thumbs. Come on, Paulie. Besides, I was *not* late," I protested. "I'm supposed to have until midnight."

"Duke, I love you. You know that. And I love your moron of a father like a brother—"

"That's because he *is* your brother."

"—but you've got to know this doesn't look good. I can't have my nephew going around making me look weak. It's bad enough that I'm already giving you a discount on the vig." She didn't bother repeating to me that it was worse for her because she was a woman. It meant she had to be twice as tough. She could never make a threat without following through. "If you weren't family, I'd have—" she said. "That reminds me, dinner at my place tomorrow? Charles is making lasagna."

"Can't," I said. I was used to the way she casually slid between being my aunt and a crime boss. "I'll be out of town. I've got a job.

How do you think I got enough money to pay off my debt? And how do you think I'm supposed to work if Rick pulls my thumbs off?"

I handed her the envelope.

"Honestly? No idea how you came up with it." She shrugged. "I've offered you plenty of jobs, and you always claim you're a hundred percent legit. Which is clearly a lie."

She picked up her phone. "Those pictures you texted me?" She held up her phone and showed me one of the photos of Baker and Cleary that Mimi had snapped for me at the Market House. "What's going on, Duke?"

I told her. From Baker and Cleary tailing me in their SUV to the deal we'd worked out: twenty grand upfront, forty more when I finished the job, and Dad getting time served. I did it as quickly as possible, conscious that I had to get to the airport.

While I talked, she bounced the envelope of cash I'd given her back and forth between hands. When I finished, she tossed the envelope on the desk.

"Can you back out of it?"

"Paulie—"

"I'm not joking, Duke." She reached out, sliding the envelope of cash back in my direction. "Pay them back and say whatever you need to get out of the job. I'm sure Rick's already told the rest of the boys that you showed up with enough cash to line your name out of the books. We can keep this between us."

I thought for a second. One of the mistakes I'd made in the first place was placing my bets with one of Paulie's bookies down the chain instead of dealing with Paulie directly.

"You know," I said, "you could have offered me that deal back when it was just about gambling debt."

"That was on you," she said. "Tough love, kiddo. If your mom was still alive, she would have said the same thing." I glared at Paulie, but she ignored me, and said, "You need to learn that gambling isn't for you. And that reminds me . . ." She picked up her cell phone and banged out a quick text.

"What was that?"

She put her phone back down and picked the remote back up. "I told Lily"—one of her top lieutenants—"to spread the word that you were square, and that you were officially blacklisted. Anybody who takes action from you is going to get retired. Should have done that a long time ago." She looked at me with a mix of love and pity. "You've been reckless since your dad got popped and Ginny got worked over. I get it with trying to even the score. You were trying to atone. But you went about it like a maniac. And since you played out that string, even though you're straight, you've been looking for trouble. Like it or not, I'm in a position of some responsibility for you. At the very least, if you can't learn to keep yourself out of trouble, I can make sure that your trouble isn't part of my doing. Frankly, you need to learn a lot of things. You're still the stubborn idiot who thinks poking a wasps' nest is a good idea."

17

THAT'S THE PROBLEM WITH FAMILY. They remember what you did when you were a little kid, which, in this case, was that when I was five, I'd taken a stick and whacked a wasps' nest. I'd had to spend three days in the hospital and still had some scars on my back from the stings. After, my mom asked what I'd been thinking. Supposedly, I told her I wanted to see what would happen if I hit a wasps' nest with a stick, and she said, didn't you know the wasps would attack you? And the legend is that I said, yeah, but how was I supposed to know *for sure* if I didn't try? Which caused my mother to sigh, turn to my father, and say, "He gets that from your side of the family."

"I'm serious, Duke," Paulie said. "You shouldn't have started gambling again. The house always wins. You know that, and I thought letting you face the natural consequences would save you trouble down the road. But this . . ." She poked the envelope again. "I don't know. It's not right. It doesn't pass the smell test. Give the money back."

"Paulie. I appreciate the offer. I do, but you know it's not just the money."

"It's a rush job. Rush jobs get you killed," she said. "I understand why you're doing it, and the money itself isn't as much of a red flag given what they need you to do. Who else are they going to hire? Shirlene Van?" The name came out of her mouth dripping with scorn. Which was fair. Shirlene was good, but not *that* good.

Paulie continued, "But it doesn't make me any less nervous. If whatever is in that safe is something the feds want *this* much, then whoever owns the safe probably wants to keep you out just as much. You're whacking a wasps' nest again, sweetie. I don't like this at all."

"Me either, Paulie, but I've got to try. I owe it to Dad."

She stared at me for a few seconds. Finally, she said, "Yeah. You do." She took a deep breath and then added, "Be careful, Duke, okay? The truck is fine in the lot but be careful."

I leaned in and kissed her on the cheek. "Thanks, Paulie." She nodded. I kissed her cheek again. "Can you call me a cab? My cell phone is in my truck. I've got to go. I'm on a timeline here. With a little luck, I'll be back in a few days and Dad can join us for our next family dinner."

She laughed and said, "I've seen the bets you make, Duke. I wouldn't count on you having much luck. Just . . . don't push it, okay?"

She picked her phone up off her desk and sent a quick text. "Forget the cab. I'll have one of the guys give you a ride to the airport. Be smart, and don't be as proud as your goddamned sister. Call me if you get in a jam."

I nodded. We had a whole system set up for emergencies, even before Dad got busted. I could get in touch if I needed. "Keep an eye on Ginny for me? And Dad?"

"Of course. Anything. We're family."

I started to leave but stopped when she called me back.

She was holding the envelope of cash. "Just wait until I count this."

So much for family.

18

BETWEEN PAULIE'S DRIVER TAKING THE WRONG EXIT, Los Angeles traffic, and a full pat down at security—I was pretty sure my lack of a carry-on beyond my passport raised some suspicion—I barely made the plane. I didn't even have time to break the fifty-dollar bill Baker had given me to buy a paperback.

The flight attendants ran through the usual safety rigamarole, and then we were on the runway and in the air. I ordered dinner and champagne and thought about the first trip I had taken to Switzerland, when Ginny and I were both teenagers, back when I thought we were both invincible. Everything seemed like a lark, and we were bulletproof.

Dad had his own gig he was working in Liechtenstein, but he'd brought me and Ginny because there was a nice, low-stakes setup in Zurich that he thought would be a good test for the two of us. He planned the whole thing and then gave it to us to complete. All we had to do was follow his play and, once we were done, hand the necklace off to the fence. Our end wasn't going to come out to more than forty thousand dollars, which would barely cover expenses, but that wasn't the point. Even though we'd been working *with* Dad for years, he was just beginning to let us work on our own. That was why he'd designed everything and wasn't giving us any latitude on how to make it happen. It was his version of schooling and just another one of the steps along the way to prove to him we were ready to both pull jobs and plan jobs on our own.

It was a paint-by-numbers robbery. Child's play. A classic double-box: safe, simple, and almost foolproof.

It was also an extremely boring way to steal a necklace.

Which is what I said to Ginny while we were waiting for Dad to get back from Liechtenstein, so she said, "Do you want to make it more interesting?"

"What, like a bet?"

The hotel we were working was extremely expensive, and befitting the exorbitant nightly rate, hard-pressed against the river. We were eating dinner in the hotel's Michelin-starred restaurant, seated at a two-top by the windows. A small boat decked out with twinkling lights moved slowly past. The dining room was set back a bit, with a promenade along the banks, but the upper floors hovered over the water. If you dropped a coin straight out your bedroom window, you could make a wish. In the dining room, the underpowered European air-conditioning was struggling to keep up with an unexpected heatwave. My hoodie was draped over the back of my chair, and I was sweating. A swim sounded nice.

"Well," she said, "I was thinking more of a competition. See who can steal the necklace first. But you have to do something other than use the double-box." Without making any kind of movement to give away the fact that she was watching the lobby, Ginny added, "She's back. You game?"

The mark was wearing a black cocktail dress and a fur stole that she certainly didn't need with the unseasonable heat. The expensive ice around her neck was keeping her cool, however. She was at the front desk with both hands clutching shopping bags. She said something to one of the attendants, who nodded, and came around to take her bags for her. She turned on her heel and marched to the elevators so she could return to her room.

That was what we were waiting for: all she had to do was put the necklace back in her room safe and we were in business.

The double-box was basically a magic trick. While the mark was out shopping, we'd modified her room safe so that we could reach into it from the suite next door, which was our room. Once the necklace was in the safe and we figured the mark was sleeping, we'd nab the diamonds from our side, make the safe whole again, patch the wall, and walk away. In the morning, Sleeping Beauty would open an empty safe and we'd be gone without a trace. The hardest part was matching the paint color for when we repaired the wall.

Like I said, simple, risk-free.

And completely boring.

"Dad's not going to like it."

Ginny said, "So we don't tell him."

We watched the mark get on the elevator, the desk attendant carrying her shopping bags and stepping in behind her. As the doors closed, I saw her pull a tissue from her purse and dab at her face. I was sweating and she was sweating. She probably wanted to take a bath.

"You really think you can steal the necklace before me?" I asked.

She said, "I'm getting dessert. Do you want some? And yes, I am absolutely, positively certain I can steal it before you can steal it."

"What are the stakes?"

"You win, and you can have my car."

She caught the waiter's eye and ordered herself the lemon tart and an espresso. I was full, so I skipped the dessert and just asked for the espresso.

I waited until the waiter left and said, "You sure? It's a nice car." It was. A Mazda Miata convertible that Dad had given her a few weeks earlier for her eighteenth birthday. He generally tried to get us to keep a low profile, but in Los Angeles, a Miata wasn't particularly overboard.

"I'm sure, but if *I* win," she said, leaning forward and grinning, "you have to shave your eyebrows." She stuck out her hand.

"You don't want my car?" I was driving an eleven-year-old Civic with a hundred and sixty thousand miles on it. I was very much looking forward to my eighteenth birthday.

"Eyebrows."

I should have known better. I *never* won against Ginny, but the odds she was offering were absurd. Her car against my eyebrows? Plus, all I had to do was get to the room before Ginny and I was golden.

I shook on it.

Then I stood up, grabbed the hoodie off the back of my chair, and said, "Be right back."

19

AS I WALKED TO THE ELEVATOR, I shrugged on my hoodie and put the hood up. I got on the elevator, turned around, and saw the waiter delivering our coffees and Ginny's dessert. As the doors started to close, Ginny gave me a friendly wave and a smirk that should have made me hesitate.

The heat was stifling, but even though the hotel didn't seem to have cameras in either the elevators or the hallways, I kept my hood up and my face down.

I got off on the top floor, walked down the hall past our adjoining room, and then unlocked the mark's door with the electronic key card Ginny and I had cloned three days earlier. The suite was the mirror image of ours: a bedroom with a sitting area, an expansive living room, a bathroom, a walk-in closet with a safe bolted to the wall. A balcony ran the length of the entire suite, with three sets of French doors in the living room and two in the bedroom. She had the air-conditioning running, but she had also opened the living room balcony doors to the night air. There was a lazy breeze that moved the curtains like slow ghosts, and I could feel that the temperature outside had finally dipped to a reasonable level.

She hadn't closed the bedroom door, and I could hear the water running from the bathroom; I'd been right about her wanting to clean up.

I could see the bed from where I was standing in the living room. She'd thrown her dress and fur stole casually across the covers. I took a few more steps until I could see that the bathroom door was closed but not latched.

She'd opened the balcony doors in her bedroom as well, and I wondered if anybody across the way had watched her undress. It was a scenic view over the river. The same view from the living area of the suite, and the same view that Ginny and I had next door. On the other side of the water, the lights showed a city alive at night. People were eating and drinking and making love and all of them—including the woman in the shower—were oblivious to my larceny.

I started to move to the closet. I didn't exactly have to hurry, but there was no point stalling. Unless she was really going to rush her shower, I figured I had at least five minutes to open the safe, grab the necklace, and get out. Plenty of time.

Except as I turned toward the closet, I realized I didn't even need five minutes: she'd left the diamond necklace sitting out on the dresser.

Well then.

For once, I was going to win a bet against Ginny. I was going to enjoy the hell out of driving her convertible.

I put the necklace into my pocket and walked back out into the living room.

There was a man standing in the entrance to the suite. He was tall and thin. He was wearing a pair of black pants and a black shirt.

He was also wearing a ski mask.

I probably should have been worried, but even though I was only seventeen and still growing, he didn't look like much.

Then the beanpole stepped into the room, and right behind him was another man, also wearing a ski mask. The good news was that neither of them appeared to be working heavy. The bad news was that the reason they weren't carrying guns was because with the second guy on board, they didn't need them: he was approximately the size of a commercial refrigerator. I could see the muscles through the strained fabric of his shirt, and I wasn't entirely sure he'd fit through the doorway.

It took me a quarter second to realize that the ski masks meant they were here to steal the necklace. It took me another quarter second to decide that while I was perfectly happy to kick the tall guy's ass, the other guy looked like he could bench-press a car, and he was very much blocking my exit into the hallway.

Plan B.

I turned on my heel, ran through the open balcony doors, hoisted myself onto the railing, and jumped.

It was only as I was launching myself that I realized I had no idea if the river was deep enough for me to land safely.

20

SIX STORIES IS ROUGHLY EIGHTY FEET, and physics dictated that 2.2 seconds later, I was very pleased to discover that the river *was* deep enough, at least in this spot.

When I surfaced, Ginny was standing next to the bank of the river. "I drank your espresso," she said.

I coughed a bit. I'd gotten water up my nose and gotten the wind knocked out of me. Eighty feet is a long way down. I said, "We need to get out of here."

She looked surprised. "The mark saw you? Sloppy." She leaned out so she could look up past the hotel overhang and see where the hotel jutted out toward the river.

"No," I said. "But there were two men coming in just as I was leaving."

"Whoops. Gentlemen callers?"

I laughed at her language. "I don't think so. They were both wearing ski masks."

"Competition?" Ginny said.

"That's my assumption."

"Armed?"

"Nah. Not that I could see. One of them was lanky. A broomstick with legs. He didn't seem like a problem, but the other guy looked like the Hulk. Prison muscle." I hauled myself out of the water and got to my feet.

"Here." I pulled the necklace out of my pocket and handed it to her. "See? Sometimes, Ginny, things work out fine even if they aren't planned to perfection. No hesitation, just action. Which means I stole the necklace first, and I win. You can give me the keys to your car as soon as we're home. Now, can we get the hell out of here before the ungentlemanly callers come looking?"

Ginny took the necklace from me, spun it around on her finger, and then tossed it into the river.

It landed with a small splash and promptly sank out of sight.

I brushed my hair back and used my hands to squeegee some of the water off myself. "You realize I just got *out* of the river. Any particular reason you threw the diamond necklace back in?"

"Because it's fake," Ginny said. "Sometimes, Duke, things work out exactly the way they should when they are perfectly planned. Well, not exactly. I wasn't expecting you to jump in the river or for there to be other people trying to steal the diamonds at the same time, but the rest of it went exactly as scripted. I knew I was going to win the bet before we even made it. This is what we call 'playing the long game.' And you, Duke, were played."

"Wait . . . what?" I took a step toward the river, stopped, and then turned back to her again, my shoes squelching with each step.

Ginny had a mischievous look on her face. "I stole the real necklace two nights ago and replaced it with the one I just threw in the river. It was a fake."

"A fake?"

"A fake," she agreed.

"You stole the real necklace two days ago?"

"That is correct, dear brother of mine. Which means I stole it first and *I* win. Alas, I shall be keeping my keys. And at some point, when I decide the time is right, you are going to have to shave your eyebrows."

21

IT SHOULD HAVE JUST BEEN a funny story. The kind of tale I trotted out to explain what it was like having a sister like Ginny.

As we walked down the promenade, she told me the whole con. She'd been planning it from the first day Dad had told us what we were going to be doing in Zurich while he was working in Liechtenstein. She commissioned the fake necklace from a friend in Los Angeles, then, once we were in Zurich, she waited until I was otherwise occupied so she could make the switch.

It wasn't hard to get rid of me for a night. I was seventeen, and while Ginny and I were sightseeing and waiting for the mark to check into the hotel, we'd run into a gaggle of German girls who were roughly the same age as us. I had eagerly accepted their invitation to go clubbing, and Ginny had declined. While I was out dancing, fruitlessly hoping it would lead to an invitation back to the German teens' hostel for a night of debauchery, Ginny was sneaking into the sleeping mark's room, opening the safe, and swapping the real necklace for the fake.

She'd already delivered the diamonds to the fence.

Sigh. Sisters. They're the worst.

As we walked away from the hotel, I was dripping, and Ginny was laughing at me. By the time we rounded the corner to go down a narrow alley between the hotel and the next building over, I was already starting to see the humor in my own gullibility, and an annoyed smile was creeping onto my face.

And then I got serious. Because there was an extremely large man heading down the alley toward us. Even without the ski mask, I recognized him by his musclebound walk. He was still thirty or forty feet away.

"That's one of the guys from the room."

We both spun, ready to run, but when we did, the other guy was right there, blocking our retreat. The tall, skinny one.

He said . . .

Actually, I have no idea what he said, because it was in Swiss German.

I glanced back over my shoulder. The behemoth was stopped about ten feet behind us. He was looking at his partner for a cue.

Which was *our* cue.

Our dad had taught us that when you're in a pinch, it's always better to act than to react.

Ginny said, "You take Captain Steroids. I get the easy one." She got into a fighting stance.

By the time I turned around, the big boy had already figured out what was happening and was closing the distance.

He went for the kill shot right away, throwing a heavy, slow round punch. If it had connected, it would have put me down, but it was clumsy. I stepped past the swing, trying to keep a little space.

The last thing you want to do when fighting somebody who has a distinct size advantage is to get in close. I was screwed if we got into a clutch. But he was slow. And from his stance and the way he held his hands, he was untrained. He was used to winning fights by being bigger than everybody else.

You can build muscles everywhere except your testicles. Which is right where I kicked him.

When he bent over, I clasped my hands together and used them to throw my elbow like a wedge into his nose.

He folded to the ground and went to sleep curled up on his side like a giant baby.

When I turned around to check on Ginny, her guy was on the ground too. The difference was that her guy was on his back, breathing in wet gasps, holding on to the hilt of a knife buried in his belly. His eyes weren't focusing.

"Shit," I said. "That your knife?"

"His."

I looked at my sister. She was holding her side. Her shirt was soaked with blood.

Very calmly, she said, "I'm going to need a vet."

22

I HELPED GINNY walk out to the street. I'd wrung out my hoodie the best I could and given it to her so she could hide the blood weeping out of her side. She was walking okay, but I was keeping an eye on her.

"There," she said, pointing out a fleet little sports car. It was parked on the street, but in an island of shadow that gave me space to work. I had a set of lockpicks in my pocket—I almost always did—and I got the car open and Ginny inside as quickly as I could. I hustled around to the driver's side and Ginny gave me her phone.

Dad picked up almost immediately. "Emergency?"

"Ginny's hurt."

"How bad?"

"Stable," I said, "but stitches. We got in a fight. Two guys. One of them had a knife. We need a vet."

The vet wasn't really a veterinarian, of course. Occasionally you'd end up with an actual animal doc, but that was rare. Most of the time it was an MD who'd either lost their license or needed cash for all the usual reasons. But we called them vets because that's what Dad and his old-school buddies called them. Dad never worked a job without having a vet lined up, but because Liechtenstein was so close, and because Ginny and I should have been safe as apple pie with the double-box play, we didn't have our own vet on tap in Zurich. We were reliant on Dad's. "Call me back in two minutes," he said.

"Okay."

"Duke," he said, his voice dropping a bit. "Do you need to clean up before you leave?"

I looked at Ginny. She had done up her seat belt, but she was leaning back with her eyes closed, breathing evenly. She looked peaceful. Almost like she was napping. Except for the hand pressed tightly against her side. "Clean up what?"

"You said you got in a fight. And? Ginny got cut and the guys you were fighting with just walked away? That's it?"

"The one who stabbed Ginny is dying. Probably dead by now."

"The other guy?"

"Unconscious."

"Can he make you? Did he see your faces?"

I didn't say anything. I looked out the window toward the mouth of the alley. It was dark and quiet. No screaming. No pedestrians.

Dad said, "You know what you've got to do. I'll call the vet. You call me back when you're done, and I'll tell you where to meet him."

I hung up and looked at Ginny again. "I'll be right back," I said. "You okay?"

"I'm okay," she said. "You okay?"

I knew what she was asking. And I didn't answer.

I got out of the car and went back into the alley. The man with the knife in his belly had a stillness that was unmistakable. I reached down, closed my eyes, and pulled the knife out of his belly.

The big guy was starting to stir. He was still on his side, but he was reaching out with one hand and clawing weakly at the pavement, as if he could drag himself back to consciousness.

I took the knife and pressed the point into his neck. I kept pressing until he was as still as his partner. Then I threw the knife into the middle of the river. It sank, keeping company with the fake necklace.

I walked back to the car, got in, called my dad for the address so we could meet the vet, and started driving. I kept a tight grip on the wheel.

23

WE MET THE VET HALFWAY between Zurich and Liechtenstein, at a parking lot at a small grocery store in a tiny lakeside village called Mühlehorn. The vet was quiet, but he didn't have any wasted movements, and he was quick to say that other than a scar from the stitches, Ginny would be fine. She looked shaky to me, but she gave me a wan smile, and the vet numbed her up and started stitching.

Dad arrived just as the vet was cleaning up.

He waited to say anything until the vet was gone and the three of us were in his car. Ginny was in the front, with her seat reclined a bit. She had her eyes closed and was breathing slowly and evenly even though she claimed she wasn't in too much pain. The cut had been relatively shallow but long—it took ninety stitches—which was still better than a deep puncture, but it had bled a lot. She was still pale, but she'd forced down a candy bar and some water, and said she was good to go.

The car was running, but Dad left it in park. We were next to the lake. Any other time, it would have been a nice place to visit, but Dad's anger thrummed over the engine.

He stared straight ahead through the windshield.

His voice was deliberately quiet. Controlled.

He said, "I've never been more disappointed in you."

I slunk down lower in the back seat. I could feel the burn in my throat as I kept myself from crying.

There had been a wet, gurgling sound when I'd pressed the knife into the man's neck.

Ginny shifted in her seat, grimacing. "Dad, come on. It wasn't all Duke's fault."

He pivoted, looking at me and then her. "Oh, do you think I'm just talking to your brother?" He sighed. "I've never laid a hand on either one of you. Not in anger. Not outside of training, and that's different, but I have half a mind to spank the both of you."

"Dad . . ."

He glared at me and then back at Ginny. "You put yourselves in danger because you were screwing around. You know me. You know that I'm all for having fun, for playing around. But this isn't a game."

I said, "I'm sorry."

Ginny said it, too, a sort of whisper. I could hear that she was also struggling not to cry.

Dad leaned his head back against the seat. He sighed, and when he spoke again, he sounded more sad than angry. "When your mom found out she was pregnant the first time, she said, 'Well, I know who I married, and I know what kind of kid this is going to be.' And when she found out she was pregnant the second time, she said, 'At least they'll always be able to take care of each other and keep each other safe.'"

Nobody said anything for a bit, and then Dad straightened up. "We break the law, but we don't break those rules. Do you understand? Those are the only unbreakable rules. Take care of each other. Keep each other safe. Nothing else matters if you don't keep each other safe."

And we did.

We looked out for each other.

We kept each other safe.

Until one day, about twenty months ago, I was a second too late to see it. A second too late to stop her from getting hurt. Again.

24

WHEN THE WHEELS HIT THE TARMAC, I was exhausted from being ruthlessly pampered. I'd gotten used to living an exorbitant life funded by thievery, and then I'd gambled it away; I hadn't been relishing the relative austerity, so the flight was enjoyable. Business class meant that about every fifteen minutes somebody came by to feed me and give me something to drink, and there was an infinite supply of movies to watch. The ticket was round-trip, and there was a part of me that was already looking forward to the bottomless champagne I could drink up on the way home in a congratulatory silent toast to myself for earning the rest of my pay and springing my dad.

Agent Cleary met me outside of customs. He was carrying an inexpensive duffel bag but had ditched the cheap suit. He looked at home, wearing Euro-cut clothing; he could have blended in anywhere from Rome to Berlin, but he still looked like he was in a bad mood. Even with the new set of duds, I figured he and Baker had flown something military courtesy of good old Uncle Sam. Fast, but not as nice as sipping bubbly at the front of a plane. A private jet would have been even faster, but I was pretty sure the United States government didn't spring for that kind of thing for mooks like Baker and Cleary.

He took me to the garage and stopped in front of a zippy-looking car. He'd parked in a back corner that was deserted.

"Take off all your clothes," he commanded.

"I'm usually a second date kind of guy," I said, "but if you buy me a nice dinner, I'll consider it."

"You think you're hilarious, don't you?"

"Mostly," I said. "You don't?"

He threw the duffel bag at my chest. "Strip down and change into the outfit in the bag. There's a garbage bag in there. Everything goes into the garbage bag."

"And I'll get that back when we're done?"

He rolled his eyes.

"Give me your passport." He pulled out a pack of Winstons and lit up a cigarette while I stripped down. I thought about asking him to back up a bit—I've never been a fan of the smell of cigarette smoke—but he seemed like the kind of guy who'd be an asshole about it. Frankly, he seemed like the kind of guy who'd be an asshole about everything.

Like they'd told me, I hadn't brought my phone, and aside from my passport and the fifty bucks Baker had given me, I was empty handed. But empty handed wasn't the same thing as unprepared. If I could have figured out how to bring it, I would have tried to sneak my Glock, but assuming they weren't smart enough to understand everything I'd asked for in my tools and materials list for the job, I had a backup plan for self-defense.

I used the car to give myself a modicum of privacy from anybody who might decide to walk by while I was shimmying out of my pants. Cleary kept a close eye on me. I started pulling on the pants when Cleary stopped me. I thought he was going to make a comment about my old scars, a road map of my bad decisions, but he didn't.

Instead, he said, "Everything."

I looked down at my trunks and sighed.

"Those Baker's orders?"

He pushed his chest out and showed me his teeth. "What, you think Baker's the only one calling the shots? Now, get on with it. We don't have time to waste."

The new clothes fit surprisingly well. Even the underwear. Honestly, all of it was nicer than what I usually wore. The shoes were a problem, though. I held up the pair of pointy-toed dress shoes they'd picked up for me. They were at least a size thirteen. "Do you guys think I play in the NBA or something?"

"Whatever," Cleary said. He was itching to get moving. He threw the rest of his Winston on the ground and crushed the cigarette butt under the sole of his shoe. It saved me the trouble of taking it away from him if he'd tried to bring it into the car with me.

I was perfectly content to keep my original kicks. They were old-school sneaky, with a hollow under the left heel. You had to know where to press and how to twist to get at it, but it was just big enough to hold a plastic handcuff key. It wasn't much, but it was something, and it was just dumb enough and old-fashioned enough that people usually missed it. I'd learned the hard way that having a quick and painless way to get out of handcuffs was always a good idea.

Once I'd changed and gotten in the car, Cleary didn't say much beyond that it was going to be a thirty-minute drive. I mostly just looked out the window, taking in the sights.

25

BY THE TIME WE ARRIVED, my eyelids were starting to flutter closed.

The warehouse they were operating out of was about ten thousand square feet and mostly empty: the back corner had been walled off into a separate room with a metal security door, there were three identical BMW sedans parked against one wall, as well as a white, windowless box truck and a matching gray box truck. And that was it. Except for a few tables and a mountain of safecracking gear plus all the specialized equipment I was going to need to get into an American Castle Galaxy Nine without anybody noticing.

Which, again, was supposedly impossible.

I needed to get my shit together.

I needed some caffeine.

Or a nap.

Besides Baker and Cleary, there were two men I'd never seen before at the far side of the garage. They were standing by a workbench, chatting quietly. They were both white, dressed in the same European-cut clothing as my American friends had changed into. The two men had short hair—one of them was going gray—and military bearings. Otherwise, the space was empty and immaculate.

"We got everything you asked for," Baker said, "and then some, just in case."

I didn't want to show that I was impressed. Even if they'd hightailed it straight from the Market House to an airbase, they would still only have been a couple of hours ahead of me. Then again, if

I had the entire United States government at my disposal, I could probably get more stuff done too.

Evidently, trying not to show I was impressed wasn't the same thing as not actually showing I was impressed, because Baker grinned. "It's all here. Put together whatever you need plus whatever you *might* need. Pile it up right here," he said, pointing to the ground in front of the gray van, "and my guys will load it up. And get a move on. I want to be on the road within the hour. Let me know if you need anything else."

"Just a coffee. A soy latte would be killer, but I'll settle for a standard cup."

"I'm sure we can rustle something up," Baker said. He looked me up and down and then shook his head with dissatisfaction. "But first, just to be sure you didn't try anything cute, we're going to have to frisk you."

Cleary said, "I saw him change. All new clothes."

"Frisk him anyway."

Cleary shrugged and walked over to the man with the gray hair and whispered something in his ear. The man took his time, going inch by inch without saying a word. Very professional. I might have been able to sneak something small by him if I'd tucked it into my waistband, but I doubted it. But he didn't find the key hidden in the heel of my shoe. Score a win for Duke. When he was finished, he nodded at Baker and then went back to whatever he'd been doing across the room.

"And now, I'm going to have to get you to take off your shoes," Baker said.

I wrinkled my nose. So much for a win for Duke.

Baker misinterpreted my response and said, "Sorry. When I said everything, I meant everything. I'll have new shoes for you before we leave."

Even in my stockinged feet, I had the gear piled up in fifty-nine minutes. I could have done it quicker, but I spent a few minutes looking at the extra gear that was there that I *hadn't* asked for. There were some tools—a suction drill rig, a lock decoder—that were custom made. Not the sort of thing you could pick up off a shelf, even a very specialized shelf, and not stuff that had been on my list of requests. Who the hell had they been made for originally?

And more importantly, what had happened to the guy who *had* requested that stuff? Or more likely, given the nature of the gear, who had made it himself. Or herself.

But I was in a hurry and didn't want to think through the implications of those questions, so mostly I just concentrated on checking off my items. There were a few extra things that weren't exactly necessary for the job at hand but that I thought might be useful. For self-defense. Just in case.

I was focused on organizing and selecting tools, but neither of the two new fellows ever came over. At one point, one of them let himself into the room in the back corner and I caught a glimpse of a desk and a chair and a blank wall behind them. Not much to go on, and it was obvious that they were deliberately keeping their distance. Cleary came back with my coffee, but mostly I just stayed in the zone.

When I was ready, Baker told me to use the bathroom. When I came out, he handed me three shoeboxes. The first box had a pair of black oxfords that fit fine, so I kept them on. They had rubber soles, which meant I could run well enough in them if I needed to, plus they looked good with what I was wearing. When the job was over, I was going to keep this outfit.

"You're going in the back of the white van," he said.

I'd figured as much when I watched the men load up: the white van had a bench seat in the cargo area that ran the length of one wall.

"Also," Baker said, "this." He handed me a hood. "Sorry. For your own protection. You're going to need to wear it the entire time until we get there." He showed me a plastic zip tie. "I'll be securing the hood, just in case. It's not that we don't trust you, it's, well . . ."

"It's that you don't trust me."

He laughed. It seemed like a genuine laugh, his eyes finally softening for an instant. "Yeah. Fair enough. We did our research on you. You aren't exactly trustworthy."

I had to give him that. Up until almost two years ago, I'd spent my entire life either training to be a criminal or actively *being* a criminal. I liked to think of myself as a good guy, but I'd done a lot of things that should have disabused me of that notion.

Baker continued, "Realistically, the less you know, the less of a need there is to take you out in a field and shoot you in the back of the head when this is all over."

"Your bedside manner sucks," I said.

"I've been told. But hey, I've already given you twenty thousand dollars in cash, and there's forty thousand more waiting for you when this is all over. Isn't that enough?"

"Plus, my dad will be let out with time served."

"A deal's a deal," he said. "Listen, it's going to be a long drive. Get some sleep. Just bang on the wall between the back and the cab when you need to take a leak."

Reluctantly, I put the hood over my head, let Baker cinch it closed, and then laid down on the padded bench.

I was asleep before we hit the highway.

26

I WOKE UP WITH A FULL BLADDER. I figured I'd been sleeping at least six or seven hours. Best sleep I'd had in months. It felt good to be doing something other than another boring, legitimate job for a suburban homeowner.

I had a faint recollection of stopping at least once, but I could hear the hum of tires. We were still on the highway.

I sat up and felt my way along the bench until I could bang my fist on the metal a couple of times. One of the men up front knocked back.

After another five minutes, I felt the van slowing down and then exiting. A few turns, and then they backed it in somewhere. The engine shut off. I heard the back door open, felt the cool air.

"You just need to take a leak?" It was Cleary's voice. He didn't sound happy.

"Yep. Though I wouldn't say no to a donut and a bagel. And another cup of coffee."

"You'll have to settle for going to the bathroom. Here's a bucket," he said, banging the hard plastic into my shins.

"Are you going to take the hood off?"

"You don't need to see to piss in a bucket."

I thought about saying something smart back at him but given that I had a hood over my head, and he seemed like the kind of guy who would punch me in the gut just because he could, I decided to keep my mouth shut.

I did my business, and then, wordlessly, Cleary took the bucket and then slammed the back doors closed again.

I guess I could understand why he wasn't thrilled about being in charge of the piss bucket.

From there, it was another two hours of highway driving and then another forty minutes of city stop and go. I was doing my best to pay attention, but I knew it was essentially useless. I was only guessing at how long everything was taking. I had a decent internal clock, but if we really *had* been driving for nine or ten hours at that point, we could be almost anywhere in Europe. We could have made it to Rome in that time.

We made a turn, and I felt the gentle thump of tires going over a poorly cut curb, and then the van going down a ramp. Parking garage, I thought. We made left turn after left turn, and even though I lost count, I figured we'd gone down at least four levels. Wherever we were, we were in the absolute basement.

They parked the van, and then a few seconds later, the back doors opened. This time it was Baker's voice. "Keep the hood on," he said. "I'll lead you in. I'll have somebody bring in the tools for you."

He kept his hand on my elbow as he helped me down and then marched me along. I could feel a temperature change and hear the hollow echo of the parking garage fall away as we entered a building. We went down a long hallway and then turned and turned again, doors opening and closing.

"Watch your step," he said.

There was a bit of loose grit underfoot. Like small bits of gravel. I didn't like being unable to see, and there was something I didn't like even more: I could smell something that had been burned. Scorched plastic. Maybe wiring. Somebody had been working in here with a torch. The smell of drywall dust and broken concrete too. Not gravel. Debris. They were clearly trying to sneak us in somewhere.

And then more walking, a few doors, another temperature change.

"Hold," Baker whispered. We waited, I heard what I thought might have been footsteps at a distance, and then after a couple of minutes, Baker hustled me along.

I didn't like doing covert work with a hood over my head; if they took off my hood and told me to run for it, I'd be hopelessly lost. I was at their mercy. But it was worth it. That's all I needed to remember. I'd paid Paulie off, and the rest of the money I'd get when the job was finished meant I could catch up on my rent for the year and buy a new—used, but newer—truck. Maybe even a new surfboard. And, most importantly, my dad walking free. I kept repeating it to myself like a mantra: a fresh start.

Redemption.

Baker stopped me. I felt his hand on the back of my head and then a little pressure before the snap of something cutting the zip tie securing the hood. "Okay," he said. "You can take it off."

I undid the straps of the hood. I stood there for a few seconds with my eyes squeezed tight against the glare of the ceiling lights.

When I opened my eyes, I was staring at an American Castle Galaxy Nine.

It was beautiful.

And impenetrable.

And I was going to open it.

Baker chucked me on the shoulder in a friendly manner, but his eyes had gone cold again.

He said, "Let's go. You're on the clock."

27

"FIRST THINGS FIRST," I SAID. "I need a double espresso, a sandwich for later, and a couple of donuts for right now."

"Donuts?"

"Or some muffins. Whatever. Something in the same ballpark. I don't care what as long as it gives me a quick hit of sugar."

I was wide awake. I'd slept solidly in the van, but there was nothing that woke me up quicker than a puzzle I had to solve. I was hungry, though, and I figured wherever we were, it was Europe, so they'd probably have good espresso.

He didn't move.

"Look," I said, "once I get started for real and seal it up, nobody's going to be going in or out. You said I've got a ten-hour window. I haven't eaten since I got off the plane, and other than the cup of coffee you gave me back in the garage, nothing to drink. This is going to be a long haul. You guys can sit in the van and eat Twinkies all night, but I'm stuck here. I need some sustenance. You guys thought of everything else, you should have thought of this too. Espresso to get me started. A sandwich so I don't bonk. Donuts for now *and* for later, when I start getting cranky. And get a couple of bottles of water. Plus, once I get going, I'm not going to be able to stop. It would probably be good for me to have that bucket. My bladder isn't made of steel."

He almost smiled. I didn't bother watching him leave the room. I was looking at the safe.

The American Castle Galaxy Nine posed two major problems for a safecracker. The first was the most obvious one: I had to unlock it.

And unlocking it meant three separate issues.

If all you wanted to do was to open the safe, and if you didn't have a problem with destroying the safe—or, at the very least, making it clear you'd done an intrusion—it was a cinch. You could do almost anything if you had enough time and the right drilling rig and drill bits. And then there were explosives, thermal lances, pressure breaks, liquid jacks, all the flashy stuff you saw in movies.

But *opening* a safe and *unlocking* a safe are very different things. I had to unlock the safe if I wanted to get us in and out without leaving a trace.

Any cheap safe that opens with a key—and only a cheap safe relies on a key—is simple to unlock. Almost anybody can get into one in half an hour with the help of a YouTube video and a set of twenty-dollar beginner picks. For somebody like me? Butter in a microwave: melted in thirty seconds or less.

For amateurs, electronic keypads look scary, but they can be some of the easiest to crack. Low-end safes like you find in hotels have a pin-hole for an electronic lock bypass in case you change the factory-set master code—which, frankly, most hotels don't—and then forget it, or if the battery dies or something shorts out, but it also makes it a breeze for a professional to get in.

A higher-end safe with an electronic keypad or biometric lock and no physical bypass will keep out your garden-variety locksmith and even most professional burglars, but every commercial-grade electronic-based lock that I knew about had at least one weakness that I could exploit in less than five minutes. Even military-grade electronic locks had exploits if you knew what you were doing.

Dial locks, however, couldn't be solved with software. Not exactly. And the first problem I had to solve was that the American Castle Galaxy Nine used a dial lock.

Three turns to the left, two to the right, that sort of thing. On pretty much anything that you'd find in a standard home or small business you could chuck on a robotic safe dialer—an automated wheel that spun the dial until it had gone through every single possible combination—and then read a book until you heard the click that signaled victory. If you wanted to get technical about it, sure, you were using software to find an exploit. Good safes, however, used dial locks that were supposedly proof against manipulation. The key word being *supposedly*. If you knew how to creatively modify an Angler 96 Robo-Dialer, you could dial an American Castle Galaxy Nine.

The second problem was that it wasn't a normal dial lock. Your standard-issue combination padlocks, like what you'd put on a gym locker, had a three-number combination on a forty-digit dial, theoretically limiting the number of possible combinations to about sixty thousand. With the American Castle Galaxy Nine, even though I could use a robotic safe dialer, it used a five-number combination on a sixty-digit dial.

In other words, I was looking for a match of five sets of numbers from zero to sixty—say 54, 24, 34, 17, and 9. That meant the possible number of combinations was $60 \times 59 \times 59 \times 59 \times 59$.

Which was somewhere in the magnitude of four point two *billion* possible combinations.

It would take the Angler 96 about two and a half *centuries* to dial all those combinations. I only had ten hours. Finding two numbers on my own would leave me with a much more manageable number of combinations for the Angler 96 to dial through. Call it two hundred thousand and change. With my modifications, the Angler 96 was extremely fast, but that still meant that *if* I didn't mess up, and *if* the dialer had to go through each of those two hundred thousand possible combinations, that would leave me . . . about six minutes to spare.

I was gambling on the fact that the odds against needing to dial all two hundred thousand combos were pretty low. And who knows? Maybe I'd get lucky, and the dialer would hit it after forty or fifty thousand tries.

The third problem, and the one I'd be working on while the Angler 96 solved the combination for me, is that the American Castle had a random access code generator companion lock. Basically, even if you had the five-number combination for the dial lock, you also needed a key fob that was synced to the safe and came up with a random number that matched. When you had the combination dialed in, you then had to press a button on the key fob, and then had thirty seconds to type in the code from that into the safe's companion electronic keypad. If you got it wrong, you got a second try. But there wasn't a third try. If you got it wrong on your second try, it activated the relocker, shooting extra bolts through the door. At that point, there was no way in but brute force, and *that* would leave a mark.

Weirdly, this was the easiest part if you knew the secret. The trick with a random number key fob was that they had to be synced to something. In other words, the random number was *not* actually random. All you needed to know was the anchor number and the formula.

Which I did.

Like I'd said to Baker and Cleary at the Market House, there were maybe twenty people in the world who could open an American Castle Galaxy Nine. Sure, with an unlimited amount of time, like a week or two, there were probably more like fifty people who could do it. But in ten hours? That was a very short list of people.

And opening it in ten hours without anybody knowing you'd ever been inside?

That list used to have two people on it: Ginny and me.

The problem was that I couldn't just open the safe. Even once I solved the combination on the main lock and the random number generator for the companion lock, as soon as I pulled the airtight door open, the argon gas inside would release, the pressure would drop, the counter would click over, and we were blown.

Which meant keeping the pressure up.

28

CLEARY AND THE TWO MEN from the garage came in carrying duffel bags and toolboxes. I'd sorted things carefully before we left the warehouse so I could get to work immediately. One of the guys turned around right away for another load, Cleary following, but one of the unnamed guys—he was wearing a black sweater and black pants, and I assumed he had his pistol holstered in the small of his back—sat down on one of the toolboxes to watch.

"I guess you're my minder?"

He didn't say anything. He didn't react at all. I might as well have been speaking Greek to him.

I decided to pretend like he wasn't there and started working on getting the last number in the combination. It was a piece of cake thanks to a trick that Helen MacDonald figured out a few years ago. Helen was pushing eighty, but still working. She was the person who'd trained my dad, and a sort of honorary grandmother to me and Ginny. Dad sent me to stay with Helen while Ginny was recovering from our little adventure in Zurich. I'd ended up staying with Helen for the better part of a year, a sort of apprenticeship. She was both old *and* old-school, but she hadn't slipped at all in her senior years. Only last year she'd done a job at a museum in Thailand that netted out close to four million dollars.

Allegedly.

We still talked a few times a month on the phone.

I took a ruler and a roll of masking tape out of one of the toolboxes and marked a spot with the tape six centimeters to the left of the dial. Then I took a small tank of liquid nitrogen out of a duffel, put on a pair of thick, leather welding gloves, and shot the piece of tape with a nice, long squirt. It frosted up and turned white.

And then I took the dial and gave it a healthy spin. It stopped on the number 29.

The combo was X-X-X-X-29.

One number down, two minutes off the clock. I was making it look easy.

The next trick was something Ginny and I had figured out together: a cheat for the first number.

I pulled out a precut piece of glass about the size of a paperback book and then grabbed my propane torch. I fired up the torch and then, with my free hand, held the glass over the tape, keeping my fingers as far to the edge as I could. The glass was just enough of a barrier to stop the torch from tripping the thermal fuse inside the safe door; once that was tripped, safety bolts automatically slammed home, and if that happened, there was no way to open the safe using the main dial. I counted to twenty while heating the glass and the metal beneath it. As soon as I hit twenty, I dropped the glass, not worrying about shattering shards—I'd clean that up later and didn't have any time to waste before the heat wore off—and then gave the dial a spin in the opposite direction. It stopped on 11.

11-X-X-X-29.

Cleary and the second man came back in pushing the rest of my gear on a rolling cart. Everything was here. Eleven duffel bags, four rubber totes, and twelve canisters of gas and air. None of the men made any move to leave the room.

"Are all three of you going to sit here and watch me?" I asked.

"You worry about your business, and we'll worry about ours," Cleary said.

The second quiet guy made himself comfortable sitting on another one of the bins, while Cleary leaned against the wall. Cleary was looking fidgety. I wondered if he'd had a chance for a smoke during the drive or while he was unloading. He was probably craving another Winston, but the smell of cigarette smoke lingers.

I had already pulled out the robotic safe dialer when Baker came back in.

"Coffee, water, a sandwich, and some pastries. Sorry. No donuts."

I thought about making a half-assed joke about sending a guy named Baker out for baked goods, but he had that cold look in his eyes again. Instead, I took the food and the espresso with a nod of thanks.

I downed the espresso and put the bag of food down off to the side, trying to look like I was concentrating fully on setting up the dialer. But they'd made a mistake. The name of the bakery was in small letters on the paper cup, and I knew something I hadn't known a few minutes ago: we were in Germany.

29

THE ANGLER 96 WAS ALREADY twenty thousand attempts into solving the combination by the time I was ready to finish sealing off the safe.

There was no way to circumvent a pressure drop from triggering a click on the counter, and once that click was logged, it was counted and couldn't be erased. That meant there was only one solution: make sure there *wasn't* a pressure drop. Essentially, I'd created a hermetically sealed bubble of heavy-duty plastic sheeting around the safe. An airlock of sorts. The bubble attached at the top and sides of the safe and then to the floor around me. I had also used lightweight aluminum scaffolding to make a workspace in front of the safe and to keep the bubble big enough; I needed space to solve the combination and to be able to punch in the random number access code. Also, I had to be able to actually *open* the door of the safe, not just unlock it. The bubble wasn't the slickest thing in the world. It looked like a blanket fort made by a couple of rambunctious eight-year-olds. It didn't matter what it looked like, though. All that mattered was that the seams were sealed properly.

Once I had the safe unlocked, I could open the door, take out whatever was inside, and then close up shop behind me without there ever being a change in the level of argon in the safe. No change, no pressure drop, no click on the counter, no clue that we'd ever been here.

Grantchester Ducaine: The Ghost Who Walks through Walls.

Yes, I was pleased with myself.

"Okay," I said. "Time for all of you to get out."

"We're not going anywhere," Cleary said.

"Fine with me, but if you stay in here, you'll asphyxiate pretty quickly."

Baker, who had been watching me carefully the entire time, narrowed his eyes. "What are you talking about?"

"Didn't you guys look at the list of stuff you got for me? The argon gas? The scuba kit and all the canisters of air? You thought we were going swimming."

"Son of a bitch," Baker said, shaking his head, but he looked impressed. "That's how you're doing it. That's what all this crap is? You're a smart one, aren't you?"

I grinned, but the truth was that the compliment should have gone to Ginny. We'd been drinking beer a few years ago and talking about the white whales of safecracking, and she was the one who'd come up with the way to beat the pressure drop. She'd never had a chance to test it out.

Cleary pushed away from the wall. "What's he talking about? We're not going anywhere."

I gestured to the bubble and the aluminum scaffolding. "I'm going to fill this with argon gas to equalize the pressure out here with what's inside of the safe. That way, when I open it, it doesn't trip the pressure sensor. You can stay in here with me, but once I seal it up and get started, you won't have any air to breathe."

Cleary shook his head. "There are plenty of canisters of air."

"Sure. But there's only one regulator." He looked at me blankly. Helpfully, I said, "The breathing thing you stick in your mouth? Sorry. I'm going to have to be in there by myself unless you feel like committing suicide. Which, you know, personal choice and all that."

I didn't bother waiting for him to think it through. I moved two of the duffel bags and one of the totes inside the bubble, and then all the canisters of argon and oxygen.

Baker grabbed my arm. "One thing and one thing only," he said. "It's a metal box."

"It's going to be obvious?"

He gestured to Cleary, and Cleary took a small bag off the rolling cart. It wasn't one of my bags. When he opened it, I saw there was some sort of a nasty-looking compact machine gun in there as well as several magazines of ammunition. Cleary pulled out a small plastic box, opened that, and from a foam nest, pulled out a smaller box that was made of stainless steel. It was about the same size as a ring box, like what an engagement ring came in. If he dropped to one knee, I was going to say no.

Baker took the ring box and handed it to me. "It will look exactly like this. Swap it out. The whole thing. No need to open it." He was still holding my arm with one hand, and he gave it a squeeze. "Nothing fancy. No games. We aren't playing here, Duke. Remember the money. And remember your dad. The rest of his life depends on it."

"Are you threatening me?"

"Do I need to threaten you?" he asked.

I was pretty sure he was threatening me.

But it didn't matter. It was too late to back out.

I stepped inside the bubble and closed it up behind me.

30

THE PLASTIC SHEETING that formed the bubble was frosted and double layered. Translucent enough to let light in, but not enough for them to see in or me to see out. I could see silhouettes of Baker and Cleary and the two other men, but it was only shadows and shapes, no way for them to tell exactly what I was doing. Which was something I was counting on. I had a little side project I wanted to work on while I was waiting for the Angler 96 to do its job.

Pressure first.

I set up my oxygen tank, put the regulator in my mouth, and then started filling the bubble with argon. There was some wiggle room with the pressure sensor in the safe, but a big, quick drop would be a problem, so I had to be careful. I used about half a tank before I stopped and took a pressure reading. I needed to wait fifteen minutes or so before I took a second reading to make sure the pressure was holding, so I used that time to work on my double top secret project for self-defense: I made a stun gun.

Buried in the list of things I'd needed were a few nine-volt batteries and a basic kit of electrical components.

Which, I realize, sounds unimpressive if you don't understand how a stun gun works.

I was counting on Baker and Cleary and whoever was helping them get my gear together not knowing how a stun gun works.

Almost all the extra stuff I was using were items that I might arguably need to open *a* safe, but none of it was needed for *this* particular safe. But it was exactly what I needed to make a homemade stun gun. With the right circuitry to reduce the amperage while simultaneously boosting the voltage, a nine-volt battery, an oscillator, and a capacitor, you could do some damage. Put the electrodes against a grown man—it doesn't matter if it's through the clothes or on the skin—and trigger the charge. You could be the toughest son of a bitch in the world, but electricity is wonderful stuff. Once it was completed, I could put any man on the ground and out of it for at least a few minutes.

Bonus points if it was Cleary, because there was a chance this sucker would make you lose control of your bladder.

Was it paranoid to build myself a homemade stun gun?

Sure.

If I didn't need it, no harm, no foul. I'd asked for the components back in the Market House when we were still in Los Angeles, back when I'd just been a *little* nervous. But since then, there'd been a bunch of red flags, and I had a fully wired stun gun ready to go by the time fifteen minutes were up. It didn't look like much, and it was small enough that I could slip it in my pocket, which was part of the charm.

The pressure in the bubble was holding, so I dumped the valve in the argon tank open again, keeping an eye on my readings. I had three full tanks, but even with my back-of-the-envelope math, I was pretty sure I wouldn't use more than one and a quarter.

"How's it going in there?" Baker's voice through the bubble. Muffled, but understandable.

I pulled the regulator out of my mouth. "Good. Time?" I shoved it back in and took a breath.

"Eight hours."

Which, I suddenly realized, really meant I needed to be done in seven, because it was going to take a little while to undo everything.

I pulled the regulator back out. "No more questions. Can't talk and breathe at the same time."

I popped the mouthpiece back in and took a deep breath. I hadn't really needed to ask him the time since I had my own timer, but I wanted him looking at his watch too. It gave him something to do other than imagining what I was up to in here.

Regardless, I was in good shape. There wasn't much else for me to do other than make sure I was ready to outwit the random number generator. I had Ginny to thank on this one too. Like I said, what the American Castle corporation called a random number generator couldn't be entirely random. It had to sync up with a matched key. Lots of banks used versions of them for business accounts. The account holder has a key fob with a button and a basic LCD screen. Log in to your account and the bank pops up a verification screen. Press the button on the key fob, and voilà! A code. Except for you to be able to match it up, there had to be some sort of base number that both devices were working off at the same time.

American Castle used a three-digit base number, and the formula was simply the base number multiplied by the combined day, month, and military time of day, all written sequentially. For example, if the base number was 829, and it was July 7 at 16:52, the code was 829 x 07071652, or 5862399508. Because I was limited to two tries, it was impossible to hack.

Unless you knew the base number.

Which I shouldn't have known, because American Castle should have chosen the three-digit base code randomly for each safe. Except they didn't. Somebody, somewhere at American Castle, had decided to tie the serial number to the base code. It made a sort of sense: if somebody lost their key fob and needed another one, all American Castle required was the serial number to send you out a new one.

But you had to have more than just the serial number—which was plainly and stupidly visible on the front right bottom corner of the safe—to figure it out. You needed to know the equation they used to convert a twelve-digit serial number into a three-digit base code.

Ginny had figured it out.

She was better at math than I was. Better at most things.

Just not as lucky.

The thought made me laugh. It had been a long time since I'd thought of myself as lucky.

31

THE AUTO-DIALER KEPT A PLEASANT HUM as it worked to untangle the rest of the combination. Between that and the sound of me breathing through the regulator, there was a sort of rhythmic music to it. It was almost relaxing.

There wasn't anything to do but wait. An occupational hazard of thieving. There was a *lot* of waiting for things to happen when you were stealing stuff. It was something I struggled with when I was younger; I wasn't a naturally patient person. It was something I'd worked on with Helen, though. Both she and my dad were avid readers, and Helen had turned me into one as well during the time that I apprenticed with her.

Thinking of Helen made me take another look at the detritus of gear and tools around me. I could hear her voice: "A messy workplace makes for a messy mind."

Even with the regulator in my mouth, I had to smile.

The time I'd spent with her had felt so different from what I was used to with my dad and Ginny. Helen kept me working on technical skills, of course, but she insisted we focus on soft skills as well. Going to museums and galleries so I could understand art, bringing me to ballet recitals and modern dance performances, even making me take cooking lessons.

"If you're going to steal from the wealthy," Helen liked to say, "it's much easier if they think you are one of them." It was one of the reasons why both my dad and Helen insisted Ginny and I go to an elite college.

But I don't think it was just learning how to pass. In a lot of ways, the difference was that my dad taught me how to have a life as a criminal, but Helen taught me how to have a *life* as a criminal.

I remember one day when we were in Rome, part of a long con that Helen was in the middle of. I think Helen was passing herself off as Lady Herirshare, and I was supposed to be her great-nephew and the last heir to some sort of American railroad fortune. But we were having lunch at an exorbitantly priced bistro around the corner from our equally exorbitantly priced hotel when I asked her what the point was of all the extracurricular activities she was making me do.

She took a bite of her salad and considered me. "You can't see it because you're still a child," she said, despite me being close to eighteen at the time. "But there are scars there. Your mom's dead. You killed your first man at eleven. And another in Zurich last year. You must know that isn't a normal childhood."

I shrugged and speared some pasta, which was, as far as I could tell, fancy mac and cheese. "What's normal?"

She raised a skeptical eyebrow. It was something she'd perfected, and it was devastating.

"We," she said, "and by we, I mean me, your father, most of the men and women you've worked with your whole life, keep a sort of loosely agreed set of ethical boundaries. You do what you say you're going to do, and you try to do it with as little violence as possible. Sometimes it's not possible to avoid, and then, well." She shrugged. "We're professionals. We're good at what we do, and we have our eyes open. It's the life we've chosen. But your father . . ."

"What?"

She looked down at her plate and then pushed it aside and reached for her wineglass. There was just a sip left. The waiter appeared as if magically summoned, asking if she wanted another glass, and in fluent Italian, Helen declined. Once the waiter had departed to a reasonable distance, she spoke again.

"Sometimes I wonder if he ever thought about the cost of making this decision for you."

I was sure my face showed how confused I felt. "What cost?"

"Oh, he's like one of those ridiculous sporting parents you have in America. That's what he thinks of himself like. You know that, yes? You must know that. He said to me on more than one occasion that if you were athletes, he'd be raising you to be the greatest of all time. You and Ginny like Serena and Venus Williams. But you can't create that kind of transcendent talent without pushing too far occasionally. There's a thin line between pushing a child to reach their full potential and abuse, and he was on that line often enough."

I shook my head. "But he was right. Wasn't he? I mean, Ginny is . . . she's going to be the GOAT." I smiled. "And come on, in any other universe, Venus would be considered an all-timer. I'll take that."

Helen leaned forward and reached across the table. I leaned in the last few inches so she could gently pat my cheek.

"I love you, Duke," she said. "You're a good kid. But did it ever occur to you *why* your dad never asked you if this was what you wanted?" She leaned back in her chair and then turned, caught the eye of the waiter, and motioned for the bill. "You can't have an upbringing like you did without it leaving scars you could see from space."

I didn't say anything to that, and it wasn't something we talked about again. At least, it wasn't something *I* talked about again. A lot of Helen's lessons came at me obliquely, and I know that she worried about the shadow of the life we lived hanging over me, but I didn't see the point in dwelling on it.

Violence was just the cost of doing business.

32

THE ANGLER 96 ROBO-DIALER BEEPED to let me know it had a hit. It happened much quicker than I expected. The dialer had only needed to go through seventy thousand, or around 35 percent of the possible combinations before unlocking the safe. Pure good luck that made me look better than I was.

Outside the bubble, I saw one of the shadows stand up and try to peer in. I was sure they could only see what I could while looking out, which was vague shapes and movement. No way to tell what I was really doing. But there was no way for me to tell what *they* were really doing either.

I moved my homemade stun gun into my right back pocket, and then put a couple of lockpicks—not something I needed for a safe, but in the same way they hadn't questioned the nine-volt batteries, they hadn't questioned that request either—in my front right pocket. I'd fashioned a handcuff key using a pair of pliers and one of the picks while I was waiting for the robotic dialer, and I put that into my other back pocket.

I was on edge.

I double-checked the pressure to make sure the argon was still holding steady and didn't need another top-up, did the math to figure out the access code, punched it into the keypad, turned the lever, and I was in.

It was anticlimactic, but I hummed a few bars of the fourth movement of Beethoven's Symphony No. 9 through the regulator anyway.

Ode to Joy has been every safecracker's anthem since *Die Hard* was released.

I'm pretty sure I'm one of the few people rooting for Hans Gruber when I watch that movie. It would have been a fantastic heist except for Bruce Willis ruining everything as his John McClane character. Aside from the part of the plan where Gruber was planning to blow up a whole bunch of people, I thought the people doing the stealing were the good guys.

The door to the Galaxy Nine weighed hundreds of pounds on its own, but it was so well balanced that it floated open like a paper plane gliding through the air. I could have opened it with my pinkie finger.

"Are you in?" Baker's voice, still muffled.

I pulled the regulator out, called, "Working on it," and then shoved the mouthpiece back into my mouth.

The safe was completely empty, except for a small metal box that looked like a dead ringer for the one Baker had given me to switch out.

No papers, no cash, no jewelry, no weapons.

Nothing except for the box.

And a tiny motion-activated camera.

Uh-oh.

Too late, I turned my face away.

33

THE CAMERA WAS SIMPLY RESTING on the shelf next to the metal cube. It was small. Like a deck of cards. I snatched it, turning the lens away from me. I popped the battery out and opened the camera up with a screwdriver from my kit. It had a Wi-Fi chip. There was a good chance the video it had gotten of me was already floating in the cloud.

I thought about it for a few seconds, then did a quick check to make sure it didn't have a GPS chip working on a separate battery. It was flat enough that I could stuff it in my front left pocket—with the lockpicks, the stun gun, and the handcuff key, it was the only pocket that was still empty—without an obvious bulge. I sure as hell wasn't telling Baker about it. The deal had been to get in, get out without anybody knowing. As far as he was concerned, I'd held up my end of the bargain and he owed me forty thousand dollars. I wanted every penny of it and for my dad to walk free.

But the camera meant that I didn't know how long we had before the bad guys came rolling in. If tripping the motion sensor just automatically sent the video or photo to storage somewhere, it might be days or weeks before anybody noticed. But if it triggered an actual alert, and if there was somebody who was supposed to be watching for alerts, it could be sooner rather than later.

Time to hurry.

I swapped out the silver cube for the one Cleary had handed me, checked the gas to make sure I was good, and then closed the safe back up. Once it was closed and locked and I didn't have to worry about the pressure drop, I opened the bubble.

"You got it?" Baker said as soon as he saw my head poke out of the opening.

"Keep the door to the room open," I said, pulling the regulator out of my mouth. "The argon will dissipate pretty quickly, but you don't want us all passing out." I handed him the silver cube. "Here you go."

He held it up in front of him. Cleary and the other two men huddled around him, staring at it as if they'd finally found the Holy Grail. It was a comical sight: four grown men looking at a little metal box as if it was the most amazing thing they'd ever seen.

Cleary pulled the plastic box with the foam nest back out of the duffel bag, and Baker put the ring box inside. Cleary closed the protective case and then slid it into his voluminous jacket pocket. Evidently, he and Baker thought the real deal was safer on Cleary's body then in a bag with the rest of the tools.

I turned my attention to packing up the gear. I could feel the camera in my pocket, and it was making me nervous. I wanted to get out of there as soon as possible, and I sure as hell didn't want Baker finding out about the camera and deciding I wasn't getting the rest of my payment.

As soon as the last piece of gear was squared away and ready to be taken out, Baker held up the blackout hood and reached to slip it over my head.

I pulled back.

"It's for your own protection," he said. "You know the drill. If we told you, we'd have to kill you." He smiled, but his eyes were diamond cold again.

Those eyes were the last thing I saw before the hood came down over my head and he cinched it closed, once again using a zip tie to secure it.

Which would have been more dramatic, except that he took my elbow and walked me carefully back to the van.

I made it more awkward than I needed to, because I kept my hand low and near my back pocket where my homemade stun gun was riding shotgun. I only relaxed once he got me situated on the bench. If they were going to kill me, they weren't going to do it now. Though, that made sense: a bunch of blood and my dead body might be a giveaway that something interesting had happened near the Galaxy Nine.

The back doors of the van thumped shut. A few seconds later, we started moving. I gave it ten minutes before I decided I wanted a look around.

I was surprised they hadn't frisked me before putting me back in the van. They'd been so careful on the way here, making me leave my cell phone at home, not letting me take any of my own gear or tools, having me strip down and change into clothes they provided, even going so far as to pat me down again and then pick up a new pair of shoes that fit in the hour I was given to sort stuff at the warehouse. But the fact that they weren't being careful anymore left me with a hollow feeling in the pit of my stomach.

Maybe they were being less careful because the job was over and all we had to do was make a clean getaway, but maybe it was because they were going to dump my body.

But not being frisked meant that I didn't have any problem with the hood. I pulled the lockpicks out of my right front pocket and felt for one of the tension wrenches. It was a hardened, flat piece of metal with a small ninety-degree bend at the end. People like to use zip ties for restraints because they ratchet closed. The easiest way to get them off is with a pair of wire cutters. Or, by simply reaching up, slipping the end of something thin and strong—like, say, a tension wrench—under the ratchet tab, and then gently pulling the zip tie open. That way you could reuse the zip tie if you didn't want anybody to know you'd taken a peek around.

It was pitch black in the van.

Right. No windows in the cargo area.

I sighed, put the hood back on over my head, zip-tied it shut again, and lay down on the bench. There wasn't anything to do but go to sleep.

34

I WAS SORE, TIRED, HUNGRY, THIRSTY, and cranky by the time they let me out of the van.

We'd stopped twice, both times Cleary impatiently handing me the bucket so I could go to the bathroom, but there was no offer of anything to eat or drink. The second time, I felt him grab at the zip tie on the hood, making sure it was still securely fastened.

All I wanted was my passport back, my ticket home, and a bag full of cash waiting for me when I got off the plane. My plan was to pick my dad up at the prison, stop for a visit with Ginny before taking Dad out for dinner, and then to skip town for a month in case this blew back at me.

It was the damn camera.

Sure, I'd had the regulator in my mouth, but that didn't really hide who I was. The best-case scenario was that there was no automatic notification, and because nobody suspected a break-in, they wouldn't check the camera feed. And maybe, like a lot of security systems, they only kept a week of data. As long as they didn't check the system, I was pure and free.

Except I was an idiot.

I'd *taken* the camera. While I was sure Baker's duplicate box could pass the sniff test, the next time whomever it was opened the safe, they'd see the camera was missing. If that happened before the security system data rolled over and erased the photo . . .

The clock was ticking. I wanted to get my feet back on US soil as soon as possible. I figured that whatever agency Baker and Cleary were involved with, the person or company—or, more likely, country—we'd hit wasn't going to take kindly to the intrusion. I was certain we'd been in Germany, but it could have been anybody: the Russians, the Chinese, the Japanese. Not that it mattered. German bullets killed you just as dead as bullets from any other country.

"Hold still," Cleary said. I heard the snip of wire cutters going through the plastic zip tie and then he pulled the hood off my head.

We were back in the same warehouse. Two of the BMWs were gone, as was the other van. There was no sign of Baker, but one of the quiet guys, the one whose hair was going gray, was already busy at the workbench. He was leaning over some kind of an assault rifle. Next to the rifle, I could see the protective case holding the silver box I'd taken from the safe.

"Where's Baker?"

"He's at the ATM, taking out your cash. I hope small bills are okay," Cleary said.

He grinned at me. I didn't like it. Cleary had been an asshole the entire time, and suddenly he was Captain Hilarious? Maybe it was because he'd been stressed out about the job, but maybe not. He didn't seem like the kind of guy who got too nervous about doing a mission.

Maybe he was happy because he was about to be able to get rid of me.

He reached into his jacket pocket and his smile turned to a frown when he realized his pack of Winstons was empty.

"Yo!" He called across the warehouse to the guy working on the rifle. He held up the empty pack of smokes. The man nodded and pulled out his own pack. They looked weird to me, but from a distance, I couldn't quite figure out why that was.

Cleary walked over and lit the bummed cigarette. Then he opened the protective case and pulled out the silver box. He came back looking even happier than he had a few seconds ago when he was joking about my money.

I couldn't decide if it was the box from the safe or the cigarette that was making him so happy.

"Come on," he said. He slipped the box into his pocket. "We'll have you wait in the office." The smoke from the cigarette was acrid and biting.

He motioned me ahead of him toward the room in the corner.

I didn't like it. They hadn't put me in there before, so why now? Why show me another part of the warehouse. I had my hand in my back pocket, holding on to my homemade stun gun. Once we were inside, I was planning to pull it out and keep it under my leg. Handy in case I needed it.

I didn't get a chance.

As soon as I was through the doorway, Cleary hit me in the kidney.

35

IT FELT LIKE I'D BEEN HIT with a sledgehammer. I went down hard.

For the record, if you've never had a full-sized man who knows how to punch hit you in the kidney, it sucks.

Cleary used a smoothly practiced move to slap the shackle of a handcuff over my right wrist, then drag me a couple of feet across the floor, and then lock the other shackle onto a bolt sunk in the wall.

I did not take it as a good sign that there was a bolt sunk into the wall for just this eventuality.

"No smart comments now, huh?"

"You punch like a baby." The effect I'd been hoping for was muted by the fact that I more or less had to gasp the phrase out.

He laughed and then stepped toward me, leaning over, but careful to keep enough distance that I couldn't get to him. "You have no idea what this is about," he said, patting at the pocket of his jacket where he'd stashed the box. "No idea at all. Now just sit tight, and I'll be back to take care of you in a few minutes."

I waited until the door had closed behind him to moan, "Asshole."

I was pretty sure I'd be pissing blood for the next week.

If there was a next week.

That whole, "I'll be back to take care of you in a few minutes" thing didn't sound promising.

I spent a couple of seconds catching my breath and then took stock. There wasn't much in the room: a desk with a folding chair, a phone charger plugged into the wall with a cord that was long enough so that you could charge your phone on the desk, a second folding chair that was just out of reach, and a tall, narrow metal storage cabinet that was padlocked shut. The only thing I had going for me was that I was handcuffed on the blind side of the door. When the door opened, I'd be shielded from view; whoever came in next would have to step all the way in before they could see me. Not a problem if the person you were coming to deal with was handcuffed to a wall, but there was no way I was staying handcuffed.

Baker's joke about taking me out in a field and shooting me in the back of the head didn't seem like much of a joke anymore. This was why I didn't like to deal with cops and feds. At least with criminals you go in *expecting* them to screw you over.

In a way, bringing me back here made sense. I figured Baker had decided to drive me all the way back here because it was home turf for them. Why take the risk of killing me and trying to dump my body before they handed off the ring box we'd taken from the safe? The whole point of using me was so that we could get in and out without anybody noticing. If you had an unbreakable safe holding something that you very much did not want to get stolen, and then you heard that a relatively famous safecracker was found dead in the general vicinity, well, that would raise some questions.

And now that we were back at the warehouse hundreds of miles away from the job and I was safely handcuffed to the wall, they had all the time in the world to take care of me. Why rush? I was handcuffed to the wall. They figured I wasn't going anywhere.

Which, come on, seriously?

It was as if they'd never even thought about who I was or why they'd hired me in the first place.

Incredibly disrespectful.

I'd just done something impossible with one of the best safes in the world, and they thought a pair of handcuffs was going to slow me down?

36

ONCE I WAS OUT OF THE HANDCUFFS, I spent a few seconds massaging the spot where Cleary had sucker punched me, but then I heard the exterior rolling garage door opening. I didn't know if that was somebody leaving or somebody coming back, but it didn't matter: they might think they had all the time in the world, but I knew I didn't.

The desk drawers were empty except for a few chocolate bar wrappers. Snickers, but with what looked like Russian written on the wrapper. I thought about trying to use the phone charging cord as a garrote, but my homemade stun gun would be quicker and more effective. Slowly strangling somebody to death in a fight was cinematic, but it was, well, slow. Being slow was a good way to lose a fight.

That didn't stop me from taking the phone charger and stuffing it in my pocket with the camera, though: I needed a new charger, and a decent one was like thirty bucks.

I walked over to the storage cabinet. It was tall, shallow, and narrow. If it weren't for the high-security padlock holding it shut—and the fact that I was doing work for some sort of American agency that was willing to murder me to keep a job secret—I would have assumed it was full of office supplies. But nobody used a hardened steel six-pin padlock to keep their staples and sticky notes unpilfered. I gave the top an experimental tug. The cabinet was bolted to the wall.

The quickest way through a standard padlock is a pair of long-handled bolt cutters. Cutting through the hasp of your every-day Master Lock gym lock with bolt cutters was something even a ninety-eight-pound weakling could manage. But aside from not having a pair of bolt cutters handy, the hardened steel of the high-security lock made that impossible without an industrial-grade pair of bolt cutters with three-foot handles. So, there was that. And the six-pin tumbler was also enough to stop your garden-variety locksmiths.

I was always shocked at how bad so-called professionals were at picking locks.

It only took me thirty seconds.

If opening the American Castle Galaxy Nine had meant the *Ode to Joy* played in my head, seeing what was inside the cabinet almost made me sing it out loud.

It was completely full.

And when I say completely full, I mean *completely* full.

Top to bottom.

With money.

Cash.

Every shelf was stacked with bank-wrapped bundles of American twenty-dollar bills.

I did a quick and dirty estimate. The bundles were stacked three deep, fifteen high, and ten across. Call it four hundred and fifty bundles per shelf, six shelves high. A bank bundle was one hundred bills, so each bundle was two thousand dollars, which meant . . .

More than five million dollars.

And that's when I heard footsteps.

37

I BARELY HAD TIME to press myself against the wall by the door.

The instant it opened, I jabbed my homemade stun gun into the chest of the person standing there and hit the trigger. I kept it pressed hard against his chest until he hit the ground, flopping and jerking around.

It was Cleary.

I didn't have any kind of a plan past that, so I was profoundly relieved to look up and see the warehouse was empty. The sound of the garage door opening and closing had been the gray-haired man leaving.

I grabbed Cleary by the collar and hauled him over to where the one end of the handcuffs was still secured to the bolt in the wall, and then I closed the free shackle over his wrist. I went out to the main room and rummaged around on the workbench until I found a box cutter and then went back into the office. Cleary was starting to stir, so I hit him with the stun gun again. It might have been overkill, but I wasn't taking any chances.

I used the razor to cut off all his clothes, including his underwear. Unless he kept a handcuff key tucked into his cheek like a squirrel, I figured he wasn't going anywhere until help arrived. Leave me alone naked with a pair of handcuffs and I'll still figure it out, but for most people, without a key, handcuffs do the job just fine.

Just in case, for good measure, I took two lockpicks and broke the tips off inside of each of the key passageways. Even if he had a handcuff key squirreled away or Baker showed up with his own, Cleary wasn't getting those handcuffs off without a hacksaw.

I had a sudden thought and then reached for the pocket of his jacket where he'd stashed my passport.

It was still there, so I took it.

And then I had another thought.

The ring box was also still in his pocket.

I said, "Holy crap," aloud, which made me feel kind of silly since Cleary was too out of it to appreciate my gleeful surprise at finding the ring box.

Normally, I went for the whole "honor among thieves" thing. Which wasn't much of a thing, criminals being generally willing to play fast and loose with social conventions. That being said, word did get around if you had a habit of screwing your partners; if you knew your partners, you could usually trust them to be square. But there were a few compelling reasons for me to take the box. First of all, these guys had already decided to screw *me* over. Once your partners make it clear the plan is to squeeze a few rounds into your head and hide your body, all bets were off. And second of all, honor among thieves only applied to thieves, not feds.

The only chance I had at getting out of this alive was to make it back to the continental United States and to hope that because Baker and Cleary were government suits, they'd live and let live. I had the pictures from the Market House that Mimi had gotten for me, but the ring box was my biggest bargaining chip; I was holding out hope that if I could get home safely, I could use it as leverage to hold them to their deal.

I looked at Cleary unconscious on the floor, splayed out, his legs spread. What an asshole. I hauled off and kicked him squarely in the nuts, following through like I was trying to sink a fifty-yard field goal to cover the spread.

He'd feel that when he came to.

Okay. Home.

I needed two things. I needed to get this box off my person and somewhere safe, and now that I had my passport back, I needed funds to get myself home.

Well. The second part was easy. I stepped over to the supply cabinet.

It was physically painful to stand in front of that much money. But I couldn't take it: there was no way I could carry it. A million dollars in one-hundred-dollar bills fits neatly in a small bag and weighs a little more than twenty pounds. The same amount of money in twenty-dollar bills weighs more than Ginny and is about as easy to stuff in a duffel bag. Five million dollars? Five million in twenty-dollar bills weighs about five hundred and fifty pounds.

The other concern was that even if I could carry all of it, I had to get it through customs. I was in Zurich. I had to get it back to the United States. If I'd known I needed to transport that much cash ahead of time, I'd have figured out arrangements, but whatever I took now was going to have to fly commercial right alongside me. I wasn't going to try to pass five million dollars through the X-ray machine. I was pretty sure that would get me pulled aside for some extra security screening. And checking it as luggage didn't seem any smarter. Anything to declare? No, nothing other than five million bucks in cash in these half dozen oversized suitcases. All of which was compounded by the fact that, last time I'd checked, it was still illegal to cross the border with more than ten thousand dollars.

The other option was to take all of it and just vanish. Except that came with some caveats.

You *can* disappear on five million dollars, even if the United States government is hunting you, but only if you are willing to truly disappear. When the USA wants to find you, they *will* find you, unless you go all the way: you've got to ghost forever. Off the grid. No letters home, no phone calls. And you can't live it up like you've got five million dollars in cash. You've got to keep under the radar. Go somewhere you won't stand out, stay low-key. Be so damn boring that you're invisible. Which makes having five million dollars not very fun.

But even if I thought I could hack a life on the run, I wasn't willing to do it. I wasn't willing to leave my friends and family behind. That was no life at all.

The only way out was through.

I had to get back home. Dropping my body in some dark alley in Europe was one thing, but—and maybe I was being naive—doing it back in LA felt like more of a stretch for a federal agency.

Okay. Almost certainly it was naive. But I wasn't sure what choice I had other than to try to get back home.

I went back to the workbench and found a roll of clear packing tape, and then dumped one of the duffel bags out. I put the packing tape inside and then fished the phone charger out of my pocket and put that inside as well. Next, I took twenty bundles of cash from the storage cabinet and filled the bag. I was unreasonably mad that the money was in twenties instead of in hundred-dollar bills, but cash was cash. Twenty stacks added up to the forty thousand dollars I was still owed for the job, but the second Cleary had cuffed me to the wall, my fee had gone up, so I grabbed another twenty stacks. I would have taken more, but that was about as much as I thought I could sneak through the airport.

As soon as the money was in the bag, I got the hell out of there.

I thought about taking one of the BMWs, but I suspected the cars had GPS trackers. Even though they'd cancel my plane ticket, Baker would probably look to the airport right away. I was hoping to slip through—pay cash for a new ticket—and maybe Baker would think I'd gone to ground. No sense tipping them off; I wanted as much of a head start as possible.

The neighborhood was industrial, but there was an older woman getting into a newer Fiat just down the street from the door to the warehouse.

She spoke enough English for me to determine that yes, in exchange for one of my stacks of twenty-dollar bills, she would be more than happy to take me to the airport and make any stops I wanted along the way.

38

I WISHED I'D HAD A DIFFERENT PASSPORT, but I had to work with what I had. For thirty-eight hundred dollars in cash—well, technically, I had to convert it into euros first—I booked a one-way business class ticket under my name on the next flight direct to Los Angeles. It left in forty-eight minutes.

I ducked into the bathroom, shoved the change from my ticket conversion into my pocket, and then used the tape I'd taken from the warehouse to secure the rest of the money around my stomach. I got everything except for one stack of bills taped securely, and I stuffed those in my pocket along with the loose bills. The money taped to me would be uncomfortable to peel off my body when we landed, but at least I was pretty sure that I'd be able to get through airport security here and customs in the US with it. I suppose I could have shipped it along with the cube, but I just couldn't force myself to part with the cash. Besides, the ring box looked like a generic thing, while cash looked like, well, cash. There were much better odds the cube would make it home if it wasn't in the same package as the twenty-dollar bills.

Security was a breeze. There was a separate line for business class passengers, and nobody seemed to notice or care that I was looking kind of lumpy or that I was traveling with a duffel bag that only held the phone charger I'd snagged back at the warehouse. Everything else had gone into the trash.

I had a few minutes at the gate, so I stepped into a small store selling tourist knickknacks and menswear. I bought a zippered hoodie that was two sizes too big, a few button-downs, a pair of pants, a couple of pairs of socks and underwear, and a toiletry kit. Then, on a whim, I stopped in the duty-free store and got a nice bottle of whiskey for Paulie.

I didn't actually want any of what I'd bought. Other than the whiskey, I was planning to toss everything once I was on the other side at LAX. But the hoodie would help smooth the contours of my cashed-up body, and the other crap was so that I could leave LAX without getting strip-searched; when you come back from Europe, and customs and immigration sees the only things you're carrying are a phone charger, an empty bag, and a passport, you tend to get pulled aside for enhanced screening.

By the time I was finished shopping, the plane was loaded up. I boarded, tossed the now partially full duffel bag in the overhead compartment, buckled up, and accepted a glass of bubbly and a complimentary amenity kit from the flight attendant.

Business class was the best.

It was barely more than two hours since I'd cuffed Cleary to the wall. By now, somebody was sure to have found him. I had a new ticket and had made it onto my flight, but I was sure Baker had flagged my name; I could get out of Europe, but the second I landed in the United States, there'd be somebody waiting to meet me. If it was Cleary—if he somehow beat me back to LA—I was going to be in for a world of hurt. I was hopeful they wouldn't just murder me, not on American soil, but there wasn't much I could do about it now, and I had fourteen hours to kill. I stopped a flight attendant and ordered a gin and tonic.

And then I changed it to a double.

I wondered for a few seconds what agency it was, exactly, that Baker and Cleary worked for. CIA, NSA, Department of Defense, Homeland Security?

Why had I never asked to see their ID?

Not that it mattered. They were probably CIA, but in the years since 9/11, there'd been such an expansion of intelligence services and agencies that it was impossible to tell for sure. All I knew is that they didn't work for the National Park Service.

Stupid. Stupid. Stupid. What was I thinking, heading home right away? I didn't have to disappear completely and forever. Just for long enough so that things could cool down. I could have taken some of the money and laid low for a few months. Vacationed in Italy. Rented a flat somewhere in the French countryside. Gone to Barcelona and gotten fat on . . . what kind of food was Spain famous for?

I sighed. No. I couldn't have done any of that. I couldn't have done anything except gone home. Already, this was the longest I'd been gone from Ginny since everything had turned to shit. It didn't matter that I wasn't even sure she knew I was gone. *I* knew I was gone, and that was enough.

All I could hope for was that a direct flight to Los Angeles and the United States mainland would make it harder for Baker to simply have me disappear. Maybe instead of killing me, they'd just lock me away for a few years. With a little luck, I thought, surprising myself with a smile, instead of whisking me away to some off-the-books dark site, they'd send me to the federal pen, and I'd end up getting to spend time with my dad. Paulie could visit us both at the same time. Not a great ending to this little escapade, but it beat rotting in a shallow grave or having my nipples clamped to the business end of a twelve-volt battery.

I drank my G&T, ordered another double, and then started to figure out what my options were for avoiding prison.

It helped that I had an ace up my sleeve.

Or rather, it helped that I'd gotten rid of that ace before stepping foot on the plane. Even I wasn't dumb enough to just fly home with the prize in my pocket.

As long as they brought me in alive, I had something to negotiate with, because I was certain they wanted that box back more than they wanted me dead.

Certain was the wrong word. More like, hopeful.

But just in case, I was going to try to figure out how to leave LAX without getting picked up.

39

THE BEST IDEA I COULD come up with was to hide in the airport bathroom for a few hours before I went through customs.

It was not a particularly good plan, but I thought that maybe if I waited long enough, whoever it was that Baker sent to the airport would get bored and leave.

I didn't even get the chance to find out how dumb my plan was.

When the plane came to a stop, the pilot asked everybody to remain seated.

"Just a small security issue, ladies and gentlemen."

I was ready when the two agents came to my seat.

They were a man and a woman.

The guy was Asian. Korean descent, I thought, close to six feet tall, a little younger than me. He had a pretty-boy smile and was wearing a suit that had obviously been tailored. He seemed like he was in a good mood, which was . . . reassuring?

The woman was a few years older than me, mid-thirties, with the first hint of wrinkles around the corners of her eyes. I had no clue what the difference was between laugh lines and frown lines, but she looked pretty. And serious. Pretty serious. She seemed to be very much in charge. The kind of woman who either found me charming or wanted to push me in front of a bus.

I was hoping she was the former.

Passengers were craning their heads to watch the two agents usher me off the plane, but as soon as we hit the jet bridge, I was filled with an unaccountable sense of optimism: there were four uniformed police officers waiting as backup.

If they were going to kill me—or even black-site me—they'd get me out of there as quickly and cleanly as possible, with no witnesses. Plainclothes agency muscle and an unmarked van, not boys in blue on standby.

The woman had her hand on my elbow. "Let's do this with a minimum of fuss, Mr. Ducaine. Okay?"

"It's Duke."

"We know. Your file is extremely comprehensive, and we know you go by Duke rather than Grantchester, but at least for the time being I think we'll stick to Mr. Ducaine and the illusion of formality that accompanies it," she said.

Huh. Interesting.

"I'm Greaves," she continued. She had the flat accent of a native Midwesterner. If I had to guess, I would have said Iowa. "And my associate is Agent Park. FBI. He'll show you identification as soon as we are out of public sight. But in the meantime, can we agree that you won't be a problem?"

"You aren't going to cuff me?"

Park laughed. "What's the point in cuffing you. You'd be out of them before we even clicked them shut. You're famous, man."

I liked this guy.

"But I'm under arrest?"

"We just want to have a few words."

Park had that smooth California accent that spoke of a childhood of sunshine and surfing, and I would have bet good money that he was a fun guy to have a beer with.

Though, realistically, I probably wouldn't have been in this mess at all if I could just stop betting on things . . .

Greaves kept her hand on my elbow, Park walking on the other side of me. Two of the cops walked in front of us, two behind, and they took us down a side corridor, away from the official immigration and customs lines.

"You'll have to forgive Agent Park," Greaves said. Her serious facade cracked a little. "He worked robbery for a couple of years. He's a fan."

"Of your dad, really," Park said. "He was the best. I still can't believe when he finally got popped it was for something so sloppy."

I kept myself from reacting.

Park continued, "It was a pleasure to get to meet him, though. No joke. He's an artist."

I glanced at him and saw him shaking his head, but with a big smile plastered across his face.

My dad had that effect on people. He wasn't just good at getting safes and locks to open. He was one of the best confidence men working. Or, he had been. Before he relocated to FCI Terminal Island.

Obviously, I wish my dad wasn't in prison, but at least it was conveniently located, close enough to Long Beach that when I went on my monthly visits I could also hit up my favorite taco joint. I could do a lot worse than getting thrown in there with Dad. As far as federal correctional institutions go, while FCI Terminal Island didn't live up to the old "Club Fed" nickname it had in the 1980s, it was still pretty cushy.

Greaves gave my elbow a squeeze. "Sorry, Mr. Ducaine," she said, "but you didn't answer my question. I'm going to need to hear you say out loud that you're not going to be a problem. You're not going to try to run, right? Because that would be a pain in the ass, and honestly, we'd just catch you. I ran track at Georgetown, and Park was on scholarship for D1 basketball. I promise, we're both faster than you are." Now she was actually smiling a bit.

The smile seemed genuine.

Which, for some reason, was deeply unsettling.

What the hell was going on?

I glanced at her partner. "You played Division 1 basketball?"

Park smiled again. He was a remarkably happy guy for an FBI agent. "I still hold the school record for most assists in a season. Good university, lousy basketball team. But hey, it was either be a starter there or warm the bench at a bigger name school that wasn't as good academically. Four-year starter and I graduated without any student debt. All in all, a good deal."

The cops in front of us turned left and opened up a door into a conference room. Greaves marched me around the table and sat me as far away from the door as possible. Park shut the door, leaving it so it was just me, Greaves, and Park.

Park pulled out his ID and showed it to me.

I didn't really know what FBI identification was supposed to look like, but it was either the best fake I'd ever seen or the real deal. The lamination showed wear, and the picture was just enough out-of-date—Park had grown his hair out from a buzz cut—to convince me.

"Can we get you something to eat or drink?" Park asked. He'd taken out a notebook and pen and put them on the table in front of him. This was going to be official.

"I'm good," I said. "For now. I got to fly business class, so I probably ate better than I usually do. Slept too. And right now, I'm kind of wired, but I might need a coffee if this goes long." I put my hands on the table and leaned forward. "Let's cut to the chase here. What do you want?"

"What do we want?" Greaves asked. She looked surprised. "Look, we clearly know who you are, even if Park has a bit of a fangirl crush going on, and that means we know enough about your history to know that you've been mostly playing it straight since what happened with your sister and your dad getting popped."

She stopped talking and stared at me, narrowing her eyes. "Sore spot?" she asked.

She'd caught a glimpse of something that I'd been taught to keep hidden.

40

THE GUY WHO MY DAD HIRED to teach me and Ginny to shoot when we were kids told me it was my "whatever needs to be done" face.

And he'd also told me to make sure nobody else ever saw that face.

He was a former SAS instructor with forty-two confirmed sniper kills.

"Don't telegraph it," he'd said to me after a few weeks, when we'd started working on close-quarters firearms combat. "It's written on your face."

"Telegraph what?" Ginny had asked.

"That he's about to pull the trigger," he'd said.

The truth is that these training sessions weren't at all unusual. Just like Dad hired us tutors for Spanish and trigonometry, we had tutors for shooting and other tricks of the trade.

Ginny tilted her head. "And you don't think I'd pull the trigger?" she asked. She was genuinely curious. She was always more curious than I was.

"That's not really what I'm talking about, Ginny. You'd kill somebody if you thought it was important. You'd think about it, and if you decided there wasn't any other option, yeah, you'd kill somebody. No question. But," he'd said, "you wouldn't telegraph it. If you needed to do it, you'd just do it. Duke takes it personally."

"And?" she'd asked, still curious. "Is that a good thing or a bad thing?"

"Depends," he'd said. "Every strength is a weakness in the wrong circumstance, and vice versa. Though, in this case . . ." He looked at me and said, "Don't take this the wrong way, Duke, but your sister is smarter than you."

I didn't take it the wrong way. Ginny *was* smarter than me.

"You'll be fine if you're working together because people will take you as the bigger threat, and while they are trying to eliminate you, Ginny can watch your back. But you're still better off keeping it hidden, so that nobody's trying to eliminate you.

"The truth is, if you've got the time to think your way out of a bad spot, it's always cleaner not to have to fire a shot. Because I will tell you, the second you start shooting is the second when whatever you are doing has escalated to the point where there is no return and where you, yourself, might get shot. And getting shot, my young friends, is unequivocally a *bad* thing."

He was an interesting guy. He never condescended to us, which was a bit of a rarity coming from adults, particularly when we were still so young. We had a certain amount of standing because of our dad, but none of the other professionals we met could look past our age and relative lack of experience. But I think he saw what my dad was doing in terms of getting us ready for adulthood, the inexorable path we were walking down. He understood what his role needed to be in our education. He knew that, sooner or later, following in our father's footsteps, we'd need to use the skills he was teaching us. It was a serious job, and he took it seriously.

He was probably in his early fifties at the time, bored, and discovering late in life that he should have been a teacher instead of a soldier. He only stayed with us for four months, but I still get holiday cards from him, and when I took a year off to travel Europe while I was in college—thanks to years of top-rate academic tutors, and at Helen's insistence, it was the same fancy schmancy liberal arts school Ginny went to—I dropped in on him and his wife up in the Highlands.

"But," he'd said to Ginny, "sometimes, having Duke show that face will stop somebody from deciding that killing the two of you means they don't have to split the pie. People will interpret that look on Duke's face as something to take seriously. I'll tell you this," he continued, "nobody who has ever claimed to be an alpha is actually an alpha. To the last, people who say they are alphas are terrified of how weak they themselves are. But that look, Duke . . . *that* look says it all. Just remember, being an actual alpha makes you both a threat and a target."

Ginny sounded a little peeved when she said, "So you don't think I'm an alpha?"

He'd smiled, and he'd said, "Ginny, you, my dear, are the omega."

God, we both loved him. He was a good teacher and a good dude.

I'd learned to hide the look.

Most of the time.

When I was busy trying to track down the men who'd hurt Ginny, earning my nicknames—both of them—I didn't stop to think, and I didn't try to hide that look on my face.

I *wanted* them to know who they were dealing with.

41

BUT THIS WASN'T THE TIME OR PLACE FOR IT.

"How about you move on from my father and sister," I said.

"Fine," she said. "The point is that, near as we can tell, you've been a virtual Boy Scout since then. For like a hot minute, we thought you were part of the Flanigan heist in Boston last year—"

I started to protest—I'd heard about it, and frankly, I was insulted they thought I would have been part of that ridiculous mess—but Greaves held up her hand and kept talking.

"But we know you aren't that sloppy. So as far as we can tell, until a few days ago, aside from some gambling issues—"

I tried to speak again, but once more she held up her hand, stopping me.

"We know about your aunt. Not just the bookmaking and the fence stuff. All of it. And we know you settled your debt with her."

I made a mental note to tell Paulie that she was either wiretapped and her office bugged out the wazoo, or that somebody on her payroll was an informant.

Greaves kept talking. "We know what kind of jobs you pulled before things went wrong with your sister, even if we don't have the kind of proof that is required by a court of law. But like I said, it's been a while. And then, all of a sudden, you show up at your aunt's office with twenty thousand dollars in cash. And there's no way for you to come up with that kind of money legally."

"You'd be surprised how motivated I can be to work hard when my bookie threatens to break my thumbs off."

Park laughed. "Your aunt threatened to rip your thumbs *off*?"

"Not her personally."

"Fair enough, but there isn't a legal job in the world that pays that well. Or in cash. So, where'd you get twenty thousand dollars in cash to pay off your gambling debts?"

Huh.

That was interesting.

The question meant two things: first, while there might be a bug somewhere in the building, Paulie's personal office was clean, and the most likely reasons the feds knew I'd paid off my debt was because of an informant. And second, Park and Greaves didn't seem to know about the job I'd just pulled for Agents Baker and Cleary.

I was suddenly very uncomfortably and acutely aware of the cash taped around my stomach. I'd obviously had to ditch the stun gun, camera, and the tools before going through security, but if these two weren't here because Baker and Cleary had sicced the dogs on me, then why had the FBI picked me up?

It couldn't be simply that I'd paid off my aunt and gone on a trip. What was I missing? And more importantly, did I want to stick around to find out?

I decided I didn't.

"Am I under arrest?"

Park's smile wasn't as warm this time. "Not yet."

I stood up. "Well then, if I'm not under arrest, I think I'm going to head home. I'm beat. If you want to talk tomorrow after I've gotten some sleep, I'll be happy to do so. But I'll be bringing my lawyer."

Neither of the two agents made a move to stop me, but Park looked deferentially at Greaves. She was obviously in charge.

Greaves said, "Sit down."

"I know my rights. If I'm not under arrest, I can walk, and if I'm under arrest I want a lawyer." I said it confidently, but I didn't feel confident.

"Yeah," Greaves said. "This isn't one of those kinds of situations."

She said it in a friendly manner. There wasn't the undercurrent of threat that came from Baker, let alone the overt threats of violence that Cleary tried to wield, but somehow that made it a little scarier. Park was fidgeting a little, but Greaves seemed utterly and completely in control.

The fact that they hadn't cuffed me, that they didn't have any backup other than a couple of uniformed cops who probably spent more time issuing traffic citations than anything else. And the fact that they seemed to know an awful lot about me . . .

"Okay," I said. "Let's just have sex."

Park tilted his head. "Sorry. What?"

I sighed. "You know that feeling when you're out on a first date and everything's going well? You hit it off, the restaurant's romantic, the weather is beautiful, and there's that tension that comes with being with somebody you know is attracted to you and vice versa. You sit there eating dinner and chatting and laughing at each other's jokes, but you're both just waiting because you know—and you knew almost from the first of it—that this night was going to end up with the two of you in bed together. You know what I mean? That kind of first date, when you know how it's going to end before you've even got the menu open? And sure, there's something fun about the tension, but really, you just want to get it over with so that you can relax. That feeling."

Park shook his head and said, "Honestly, not really. My wife asked me to be her buddy on a field trip to a museum in the eighth grade, and then told me that I was her boyfriend, and that was it. I've never been on an actual first date."

Greaves put her hand on Park's arm. "He's trying to make some sort of clever point that he knows he's going to get screwed, so we might as well just ask for the bill. Is that it?" She looked at me.

"Something like that."

"Fine," she said. "If you think you're going to get screwed, take off your clothes."

42

IF I'D BEEN DRINKING COFFEE, I probably would have spit it out. "I didn't mean literally," I said.

Greaves stood up now. "I did. You can either strip so we can search you properly, or you can just hand over the cipher."

Uh-oh. Maybe I'd underestimated what was happening. Was Greaves playing me? I didn't know, but I thought I'd give acting dumb a chance. "What cipher?"

Park pushed his chair back and then swung his feet up onto the table. "Give us a break, Duke. We aren't stupid, and neither are you."

So much for playing dumb.

Greaves reached into her jacket pocket and pulled out a folded piece of paper. She handed it to me.

I unfolded it.

Oh.

It was not a particularly flattering photo. I was sweating from working in the bubble, and the regulator in my mouth made my lips bulge. It didn't help, either, that I'd been surprised to see the camera sitting in the safe.

"I was kind of hoping the camera didn't have a chance to transmit the photo." I handed the piece of paper back. "Sorry. I wasn't trying to be cute. I didn't know if you knew about Baker and Cleary or not, if they were the same agency or whatever. Also, I didn't know it was a cipher. I mean, if by 'cipher,' you mean some sort of encryption device. I guess I figured it was that or a virus or a code breaker or something like that. I mean, it was too small to be anything of real value if it was just a physical object. And I'll tell you, Baker sure acted like—"

"Who are Baker and Cleary?"

I sat back down. "I think there's some confusion going on. I'm on *your* side here. Baker and Cleary are feds. This is all legit. I mean, I didn't write up an invoice or anything, but you guys hired me to do off the books work, so the miscommunication is on your end. It happens all the time between federal agencies, right? You guys don't always play nicely together, and maybe you didn't get the memo, but I was working for the home team here. I didn't do anything I wasn't supposed to."

Which wasn't *strictly* true because, well, I did hit Cleary with a stun gun and then sort of stomped him in the nuts while he was unconscious but, come on. Like I was supposed to just let them take me out to some field somewhere so they could file me under "dead end" with a bullet? And sure, I'd stolen the box—or the "cipher"— off Cleary while he was down, and I'd helped myself to some of the cash in the storage locker. Oh, plus, I'd taken the phone charging cord, though, all things considered, I doubted that was tops on the list of the government's grievances.

I saw Agent Park look at Greaves for guidance, but Greaves was staring directly at me. She appeared to be thinking furiously. I'd thrown her some sort of a curveball.

"We aren't really interested in you. Give me the cipher, and we can talk about it."

"I don't have it."

"*Excuse* me?"

I was already feeling like things were spinning out of control, so the look of pure panic on Park's face did not help.

"I mean, I don't have it on me," I said. "It's in the mail."

Park looked at me incredulously. "You *mailed* it? Are you out of your fu—"

Greaves silenced him with a look that was truly scary. It was stunningly clear that she and Park were not equals. Then she turned that same gaze on me. "Explain."

"I mean, not the *mail* mail. I overnighted it. For what it's worth, I paid for extra insurance."

"Okay," she said. "We're still going to need to strip-search you, but . . ." She sat back down again herself and then leaned forward, earnest. "Duke, did you know what was in the safe before you went in?"

I shrugged. "A payday. You guys—I mean, not you and Agent Park specifically, but Baker and Cleary—came to me and offered me a deal that was too good to pass up. And I figured, okay, I've been a good boy, but if the feds want me to do a job and are willing to pay for it, no harm, no foul. The deal was, I show up, I open the safe without anybody finding out, I get what's promised to me. What did it matter to me what was in the safe? It was a pure contract job, and it paid a lot better than any other honest work I could find."

"What did they offer you?"

"Sixty thousand dollars."

Greaves's face tightened and she shook her head. "Sixty thousand dollars?"

"It's the truth. Not many people could have pulled it off." I was trying to play it cool. Even though she was intimidating, I kind of wanted to impress her, and I thought saying that *nobody* else could have pulled it off would have sounded like I was bragging. "Sure, sixty thousand dollars sounds like a lot, but I had them over a barrel."

She shook her head. "Good god, Duke. I would have believed you if you'd told me they offered you ten million dollars. But sixty thousand dollars?"

"Uh . . . I'm not following. Look, I had some debts. Sixty thousand dollars is a lot of money." I felt defensive. "I am not, in any way, admitting that I have ever broken the law in any manner, but it can be hard to make a living doing honest work. I charge good rates for my services, but there are only so many jobs in the Los Angeles area installing safes or helping people who got locked out that need my level of expertise. Sixty thousand dollars was hard to turn down."

I didn't want to admit that sixty thousand dollars had seemed like *too much* money, that it was enough to scare me, and I would have walked away if Baker hadn't offered me the chance to get my dad out. If Baker had offered ten million dollars, I would have run screaming.

"Sixty thousand dollars," she said, shaking her head with disbelief. "You're telling me that they offered you sixty thousand dollars to waltz into Berlin, break into a CIA black site, and crack one of their safes, and you took the job?"

43

I DON'T HAVE THE BEST POKER FACE. It's why I mostly bet on football, baseball, and basketball instead of playing cards. But I was too stunned to react beyond blinking a couple of times.

It only took me a couple of seconds to process the news that I'd broken into a safe that belonged to the CIA, but a few seconds of silence can feel like an eternity. Good interviewers know that half the secret to getting somebody to talk is to simply wait; quiet makes people uncomfortable.

It made me uncomfortable, and I blurted out, "Oh, shit."

Greaves and Park exchanged glances. The color in Park's face bled away.

Greaves spoke first. "Oh my god. You really *didn't* have any idea, did you? You seriously agreed to do this job for sixty thousand dollars, and you had no idea what you were getting into?"

I said, "I'm sorry. You're saying I . . . you're saying the safe I opened belonged to the CIA?" I was forgetting myself, but I was about as confused as I could get. "But Baker . . ."

Park picked up his pen and then put it back down. "Again, who's Baker?"

"Baker was the agent in charge. Him and Cleary, but Agent Baker was running the show." I felt like I was falling down an endless elevator shaft. "This doesn't make any sense. I wasn't stealing *from* the CIA. I was working *for* the United States government. Why the hell would we hit one of our own agencies?"

Greaves spoke slowly, like she was talking to an infant. "That safe—a supposedly impenetrable safe that belonged to the CIA—was inside a CIA black site in Berlin. Nobody was supposed to know about the facility, let alone the safe or what was inside of it. And, honestly, it was a brilliant job. We still haven't figured out how you got in and out of the building." I thought about the smell of drywall and the rubble underfoot. With the hood on, I couldn't fill in any gaps. Greaves continued, "If it weren't for the camera in the safe, I think you would have gotten away with it."

I wasn't completely naive. I'd figured we were hitting some sort of state actor. If not the Russians or the Chinese, then the Saudis or Iranians or something. And if not a state actor, then maybe a terrorist organization. The whole point of breaking in without leaving a trace was so that the American government could play its little spy games without anyone the wiser.

But Greaves was telling me we hit the CIA? Why would Baker hire me to break into a safe that belongs to the CIA?

And then, like the bolts of a vault door slamming shut, it hit me what Greaves and Park were *really* saying, and I felt like an idiot for being so slow on the uptake.

I'd never actually asked Baker and Cleary who they were or who they worked for. I'd just seen their SUV and pegged them as feds. They looked and acted like government suits, but if they were working for a government now, it wasn't for *our* government.

However bad I thought this was, it had just gotten a whole lot worse. I hadn't just broken into a safe and run from my handlers.

I'd committed treason.

44

NOT GOOD.

"I, uh, I think I need to talk to a lawyer."

Greaves said, "No."

"No?"

"No," she said. "You're not going to be talking to a lawyer."

Park interjected. "But—"

Greaves steamrolled over him, once again making it clear she was operating on a different level. "No. This isn't one of those 'I want my lawyer' kind of deals," she said.

Not a lot of this was making sense to me, but I understood what Greaves was saying: I'd broken into a CIA black site, and unless I got really, really lucky, I'd spend the rest of my life detained in a different black site. That or Guantanamo. Or pushed out of a helicopter over the open sea.

"What are my options?"

That, clearly, was the right question.

"You play ball," Greaves said.

"Meaning?"

"Meaning," Greaves said, "until we get back what you stole, you work for *me*."

Not us, but "me," Park only here in a secondary role.

She continued, "I can offer you any support you want. The full might and force of the United States government is at my beck and call until we get it back. You give me the cipher and you can walk away, free and clear. No charges. No time."

"Okay."

"Okay? That's it?"

"Okay. But there are a few conditions."

Greaves actually laughed. "Duke, come on. You're not really in a position to make any demands, are you?"

"Actually, I think I'm in the perfect position to make some demands," I said. I stood up and pulled up my shirt so they could see the cash taped to my torso. I started feeling for the tape. "First of all, I'm keeping this. I earned it, fair and square." I winced as I pulled the tape from my skin. "Well, maybe not fair and square, but I earned it. This was part of what I was getting paid for the job, and it's mine."

"Duke—"

I shook my head. "I know what you're going to say, but you need my help more than I need yours. The only reason I'm not already in jail or, yeah, disappeared somewhere and locked in a windowless room with a bag over my head, is because this cipher is so valuable that you'll do whatever it takes to get it back. Like you said, full might and force of the US government. That means getting done whatever needs to get done. Including cutting me the kind of deal that makes me work with you. Because if you guys had any other leads, you'd be pursuing those first and just let me cool my heels somewhere secure."

I'd unwound the tape and had the stack of bills on the table now. A lot of money for me, but Greaves had been right; there was no way I would have jumped into this for any amount of money if I'd known what was waiting for me. Still, I'd jumped, and as long as I was in a pool full of piss, I was going to go for a swim.

"I keep the money."

Park rolled his eyes, but it really did seem like he was at least a little amused by all of this, like I was putting on a show for his benefit. I made a mental note to ask my dad if Park had been such a fanboy when they'd met.

"Fine," Greaves said. "You can keep the money that you very clearly were intending to smuggle into the country. You know it's illegal to cross the border with more than ten thousand dollars without declaring it, right?"

"Yeah, that's the worst of my problems right now," I said. "Second: Ginny."

Park frowned. "Your sister? What about Ginny?"

"I do this, if I help you, then *you* help me."

"With what?" Greaves asked.

"Right now, my aunt's paying. It's the best place in LA. But it shouldn't be on my aunt. I cooperate, Ginny gets to stay there, on the government's dime. For as long as it takes. And any medical procedures she needs. Again, best available."

"Okay," Greaves said.

"Okay? That's it? You don't need to get some sort of approval?"

She bit her lip. "Look, Duke, if we're going to work together on this—and we *are* going to work together on this, because you're right, this cipher is a big deal—it's going to help if we can trust each other. I'm authorized to approve it."

"Want to save me some time and just tell me what else you're authorized to approve?"

She glanced sideways at Park and then said, "What else do you want?"

"One more thing," I said.

"Your dad."

"Saw that one coming too?"

"He's not even two years into an eight-to-twelve," Park said.

"Time served. That's what the morons who fleeced me were offering."

Greaves laughed. "They can't have been that big of a bunch of morons since they *did* manage to trick you."

She had a point.

"I'll start cooperating with you right now, but I want him out by the end of the day."

"Nope," Greaves said. "He walks *after* we've got the cipher and you've cooperated."

I had to trust her. Which was hard, given that I had just been burned by . . . Who the heck had I been burned by?

"Oh, for crap's sake," I said. "I really am a moron. The cigarettes."

45

"WHAT?" GREAVES FOLDED HER ARMS OVER HER CHEST.

"The cigarettes," I said again.

In different circumstances, I might have asked to buy her a drink. She was attractive in the way that fit, healthy-looking people are attractive, radiating a sort of well-being. It wouldn't be a shock to find out she played in an adult soccer league twice a week and ran 10K races on weekends when she wasn't at the gym practicing jujitsu. I'd seen plenty of FBI agents and cops who'd let the slow march of time creep up on them, but Greaves was trim and solid. She'd be able to hold her own in a fight, I thought. And she was clearly smart, competent, and in charge, with Park almost an accoutrement as her young-gun sidekick. Her confidence might have been the most attractive thing about her.

I didn't always have the best judgment in women, but I'd never been interested in the kind of woman who'd bend her life entirely around mine. It never bothered me to date somebody who was smarter or more accomplished than me, let alone somebody like Meg who was better at most things. And it certainly never bothered me to date somebody who was more financially stable than I was; if it did, that would have severely limited my current options. I didn't have a type, not exactly, but if I was pressed to say what it was that I looked for in a woman, it was somebody who knew who she was. And Greaves had that.

She also might have me on charges of treason.

I didn't want to forget that.

"The cigarettes," I said. "And the Snickers wrappers."

Park looked at Greaves and then at me. "Care to explain?"

I pictured Cleary walking across the warehouse to the workbench to bum a cigarette. I knew the package had looked funny. I said, "I think the cigarettes were Russian. The Snickers wrappers too."

Park was writing away in his notebook. It seemed redundant—I was sure they were recording everything—but it was kind of charming in an old-school way. He said, "Russian?"

Greaves placed her hands flat on the table. "Tell you what, Duke. Why don't you start from the beginning?"

I did.

I told them *almost* everything. From the first time Baker called me from a blocked number all the way through me cuffing Cleary to the wall. I omitted the part where I kicked Cleary in the nuts, but not only did I tell them about the quick stop I'd made at a package shipping store, but I even handed over a receipt with a tracking number.

46

ABOUT THREE HOURS IN, when I'd answered most of their questions mostly truthfully, Greaves's phone pinged. She looked at it and said, "Okay, I think we're done. You can go."

"I take it that text means the surveillance is in place."

She held my gaze. I counted off five seconds in my head before she finally shook her head. "God, you are exasperating." Her tone didn't match her words.

I said, "I'm surprised you're letting me go."

"No, you're not," she said. "Think it through."

I did, and then I nodded. "The cipher. You don't trust that I'm telling the truth about it being in the mail. You're going to keep me on a leash until you have it in your hands, in case I've somehow managed to slip it past you." Which, to be fair, was what I was trying to do. I hadn't been dumb enough to mail it to my apartment, and the tracking number they had was just going to lead to disappointment.

"Come on, Duke." She gave me an enigmatic smile. "You can do better than that. If the cipher was all we wanted, we'd just keep you locked up for a few days. You know why I'm letting you walk out of here."

"I'm bait."

"Bingo."

I smirked. "I've got to say, that's a little hurtful. I thought you cared about me."

"Does this 'I'm so charming' thing usually work for you?"

"You'd be surprised."

"Probably," she said, smirking right back at me. "To answer your question, yes, we've got our surveillance set up and ready to run. While I don't want to see you get hurt, I *am* willing to dangle you out there as bait."

To Park's credit, Greaves's statement seemed to make him uncomfortable.

"You're wasting your time with the surveillance," I said. "I'm headed straight home. Maybe a quick stop at the market for a six-pack, but otherwise, delivery, some combination of television and reading a book, and then bedtime. Jet lag is a bitch."

She looked surprised, which was . . . surprising.

I narrowed my eyes, suspicious. "What?"

"Straight home?"

"Straight home," I agreed. "What aren't you telling me?"

"Oh, crud," she said. "Duke. I'm sorry. We thought you knew."

"Explain. Now."

She nodded at Park. He said, "Your aunt is in the hospital."

Greaves reached out, gently touched my shoulder, and then lowered her hand. "You really don't know? I can't believe nobody called you."

"Don't take this the wrong way, Agent Greaves," I said, trying to keep calm, "but if you don't tell me what the hell you're talking about, I'm going to lose it." I didn't bother reminding her that she and Park had searched me thoroughly enough to know I wasn't carrying a cell phone.

"Eight or nine hours ago, somebody called 911 from your aunt's office," Park said. "They only said three words: 'send an ambulance.' When EMTs showed up, they found three of your aunt's men laid out, dead. Professional job. As for your aunt, she was beaten almost to death."

Greaves jumped in. "The key word is *almost*. She's at Cedars-Sinai. In the ICU. She's in serious condition, which is better than critical, but still not good. My guess is that the guys who hired you came looking for the item you were supposed to steal *for* them, not from them."

Greaves went over the injuries: broken arm, lacerated spleen, broken nose, fractured skull, contusions, you name it. Paulie had gotten the shit kicked out of her.

While Greaves spoke, I felt myself go calm. Cold. This wasn't the time for me to be upset.

But I knew Greaves was right. There was no chance this was random; I'd brought this onto Paulie as soon as I'd sat down to talk with Baker. Not that either Baker or Cleary had personally done the dirty work at Paulie's. It was a twelve-hour flight direct. Even if they had access to a private plane, there was no way they could have beat me back to Los Angeles in enough time to have done the work themselves—but it was still on Baker and Cleary. And on me.

And now that I'd spent more than three hours sitting in this room with Greaves and Park, even if I originally had a head start, I was almost certain that Baker and Cleary were boots on the ground in LA and on the hunt with whatever crew they'd used to descend on Paulie. But the upside of knowing that Baker wasn't a fed was that I was no longer worried about him picking me up at the airport. Too public.

"If we're done, I'm going to go visit my aunt." I picked up my duffel bag.

Greaves nodded. "You want Park to give you a ride or have one of the cops take you in a cruiser?"

"I'll cab."

"Fair enough," Greaves said. "I'll call over to the hospital and make sure they let you in. There's a uniform standing guard at her door. And don't forget to text me a photo of the man who recruited you. Baker. It would help if we knew who to be on alert for while we're watching you. Believe it or not, we do want to keep you safe," she said, not unkindly. "Here." She reached into her pocket and pulled out a business card. "Take this."

I took the card. The address had her working the FBI Los Angeles division building on Wilshire. "I doubt I'll be calling."

"Maybe not, but call me if anything comes up. Or," she said with a resigned tone, "just flag down somebody on your surveillance detail and tell them you want to speak to me."

47

LA CIENEGA BOULEVARD WAS UNUSUALLY CLEAR, and I was at Cedars-Sinai twenty-five minutes after walking out of LAX.

As I took the elevator up to my aunt's floor, I realized I hadn't asked who the three men were that had gotten killed at Paulie's office. I wondered if Rick was one of them, or if he was off his shift. I was still a little sore from where he'd clubbed me.

Paulie's lieutenant, Lily, was sitting outside Paulie's room with two of her men. I greeted Lily, and then handed my passport to the LAPD uniform ostensibly on guard duty despite the presence of Lily and the two goons. The cop looked like he was in middle school. He examined my passport and then, thanks to Greaves's call, he let me in without any hassle.

It was a private room, though I'd never been in the ICU at Cedars-Sinai before, so for all I knew they were all private rooms. There were already five different bouquets of flowers on the windowsill. I expected more to show up soon. Word travels fast, and Paulie was both respected and feared. At least half of the flowers would come from people who genuinely wanted to send them, and the other half would come from people who were afraid that when my aunt pulled through, she would start asking why it was that somebody hadn't sent her flowers.

I saw a cardigan neatly folded and draped over a chair in the corner. The chair was blue and vinyl, a recliner that could convert into a bed for family members who wanted to stay close. I put my duffel bag on the chair and lifted up the sweater. I recognized it as one of my uncle's, and I suddenly realized I hadn't even thought about his safety. He wasn't involved in Paulie's business—he was as straight as you could be, married into the Ducaine family—but even though the violence would have occurred after hours and he never went past the first floor of Charlie's up to where Paulie did her less legitimate business dealings, it was still a relief to see proof that he was alive. I figured he'd ducked down to the cafeteria to get something to eat or drink.

I loved Charles. He was Paulie's second husband. Her first husband had gone down in a bad bank job when I was too young to remember him, and Charles had been around since I was six or seven. He was quiet, content to be by himself when Paulie was working, but he was also a warm man, thoughtful and considerate. I think, sometimes, because of the world Paulie and my dad moved in, people thought he was weak, but I never thought that of him. He worked as a luthier, repairing stringed instruments, splitting his time between high-end jobs, and doing free work for Los Angeles area public schools that couldn't afford it. He had long, elegant fingers and played a beautiful game of billiards. He saw all the angles. He had the kind of mentality that would have made him a good safecracker if he'd been interested.

But I was glad he wasn't in the room right now, because I needed a minute to regain my composure.

My aunt looked like hell.

Paulie's face was swollen almost beyond recognition. I wasn't sure I would have recognized her if I hadn't known who I was looking at. She was intubated, and the mechanical sound of the ventilator filled the room. I spent a few seconds looking at the electronic monitor as if that would tell me anything.

When I looked back at her, Paulie's eyes were cracked open.

I realized I was still holding Uncle Charles's sweater. I folded it as well as I could and put it back on the chair. "He's okay?"

She nodded as well as she was able, and then she lifted up her good arm—the other one was in a cast already—and made a writing motion.

"It's okay, Paulie," I said. "Just rest. We don't need to talk. Lily's outside with two guys, plus the cops put a uniform on the door."

She made the writing motion again, and when I started to say it could wait again, she gave me a look that could only be interpreted as a terrifying command.

"Right," I said.

Even on a ventilator, with a broken arm, in the ICU, touch and go, face swollen, Aunt Paulie was scary when she wanted to be.

Fortunately, there was already a pad of paper and a pen on the bedside table. I had to put the pen into her hand and close her fingers around it. She tried to write while I held the pad for her, but it was her nondominant hand and it was just chicken scratch.

"Sorry, Paulie," I said. "I can't read it."

She gave me the intimidating look again.

"Okay, okay. Just a second."

I took the pad of paper and wrote out the alphabet, and then I held up the pad for her. "Just tap the letters with the pen. Spell it out. If I ask a yes or no question you can tap *Y* or *N*, okay?"

She tapped the *Y*.

The mechanical click and whir of the ventilator played an ugly symphony with her vital signs. There was no question she was in pain, even though it looked like she had something serious plugged into her IV drip.

It was slow going. It took her a few seconds to find each letter and then to get the tip of the pen to settle on it.

"Called," I said.

She tried to nod again, but it was hard with the ventilator, so she touched the *Y* again and then kept moving the pen.

"Knox."

My dad's name. Knox Ducaine. As in Fort Knox, the fabled repository of much of the United States' gold reserves.

"You called Dad. Or, I guess, Charles called Dad."

Y.

"He knows?"

Y.

"Okay," I said. "Charles can tell me more?"

Y.

"New thing?" I asked.

Y.

She tapped.

"Safe."

Y.

"Charles."

"Safe. Charles. You're saying Charles is safe?"

N.

I looked at the sweater neatly folded on the chair. "That's his sweater."

Y.

"So, he is safe."

Y.

"But that's not what you're trying to tell me." I thought for a second. "You're not saying *he's* safe. You're saying *a* safe. It's a safe that Charles knows about?"

Y.

"That means it's at your house, not the office?"

Y.

"What's the combo?"

She glared at me.

Not in a joking mood.

"Okay. I'll get him to show it to me. Will I know what I'm looking for when I see it?"

Y.

I heard the door open, and I turned to see my uncle. He was carrying a cup of coffee and looked like he hadn't slept in a century.

48

A STORY MY DAD TOLD ME ABOUT MY UNCLE.

After Charles proposed, my dad took him out for drinks one night. Gave him the whole "if you hurt my sister, I'll kill you" speech. Keep in mind, by this point, Charles knew who Paulie was, knew who my dad was. When I say he knew who they *really* were, I mean all of it.

But, my dad said, he gave Charles the whole speech, and Charles just stared at him, taking his time to think about it.

For context, I should say that Uncle Charles looks exactly like you think somebody like him would look like: a neatly trimmed silver mustache; bifocals; a pressed, solid-color shirt; khakis. He's got a full head of hair, and while he's handsome, he's not exactly rocking the animal magnetism. He's maybe five foot seven and is a whippet of a man. Nobody would ever mistake me for his son. At first glance, he *seems* like the kind of guy who's a bit musty and fussy, and he says things like, "oh geez," when he hits his thumb like a hammer. But not in a jerky or off-putting way. He was nice. No other word for it. Warm, contemplative, a great uncle. But more than anything, he was just . . . sweet.

Which is why my dad loved this story so much. I probably heard him tell it a hundred times.

"So," my dad would say, "Charles mulls it over, taking his time, and then he leans forward, and he says to me, 'No, I don't think you understand. You've got it all backward.'" And here, my dad always paused for emphasis before continuing. "And he says to me, 'If *you* ever hurt Paulie, if you screw up and she ends up going down for it, if you make a mistake and it means she gets hurt, *I'll* kill *you.* I will come after you, and there will be nothing you can do to stop me.'"

Dad laughed whenever he told the story, but privately, he said it was the only time when there wasn't a gun pointed at him that he's ever truly felt scared by a threat.

49

WE HUGGED, AND I TOLD HIM what Paulie had spelled out.

"I can take you over now," he said. "We should really let your aunt rest."

Paulie grunted and made a motion with her hand. I got the pen and pad of paper with the alphabet written on it. She pointed at Charles. Then she spelled out the letters.

R.U.N.

To which, Charles took off his glasses, leaned over his wife, kissed her on her forehead, and said, "As always, thank you, my dear, but I'm not leaving you alone."

She moved the pen again, but Charles took her hand gently in his.

"Now you know how rarely I say no to you. And you also know that the few times I have said no, I've meant it. I love you. Forever. No matter what. I knew what I was getting into when I married you, and I'm not leaving you."

I turned my back for a couple of minutes so that they could compose themselves.

"Duke," my uncle called.

I turned.

"Paulie wants to spell out another thing for you."

"Thanks, Uncle Charles."

Paulie moved the tip of the pen across the paper.

"Safe," I said. "Yeah. I got it. Charles is going to take me to the house as soon as we're done."

N.

"No? You want him to stay here?"

N.

"Uh . . ."

Y.

I got it. "This is something else about the safe."

Y.

"About what's in the safe? Information?"

Y. Y.

"You want me to know something about where you got the information from?"

N.

"No. Okay. Not where you got it. That's not what's important. But there's something you want me to do with the information in the safe once I have it?"

Y.

She moved the pen.

"Burn?"

Y.

"Them?"

Y.

"All?"

Y.

She moved her pen four more times, but this time I didn't have to ask. I knew I was right.

"Down," I said. "Burn them all down."

Y.

Y.

Y.

Burn them all down.

I could work with that.

50

MY UNCLE, WHO HAD BASICALLY just told my aunt he'd both die and kill for her, drove a minivan.

To be fair, minivans *are* comfortable and convenient for running errands, and Charles needed cargo capacity for when he was picking up cellos and basses to repair.

"You talked to my dad?"

"I used one of the emergency numbers you guys have set up. I told him about Paulie, and he told me he'd be okay. Said he's got something worked out." Which meant he'd lined up protection for himself in case Baker decided to make a run at him inside FCI Terminal Island. "He said not to worry about him, and to just take care of Paulie."

Sounded like my dad. I made a note to call him as soon as possible.

Charles said, "You know it's not safe to see Ginny, right?"

"I know," I said, and we drove in silence.

At the house, Charles walked me up to their bedroom and pulled aside a photograph of a barn hanging on the wall to reveal the safe. Any burglar worth their salt would find it, but it was an IronClad 3600 series with a digital keypad. Easy enough to get into with some decent tools, but solid enough that it had to be somebody who knew what they were doing. It would keep out your average lookie-loo pop-in with a crowbar, but anybody who broke in knowing it was Aunt Paulie's place would have it open in less than ten minutes. Not, by any stretch of the imagination, high security.

"Oh," I said. "I can't believe she keeps anything important in here. That's terrible. And you didn't need to show me this. I *installed* this safe for her."

"No," he said. "You didn't install *this* safe for her."

If I'd still been a teenager, I would have let out an exasperated sigh. Of course I'd installed it. I recognized my own work. "It's not even locked. You know that safes work better when you lock them, right?" I reached out and pulled open the door of the wall safe.

There were stacks of cash inside, plus a half dozen passports rubber-banded together, and a compact Heckler & Koch 9mm pistol.

"It's about a quarter million," Charles said. "The pistol is lawfully registered to me, and the passports are perfect and legal. Nothing we could get in trouble for if cops showed up with a search warrant. Turns out a lot of countries will sell you citizenship for enough money."

Nothing else.

I looked at my uncle. "I don't get it. This doesn't make any sense. Why would you leave it unlocked? And you really shouldn't leave it unlocked with a nine-millimeter inside. The math on gun ownership is unambiguous: you're way more likely to get shot with your own gun than you are to somehow thwart a robbery. I mean, do you even know how to fire a gun?"

I picked up the Heckler & Koch. The weight was off. I checked. Empty chamber, empty magazine. Unloaded. And there wasn't a box of ammunition in the safe.

I looked at Uncle Charles quizzically. "Okay. I'm officially confused. An unloaded pistol? An unlocked safe? And this is the same make and model as the safe I installed."

"Same make and model," he agreed. "But that doesn't mean it's the same safe that you installed. And this stuff is all in here"—he waved his hand at the stack of cash and at the pistol I'd returned to its perch—"because Paulie thought that anybody who broke in would think it was their lucky day. It's an extra insurance policy. We always leave it unlocked, and the gun is unloaded because the whole point of it is for somebody else to find it. And yes, I am very aware of the statistics surrounding gun ownership. Getting shot by my own pistol is very low on my priority list."

I was sure I looked as dumb as I felt. "I'm sorry, Charles, but all I'm seeing is a bunch of money and some passports. And loaded or not, that's a decent pistol." The HK VP-9 had a paddle-style magazine release, but this was the push-button model with night sights. It probably retailed for eight hundred and fifty dollars. "Seriously, though. Do you know how to use it?"

"Yes, I can use a pistol. Just because I stay out of Paulie's business doesn't mean I'm a helpless lamb. That was one of her conditions when we got married, that if I was going to be with her, I had to learn how to protect myself. But let's hope it doesn't come to that. And that's not why *this* pistol is in the safe. If I'm going to shoot somebody, it's not going to be with a pistol registered to my own name. Even *I'm* not that naive." He shook his head and then smiled briefly. "Your aunt, as usual, was right. It's a honey trap."

51

"UH . . ."

"Not that kind of a honey trap, Duke. Your aunt's point was that a pile of cash, a few passports, and a nice pistol would be an obvious jackpot. You open the safe and there you go," he said, in what I thought of his "kindly teacher" voice. "No reason to keep searching. That's the point. And, point made, since even you aren't looking past it. Take your time. Look closer."

I looked at the safe again. And then I looked at the open door of the safe.

Sneaky, sneaky.

It was subtle. Very subtle. No way I would have noticed if Uncle Charles hadn't told me that I was looking for something unusual: the door of the safe was about a quarter inch too thick.

There was a false panel built into it.

I ran my fingers under the door of the safe, stopping when I felt the combination lock embedded in the metal.

"Before you ask," my uncle said, "no, I don't know the combination. But Paulie told me that if I ever needed to get it open in a hurry, all I had to tell you was 'Kyoto,' and you'd know what that meant. So, Kyoto? Do you know what that means?"

A job Ginny and I had done together about a year before things went sideways. Nothing about the job was particularly remarkable except that it had been in—drumroll, please!—Kyoto, and that the safe's digital alphanumeric keypad used a five-digit combination of 44669. Not that the combination was particularly unusual or noteworthy other than the fact that 44669 on an alphanumeric key-pad spelled out Ginny's name.

I had to kneel down to get a better look at the combination dial on the underside. It was not an alphanumeric keypad. Instead, it was a five-dial, like the kind of thing you'd find on a luggage lock or a suitcase. Made sense. The door was too thin to easily support something more complicated, and the point of the lock on the door panel wasn't really to keep anybody out who was hell-bent on getting it open—the only way to keep the secret panel secret was to use steel thin enough that you could pry the back off with a screwdriver—but rather to prevent the casual snoop.

I dialed in 44669.

It didn't open.

Because I was a jet-lagged moron who was looking at the numbers upside down.

I did it again, reversing the numbers, and with an audible click, the panel opened.

There wasn't a lot of space, which was fine, because there wasn't a lot inside: just two manila envelopes.

One of them had my name written on it.

The other had Ginny's name.

52

WE SHOULDN'T HAVE BEEN DOING the job in the first place, but I'd guilted Ginny into it because I needed the money.

I was coming off a bad streak in Las Vegas after a string of bad streaks. Gambling wasn't new for me, but where it had always been up and down before, this time I'd chased the sports bet all the way to the bottom. It happened fast, and I was basically broke. I wasn't dumb enough to take a marker at the casino, not with what I already owed my bookie, but if my bank account was a roulette wheel it would only have had double zeroes. Ginny decided she preferred lending me money to cover my rent as opposed to having a nonpaying roommate, but still, at first, despite my rapidly spiraling debt to her, she said no to the job.

The actual heist looked good. It was work-for-hire. All we had to do was steal an oil painting from a private collection and hand it off. A small Degas that would have gone in the neighborhood of twenty million if it went to auction legally. The problem, and the reason Ginny was saying no, was that the contract came through a man we'd never worked with before. And red flag: he'd come looking for us. A fixer named Janus. We didn't even know where he operated out of. The name should have been enough for me to want to walk away. Ginny even made a joke about the Roman god Janus being two-faced.

But I was blinded by desperation. I didn't want to have to face Dad's disappointment when he found out how deep I'd gotten betting the sports book after he'd already read me the riot act about using a bookie. Four days in Vegas and I was cleaned out. If I didn't want Dad hearing about the job ahead of time and putting the kibosh on it, I couldn't go to Paulie or any of the other setup people we usually worked with, and I didn't have anything of my own on tap. Which meant taking a contract from a contact we didn't know. Janus had reached out at exactly the right time for me to want to take it.

Ginny and I argued about it, and then, finally, I guilted her into agreeing.

The fact that we were stealing it from a private collection helped: private collections were always better than museums. When you stole a painting from a private collection, it made the news. But when you stole a painting from a museum, particularly if the piece of art was famous, then it made the news *worldwide*. You'd be looking over your shoulder basically forever.

Occasionally, I'd read news stories about crime rings pulling art theft jobs and then panicking because they couldn't find a buyer, and sometimes that meant that they'd burn the painting to hide the evidence as the cops closed in. But in the world of art theft, as organized as those crime rings were, they were amateurs. Professionals never stole a piece of art unless they already had a buyer lined up.

But the beautiful thing about this job, and what tipped Ginny into the yes column, is that we didn't have to worry about publicity of any kind, and we didn't have to worry about the owner running to the cops.

That was because the painting was in a very, very private collection: the work of art we were supposed to steal was already stolen.

The man who was in possession of the painting had commissioned its theft more than thirty years earlier, and even then, that had been from a private collection too. I had no clue who the client was behind Janus, or how they had found out where the stolen painting was in the first place, but it meant it took a lot of the heat off us after the job; it wasn't like the guy who had the painting stolen in the first place thirty years ago could call the authorities and complain that somebody had stolen his stolen painting.

Plus, it didn't hurt that the job was in Paris, one of Ginny's favorite cities, and I'd promised to spend some of my end on a vacation for us afterward.

It was a cake-mix job. Janus had provided us with all the details as well as a small group of professionals working support, plus a driver. Ginny and I were the oil and eggs. A week of prep, and then we baked the cake. All told, day of, it was six hours of the crew sweating bullets as they moved to the tune Ginny and I played. The vault was a Ridgewood 4, and Ginny made it dance the jig.

Afterward, we split up. The driver and crew from Janus dispersed, taking the gear and weapons, and disposing of them along with the vehicles. Ginny and I took the painting to a cool-out that Janus had also arranged.

The cool-out was a sixth-floor walk-up apartment in the Latin Quarter. Technically, the building had an elevator, but it was one of those Parisian retrofits where you could only squeeze in two people who are intimately comfortable with each other, and it rattled and wheezed when it was in operation.

We were right across the street from the Seine, and I'd spent most of the afternoon sitting in a lounge chair by the Juliet balcony. The 5th arrondissement was also a good place for people watching.

Ginny was in one of two bedrooms catching up on her sleep. Between jet lag and working into the wee hours of the night to steal the painting, she was wiped. I'd caught a few hours already and felt pretty good, though. Relaxed. Besides, I wanted to be awake and alert when the collector showed up. Once they verified the painting, we'd get our fee, and we could split. Cash on the barrel. I'd insisted on it since we didn't know Janus. One of the things that had gotten

Ginny to let go of her misgivings. For this job, we'd already worked out how to get the bills back into the country and how to wash it. Routine stuff. At this point, all Ginny and I were doing was waiting to get paid.

I read a few more pages of my novel—like my dad and Helen, I mostly preferred mysteries and thrillers, but on any job, the amount of waiting around meant that I was willing to read almost anything I could put my hands on—and then I heard the whir of the old elevator in the hallway. I listened carefully until it stopped on our floor. The elevator door opened and then closed. I put down my book.

Maybe it was Ginny's hesitation at doing the job in the first place, or the fact that even as it went along there were some things that felt off, things that we'd chalked up to working with a new crew, but in that instant, I had one of those unexplainable niggling doubts. It had made sense to give all the gear and guns to the driver and crew to dispose of so that Ginny and I could travel clean as soon as we handed off the painting, but I was suddenly unhappy that neither of us was heavy.

I hustled into the kitchen and palmed a paring knife. Not as good as a gun, but better than nothing and easy to keep hidden in my hand.

The rap at the door sounded exactly like the man in the hallway: short, neat, and polite. He came in trailed by a gorilla. We exchanged pleasantries, and then he examined the Degas on the dining room table. He used a loupe for about five minutes, and then took a microscopic sample of paint and ran a few chemical tests.

By the time he was finished, Ginny was up. She was drinking a cup of coffee and standing by the railing of the building. I noticed the bodyguard paying special attention to her, and I tried not to laugh. He was not Ginny's type. He was a big boy, though. A little bit gone to seed, but he had the look of somebody who'd played football in college. Except we were in France, and the few words the guy had said marked him as British, so it had probably been rugby. He had come in carrying a leather weekender bag that presumably held our cash, and I'd relaxed a little as soon as I'd sized him up: he either had an excellent tailor or wasn't carrying a gun anywhere obvious.

The collector said, "Good," and then, to the muscle, he said, "We're all done. Let's finish up."

Ginny, from where she stood next to the Juliet balcony, said, "I think we'll count it. Bring it over."

The bodyguard looked to his boss. "Go on," the man said. "Get it over with."

The goon strolled over to Ginny. He set the leather bag in front of her and then stepped behind her.

From there, things moved fast.

And I hesitated.

Again.

53

I STILL DON'T KNOW IF IT WAS the first brush of surprise on Ginny's face or the way the leather weekender came up from the floor in her hands with such ease that I knew the suitcase was stuffed with bubble wrap or crumpled newspapers instead of US dollars.

As soon as she registered the weight—or lack of weight—in the bag, she started swinging it, trying to use it as a distraction, but the man had already moved in. He wrapped his arms around her from behind and lifted her feet off the ground.

Ginny snapped her head back. She made contact, and I saw blood spray from the man's nose, but he didn't loosen his grip. He arched his back and lifted her higher. He was too close and had too much size on her.

I started moving.

I had the kitchen knife I'd palmed in my hand. The man was twisting himself and Ginny around, showing me his back. Her arms were pinned against her body. He had weight and size, and his hands were locked together, so her torso was immobilized. As long as he was willing to withstand the barrage of her heels smashing into him and her thrashing her head back in an attempt to bloody him further, all he had to do was keep squeezing until he either crushed her rib cage or she ran out of breath. But he wasn't waiting. He was already angling her toward the railing of the balcony.

He was tilting his head away as best he could as Ginny thrashed, trying to avoid another strike of her head against his face. He was arched backward so that he could lift her all the way off the floor. His throat was exposed. All I had to do was get there, grab his hair, and pull, keeping his throat available for me to slice it open from ear to ear. Simple, brutal, and quick.

I hadn't hesitated for more than a second.

But a second was too long.

A second too late.

He tossed Ginny over the railing of the balcony.

I screamed Ginny's name as I buried the knife in his back. He gasped and tried reaching back for the knife, but I pulled the blade out and used the opening to stab up under his arm, through the armpit so I'd miss the rib cage, and then again in his stomach. He swung his arms wildly, but I ducked and stabbed and then, finally, I slit his throat, pressing hard, sawing through the flesh and cartilage. The blood-slicked blade skittered out of my hand at the same time he collapsed to the floor.

I put my hands on the railing and looked down.

I'd heard shattering glass and bent metal when Ginny fell, and I knew what I was about to see.

I was right. She was on her back on the roof of a panel van parked alongside the curb on the street below, Quai de la Tournelle. She looked twisted. Broken. There was blood on her face. One of her legs was at an awkward angle. There were already people rushing over to her. I screamed her name again.

And then I saw her arm move.

She was still alive.

I let go of the railing and turned so I could go to her.

When I did, the neat, polite little man who'd authenticated the painting shot me in the chest.

54

ACCORDING TO THE DOCTORS, we were both lucky.

The bullet was a through and through and had missed my heart by a sixteenth of an inch. It was going to be a hard two months of initial recovery for me, but I was going to be fine.

By all accounts, Ginny should have been dead. Instead, she was in a coma. In something approximating a miracle, she didn't seem to have a spinal injury. There was a litany of broken bones and other insults to her body, a laundry list of surgeries she'd need, but her spine was intact.

The real danger was her brain. The doctors had to drill a hole in her skull to relieve the pressure. There was no way to know when— or if—she'd wake up. But if she did come out of the coma, the neurosurgeon said it was impossible to know whether or not she'd have lasting brain damage.

Some luck.

Ginny and I both had pristine IDs. Other than taking a statement from me—it was a short statement, because I told them that after a morning of sightseeing, I couldn't remember a thing that happened in the apartment—the cops left us alone. As far as they were concerned, we were American tourists, and we'd been followed back to our rental by opportunistic thugs. The dead bodyguard had an extensive criminal history. The police decided the whole thing was a simple robbery gone wrong. The way they figured it, there had been two of them: the dead man and an accomplice. The two partners had some kind of a fight that ended in the bodyguard stabbed to death,

Ginny tossed over the railing, and me shot and left for dead. My prints were on the knife because I'd been staying there, but Ginny and I were innocents caught in the middle of a dastardly plot. The police didn't have a lot of confidence that they would be able to find the shooter. I didn't offer them any information that could have helped.

The second day in the hospital, I got a phone call from Aunt Paulie. She spoke carefully, but I got the gist. Dad wasn't coming. He'd been in the middle of a job of his own, and when he'd heard the news, he pulled the plug so he could rush to Paris. Only, in his hurry to get to me and Ginny, he'd made a mistake and gotten picked up dead to rights. She told me she'd be there as soon as she could, but even with the best lawyer money could buy, Dad wouldn't be going anywhere anytime soon.

Two more lost bets I'd be paying interest on for a long time.

The recovery left me with a lot of time to think.

A lot of time to find blame.

And to figure out where to start inflicting pain.

That had been twenty months ago, and I'd worked my way along the string as far as I could, but the trail had gone completely cold.

I'd killed my way to a dead end.

Or at least it *had* been a dead end—until I opened the envelope from Aunt Paulie's safe that had Ginny's name written on it.

55

UNCLE CHARLES DROVE ME from his place to my truck.

The surveillance team Park and Greaves had ordered was trying, but they weren't good enough. It was a moving box, but they were only using three vehicles. I don't think Uncle Charles noticed them, but I made them immediately. Not that it mattered. I wasn't trying to shake them. Not yet.

Charles and I were both quiet. He'd told me the names of Paulie's men who'd been killed when she was attacked. I felt a small surge of relief to hear that Rick had been off duty; I was still angry about him getting ready to rip my thumbs off, but I also knew he had young kids, while the other guys were all single.

Mostly, though, I was sure Charles was thinking about his wife. It couldn't have been easy for him. My dad had always been honest with Ginny and me about how difficult it had been for our mom when he was working. That even though she'd understood what our family was like, and accepted that it was who her husband was, and soon enough, who her children would be, it wasn't where she came from.

Love sure was a funny drug; it made people agree to all kinds of things.

While Charles was thinking about Paulie, I was thinking about the information inside the envelopes she'd left for me. Both the envelopes.

I hadn't told Charles what was in them, and he had known better than to ask.

I started to get out of my uncle's minivan, but he stopped me.

"Be careful, Duke," he said.

It was almost too much to bear. My aunt was in the hospital because of me. She could have been—should have been—dead. And my uncle was telling me to watch out for myself. And he meant it. He wasn't angry at me. He just loved me.

Maybe I didn't have a conventional family, but still . . .

I watched him drive away and then got into my truck. I hadn't bothered locking it, and I'd left the key in the cup holder.

Yeah. I know.

I grabbed my phone from the glove box. The card Baker had given me at the Market House was in there. I spun it around and around in my fingers, thinking. He'd tried to send me a message by going after Aunt Paulie. And, looking at my phone, I saw that he'd left me several messages, but these ones were literal.

The messages were all versions of the same thing: hand the cipher over or it would get worse.

I wanted to call the number, to send him a message back, but I knew it wasn't the right play. I had to start thinking three steps ahead.

I committed the number on Baker's card to memory and then tossed it back into the glove box. I set aside the phone to bring it inside when I got home.

The drive to my apartment was boring. The cars tailing me did an adequate job, and traffic was light. I was able to snag a spot right out front of my building, but instead of going home, I headed down the block to Kim's Market, giving a sarcastic wave to one of the sur-veillance vehicles—a late-model Jeep with two women in it, both unmistakably FBI agents—before stepping inside the store.

Kim's Market was one of those neighborhood places that had a little bit of everything. Toilet paper, canned tuna, cold drinks, light bulbs, condoms, plus a deli counter serving sandwiches, tacos, and Korean food. More importantly, Mrs. Kim owed me a favor for straightening out her grandson and extricating him from the gang life when he started doing some light banging a couple of years ago.

There were only a few shoppers milling around, and Mrs. Kim came out from behind the deli to give me a hug.

"Let me get you something to eat," she said, which was her way of saying hello. "The tacos are good today. Pulled pork with a gochu-jang sauce."

"No thank you, Mrs. Kim," I said, and then waved to her daughter, Soo-jin, who was working at the register. It had been Soo-jin's sister's kid that I'd straightened out, but the two of us had been friendly even before I'd stepped in. In fact, being friends with Soo-jin was one of the reasons I *had* stepped into something that wasn't my business.

Mrs. Kim's face showed that she was hurt. "You don't want my pulled pork?"

"It's not that, it's just that I'm actually in a bit of a hurry. I only came in because I need to grab something from the office."

Mrs. Kim looked relieved. "In that case, I'll just make you some tacos to go, then," she said, dismissing me and heading back behind the counter. Soo-jin winked at me, and I smothered a laugh. Her mother had never once let me leave the store without feeding me. Soo-jin liked to say that the way to tell when her mother loved somebody was when she tried to fatten them up.

56

I LET MYSELF INTO THE OFFICE using the keypad I'd installed for them. There was a reasonably secure safe I'd given Mrs. Kim that was against the wall. They used it to keep cash and receipts, but I ignored that and climbed up onto the desk. I popped up one of the ceiling tiles and then opened the lockbox I'd bolted to the rafters. I pulled out a small backpack, closed the lockbox back up, and then replaced the tile.

I sat down at the desk and then unpacked the backpack. There wasn't a lot in it: a burner phone and a charger, a set of picks, a pair of work gloves, a Smith & Wesson 9mm with three empty magazines, and a box of bullets. The pistol had the serial numbers filed off—which made the pistol very illegal—but it was completely clean otherwise. Better than the Glock in my truck, which wasn't exactly legal, either, but was traceable. I used to keep ten thousand dollars in there in cash, too, but I'd raided that early during the first blush of my bad streak betting on ball games.

I plugged in the phone and waited for it to start up. I hadn't checked the backpack in more than a year, but it was good to see that the phone had mostly held its charge. That was one of the best things about cheap burner phones. They didn't do a lot more than make phone calls, so if you left them turned off, the batteries lasted forever. I put on the gloves and then fieldstripped the pistol, inspected it, and then reassembled. Then I opened the box of bullets and loaded the magazines. While a burner phone does fine just sitting for a year, leaving a magazine loaded indefinitely theoretically increased the chances of having the spring in the magazine fail. There was some debate on it, but it wasn't like it was that difficult to load three magazines. I was hoping I wasn't going to need the pistol, but if I did, I wanted to avoid a misfire.

I put the pistol and the loaded magazines into my duffel bag, took off the gloves and laid them on top of the phone where I wouldn't forget them, and then left the office to go shopping. I took two more burner phones from behind the counter and asked Soo-jin if she could activate them, plug them in, and make sure they were working while I grabbed what I needed: a roll of duct tape, a box of Cheerios, a jug of milk, and a can of shaving cream.

Mini-marts are mini-miracles. Everything you need, nothing that you don't.

Though, technically, the only thing I needed other than the phones was the duct tape. The Cheerios, milk, and shaving cream were strictly for personal use.

I brought everything up to the counter and dumped it in front of Soo-jin.

She reached down to get the notebook where they kept my tab, but then stopped and squinted at me. "What?" she said.

"Believe it or not, I can pay my tab."

Normally, this should have brought forth a smile, but instead, Soo-jin scowled at me.

Frankly, if it were up to Mrs. Kim, I probably would never have paid for anything again as long as she was breathing, but I didn't feel right about just taking stuff. She'd busted her ass to give her kids and then their kids a better life. She didn't deserve to lose a grandson to a gang. Other than one of her grandson's gangbanger pals sticking a pistol in my face—a rash decision on his part that cost him two months in a cast—it hadn't been a big deal to help Mrs. Kim out.

That being said, I had taken advantage of her offer to let me run a tab until, as she charitably put it, my "cash flow issues" were resolved. But Soo-jin was less charitable about my gambling.

"It's not like that," I said. "Honest money."

Well, I thought, honest enough.

At that, her glower dialed down to a something more like a combination of a frown and that look babies get when they are gassy. While she totaled up the ledger, I went back into the office, opened the new burner phones, and confirmed they had enough of a charge. Then I pulled out one of the stacks of twenty-dollar bills from my duffel bag, put a thousand dollars into what was now an empty backpack, and returned the backpack to its hiding place in the lockbox in the rafters. I'd have to remember to replace the gloves, pick set, and pistol later, but it never hurt to have a little cash set aside somewhere safe.

By the time I was done, Soo-jin had totaled my tab. With the new purchases, I almost zeroed out the other half of the stack of cash I hadn't put into the backpack. It was immensely satisfying to count out the money and square my accounts.

But still, Mrs. Kim wouldn't let me pay for the tacos.

57

THE TACOS WERE PHENOMENAL.

I realized I had other priorities, but oh man. The pork was juicy and tender, double-wrapped in fresh tortillas, with a salsa that was some sort of pineapple Korean fusion, the gochujang spicy enough to keep me interested, and with a nice crunch from some sort of cabbage. I was glad Mrs. Kim had included a generous pull from the napkin dispenser. She'd also thrown a bottle of seltzer water in the bag, which was a nice touch.

I ate while I sat on the front steps and watched the FBI watching me.

Aside from the Jeep with the two women in it, there was the dark gray cargo van with a vinyl graphic of a bouquet and floral creations splashed on the side, conveniently parked across the street and just down from my building.

Because a flower delivery van parked for hours and hours was completely inconspicuous.

Then there was a plain sedan that might as well have had "Hello! I am an unmarked government vehicle!" spray-painted on the hood. The guy behind the wheel was sort of slumped down, as if that made him less suspicious.

Finally, I could see two agents—clearly trying to pass as a couple—sipping drinks at a table outside the coffee shop on the corner.

I waited a few more minutes and then Taneesha and her younger sister, Maya, walked around the corner. They stopped in front of me, and Taneesha shook her head.

"They've got the back blanketed. Cars on either side of the alley. One's a black Chevy SUV, the other's a gray Ford sedan. You want the plate numbers?"

"Nah," I said.

Taneesha and Maya had come home from school and found me sitting on the steps. I'd asked them to do a loop around the building to see how tight of a net the feds had put up.

Ginny and their dad, Jameel, had dated for a few months when they were in college together, and it had been, to put it lightly, not a good relationship. But they found that once they weren't dating, they got along incredibly well. As boyfriend and girlfriend, it was gasoline and a bonfire, but as a friend, he was as good as it got, and being friends with Ginny meant I was part of the package. Jameel was the one who told me about the apartment when it became available. He even helped me move in. I functioned as a sort of honorary uncle to Taneesha and Maya, and they'd often come hang at my apartment when Jameel had to work late. Taneesha was in eighth grade and smart as a whip: she was in the gifted and talented program, already taking AP calculus, knew three programming languages, was fluent in Spanish and French, could read Latin, and could get by in both Korean and Mandarin. Maya was only in second grade, but clearly just as smart as her sister.

Taneesha continued, "There's also a guy standing in a doorway in the alley, pretending like he's staring at his phone, and there's a woman walking laps around the block with a dog. Either they just moved here, or they're part of the team."

"Thanks, kiddo," I said. "And what about the other two? Need me to show you the pictures again?" I'd shown her the photos I had of Baker and Cleary on my cell phone.

She rolled her eyes. "Please. I'm not a baby, Duke."

"Sorry," I said. "You're right. And nice work. I'll be up in about half an hour. That okay with you?"

"Sure," she said. "I'll make Maya an after-school snack and get her started on her homework."

They headed inside, with Maya complaining that she didn't want to do her homework and Taneesha patiently offering to read aloud to her if that was easier.

Good kids.

I looked back at the van with the flower delivery decal on it. I sighed unhappily.

Being used as bait didn't bother me. But the whole point of being bait was to get some bites. I don't know what I'd been expecting, because even if I thought Cleary was the kind of hothead I could take advantage of, Baker was too sharp to just be caught waiting outside my apartment. Still, it was disappointing; after seeing what they'd done to my aunt, I *wanted* Baker and Cleary to try to come for me.

Baker and Cleary aside, the scale of the surveillance operation Greaves and Park had been able to throw together so quickly was concerning. They had to have at least a dozen agents working me directly, maybe more, plus off-site support.

Which said two things. The first was that when Greaves told me the full might and force of the United States government was bearing down, she wasn't lying. Surveillance operations are expensive. Even simple wiretaps and video still require someone to sort through the information. But something like this ate up man-hours and racked up overtime like a New York City sanitation worker. Sure, constitutional rights and all that stuff, but one of the main reasons it's hard for law enforcement to get authorization for this kind of surveillance is simply that it costs a lot of money.

The second thing the scope of this told me was that there was something going on with Agent Greaves that I didn't understand. Park felt like standard FBI to me, but Greaves was playing in a different league altogether. Unless she was lying to me—and I didn't think she was—she had the ability to authorize my demands and get this surveillance up and running without a problem. If the cipher was important enough that she could give the go-ahead for all of that, then it meant it was unlikely that she was simply a rank-and-file agent. No way she was a standard-issue desk jockey or field agent working the LA bureau. I was going against something serious here.

I finished the last bite of the tacos and then licked my fingers before wiping them off with the napkins Mrs. Kim had included.

It was time to get moving.

58

I HAD A GIRLFRIEND ONCE who broke up with me because she said I was always looking for the way out. I couldn't explain to her that it was habit, nothing personal.

There's a certain segment of professionals who like to believe they can leave *everything* behind in ten seconds flat if they need to. Those people have watched too many movies. Or are psychopaths. Or sociopaths. I can never remember the difference. But the point is, unless you're willing to forswear all relationships and care about nothing and nobody, it's hard to just walk away permanently.

I hadn't ever mastered the knack of keeping a serious girlfriend, but I had a life in Los Angeles, and I had friends—Meg, Jameel and his kids, buddies at the gym, a crew I surfed with regularly, a group from college who met in Colorado once or twice a year to go snowboarding—and I had family. Even if I'd cleared out the locker in Zurich, taking those five million dollars, I don't think I could have paid the cost of ghosting forever.

But ghosting and bouncing aren't the same thing, and the bounce isn't a getaway plan either.

Getaway plans after a job are standard. A given. Guys who are ex-military—or who like to pretend they are—tend to call it an exfil plan or exit strategy, but whatever you call it, having a getaway is a given. There's no point walking into a museum and stealing a painting if you can't walk out again. Cash, jewels, exotic cars, whatever it is, you can't spend it from behind bars. If you don't have multiple getaways and cool-outs for after a score, then you won't get away.

Relying on only one getaway plan means you're relying on everything to work out, and luck runs both ways, good and bad.

But the bounce is different.

A getaway is specific to a specific job, but the bounce is the getaway you have in your pocket even when you aren't working; it's a way out of whatever situation you're in.

And the situation I was in was that I could either go hunting or let Greaves follow me around and hope that she picked up Baker before he took me out.

Act or react.

Easy choice.

It was time to slip the collar Greaves had put on me.

It was time to bounce.

59

IN MY APARTMENT, THE FIRST THING I DID was put my watch back on. I'd had to sell my pricey watches early on to help cover my losing streak, but I'd kept this one, a Dan Henry 1970 Automatic Diver. I always wore a watch, especially when I was working—losing track of time could be a lethal proposition—but I had to leave the 1970 behind with everything else when I went to do the job for Baker and Cleary. Putting it back on felt comforting, and, frankly, it looked sharp and wore like a much more expensive watch. As my dad said when I showed it to him, "Anybody with a credit card and a pulse can drop six figures to impress, but you have to have actual taste to find a watch that can hold its own for less than three hundred bucks."

Once my watch was strapped on, I took one of the burners, dialed Greaves's number, put the phone on speaker, and then turned the two o'clock crown to set the inner bezel on my watch so I could time the call.

A male voice answered: "FBI. Agent Greaves's office."

"Patch me through," I said.

"Excuse me, but—"

"It's Duke."

"Hold on."

The line clicked over in less than a minute. I used the time to walk into the bathroom, turn on my shower, and take off my clothes. Between my work for Baker and Cleary, all the travel, the questioning session at the airport, visiting my aunt, and everything else, I was ripe.

"You're not calling from your cell phone number, Duke."

"The guy who hired me called me on it. I'm assuming it's compromised. This is a burner," I said. "Call me at this number if you need to reach me." She grunted assent. "Quick question. Why is this cipher thing I allegedly stole so important?"

"Give me a break with the 'allegedly,' Duke. And you know I'm not going to answer that."

"Okay, fine," I said. "If you aren't going to tell my why this cipher thing is so important, are you going to at least tell me why it was in a nearly impenetrable safe in a CIA black site in Germany?"

"No, I'm not," she said. "What's that sound? Are you in the shower?"

"Yeah. Sorry. Multitasking. Am I on camera?"

"Probably," she said. "I'm not micromanaging the surveillance, but I'd assume they wired the bathroom along with everything else."

"Well, don't watch me shower. That's creepy. And just so you know, the first thing I'm going to do after I shower is disable all the audio and video you have in my apartment."

"Duke—"

"I wasn't asking permission. I was just letting you know so you can tell your people to expect everything to go dark. This isn't my first rodeo or whatever cliché you want me to use to make it clear that I'm a step ahead of you."

"Are you?"

"I don't like being watched," I said. "Want me to give you a courtesy call when it's done?"

"Do I literally have to say the word *sigh* to you?"

I picked up the shampoo bottle. It was empty. I'd needed to buy more for a couple of weeks and kept forgetting, which was annoying. I could have grabbed some while I was at the mini-mart. At least I wasn't out of soap. I was on a schedule, though, and I'd already soaped and rinsed. No time to just luxuriate in the shower. I turned the water off, grabbed my towel, and said, "I'll take that as a yes on the courtesy call."

"Is this really why you're calling?" Greaves said. "I do have other stuff I'm supposed to be doing. This is the most important thing on my desk right now, but it's not the only thing."

I checked my watch. Close, but I still had to stay on the line for a bit longer to make sure she'd bought in, so I said, "I want to renegotiate."

"No."

"Come on, Greaves. I don't think my dad should have to wait until you've got your hands on the cipher. Release him today on his own recognizance, some sort of probation thing. It doesn't really matter what you call it, but there's no reason to keep him locked up. You know as well as I do that if he wanted to escape from Terminal Island he could. If he was going to run, he would have already."

If my dad had wanted to break out, it wouldn't have taken much doing. But there was a reason he hadn't tried. Once the government decides it wants you locked up, you have to make a decision: do the time or spend the rest of your life on the run. Getting out of jail isn't hard. Staying out is almost impossible unless you're really willing to go all the way. For the same reason I wasn't willing to leave everything and, more importantly, *everyone* behind, my dad wasn't willing to ghost. It was why an opportunity to get him out legally was impossible for me to turn down.

She was quiet for a few seconds. I was supposed to believe she was thinking. She wasn't, of course. She was just stalling for the final seconds. Which was fine by me.

"I'll see what I can do, Duke. But don't hold your breath."

She hung up, which meant her techs had a lock on the burner phone and would be able to track its GPS location. Which was the whole point of my phone call. I wanted them focused on *that* burner phone's location.

Which was going to be in this building, approximating me being the good boy that Greaves wanted me to be.

Which I was not.

I got dressed and got to work.

60

FIRST THINGS FIRST. I SCANNED THE APARTMENT for cameras and microphones.

Given how little time they had to get in and out of my apartment, I had to admit I was impressed. Most of the apartment was covered, including, yes, my shower, and though I think I probably would have found everything doing an old-fashioned search and sweep, I would have had to work for it. Thankfully, I didn't have to do it the hard way. If you're just talking garden-variety stalker stuff that you can order off Amazon or that your friendly neighborhood creep installs in their vacation rental, you don't need anything fancy: a Wi-Fi searching app on your phone and a flashlight will sort you out. But those take time, and I still had most of my professional tools from when I was in the family business. I just did press-and-play on an electronic sniffer to find and disable. So that was five minutes.

Once I was sure the apartment was blind and deaf, I called the number on Greaves's card again. The same guy picked up again.

"Courtesy call," I said. "No audio or video in my apartment anymore. It's not a technical glitch. I disabled them, and they won't be coming back online."

"Wait—"

I hung up.

I didn't want to have a conversation about it. I wanted them to spend their time wondering what I was up to in my apartment that I didn't want them to have eyes or ears on me. They'd be so focused on trying to figure out what was happening in my apartment that they wouldn't realize it was empty.

Once that was taken care of, I prepped the package for Taneesha, and then I started putting together a kit of what I thought I needed. By the time I was done, it had been close to the half hour I'd promised Taneesha.

I needed to get out of my apartment without the surveillance team knowing, and while I'd disabled all the audio and video in my apartment, unless they were totally incompetent, I was sure there were cameras in the hallway, and Taneesha had confirmed that they had eyes on the alley, which meant shimmying out one of my windows was also a no-go.

Not a problem. There were at least three other ways I could get out of my building without being seen, but the quickest was also the simplest.

Fun fact: when it was originally built, my building had eight units, and each unit, spaciously designed for a family of four, was two stories. When it had been subdivided somewhere around 1980, instead of removing the internal stairs, the builder had simply put walls in front of them. My apartment was directly below Jameel, Taneesha, and Maya's. All I had to do was go into my closet, swing open the false wall, and climb the steps.

It was awkward closing the false wall behind me, but if, for some reason, Greaves sent in her agents, it would take them at least a couple of hours of searching to figure it out.

At the top of the stairs, the door was already open for me, and Maya was sitting on her dad's bed reading a book. She acknowledged me with a small wave and then went back to reading.

Taneesha was sitting on the couch in the living room doing homework.

I handed her the package I'd prepared. "You need to go over it again?"

The withering look she gave me would have reduced a lesser man to dust.

"Okey dokey. Hey," I said, "take this." I handed her five twenties. "Treat your dad and sister to a night out somewhere fun."

She pressed her lips together with a slight frown. "You know how stubborn Daddy is. He'll be pissed if I take money just for helping you out."

"Yeah. He's always been stubborn. The only thing that's changed about him since I first met him is that he's gotten fatter."

Taneesha giggled, and I quickly added, "Do *not* tell him I said that."

It was true that he was stubborn, though.

"Look, Taneesha, you know I love your dad, but I'm not giving you money because you're doing me a favor. I'm giving you money because I got lucky, and I've got money to burn."

Now she crossed her arms. "You *definitely* know how he feels about you gambling."

"First of all, I don't need a lecture from a twelve-year-old. And second—"

"Thirteen."

"What?"

"I'm thirteen."

Crap. "I missed your birthday?"

"Yep."

I pulled out my cash and counted out another five twenty-dollar bills. She didn't reach for them.

"Come on, Taneesha. It's not gambling money. I swear. Use the first hundred I gave you to go out for dinner with your dad and Maya.

How many times have you guys had me over for dinner? I'm just trying to repay that a little bit."

"Lord knows we don't want your cooking," she grumbled, sounding so much like an old lady that I had to laugh, even though I was a decent cook thanks to Helen's influence.

I waved the additional cash at her. "And this is for you to get yourself something for your birthday. Pretend it's a thoughtful birthday present that I spent hours shopping for."

Reluctantly—more reluctantly than I would have been to take two hundred dollars when I was thirteen years old—she took the money. "Duke," she said, "are you going to be okay?"

She'd turned the corner from being a child into acting like a young woman a year or so ago, but when she asked me that, when she asked if I was going to be okay, she sounded like a little kid again.

"Taneesha."

"For real, Duke."

I knew she was thinking of Ginny. Jameel had taken her and Maya to visit a couple of times, but it was hard on them. And even if Jameel was fine with me teaching Taneesha my trade—we'd had a long conversation about it, and he'd decided the best way for a smart kid like Taneesha to bloom was to let her follow her curiosity, even if it meant her learning how to crack a safe—he was more or less a straight arrow; still, he was as honest as he could be with Taneesha about what had happened. In the same way that I was a kind of uncle to them, Ginny was like an aunt. What happened with Ginny had hit them hard too.

"For real? I don't know, honey. But I'm trying."

She got up from the couch and hugged me. I hugged her back.

61

FROM THE ROOF OF MY APARTMENT BUILDING, it was a hop, a couple of skips, and one kind of longish jump until I was back on the ground, but now I was outside the surveillance perimeter.

I'd put some thought into what I was wearing: a pair of dark jeans, a black button-down, and a pair of charcoal-colored OluKai sneakers. Even though they were athletic, the shoes were nice enough that I could pass for business casual, which meant that with my outfit and the single-strap bag I had across my torso, I looked like I was just another slightly entitled professional with flexible working hours.

Of course, if anybody took the time to investigate my bag or search me, they'd find the Smith & Wesson 9mm I'd retrieved from Mrs. Kim's, three sets of fake identities complete with driver's licenses and credit cards, a GPS tracker, nearly forty thousand dollars in cash—I'd stashed the rest—and a few other mostly illegal goodies from my apartment.

I mean, I wasn't completely winging it. I had a plan.

Mostly.

I started walking and called Lily. She was still at the hospital, watching over my aunt, but given the state of things, she was eager to help. I explained what I was looking for, and she called me back three minutes later with a name and address.

After about ten minutes of walking, I saw a cab. Part of the process of staying out of the net the FBI had cast around me. Sure, it was a bit of a hassle, but any ride I had to call with my phone was something that could be tracked and required a credit card. With a cab, I could pay cash and stay invisible.

Traffic was heavy, even by Los Angeles standards, and I closed my eyes to gather myself.

I thought about Taneesha's question. Was I going to be okay?

I told her I was trying, but sometimes it felt like the harder I swam toward the surface the farther away it got.

Even if I managed to wiggle my way out of this mess, even if I got my dad sprung, I'd always be faced with that look of disappointment. He'd always see me and see that hesitation, see all the ways I never quite measured up, and no matter what he said, I'd know: he would be thinking it should have been me instead of Ginny.

And the worst part was, I'd be thinking the same thing.

62

THE TRAFFIC NEVER LET UP, but the driver was mercifully quiet, and when we arrived at the address I'd gotten from Paulie's lieutenant, I tipped generously, with all the flair and élan of somebody who has recently come into money. I stepped out of the cab into the mid-evening sunlight.

The house was a midsize ranch. Nothing too imposing. Nice if you didn't look too closely. The lawn was short and neat, and there was a palm tree at the corner of the lot that cut a handsome figure. The house needed a new roof, and the car in the driveway had seen better days, but unless you already knew it, there was nothing to tell you that the woman who owned the house had nearly a hundred grand in illegal gambling debts, nor was there anything to tell you that she worked at the FBI.

I marched up to the front door and rang the bell.

A woman came to the door holding a dish towel, but still dressed from work, in a professional outfit, complete with blazer. I didn't know much of anything about her except that she was FBI and mostly worked a desk job.

I was hoping she wasn't wearing a service weapon, and if she was, that she didn't decide to pull it out. I had my Smith & Wesson hol-stered under my shirt, but I couldn't see any scenario where gunplay was going to work out well.

"Theo Baggeti holds your chit," I said.

Her face flushed and she narrowed her eyes.

"This is my *house*," she hissed at me. "My *kids* are here. And I've been making my payments. What do you—"

I cut her off. "I can wipe out your debts."

She tilted her head and furrowed her brow. "What? Do you work for him?"

"Not exactly."

"Then you can eat shit," she said, and started to close the door.

"Stan Mariner."

Her face blanched. She stopped, the door still cracked open.

"You know that name, right?"

Hesitantly, she nodded. There was a sound behind her, and she turned her head. "Just a friend from work," she called out, then she looked back at me. "Yes, I know who Stan Mariner is."

Stan "the Hammer" Mariner had come up through the trenches. And if you have to ask why his nickname was the Hammer, then you have lived a very privileged life.

"I—"

"Listen," I said, "I don't know what I have to say to put you at ease, but I am not here to hurt you, and I am not here to hurt your kids. I know how much you owe, and I know that at the rate you're going, you're never going to get out from under it. All I'm asking for is some of your time, and I can get your name wiped off the books."

She stood there, holding the door, hesitating.

I said, "You know as well as I do that if I was here for bad news, I wouldn't just ring the doorbell and wait patiently outside. I know you're an FBI agent, and I don't care. If I was here to hurt you, it would have happened already. So, is there somewhere we can talk? In private?"

Her shoulders slumped, and she looked down at my feet. She said, "In the backyard. Go around the side. Just close the fence behind you. I can't deal with trying to chase down my dog tonight."

She started to close the front door, and then she stopped and said, "Do you want something to drink?"

I almost laughed; that impulse for politeness is so hard to stamp out. But I didn't laugh, because a drink sounded fantastic. "Got any beer?"

63

THE BACKYARD WAS A LITTLE OASIS. There was a wooden gate I had to go through to get in, but she had a lovely adobe fence and a thoughtful, drought-resistant garden, and smack in the middle of the yard, a modest swimming pool with crystalline water. Los Angeles in a nutshell. Her dog, a terrier mix, ran up, gave me a sniff, wagged his tail, and then left me alone.

I took a seat at a café table on the far side of the pool, far enough from the house that she wouldn't be stressed about her kids overhearing her.

She came out shortly, carrying two cans of beer. She handed me one and sat down. "I hope you like radlers."

I took a sip and nodded. It was a Two Pitchers Brewing lager with grapefruit. I didn't drink a ton of radlers—basically beer mixed with fruit juice—but it was surprisingly refreshing. "Pretty good. I've never had this before."

"They're based in Oakland, I think. My ex used to really like them. Other than the kids, these things"—she hefted her can in the air—"are about the only good I got out of that relationship."

We sat quietly for a few seconds, and it was fine. She'd been on the verge of full-blown panic when I'd mentioned Mariner, and I could see her starting to ramp down a bit.

I let her speak first.

She said, "I'm not doing anything illegal for you. I'm not going to jail for—"

"Relax," I said. "All I'm asking for is a little information. You come through, and your name gets written out of the book."

"Who *are* you?"

I debated how much to tell her and then decided my best bet was to get her to understand that I could make good on my offer.

"You know Baggeti works for Mariner," I said, "but do you know who Mariner kicks up the chain to?"

"Who?"

"Me." Not technically true. Baggeti and Mariner were on Paulie's leash, and there were still steps in between, but it was close enough to the truth.

She ran her hand through her hair and rubbed her neck. "This is all so stupid. *I'm* so stupid."

"Let me guess. You started out making small bets for fun. Maybe it was your ex. Cop, right?" I knew the answer. It was part of the information Lily had given me about the woman, but I was working her.

She nodded.

"He'd bet a bit on football games and stuff like that. Seemed harmless, and so you did it, and then you won a bit, so you made bigger bets, and then when you started losing, you chased them, figuring you could win your way out of the hole. Something like that."

"Something like that," she agreed. She took a sip from her beer, looked me up and down, and then leaned back in her chair. "Okay."

"Okay, what?"

"Okay," she said. "I'll do it."

Huh. That was easier than I'd expected. I'd had a much more complicated play ready to go, and if I'd really had to, I could have pulled my 9mm and done it all at gunpoint. I wouldn't have hurt her kids, but I wasn't above threatening to do so.

I must have shown my surprise at how quickly she'd given in, because she said, "What do you expect? I made a dumb mistake, and then I tried to fix it by making more dumb mistakes. And you're offering me a way out? I guess I could pretend like I'm going to resist or that I have too much integrity or something, but . . ."

She took another sip of her beer and then tilted her head back and closed her eyes. "I'm just tired. I've got two kids, and they're great, but they're a pain in my ass, and my ex is worse than useless. I haven't placed a bet in more than a year, and I'm in a good place with gambling, but what I owe is impossible. I'm fully tapped out in terms of equity in the house, and paying my vig, I'm barely getting by. Do you know how much better my life would be if I could wipe away my gambling debts?"

Actually, I did know, and I'd done something insanely stupid to make it happen for myself. I didn't think it would help me to answer her question, however, so I waited.

She took another sip of her beer and then said, "I won't do anything that's going to get somebody at the agency hurt or killed or that is going to get me put in jail, but otherwise, convince me you're going to do what you said about erasing my debts. And then tell me what you want so I can get you the hell off my property."

64

I REACHED INTO MY BAG, pulled out my burner, and dialed. Baggeti picked up on the first ring. He was expecting my call. I handed the phone across the table.

She took the phone, said, "Hello," and then listened.

It was a short call, but it gave me enough time to reach into my bag again and pull out the other envelope Aunt Paulie had left in her safe, the one with my name on it. I slipped out a sheet of paper. The paper was printed with a copy of one of the photos I'd had Mimi take for me at the Market House. It was a good picture, showing both Baker's and Cleary's faces.

Greaves had told me to text her the photos Mimi had taken for me, but I hadn't yet. I wanted to know more about who I was dealing with before I gave Greaves more leverage.

Written underneath the picture of Baker and Cleary was Baker's real name and as much biographical information as Paulie was able to get. Which wasn't much: six years in the Army, a general discharge—no info on why he hadn't gotten an honorable discharge—and then a decade plus of working as a private military contractor in places like Iraq, Afghanistan, and parts of Africa, and then as of about four years ago, nothing. No info on who hired Baker, and absolutely nothing on Cleary. It wasn't much, but it raised some flags; I wished I'd had time to ask Paulie to run the checks before I'd boarded that flight to Zurich.

I exchanged the piece of paper for the phone.

She was staring at me with her mouth slightly open. "Who *are* you?"

"Doesn't matter," I said. "What matters is that, for starters, I need everything you can get on these two."

She looked at the paper with Baker and Cleary's photo. "Fine. Let me get my laptop."

It was my turn to be surprised. "Really? You can just do that right here without going into the office?"

"Of course," she said. "Unless we start hitting high-level stuff, I can do it here with a VPN, and really, anything that I can't do from here I won't be able to access with my security clearance anyway. Basic background searches are fine. I can probably do all of this in an hour or so. I've got a laser printer inside."

I crossed my legs and took another sip of my beer. "Not a bad deal. An hour of work for wiping away nearly a hundred grand in gambling debt. Pretty easy."

She whipped her head up and jabbed her finger at me. "Screw you," she seethed. "If I get caught, I'll lose my job. I might not do jail time, but they'll take my *kids* from me. I made some bad decisions, but I'm not a bad person, so don't you *dare* sit there and say this is easy. You might sound polite, but I know what you're threatening when you ask me if I know who Stan Mariner is. Don't try to pretend that you're some kind of good person."

She stopped suddenly, almost as if she'd surprised herself. There were tears in her eyes.

I just leaned forward, reached out, and pushed the papers closer to her.

SHE WAS RIGHT. I WASN'T A GOOD PERSON.

Forget the stealing. I don't mean that.

What I mean is this: When I went hunting for the men who hired Ginny and then left her for dead, I didn't care who I hurt along the way. And when I shot my first man, when I was eleven, I did it because I had to, and that was reason enough. And when Ginny and I screwed up in Zurich and Dad told me to clean up the mess, there was no other option. I made my choices and I had to accept the natural consequences of those choices, accept the consequences of the life my dad had prepared me and Ginny for. Killing people was part of the deal. What was the point of second-guessing?

I'm a good thief. I'm a good friend. I'm a good son. I'm a good brother.

But I am not a good person.

I do what needs to be done, and I need to believe that I've never lost a minute of sleep over it.

WHILE SHE WORKED AT THE TABLE, I sat in a lounger off to the side, drank my beer, and thought about what needed to be done.

There was the situation I was in now, with Greaves and Park thinking I was in my apartment, and Baker wanting me to return the cipher. That was the immediate problem I needed to deal with.

But there was something else now. The envelope with Ginny's name that Paulie had left for me in her safe.

A lead on Janus.

I'd spilled a lot of blood after Ginny got hurt in Paris, trying to work my way to Janus. He'd disappeared after the incident in the apartment. I wanted to kill him for the obvious reasons, but what I *needed* from him was the name of the person who'd hired me and Ginny. I'd gone after the driver and the crew first. One of them, a weaselly man named Baptiste, had confirmed that the burn was part of the plan. I had wondered at first if it was an impulsive decision by the collector and his bodyguard—why hand over a suitcase full of cash when you can keep it for yourself?—but Baptiste had been clear that while Janus knew about it, the double-cross had been a direct order from the person who hired us. It had been baked into the whole operation. It was one of the reasons the driver and crew had taken all the gear and the weapons, so Ginny and I would be easier to dispose of. Baptiste was under a lot of duress at the time and would have said anything for me to stop, but there was no reason for him to lie about that detail.

It made a certain kind of sense. The driver and crew were all contract workers and getting paid small amounts of money. Less than twenty-five thousand dollars each. Ginny and I were the true specialists, and our unknown employer had decided it was cheaper to kill us than pay us.

When I asked Baptiste who had contracted the job, he said only Janus knew. When I asked where I could find Janus now that he'd gone to ground, Baptiste said he didn't know, but he was sure that the authenticator, the fussy little man who'd shot me, would know, and that I could find him in Bern.

So, I'd gone to Bern. My last trip to Switzerland until a few days ago.

The authenticator worked at the university teaching art history, but his flat showed the second income from his less savory work; it was the entire top floor of a three-floor building. Fifteen-foot ceilings with glass everywhere. The light must have been spectacular during the day. I didn't know, though, because I went in through the skylight while he was sleeping.

The apartment was sparely but carefully furnished. No knock-offs, and there was a pencil etching from Paul Klee—the Klee Museum was in Bern as well—that I thought was an original. The etching was small and unimpressive, about as cheap as you could get and still be an original, but even that should have put it out of reach of a professor of art history who was relying on his university salary.

I moved silently through the living room toward the bedroom. I could hear a gentle, even snoring from the bedroom. I'd been watching for days, and I knew it was just the two of us in the flat. I still had to be quiet, though. The floor below had been split into two apartments, both occupied.

I didn't want anybody to wake up and call the police.

I wanted to be able to take my time with the authenticator.

I hovered over the bed, watching his chest rise and fall. He was sleeping on his back with his left hand on his belly and his right arm above his head, with his hand tucked under the pillow. He was wearing a pair of traditional pinstriped pajamas, and even in sleep he looked fussy.

I slapped a piece of duct tape over his mouth.

He moved like a snake, whipping his right hand out from under the pillow. I blocked his wrist with my left elbow, but he kept his grip on the small, nickel-colored automatic in his hand. I pinned the pistol to the bed and threw a short right cross at his jaw. He took the punch, and then, with his free hand, he punched me in the chest, right where he'd shot me the last time we'd been in the same room.

It took me by surprise, and I let out a grunt. I kept my left hand on the pistol. He had his finger on the trigger, but as long as it was pinned against the mattress, the only thing he could shoot at was the wall. He tried to punch me again, but I caught his fist and then turned it and then pinned that arm against the bed. At which point, he let go of the pistol and went for my eyes.

I was pissed. I'd worked hard at rehab, and I'd been feeling good, but he'd caught me right on the scar, and it hurt. I moved my head out of the way of his grasping fingers, and then picked up the gun, still held sideways in my hand, and smashed it into his nose, switching off his lights.

I wrapped duct tape around his head a few times, making sure his mouth was securely covered so he couldn't scream for help when he woke up. Then I rolled him onto his stomach, taped his wrists together behind his back, and then I did his ankles.

I went out into the kitchen and spent a few minutes catching my breath. There was a dull ache where he'd punched the same scar he'd given me.

Then I spent some time fiddling with his expensive-looking espresso machine. He was going to be out for a little bit, and I wanted to be able to approach him with precision. A little caffeine wouldn't hurt me, and there was the chance I was in for a long night. It didn't matter what else happened, he was a dead man. He would know that. The only question was if he died fast or slow. I didn't care which as long as he told me how to track down Janus.

After about ten minutes, I went back into the bedroom carrying a flower vase full of cold water. I tossed the water on his head.

Nothing.

I shook his shoulder.

No response.

And then I realized that there was none of the gentle rise and fall of breathing.

I rolled him from his stomach to his side. His face was mottled, his eyes bulging out. There was a thick crust of blood from his nose from where I'd smashed him with the pistol.

With his mouth taped, he couldn't breathe through his nose. He'd suffocated.

I left his body in the bed and started searching the apartment for anything that could lead me to Janus.

But he hadn't written anything down. Whatever he'd known about how to find Janus had died with him. And without Janus, I had no way to find out who had contracted the job, who had decided that Ginny and I were expendable.

I needed to find Janus, but I'd come to a dead end.

Until I opened the envelope from Aunt Paulie.

And now I had a lead.

Florida.

I had to see a man about a boat.

BUT FIRST, I HAD TO get myself out of this mess.

Mostly, while she worked on her laptop or went in and out of the house to grab documents off her printer, I sat in the lounger snoozing. At one point she had to give me the keys to her car so I could make a run to the nearest store that sold paper and printer toner. The whole thing took her closer to three hours than the one hour she'd promised, but by the time she was done, I had a stack of printouts two inches thick.

She looked up at me over her open laptop. "Is that everything?"

I was nursing my second radler and reading through the pile of information in front of me.

"One more thing," I said. "Agents Greaves and Park. They work for you guys. I need some information about them." She started to protest, but I stopped her. "Just the basics. Nothing I couldn't find out on my own if I was willing to poke around." I had to think for the full names I'd seen on Park's ID and Greaves's business card. "Erin Greaves, Tony Park."

"And then I'm done?"

"And then you're done."

Her son wandered out from inside and asked her if he could make slice-and-bake chocolate chip cookies. She acquiesced, and then shooed him back toward the house.

I sent Paulie's lieutenant a text that the woman had fulfilled her obligations, then read quietly for several minutes before I heard her grunt. I looked up at her. She was tilted toward her laptop, fingers pinching her nose, a look of concentration on her face.

She caught me looking and said, "You sure you spelled their names correctly?"

"How do you misspell Tony Park? No. I'm sure. Those are the names."

She turned her laptop so I could see the screen. "I'm not talking about Park. He's FBI for sure. But if you spelled Greaves's name correctly, then something's wrong. There are a few Greaves, but nobody named Erin or even same initial."

I narrowed my eyes.

"Oh, hell no," she said.

"Come on. All you have to do—"

She shook her head emphatically and closed the laptop. "No way. You say you got her name off her ID card?"

"Park's ID card. With Greaves it was just a business card."

"If she was a real FBI agent, I'd at least be able to confirm that. Get her email addresses and office number, that kind of crap. I mean, whatever else we do, the Federal Bureau of Investigation is a bureau. As in bureaucracy. You can look people up. If she's an agent, she'd be in the system."

I knew she was right.

Park was confirmed FBI, but Greaves worked for the United States government in some other nebulous capacity. I didn't have any question about that. It would have been audacious to pick me up at the airport posing as FBI agents as part of a con, but it was possible. No way they could have thrown that surveillance team together like that, however, not with hired talent. Those were FBI people, or, at the very least, LAPD. And unless Greaves was the greatest bluffer of all time, she knew stuff that no freelancer was going to know. No.

Greaves might not have been FBI, but she was legit USA all the way, and she had enough juice to make a legit agent like Park do her bidding.

I wonder if I'd asked to see her ID what she would have shown me? Did she have a fake FBI identification card? Was it just her name and business card that were fake? But if Park was real FBI, then why the smoke screen with Greaves?

Oh. Maybe Greaves wasn't authorized to operate on domestic soil.

She got there the same time as I did: "CIA?"

"Yeah. Maybe."

She pushed the laptop away from herself, disgusted. "I probably already triggered alarm bells just searching for her name in the regular system. Sorry, but I'm done. I did what you asked, and I'm out. I'm not digging myself any deeper."

I nodded absently. I was thinking. When I'd called Greaves, I hadn't gotten the main switchboard, but I hadn't been put through to her directly either. The guy who'd answered had said FBI and then told me I'd reached Agent Greaves's office. Almost certainly, whatever phone number I'd called was tied to Greaves's cover. A switchboard. That number rings and the receptionist knows it's a call for "Greaves, FBI agent." If Greaves was working other covers, she'd have a different number for each one and the receptionist would answer each number appropriately.

"No," I said. "I think you're safe. She'll have kept the name out of the system. Putting her name in the system, even just so she'd know if somebody was checking up on her, leaves too much of a paper trail."

She looked a little relieved. I wasn't 100 percent sure, but it made sense.

"I didn't see any cameras outside. You have security cameras?" I asked.

She didn't say anything.

"Local hard drive, or in the cloud?"

"Local."

"Erase all the video and then reformat your computer and hard drive. Do everything on your network, reset the Wi-Fi, everything. Call it a virus. It's not perfect, but if they show up and do any kind of digging, it gives you plausible deniability. You're already a desk jockey, so if you reformat your hard drive, you should be safe enough."

"Great." She closed her eyes and let out a heavy breath. "I'm going to be spending the rest of the night reinstalling software and downloading updates, aren't I?"

Her phone started to ring, and I saw her eyes widen as she looked down at the display.

"Sure," I said, "but if that call is from who I think it is, you'll be doing it debt-free."

68

IT TOOK ME THREE PHONE CALLS to find somebody who had a contact at one of the phone companies who could access backend servers that included ownership information. I asked him for two traces: the number on Greaves's card and the number Baker gave me back at the Market House, when all this started.

My contact insisted on meeting me at a comedy club on Sunset Strip. He had five minutes lined up for the 10:30 show. He seemed more funny-weird than funny-ha-ha to me, but for five hundred dollars in cash, he gave me what I paid for.

The information on Baker's number was useless. It was registered to "Double Rhodes Holdings," which, according to what I could dig up on the internet using my phone, was a subsidiary of "Project Griffin Inc.," which was, itself, a subsidiary of "Goodman Poppy Artistic Creations," and so on. There was only so far I could trace shell corporations on my own, so I decided to cut to the chase and just give Baker a call.

I didn't want to use the same phone setup I was using with Greaves, but there was a 7-Eleven a few blocks down on La Cienega Boulevard where I bought a cheap burner. As I exited the store, two LAPD motorcycle cops cruised into the small parking lot, parked their bikes, and headed in. Neither one gave me a second look.

I dialed Baker's number.

He didn't miss a beat. "I thought you'd call as soon as you got my message."

I guess he was done pretending to be a fed.

I said, "You mean my aunt? Yeah, you should have finished the job. She's not the forgiving type."

"You know how to end this," he said.

Inside the store, one of the cops was perusing the cooler full of drinks, but I thought the second one was looking out the window. At me. Maybe he *was* giving me a second look. Time to move.

"It's only going to end one way," I said, and then I hung up. Out of reflex, I went to snap the SIM card and destroy the phone, and then I figured if the cop was watching me, that move would pique his interest. Screw it. I put the phone on a ledge next to an empty coffee cup. There were still ninety-nine minutes on the prepaid card. It would make somebody's day. Even if Baker had men in the area, the best he could do was trace it to a random 7-Eleven.

I had planned on grabbing another cab, but as I put down the phone, a couple got out of a rideshare. I flagged the driver and asked him if he'd take a cash fare.

He was a young guy, maybe twenty, Ethiopian, and spoke with an accent that was thick enough to make it clear that he'd only been in the country a short time, but however long it had been, it was long enough to know that me paying him 100 percent cash was better than whatever crumbs were left over after the rideshare company took their percentage. I realized I was starving, so I asked him if he knew a good place to eat that was open late.

Ten minutes later I was seated at his cousin's restaurant in Little Ethiopia, three miles from the 7-Eleven where he'd picked me up. I ordered a lamb stew with a side of injera. The restaurant had a small bar with three televisions showing different college basketball games. Normally, I would have had money riding on the games, but even if I had, there was work to do. Reluctantly, I looked away from the TVs and pulled out the stack of papers the wayward FBI agent had printed out for me earlier in the evening.

I wanted to think about Greaves.

The information my contact had given me on Greaves's phone number was worth the money even for nothing else but the laugh: her line was paid for by a company called "Christians in Action." I mean, they weren't trying to hide it. Christians in Action wasn't even a clever cover for the CIA back in the 1970s. The crazy thing was that the address on file for "Christians in Action" was the same address as the actual FBI Los Angeles division building on Wilshire. Stupid and sloppy. If she was based in the building, there was no reason to not just use an actual FBI number.

Unless the FBI didn't know there was a CIA pod in the building? I certainly wasn't an expert, but I was under the impression that the CIA couldn't legally conduct operations within the United States, so it could be that there was a contingent of the CIA operating secretly from within the heart of the FBI in Los Angeles, but it might also have just been a way to keep the paperwork kosher. Or maybe the Christians in Action connection was a misdirect; if it really was the CIA, it should have been harder for me to figure it out. Shouldn't it have?

Or maybe Greaves was just screwing with me. I couldn't untangle it. Layers upon layers of confusion. Mostly my own.

I took my first bite of the stew and any thought of working got chased away. The kid driving the cab had been right. The food was outstanding. I returned the papers to my bag, settled back, and watched basketball while I stuffed myself silly.

69

I FINISHED DINNER, sopping up every last bit of the lamb stew with the spongy flatbread that came on the side, and then retired to a hole-in-the-wall bar next door. The bar itself was nothing special. Just a place to nurse a beer. I was too full and too tired to think.

What I was doing was important, but it was just digging and gathering information, and I wanted to take action.

Greaves or Baker? Baker or Greaves?

I looked at my watch. It was closing in on midnight. Greaves thought I was buttoned up tight in my apartment, which meant, for now, it was time to call Baker again.

I pulled out my phone, about to dial, then remembered I didn't want him to have the same line that I'd given Greaves. Besides, it would be fun to send Baker on another wild-goose chase—I liked imagining him at the 7-Eleven where I'd left that other burner phone, checking behind dumpsters—and it would be a quick call anyway. Baker could trace it all he wanted, but I'd be gone before they ever showed up. Let him and his goons spend the night bouncing between the 7-Eleven and Little Ethiopia looking for me while I was elsewhere getting some rest.

I signaled to the bartender, making the universal symbol for phone with my pinkie and thumb.

Turns out that when you give the bartender a twenty and tell her to keep the change on a seven-dollar beer, she lets you use the house phone without giving you any dance-around about how she's not supposed to let customers use it. Or maybe she just didn't give a crap.

I set the inner bezel on my watch to track the time, and then dialed Baker's number.

"It's Duke again."

The bartender had made a point of moving down to the other end of the bar to give me some privacy, which I appreciated. It was a dim establishment. Either the owner thought it created a sense of intimacy or they were too cheap to replace burned-out light bulbs, but the end result was that I felt like I was in a little bubble. I had my duffel bag on the chair next to me, and I was still wearing the Smith & Wesson holstered against my lower back, but I felt about as relaxed as I had in days. Low-key folk music was playing on the stereo, just loud enough that I didn't have to worry about being overheard in the half-full joint. It was my kind of place.

The table near the door had five college-aged kids huddled together, and there were maybe ten other patrons scattered in twos and threes: three grizzled white dudes of indeterminate age who looked like the kind of people you'd never see outside of a bar, a young couple who was oblivious to anything other than each other, a middle-aged brunette woman who'd come in after me and who was engrossed in her phone and a full gin and tonic, a guy in his twenties who already had the hard-boiled look of a professional alcoholic.

"Duke. We were just trying to send a message. You know it was nothing personal with your aunt."

"It sure felt personal."

Baker chuckled. I decided that jovial laugh of his was going to cost him a little extra when it came time to collect. I wanted to hurt him before I finished him.

He said, "Give me what's mine and it's over."

"You know where I live. Come and get it."

"Please, Duke. We both know you aren't home, and even if you were, you've got quite a crowd parked outside your apartment."

It didn't surprise me that Baker knew my place was under surveillance, but it *was* interesting that he was telling me that he knew. I wondered how many men Baker had working for him. Baker, Cleary, the two guys in Europe, though they might have stayed overseas. And in Los Angeles, even if they were solid pros, I would bet he sent at least a crew of four to Paulie's to send Baker's message. Six guys, eight? Maybe more, depending on his resources. With Greaves's army of agents sitting watch, Baker would only have posted one guy at my apartment, which meant that the rest of Baker's crew—however many that was—was out here looking for me.

"Better make sure your guy doesn't get made," I said.

"He won't," Baker said. "I don't hire the kind of people who get made. Trust me, when I find you, you won't see it coming."

"Ooh," I said sarcastically. "Scary. Particularly after your asshat partner managed to let me get the best of him even though I was handcuffed to a wall. If Cleary is an example of who you hire, you might want to reconsider your recruitment practices."

I thought of how much I had enjoyed kicking Cleary in the balls after I'd hit him with my stun gun. Parts of my job could be extremely satisfying at times.

Baker hesitated, and then he said, "Cleary works directly for my boss. He was, well, let's say, euphemistically, Cleary was there for quality control. My employer wanted somebody he knew and trusted along on the job."

"Your employer doesn't trust you?"

"Me? Come on, Duke. You must know by now that I'm a hired gun. I'm in it for the money. Like I said, nothing personal. I'm just doing my job."

"I hope you're getting paid enough to take a bullet."

Baker spoke in a condescending tone. "Are you done with your posturing? Because I'd like to get this over with. My employer is not a patient man. As it is, the fact that you clearly did *not* manage to get in and out of the safe unnoticed has caused quite the consternation."

"Boo-flippin'-hoo."

"Because of your failure to deliver as promised in terms of getting in and out of that safe without discovery, you've left us with a very narrow window. My employer would like this resolved within the next forty-eight hours."

70

I SNORTED. "WHAT YOUR EMPLOYER WANTS is not my concern. Let me tell you what we're going to do. First of all—"

He cut me off. "You really think you're in a position to bargain, don't you? Do you know what your problem is, Duke?"

"Oh, sweet lord." I laughed. "Don't get me started. It's a long list."

"Your problem," he continued, as if I hadn't spoken, "is that you always think you're the smartest person in the room. I've met a lot of guys like you throughout my career. Good at what you do. Sometimes the best. But the same thing always happens. Because they're good at one thing, they start to think that means they're good at everything. You might be the smartest guy in a lot of rooms, but sooner or later, you walk into the wrong room and then somebody smarter than you shows up. Hubris catches up with you when you least expect it."

"Hubris? Big word."

I looked at my watch. We'd been talking for a couple of minutes, but even if he'd tracked the burner to the 7-Eleven and was racing here, I still had some time.

"You always have to be so smart, don't you? I bet your sister thought she could outsmart everybody, too, right until she hit the ground," he said.

"You—"

He steamrolled me. "You've got her in a nice facility. Classy. Not that your sister can tell the difference. I'm guessing your aunt's been footing the bill, right? No way you could afford it. No real security, though. All I had to do was sign in at the front desk. That picture on her dresser? The one of the two of you on the beach from when you were kids? You guys look like you're having fun. I'm guessing it's Hawaii, but I've never been."

"Enough. How do you want to do this?"

That's what I said, but what I was thinking was: dead man walking.

I tried to center myself. I knew I wasn't operating at full capacity. I was tired, and now I was angry. Which was deliberate on his part. He wanted me to get sloppy, and he was trying to keep me on the phone long enough that he could get to me.

Baker said, "Before we go any further, I need to know, do you have the item on you?"

The bartender had her back to me, but she made eye contact in the mirror and signaled to me, miming to ask if I wanted another beer. I shook my head at her. This was a serious drinking establishment, not the kind of place people nursed their drinks. Even if I hadn't planned on leaving as soon as I hung up the phone, with my exhaustion and with trying to get everything straight, I was struggling to keep my wits sharp as it was. Another beer wasn't going to help. Plus, there was something about what Baker said a moment earlier that was needling me. I just couldn't figure out what it was.

"Of course I've got it," I lied.

"You have it on your person?"

"It's in my pocket as we speak," I lied again.

"Deliver the package and I'll meet the original terms and throw in a significant cash bonus for any inconvenience."

"How significant?"

"Five million dollars. As I'm sure you saw when you helped yourself to the money in the warehouse in Switzerland, I'm good for it."

I was glad I wasn't in the middle of taking a sip when he said five million dollars, because I would have choked on my beer.

Also, who the hell was paying Baker? There was some serious money at play here. And what exactly did this cipher thing do?

I almost wished it *was* in my pocket.

Baker gave it a second, then said, "Say yes."

"You've just got five million kicking around?" I asked.

"Say yes, and I can meet you in fifteen minutes with the money."

He must have been close. I figured I only had a couple more minutes before I had to bounce.

I watched the bartender come out from behind the bar with a round for the three old dudes. As she passed the entrance, a blonde woman came in. She had short hair and was young enough that she was going to get carded. She was wearing a shapeless sweatshirt, like she was coming home from the gym, but she looked around the room as if she was supposed to be meeting somebody. After a second of hesitation, she moved to one of the tables that was behind me and out of my sight line, but I was already distracted: a man with a shaved head and a bulky build came through the door and sat down at the opposite side of the bar from me. He was wearing a form-fitting T-shirt that accentuated his muscles. His forearms were covered in tattoos, a complete sleeve of symbols and colors, and I saw some more peeking out from his collar and spilling up his neck. He saw me looking at him, and I moved my eyes off him and checked my watch.

I hadn't been on the phone *that* long.

My radar was up, but as much as the guy with the tats fit the profile, it was too soon. By now, Baker must have had the address of the bar, but even if he'd crashed the 7-Eleven where I'd dumped the burner I first called him from, it wasn't enough time for him to get here unless I was the unluckiest safecracker in the world and had walked into the wrong bar on the wrong night.

I figured I had at least five more minutes. Plenty of time to let Baker think he might catch up with me. An hour from now, I'd be sacked out in a hotel bed, and Baker and his men would be spending the night circling Little Ethiopia hoping they could find me crouched down in a doorway. They'd expend their energy on a wild-goose chase, and when I did come for them, I'd be rested, and they'd be running on fumes.

But right now, it was the other way around.

God, I was tired.

71

I SAID, "YOU EXPECT ME TO BELIEVE it's that simple? I give you what's in my pocket"—I was enjoying toying with him—"my dad walks free, *and* you're offering up *a bonus*?"

A bonus. I wasn't sure describing five million dollars in cash as "a bonus" was completely accurate.

"I assure you, my employer can afford it," Baker said. "But you're not really worried about the money. The question you *really* want to ask is, now that you know I'm not a federal agent, can I still come through with the part of the deal where your dad walks free?"

"Can you?"

"Yes."

No hesitation. No dissembling. That gave me pause.

I believed that Greaves could deliver on her promise. I was sure that she really was operating under the aegis of the United States government, but Baker was a freelancer. If he could really pull that off, then who on earth was he working for?

As if I was thinking aloud, he said, "I understand why you don't believe me, but I can make it happen."

"I'll believe it when I see it."

"You're going to have to trust me. I'm holding all the cards."

I shifted in my chair. I could feel my Smith & Wesson riding against my back. Something was wrong.

I couldn't figure out what it was, but something was *definitely* wrong. Baker sounded too calm. Too confident. He was acting like the cat was already in the bag. Five million dollars. If I said yes, he said he'd meet me with the money in fifteen minutes.

I looked at the new addition at the end of the bar again. He had the build but didn't carry himself like a cop or ex-military, and the tattoos were telling some sort of a story I couldn't read. None of that mattered, though: his T-shirt was too tight and tucked into his jeans. No body armor, nowhere to keep a pistol except an ankle holster. Ankle holsters were fine for a backup weapon, but they were too slow to draw from if you were expecting to need a firearm.

I turned to watch the bartender check in on the middle-aged woman, then the couple, and then the blonde, who was sitting by herself at a table behind me. The blonde in the shapeless sweatshirt shook her head no. She was a good-looking woman, and I was a little jealous of whomever was meeting her, but I figured with what she was wearing, it probably wasn't a date anyway.

The bartender drifted back to the bar to take the muscular man's order. I'd used up my time. I needed to wrap it up and get out of there. I said, "You aren't holding all the cards. The only card that matters is what I've got in my pocket."

"There you go again, Duke. Still insisting you're the smartest guy in the room."

Baker might have had a point, but on the other hand, I was the guy with the magic box that was worth five million bucks and a Get Out of Jail Free card for my dad, so maybe I *was* the smartest guy in the room.

Speaking of which, I looked at the muscular dude again. He was looking back at me. Staring. I couldn't see either of his hands.

I was holding the phone in my left hand. I started to move my right hand slowly off the counter. I could feel my pistol pressed against the small of my back.

Baker said, "You *do* have it on you, don't you?"

I said, "Where else would it be?"

"Because I'm ready to take possession of what you owe me."

The muscular dude smiled at me. A real smile. Friendly. He raised his hand and gave me a lazy wave, pointed to his drink, and raised an eyebrow.

I laughed at myself and gave him a friendly shake of my head letting him know I was flattered but he was barking up the wrong tree. It had been a busy few days, and between the constant adrenaline and the lack of sleep, I was probably just being paranoid.

But I was missing something. I knew it. Baker had said fifteen minutes. Los Angeles was a big place. Maybe he meant fifteen minutes as a generality. As in, soon. Or maybe he meant fifteen minutes as in he knew where I was.

I glanced at the muscular guy again. He was turned away from me. Not paying attention to me at all. And then something clicked.

I was looking in the wrong direction. I'd seen muscles, tattoos, and a shaved head, and I'd gotten tunnel vision. Like when I'd been at Uncle Charles and Aunt Paulie's and I'd seen the open safe. I'd seen the obvious and I'd stopped looking.

But it was right in front of me. Or, rather, behind me.

The loose-fitting sweatshirt.

Fifteen minutes, Baker said.

Sitting alone at a table.

Baker knew where I was and was closing in.

No drink in front of her.

But Baker didn't need fifteen minutes; he already had somebody with eyes on me.

The blonde.

Baker was right. I wasn't the smartest person in the room.

72

THE ONLY THING THAT SAVED ME is that I didn't stop to think. I moved instinctively, diving off my chair. The sound of the mirror shattering came to me at the same time as the sharp pop of the woman's gun.

I scrambled hard, dropping the phone and pulling the Smith & Wesson. I came up to my knees and raised the 9mm.

I felt the tug on my sleeve of a bullet passing through the cloth, but I was already squeezing the trigger. Two shots to her chest and then, as she staggered back, a follow-up to the head. Classic Mozambique drill: center mass to slow her down if she was wearing body armor under the sweatshirt, the third shot to make sure she didn't keep coming.

The bartender was screaming, and the tough-looking guy who had just come in was already running scared out the door.

I did a quick sweep, but there weren't any other shooters. It was just the blonde.

I had to move.

I was in a bad position. I didn't know how in the heck Baker had gotten somebody to me so quickly, but I knew one thing for sure: he'd believed me when I told him I had the cipher on my person, otherwise he would have never ordered her to try to take me down. Baker didn't care about *me*. The only thing he cared about was what I was carrying. It was a lot easier to get the cipher off my dead body than it was to orchestrate a fair trade.

The obvious choice was to go out the back door, but I had no clue what was back there. I'd been sloppy and hadn't cased the bar before I'd gone in. If it was an alley, I'd be bottled up, and if it was dark, Baker could have a full fire team loaded up out there. I'd be walking into a massacre.

That left the front door.

Most of the other customers were already piling out. I followed the herd.

I shoulder-rolled out the door and came up in firing position, taking cover behind the engine block of a sports car parked at the curb. I couldn't stop myself from flinching. I was expecting a hailstorm of bullets, and even though hiding behind a car was better than nothing, it wasn't much better. The engine block of a car can stop almost anything short of a tank, but engine blocks are small, and large-caliber weapons punch through a car's body like it's nothing.

Except, it wasn't *like* nothing. It *was* nothing.

No Baker. No fire team. No backup for the blonde.

The obvious thing was for me to get the heck out of there. I couldn't hear sirens yet, but it was only a question of who showed up first: the LAPD or the rest of Baker's cleanup crew.

Obvious, but I'd be wasting a golden opportunity.

I hightailed it to the corner, made the turn, and then I ducked into a dark doorway.

First things first: I switched the magazine in my pistol. I was going to wipe and dump the Smith & Wesson as soon as I could, but in the meantime, if I had to use it again, I wasn't going to start three bullets short.

The second thing I did was try to get my heart rate back down.

Doesn't matter how much you've trained or how often you've been in a situation like that, the adrenaline spike is a monster. My hands were shaking, and I could feel my pulse going like I'd just sprinted a half mile.

Goddamnit. There was just some pure dumb luck involved in me surviving, but the mistake was just pure dumb: the cell phone I'd left at the 7-Eleven on La Cienega. It was the only thing I could think of, and it made sense. Instead of snapping the SIM card and trashing the phone, I'd left it for Baker to trace.

And I'd underestimated him again. I thought it was Baker and Cleary and a few more guys at most. But he must have had an army working for him. Enough people on his team to send out a wide net. Nothing fancy. Just build a circle out from where I'd made the phone call, put his people in cars to run a grid pattern, and then wait and hope I'd call again.

And I'd walked right into it. I'd called from the bar's house phone, and as soon as Baker got the address, he sent out the APB to his teams. The blonde just happened to be somewhere on the search grid that was close to the bar. She must have been within a block or two already when I called Baker. But her being on her own, without backup, told me Baker had spread his teams thin to cover more ground. What it didn't tell me was how long until the next freelancer showed up. Was it going to be the fifteen minutes Baker had said, or sooner?

It was a gamble on Baker's part, and it had almost paid off.

If I'd been just a little slower, I'd have a nice little hole in my head.

But the next gamble was the one I was taking: LAPD or one of Baker's men? Who was going to get there first?

I holstered my pistol.

I unzipped my bag and took out the opaque plastic box I was carrying. It was about the size and weight of a deck of cards and had extremely strong magnets on the outside of the box. Strong enough that once you put it in place it would stay that way. I opened it up, turned it on, checked the power, and then closed the box back up. It was a simple slap and track unit: a battery-powered GPS tracker with cellular capabilities inside a waterproof, magnetic box. Cheap and efficient. The battery would only run for a week, but I only needed it to last long enough that I could hunt Baker and his men instead of the other way around.

No sirens, but I heard the heavy purr of an engine working hard and the squeal of tires rounding a corner, and I knew that one of Baker's guys had shown up.

I stepped out and then tried to walk as casually back around the corner as I could. I made the turn just in time to see a silver SUV rock to a stop outside the bar. The driver got out followed by another man from the passenger seat. They kept their guns low, against their legs, but even from nearly a hundred yards away, it was obvious they were holding pistols if you were looking.

I was looking.

They were both so intent on heading into the bar that neither one even glanced in my direction.

The guy who'd been driving was young, maybe mid-twenties, and wearing a baseball cap. No question from the way he moved and how he carried his firearm that he was ex-military.

But I was a lot more interested in the other guy.

The other guy?

The other guy was Baker.

73

I WAS FAR ENOUGH AWAY STILL that I had doubts, but the few steps he took from the SUV to the door of the bar silenced them. It was Baker for sure.

The smart play was to keep walking and to go ahead with my original plan: attach the GPS tracker to the silver SUV's wheel well and then hunt Baker down at my leisure.

But he'd hurt my aunt. Maybe he hadn't done it himself, but I was sure he'd ordered it. Three of Paulie's men killed, and my aunt beaten almost to death.

And Baker had threatened my sister.

He'd *been in her room.*

What would Ginny tell me to do if she was here?

She'd tell me I had the GPS unit and a golden opportunity for somebody else to take care of my problem. I didn't have to get my hands dirty beyond what I'd already done. Attach the box, walk away. Give that info to Greaves and let her wrap things up for me. Ginny would tell me that it didn't matter if I was the one who took Baker down or not, as long as Baker went down. Why take it on myself when the United States government would happily do the job?

Clean. Simple. Safe.

But it was my job to finish.

I closed the distance to the SUV, bouncing the plastic box with the GPS in my hand. The SUV was running, the key fob on the center console. The windows were down, and the doors were unlocked.

I heard the first howl of sirens drifting through the night air. The cops were at least two minutes away still. The street was deserted. Everybody who'd been in the bar when the shooting started was long gone. It was just me.

Baker hadn't been crude enough or dumb enough to threaten Ginny directly, but there was no mistake in what he meant on the phone. He'd *been in her room.* A nice facility, he'd said. He'd commented on the picture on her dresser.

That picture wasn't his to look at.

And it wasn't Hawaii, like Baker had guessed.

It was Curaçao. From before the drunk driver, from back when our mom was still alive. Pure vacation. Dad wasn't scouting a job, and Paulie didn't have anything on the hook on the island. It was just the sea and the sand and my family.

What I remember, more than anything from that trip, was my mom, dad, and Charles suiting up with scuba gear. You had to be at least ten to dive, and Ginny and I were too young, so we stayed on the beach with Paulie, who was content to read.

And my mom, with her thin, tropical weight wet suit, her BCD and tank strapped on, her regulator in one hand and her mask and snorkel in the other, looking at me seriously and telling me I had to watch over Ginny, and she had to watch over me. She'd keep me safe, and I'd keep her safe.

I put the GPS unit back in my bag and drew my pistol again.

74

BAKER AND HIS HENCHMAN CAME OUT carrying the blonde's body. The younger guy was the first one out the door. He came out backward, holding the blonde's feet and looking down at the ground so he didn't stumble. Both he and Baker were hustling. The sirens were still at a distance, but that was changing.

I waited until they were both outside, and then I shot the young guy.

Baker was quick.

He dropped the blonde's arms and went for his gun.

But not quick enough.

No hesitation: I shot him in the head.

I blinked away the burnt-in afterimage. A bullet departs a pistol moving close to eight hundred miles an hour, but the bright lick of fire stays close, a ghost to haunt the inside of your eyelids. It doesn't matter why you fired the gun. It's always there, marrying the past and the present for as long as it takes to flare away.

I thought killing Baker was going to feel triumphant, but I couldn't blink away the fury I felt for what he'd made me do.

Do not come after my family.

75

THE SIRENS WERE LESS THAN A MINUTE OUT. Just enough time for a pocket pat for IDs, but I came up empty.

Since the SUV was still running and the doors were unlocked, simply taking Baker's car seemed like the quickest and most prudent way to leave the scene. I needed some sack time, and I did *not* want to try to explain to the LAPD why I was holding a pistol and standing over three dead bodies.

Fifteen minutes later, I pulled into a parking lot in the Arts District. I did a quick search of the interior of the SUV, but it was clean. Not so much as a receipt for gas. Dead end. I might have found something if I'd looked longer, but I was worried there was a tracker on the car, and the last thing I wanted was another ambush by whomever was left on Baker's team. I wasn't naive enough to think that Baker being dead meant I was out of the woods. Baker had made it clear to me he was just a man doing a job, and I knew Cleary was still on the hunt for me; I had no doubt what he'd do if he saw me.

From the Arts District, I stole a car, drove to a Walmart in South Gate, dumped that car, hot-wired a minivan, and drove to Redondo Beach. I left the minivan running a few blocks away from the beach; I was hoping some teens up to no good would take it for a joyride and help make it impossible to follow my trail.

I walked toward the ocean and then strolled from one end of the pier to the other, discreetly dropping the disassembled components of my Smith & Wesson and the spare magazines into the water one by one. I didn't like being without a pistol, but it was time to get rid of the 9mm and pick up a clean gun.

Once I'd gotten rid of the final piece, it took me a little while to flag down a cab on Hermosa Avenue, but from there, I had the cabbie drop me off at an all-night diner on Sepulveda Boulevard. I walked straight through and out the back door. Probably more paranoid than I needed to be, but then again, if I'd been more paranoid in the first place, I wouldn't have been in this jam.

From the diner, I hoofed it over to a chain hotel. Nothing fancy, but it was only a smidge more than a mile from Manhattan Beach. At the front desk, I almost handed over my actual driver's license instead of one of the fakes I was carrying, but otherwise, it was a breeze. They even provided me with a complimentary toothbrush and toothpaste.

In my room, I thought about calling Greaves and telling her about what had just gone down with Baker, but I was wiped. Besides, I knew I'd be hearing from her soon enough. She was still waiting for me to text her a photo of Baker and Cleary, and more importantly, she was probably due to intercept the package soon. As soon as she figured out that the tracking number I'd given her was not, in fact, for the package containing the cipher, she'd get in touch.

Instead, I tried calling Helen. I hadn't talked to her in a couple of weeks, and I desperately needed some advice. With Paulie's beating and my dad hiding out—as much as he could while incarcerated—in the wake of it, I wasn't sure where else to turn.

The call went straight to voicemail. I gave her the number of the burner and told her to give me a call.

And then I fell asleep in my clothes.

76

I SLEPT FITFULLY, DREAMING of airplanes and scuba regulators, of Ginny falling endlessly, of blondes with guns, of the dark cavern I'd shot into the man's head in Portugal when I was eleven, of Baker telling me there was something I didn't understand. It wasn't all bad dreams, though: I dreamed about Agent Greaves kissing me too. That was nice.

I was woken up just after nine in the morning by my cell phone ringing.

"What the hell do you think you're playing at, Duke?"

Dream of the devil, I thought. I scratched my belly and stretched out. "And a good morning to you, too, Agent Greaves."

"Give me one good reason why—"

I interrupted. "I literally just woke up. I need a cup of coffee. I'll call you back in fifteen minutes. Hey, if I lose your card and just call the general number at the FBI building on Wilshire, can they patch me through to Christians in Action?"

"Duke—"

I hung up.

77

I WAS SURE GREAVES WAS going to be extremely pissed when I called her back, but that had more to do with me lying about the cipher and giving her the wrong tracking number than me hanging up on her. Either way, I wasn't kidding. I really did need a coffee.

I used the bathroom, dropped off my key at the front desk, and called Taneesha.

She answered in a whisper. "What?"

"You at school?"

"Why do you think I'm whispering, dummy?"

"Maya at school too?"

"All clear," she said. "Got to go."

She hung up, which was fine. I was just calling to make sure she hadn't decided to skip school or that Maya hadn't come down with a fever or something. My trust in the tactical abilities of the FBI—or whomever Greaves was using—was limited, and I didn't want to have to worry about trigger-happy feds and stray bullets. Which reminded me that I needed to make sure Jameel was at work, too, so I sent him a quick text.

Then I hopped into a cab. I could have walked, but nobody really walks in LA. Plus, it was kind of hot out.

I had the cabbie drop me off in front of a small café a couple of blocks from the water. The restaurant was quiet, so I put in my order and then sat down outside on the deserted patio. Jameel responded to my text confirming that he was at work and the apartment was empty.

Next, I checked the tracking numbers on the packages I'd sent from Zurich. One package showed that it had been delivered a little after eight this morning, and the other package . . . the other package didn't seem to exist anymore, according to the carrier. Which meant that, as I assumed, the reason Greaves sounded so pissed off was because she'd intercepted it.

When I called Greaves back, she came out firing.

"You've got thirty seconds to come out of your apartment with your hands up, or we're coming in hot."

Which made me smile, because even though *I* knew I wasn't in my apartment, Greaves still thought I was inside. The bundle I'd given Taneesha before I left was just two burner cell phones taped together: microphone to earpiece, earpiece to microphone. I'd given one of the phone's numbers to Greaves. Thanks to Taneesha and a Raspberry Pi kit—the cheap, homemade computer kits ubiquitous in middle school classrooms—when Greaves called, the other phone functioned as a physical cutout, relaying both sound and voice. A literal game of telephone. No way to trace it digitally.

Greaves continued, "And I swear to god, if you're not on your knees with the cipher in your hands, the deal's off. All of it."

"Come on," I said. "I was in Zurich. Swiss chocolates aren't a bad consolation prize. Just do me a favor and don't eat it all. It was supposed to be for a friend."

"Fifteen seconds and then we're coming in. You better be lying face down with your hands behind your head."

"There's a key under the mat," I said.

78

ONE OF THE BARISTAS CAME OUT from inside and dropped my order, two iced lattes and a breakfast sandwich, at my table. I nodded my thanks.

There *was* actually a key under the mat. One of the things you understand when you can open any lock is that locks that can be opened with keys can also be opened without keys. I had other security measures in place when I didn't want somebody coming into my apartment, but I'd planned for this. Much better to have her assault team just use the key than break my door down.

She took a heavy breath of annoyance, but she was quick on the uptake. "When did you slip out?"

"Basically right away," I said.

"How?"

"Come on. You know my nickname."

"Duke?"

"Yes?"

"No," she said. "I mean, isn't your nickname 'Duke'?"

"Wow," I said. "My feelings are actually kind of hurt. No, the nickname, 'The Ghost Who Walks through Walls.'"

She had the temerity to laugh. "Is there anything else I should know before we go through the door? If any of my men get hurt, I'm going to—"

"No booby traps." I did have booby traps, but they weren't set. "And I'm serious about the key under the mat. You really don't need to break down the door."

I heard some muffled sounds for about a minute, several shouts of the word "clear," and then a very annoyed Greaves coming back on the line.

"You are such a dick," she said.

"Granted," I said. "How do you like my place?"

"I hadn't figured you for a floral pattern. That couch is hideous."

She had a fair point about the couch. I had bought most of my furniture during my heyday, when I could afford nice stuff. Unfortunately, the couch I'd originally bought, an extremely expensive purchase from the kind of furniture shop that handed you a glass of prosecco as soon as you walked in, had been torn up by an ex-girlfriend's dog and then set on fire by said ex-girlfriend. Long story short, my current couch was a replacement that I'd procured *after* I'd picked up a gambling habit *and* had stopped stealing, which is a long way of saying, beggars can't be choosers. The couch looked like it belonged to an eighty-year-old British woman. Which was because it *had* belonged to an eighty-year-old British woman. I loved Helen MacDonald, and I appreciated the hand-me-down couch, but my mentor's taste and mine did not overlap.

"Let's just say my finances haven't allowed me to redecorate."

"Where are you, Duke?"

"Well, I'm obviously not going to answer that, but you're going to have to trust that I'm not trying to screw you over."

"Really?" she snapped. "Because it sure feels like you're trying to screw me over."

"The cipher is the only leverage I have. It's somewhere safe." I hoped that was true. "You'll get it back when I've taken care of my business. This is personal now."

"No," she said, cold and commanding, "this is not personal, Duke. That cipher is incredibly powerful. This is about protecting the United States of America."

"Sure," I said. "That too. Listen, I'll call you back in a few hours. Oh, also, Baker's dead."

"What? Are you sure?"

I thought about the sound of his body hitting the ground. "I'm sure."

"Are you out of—"

"Greaves, before you start trying to lecture me or whatever you've got in mind, I'm tired of being jerked around. I know you aren't FBI, and as long as I'm holding the cipher, I'm calling the shots."

"Duke—"

I hung up and then turned off the phone before she called back. Let her leave me a voicemail.

I was feeling nice and smug again.

79

I BOUGHT A SWIMSUIT, a Hawaiian shirt, and a pair of flip-flops at a surf shop next door to the coffee shop and wore my new outfit out of the store. I stuffed what I'd been wearing the night before in a trash can—my shirt had a bullet hole in the sleeve anyway.

Which reminded me: after dumping the one I had used last night, I needed to take care of getting a new pistol.

I made another quick stop at a "lifestyle" shop two doors down to grab an outfit for later in the day: shoes, pants, underwear, socks, and a plain, dark shirt. Not cheap, but it was easy, and it looked good. I stuffed my new clothes in my bag and headed to the beach.

On my way, I called Uncle Charles for an update on Paulie, but got kicked immediately to voicemail. I thought about trying Helen again, but if she was free to talk, she would have already called me back. And I didn't want to call my dad: he was in a defensive posture after what happened to Paulie, and there was always the chance that if I called him, I'd expose him to something dangerous.

It made me feel odd, rudderless, and adrift, this hollow disconnect. There should have been somebody else to call, but there wasn't. The only other person I wanted to talk to was the person I was already headed to see. When I hit the sand, about half past nine by my watch, Meg was just about to head into the water with a class.

We'd been friends before, but after everything went down with Ginny, it had become something more. Sometimes, I was sure I was in love with Meg, and sometimes I thought it was like I'd just inherited her from Ginny.

Or maybe it was the other way around. Maybe Meg inherited me. Because now that I thought about it, she was usually the one checking in on me, calling to see if I wanted to surf or to grab a coffee, not the other way around.

That was something to think about another time.

She told her class, a trio of wet-suited middle-aged women who were clearly new to surfing, to head out into the water and that she'd follow them. Then she turned to me.

"Give me an hour?"

"Of course," I said. I was halfway through my iced latte, and I held out the second one. "This is for you."

She grabbed it, sipped it, and then kissed me on the cheek. "Lifesaver. Can you put it with my crap, and I'll drink it after the lesson? Feel free to use the spare board. One of the clients was a no-show."

"If you don't drink it now, the ice will melt."

She waggled her eyebrows. "I've suffered worse."

She had.

I watched her head out into the ocean to join her three students.

It was probably just her name, but every time I saw Meg, I thought of the Hollywood lit versions of Meg Ryan at the height of her stardom, even though Meg, with her dark hair and surf-toned, sun-kissed body, didn't look anything like Meg Ryan. And she wasn't Hollywood at all; there was nothing staged about her. All the same, I liked to joke that if she was a movie star, everybody would believe her if she said she did her own stunts.

Yes, she was good-looking, beautiful, but it wasn't in that slick, airbrushed manner that you get on social media. She was a modern, bronzed version of California gold, but real. She moved like an athlete and was built like one. And she could shred on a surfboard. Serious, could-have-gone-pro shred, but instead she'd gone into the military and then left after what she referred to as "a series of complications." Since she was discharged, she had been living in her sister and brother-in-law's backyard, in a one-room pool house that Meg liked to call her bungalow. When she wasn't teaching surfing or mixed martial arts, or working as an unofficial fixer doing investigative work, she watched her nieces. Ginny and I used to joke that Meg was what happened when your obsessive and borderline abusive dad *isn't* a criminal.

But she was legitimately awesome, and I was at least halfway in love with her most of the time, or all the way in love with her some of the time.

Maybe if I'd met her on my own, but she'd been my sister's best friend, and if that had been a big hill to climb before, it was an impenetrable wall now. We'd turned toward each other in grief, but there was too much of herself she kept hidden. The same way I did.

I shook my head and then finished the last of my iced coffee. Good god, I was a mess.

Nothing that an hour of surfing couldn't solve.

80

IT FELT SO GOOD TO BE in the water that I was almost disappointed when Meg's class wrapped up.

Even though I loved it, I wasn't a particularly good surfer. I was okay with that, though. I was used to the idea that I'd never be much more than somebody who could cruise with a modicum of style. But something about being out on the water washed everything away. Surfing, for me, always felt like it existed out of time.

I paddled out for one last wave while Meg was talking to her clients. Sitting up on the board, I could see a small set coming, so I waited for the last and biggest wave in the set. Biggest being a relative term, since it was, at most, two feet, but I paddled hard and caught it clean, with a pop-up that I thought probably looked stylish. I saw Meg and her clients watching and cheering, and I tried cross-stepping toward the nose.

And ate it.

When I came to the surface and cleared the water from my eyes, I could see Meg and the women laughing.

Sigh.

Meg was tucking her tip into her bag when I trundled over with the board.

"Don't," I said.

"I wasn't going to say anything," she said.

"Good, because that was embarrassing."

"Yes," she agreed. "It was. The cadre of yummy mummies in my class liked the show, but yes, you should be embarrassed. Thanks for the coffee, though." As I'd predicted, the ice had melted, but she didn't seem to care. "I'm done for the day. Only the one lesson. Help me carry the boards?"

I slung my bag across my body, and she put on her backpack, and then we both hoisted a pair of boards on top of our heads. The big, foam soft tops were heavy, but it wasn't a far walk. Meg had some sort of a deal with the owners of a house that was as close to the beach as twenty million dollars would get you. I had no idea why they let her park in their garage, but it sure was convenient.

She strapped the boards down in the bed of her truck and then looked at her phone. "Waves are supposed to be good up north this afternoon. You want to go?"

"Can't," I said. "Work stuff."

"But you're here. And you clearly came for a reason. You in trouble?"

I didn't bother to answer, which was answer enough.

81

SHE PULLED OUT OF THE GARAGE, waited for it to close behind her, and then headed on Ocean Drive for two blocks before turning onto Manhattan Beach Boulevard.

The silence after her question felt heavy, so I was relieved when Meg said, "I know it's quicker to cut through the back streets to avoid the traffic, but when you do that, you miss a lot of the flavor. I like it. It makes me feel like a tourist in my own town."

I saw a mom trying to herd two little boys down the sidewalk toward the beach. She was pulling a wagon loaded with a cooler and beach toys.

I said, "We're all tourists somewhere."

The light turned yellow and then red, and Meg stopped the truck with a bit of a jerk. She looked over at me warmly and then patted my leg. "Why, Duke, that might be the most romantic thing you've ever said."

We both laughed, and then we were quiet until we got on the 405.

"You going to talk about it?" she finally said.

"Maybe in a bit?"

She nodded, and we drove the rest of the way to her place in comfortable silence.

A pool house or a bungalow, whatever you called Meg's place— it was less impressive than it sounded. The neighborhood was in the early throes of gentrification, but if you turned one way, you had apartments and pay-by-the-week motels, turn another way and it was McMansions.

Meg's sister's place was on a block that was somewhere in the middle. The house was an original 1970s ranch. They'd had to pay an arm and a leg because of the lot, not because of the house; nothing about the property was special except that there was space for the pool house to be far enough from the house that it felt like its own private residence. Meg said it was perfect because she got to live near her sister and her nieces without having to live *with* them. She could drop in for dinner or raid the fridge whenever she felt like, but if she didn't want a night of family fun—or if her sister and brother-in-law just wanted some privacy—she could retire out back.

We went past the main house and into her bungalow. She told me to make coffee while she showered and to meet her by the pool.

By the time she was showered, dried, and dressed, I was sitting in a lounge chair, drinking a cup of coffee. She brought out her own cup of coffee and sat down next to me, staring at the water. It was late morning. Just past eleven o'clock.

"I sent you a package," I said. "From Switzerland."

"Switzerland? Fancy. But I haven't seen it."

"It was supposed to be delivered this morning," I said. I tried not to let the stress sound in my voice. I had a sneaking suspicion I was a dead man if the package was lost. "I checked, and it's not on the front porch. Or by the side door."

I must not have done as good a job at sounding casual as I hoped, because Meg said, "If you're worried about it, I wouldn't be. We had a package stolen off the porch once, a few months before I moved in, but then my brother-in-law installed some cameras on the porch and there hasn't been a problem since."

I knew she'd moved in at her sister's request a week or two before her first niece was born, so that had been at least five years ago.

"It's important," I said.

"Well, there's also the el Diente thing, so I really wouldn't worry."

The "el Diente thing" was one of the reasons I'd sent the package specifically to her address. Short version was that the previous year, Meg had been giving a surfing lesson to a girl who turned out to be the daughter of Juan "el Diente" Flores. Known as el Diente, or "the Teeth," because of his penchant for feeding rival cartel members to his dogs. Some upstart gangsters tried to kidnap the girl on the beach after the lesson, but Meg intervened. In return, Flores spread the word that he'd take it real personal if anything happened in Meg's neighborhood.

Anybody stealing packages off Meg's porch had to have a death wish.

Meg tilted her head. "I take it from your concern that the package is not actually for me?"

"Honestly, I did get you something. Chocolate, in fact. Fancy chocolate. Expensive. But it, uh, sort of got lost in the mail. This is a different package."

"You sent two packages?" She paused, and then swung her legs up so they were resting on my thighs. "And the package that was supposed to be for *me* got lost in the mail, but the package that's for *you* was supposedly delivered this morning?"

"Correct."

"Can't wait to hear this story." She brushed her hair from her face, swung her legs back off mine, and stood up. "My sister probably brought it in before she left for work. Give me a second."

She walked gracefully into the house and came back a minute later carrying my package. I tore it open, and the box from the safe slid into my hand.

Meg laughed and sat down again. "You know that you just let out an audible sigh of relief?"

"It would not have been a good thing if I lost this."

"You don't seem too worked up over losing my chocolate, though," she said, smiling.

"How about a substitution? Musso & Frank?" I knew she was a sucker like me for old-school Los Angeles, and she thought the history of Musso & Frank made it a romantic dinner date.

"Musso & Frank? You win the lottery?" she said skeptically.

I shook my head, and then held up the ring box. "No, but I can afford to pay for dinner."

She put her feet back up on my legs. "Spill."

I WAS BARELY TWO MINUTES into telling her everything that happened when she called me an idiot for the first time. As I recounted what had happened over the past few days, she called me an idiot several more times.

I told her everything—I didn't leave anything out, even the embarrassing parts—and the more I spoke, the dumber I felt. When I finally finished, it was half past noon.

Meg had a creased brow and was now sitting on the edge of the pool with her feet in the water. I was floating in a lounger in the middle of the pool. She looked up at me and said, "Duke, you are the smartest dummy I've ever met. How could you miss all the warning signs?"

"I didn't miss them," I said sensitively. "I just ignored them."

She sniffed. "Sure. That's better."

That was my only defense. Baker had known exactly what to dangle in front of me to make me overrule the voice inside my head telling me to take a hard pass. Back at the airport, when Greaves and Park were questioning me, they knew it wasn't about the money because it was insane to pull a heist on the CIA just for money. There was no universe where I was going to commit some version of treason for a stack of cash, but of course, I thought I was doing something akin to my patriotic duty working for Baker. But really, it was the offer of the carrot of getting my dad out of jail that got me. That was all it took to get me to bite.

"What would you have done?" I asked.

"You mean last night?" she said.

"No." I knew exactly what she would have done last night if she'd seen Baker. She would have had the same reaction I did to Baker threatening my sister. Meg was realistic about how the world worked, and she did everything the same way she surfed: she took a direct line.

Meg shrugged. "I would have taken the money and done the job, except that I couldn't have done the job because I can't open a safe to save my life."

"You've gotten better with picks, though," I said. She mostly stuck to the right side of the law in her work as a part-time investigator, but she'd asked me to teach her some skills just in case.

She covered her face with her hands. "I literally have one of the best safecrackers, if not *the* best safecracker in the world teaching me, and it still takes me five minutes to pick a standard Yale. I'm good at a lot of things. That isn't one of them." She kicked some water at me, swiveled around until her feet were under her, and then stood up. "Let's go."

"Where are we going?"

"First, you get changed out of your suit. Then lunch. Your treat. Come on. Let's go. I'm starving."

"I'd like to note that I offered to buy dinner at some point in the future, not dinner *and* lunch."

She waved my complaint away with her hand and then poked my bag with her toe. "Whatever. You've got like forty grand in there still, plus another thirty or something at your apartment, right? And you paid off your gambling debts. You can afford to pay for both. So, what's the plan?"

"For lunch? Sushi?"

"No, you doofus," she said sweetly. "I meant after lunch, though, yes to sushi."

I'd been thinking about what to do all day. The printouts I'd gotten the night before had been as much as I could have hoped for. They'd filled in a lot of the gaps in Baker's file, including why it was he'd left the military in the first place, and a surprising amount of information in terms of what he'd been up to as a private military contractor.

The problem is that none of the information told me who Baker was working for.

And it wasn't like I could ask him.

Maybe I shouldn't have just shot him.

Except, even if what I felt at the time was rage, right now, twelve hours later, I was glad I'd done it. He was too good at his job to let him keep coming after me.

Even so, while having Baker gone meant one less thing to worry about, it didn't mean I was free of worries. I should have asked him what the hell the cipher did. Knowing that might tell me why Greaves wanted it back so badly.

It wasn't just curiosity: Greaves might have been less deadly than Baker, but she was a major problem I had to deal with.

I wanted to believe that I could just tell her to take her national security tap dance to somebody else, that I didn't care about any of that. Except, if I kept telling Greaves to stuff it, sooner or later she'd lose her patience, and then I'd be really and truly screwed. I might not be inclined to work with the law, but if Greaves hot-checked me, I'd be the priority of every cop, FBI agent, and DHS agent in the country. I was banking on her wanting to keep this quiet but given the number of voicemails she'd left for me since I'd hung up on her this morning—I'd turned the phone back on to check, and I'd been greeted by an avalanche of notifications—it was only a matter of time before she went wide. The problem was that I was still operating with too much uncertainty. There were a lot of gaps in my knowledge.

What I knew, and what Greaves had told me, was that the cipher was important enough that it was locked up in a supposedly unbreakable safe in a secret location run by the CIA. I wish I'd known how Baker had pulled off our entrance and exit—I remembered the smell of scorched wiring and drywall and concrete dust, and assumed he'd gone through a side building—but there were two things I knew *for sure*: I wasn't ready to give the cipher back until I figured out how to make Greaves honor the terms of the original deal and spring my dad, and I was absolutely certain I wasn't going to give the cipher to whomever it was who'd hired Baker in the first place.

Baker wasn't the end game. When all was said and done, he was exactly what he said he was: a hired gun. Somebody had paid him to do this. For him, it had just been business, nothing personal, despite the threats he made about Ginny, despite what happened to Paulie. And I was sure that it was just business for whomever it was who had hired Baker.

The people in power never cared about what happened along the way. Everything that didn't affect them was just collateral damage, and that included me, Aunt Paulie, Ginny, my dad, Meg, Taneesha, anybody who got in the way. The person at the top probably didn't even know I existed.

I intended to change that.

That's what I was thinking when Meg asked me what the plan was. Because while there were a lot of things I didn't know yet, there was another thing I knew for sure: sooner or later, I was going to find out who had hired Baker in the first place, and when I figured that out, I was going to do to them what I'd done to Baker.

That was the plan.

83

WE GOT SUSHI TO GO.

Before we left the house, I stashed the ring box inside her bungalow while Meg unloaded her boards to make her ride a little less conspicuous; we were just another pickup truck out on the road. After stopping for take-out sushi, I had her head toward Wilshire. A calculated bet that if Greaves wasn't working out of the FBI offices, she was at least nearby.

The intermediary handling her calls didn't even ask why I was calling. He just patched me through.

Greaves greeted me with a statement: "Five hundred thousand dollars."

I laughed. "That might be the sweetest thing anybody's ever said to me, but I don't really know what you mean."

"Five hundred grand. We can deposit it into any account you want. All aboveboard. You'll have to pay taxes like an honest citizen, but hand over the cipher right now and you'll walk away with more than enough money to change your life."

I popped an avocado roll into my mouth and grunted into the phone. I thought about it for a few seconds. When things were smooth, when Ginny and I were hopping around the globe doing exactly what we'd spent our life training to do, half a million dollars was a fun weekend in Vegas. Now, though . . .

We had a woman we worked with occasionally who did tech support who was tight with a nickel. She drove a used Volvo that she bought with a hundred thousand miles already on the odometer and had gotten papers drawn up so that she could funnel her illegally gotten money into legal retirement accounts and wash it clean. From there, stocks, bonds, real estate, and a balanced portfolio. She liked to lecture me about the power of compound interest and diversification. On more than one occasion, she told me that sooner or later I'd regret being so careless with my money.

She was right. Fun while it lasted, but the problem with easy come, easy go is that at some point it's all gone. A few years of fast living and fast spending, and then twenty months of slow living and slower earning, plus a gambling problem? I'd paid off my debts, but other than the cash in my apartment and in the bag I'd left at Meg's place—which was nothing to sneeze at—I was running on fumes. And chipping away at my insolvency working legit was going to be slow. So, yeah, half a million dollars, even after I paid taxes on it, was a lot of money.

The problem was the offer rankled me. I wanted the money, but I hadn't *earned* it. Not from her. I know that from the outside it didn't make a lot of sense, but as much as I wanted to say yes, I did have my own sort of code.

"Baker offered me five million," I said.

"And you killed him."

"Allegedly."

"You know that just saying 'allegedly' isn't some magic wand you can wave around. I've seen the body. He's dead, five million or not."

"It's not about the money," I said. Ugh. That almost killed me to say. But it *wasn't* about the money.

Her voice turned cagey. "What? You've got something else in mind? Why don't you just tell me, and then we can talk about it."

I tried to sound casual, confident. "Because it's not a negotiation."

"Are you sure? I just offered you five hundred thousand dollars, and you turned me down. It sure seems like a negotiation."

"Nope. A negotiation is when both sides have something the other side wants, and they try to find common ground. But I have the cipher, and you have nothing. Which means that I tell you what I want, and you say 'okay.'"

"Okay."

I honestly had not expected her to capitulate so easily. "Really?"

"Of course not. And there's no way you are possibly dumb enough to believe what you just said. I have *nothing*? No, I have the entire weight and power of the United States at my beck and call. When you hung up on me this morning, you said you know I don't work for the FBI. Well, if you know *that*, then you better believe that if I say the word, you're going to be black-bagged and bundled onto a plane, and when that plane lands, you'll find yourself in a foreign nation that interprets torture laws more liberally than our current attorney general."

She waited for a beat, and then said, "What, no snappy comeback?"

I did not, in fact, have a snappy comeback.

Greaves was willing to swing some heavy weight at me, and I still didn't know what all this was about. My assumption was that the cipher was some sort of cryptological device. In other words, a code breaker. A digital version of me. Able to slip through even the best governmental attempts at security. And if that was true, then it was no wonder that they wanted it back. And it was no wonder that Baker had been hired to steal it. If it was good enough, it would be invaluable. The ability to access secrets was the entire reason espionage existed, and spies always wet themselves in excitement about the idea that they could find all of the secrets at once.

84

SHE LET ME STEW for a few more seconds before offering an olive branch.

"This goes both ways, Duke. You asked for your father to be released with time served, and I can do that. You walk away without any charges." Her voice rose in anger now. "But I am tired of your adolescent crap, and if you don't give me that goddamned cipher, your dad will never take another breath of free air again, and you'll join him in spending the rest of your life in a cell somewhere."

Traffic was light by Los Angeles standards. Meg kept one hand on the wheel and reached over with the other to snag herself a piece of sushi.

"Fine," I said. "But after my experience in Germany, you can understand why I'm not exactly excited to trust you."

"I don't care," Greaves said. "We're going to meet, and you're going to give me the cipher. Now."

That was what I'd been hoping for.

"Want me to meet you at the FBI offices on Wilshire? Save you from making a drive?"

Her voice turned cagey. "If you want to walk into the Federal Bureau of Investigation with the cipher, quite frankly, that would be awfully convenient for me. I'm sitting at my desk doing paperwork right now. My office is on the third floor. Sign in at reception and I'll have somebody escort you up."

I wasn't surprised that she really did have a little CIA cell sandboxed somewhere in the building—that wasn't out of character for the agency—but it didn't matter. We both knew that I had no intention of sauntering into the FBI. But it *did* help me to have confirmation she was physically there. My plan hinged on the ability to move quicker than her.

I said, "I think I'll pass, but thank you. How about we meet somewhere outside. Your call. Pick a place. I'll come to you. But I don't want to be heading into an ambush. No agents, no spotters. Just you."

"And Park."

"And Park. If there's anybody else, I won't show."

"Give me a second."

She muted herself, and I decided to do the same so I could talk to Meg.

"Ten bucks says she picks the cemetery for the meet," I said.

Meg smiled. "Nope. The Getty. Though maybe that's just wishful thinking. Some rich dude loaned them his collection of Georgia O'Keeffe paintings for a temporary exhibition, and I've been meaning to go."

I laughed. "How about we go next week? But there's no way she'll pick the museum. It will be somewhere open, where she can have agents watching the whole thing from a distance."

Nobody ever listened to the "come alone" warnings, which was fine. I wanted her and her teams watching me. They wouldn't be looking for Meg.

We were both wrong on location.

Greaves picked a spot on the UCLA campus.

"I know it," I said. Whether Greaves was embedded inside the FBI building proper or just nearby, the bench she picked on the UCLA campus was less than two miles walking distance from the Wilshire office. It was even better than the two spots Meg and I had hoped for. Close, but just far enough that I could force her to drive over. Out in the open with plenty of escape routes. But the same thing that made it good for me also made it good for Greaves: excellent sight lines, relatively heavy foot traffic so she could have agents rotate through, and limited vehicular access. It wouldn't be easy to box me in if that was her game, but if she just wanted to take me down, she could do that from a distance. "One question: What do you guys take in your coffee?"

She growled something that made her sound a bit like a pirate. "God, you are insufferable. You can be such a prick, and then . . . Oh, whatever. Cream for me. Get Park some sort of a blended coffee drink with plenty of sugar in it. If a four-year-old would like it, that's Park's drink," she said.

"Oh," I said nonchalantly, "one more thing. Be there by two o'clock or you'll have to wait until tomorrow."

"Excuse me?"

The clock on the dashboard said 1:45. I was making a calculated gamble. We didn't want to give Greaves time to set up a proper perimeter. She'd still have agents watching, but making her rush meant Meg could take care of her end of things. That was the whole reason Meg and I had driven in this direction even before the meeting was set; I wanted to control the situation.

"Fifteen minutes," I said. "If you and Park aren't sitting on the bench by then, I'll try you again tomorrow."

"Come on, Duke, that's—"

"Ticktock."

She let out a heavy exhale. "Just when I start to like you, Duke, you do something that makes me want to kill you."

"Story of my life," I said. "See you in fifteen."

85

THEY WERE ONLY ONE MINUTE LATE.

I had the coffees on a tray. Cream and sugar for Greaves, a ridiculous concoction of sugar, cream, coffee, and chocolate chips, all topped with whipped cream, for Park.

The first thing Park said was, "You remind me of your dad."

"Is that a compliment?"

He took his drink from me. "He thought he was too smart for anything he did to ever catch up with him. And then he made one careless error because he was rushing to get to you and your sister after . . . you know. The thing."

"So, not a compliment?"

"He's serving an eight-to-twelve in a federal penitentiary. You tell me if it's a compliment."

I decided I liked Park better back at the airport, when he was still acting like a fanboy.

He stood up and then put his coffee down on the bench. "Sorry, but you know I've got to check."

I nodded. He gave me a professional pat down. We got a few funny looks from students walking past, but Park was quick and efficient. If I'd really worked at it, I could have snuck a weapon past him, but I still hadn't had a chance to replace the pistol I'd taken apart and dropped in the ocean. I was hoping I wouldn't need one with the legitimate feds.

As soon as Park finished, Greaves cut right to the chase. "Where's the cipher?"

"I didn't bring it," I said.

Park started to stand up, a peeved look on his face, but Greaves grabbed his elbow. "Give it a second," she said to him.

To me, she said, "I'm sick of your games, Duke."

"Me? You tell me you're FBI? We both know that's not true. And in the future, maybe try a little harder on your cover."

Greaves gave me an enigmatic smile. "For what it's worth, Park actually *is* FBI."

Which I already knew. I said, "Between you and me, *I'm* not the one playing games."

"Really?" Greaves said, arching her eyebrow at me. "Because it's starting to feel like everything is a game to you. Maybe if you took things a little more seriously, your life wouldn't be so screwed up."

Ouch.

It was fair, but it stung. I wanted to think I'd grown, that my dad going to jail and Ginny having everything stripped away from her would have changed me, but I didn't know if it was true. I was still shooting from the hip, still trying to make jokes as if I didn't care about anything.

Except I did care. I *was* trying to make things right. I'd been willing to take the job for Baker in the first place because it was a way of getting my dad out of jail, and now I was here, still trying to outrun my mistakes.

But, come on. Couldn't I have a little fun? And I would have bet my last dollar that as frustrated as I was making Greaves, she was *still* having more fun in her job than she'd had in years.

Of course, my willingness to bet my last dollar was part of the reason I had landed in so much trouble in the first place.

I took a sip of my coffee, turning my hip and shifting my weight a little at the same time. It seemed natural, but it meant that I could get a clear look at Meg. She was back about a hundred yards. Far enough away that there was no chance Greaves's team could make her, but close enough that she could make them *and* could give me the sign that she'd taken care of her errand.

She gave me an affirmative and then indicated the watchers: two agents on the roof, two behind me, and at least one on foot, moving around and trying to blend in with the crowd. Having Meg scouting for me meant I didn't need to look around for them. I could pretend like Greaves and Park hadn't ignored my command to come alone. Still, I was impressed with the coverage Greaves had managed to pull off in such a short period of time. Her team would have been hard for me to spot on my own without making my surveillance seem obvious.

"You'll have it by tomorrow," I said. "Scout's honor and all that."

Park looked at me incredulously. "Scout's honor? I know we said back at the airport that you'd been acting *like* a Boy Scout, but come on. You're not exactly the Eagle Scout type, Duke."

"Just get to it," Greaves said, annoyed. "I'm sure you didn't bother meeting us just to give us a whole hatful of nothing."

86

I REACHED INTO MY POCKET and pulled out an envelope. Nothing fancy. A standard white envelope that Meg had taken off her brother-in-law's desk. It held a single piece of paper.

Park looked at Greaves. Greaves made no effort to take the envelope. It made me feel silly, standing there, holding it out to them, like offering to shake somebody's hand and having them ignore you.

Greaves crossed her legs. She said, "Do you have any idea why we need that cipher back, Duke?"

"No. All I know is that I was minding my own business when I got a phone call from a blocked number, what, four days, five days ago? And now, here I am, hip deep in a pile of manure, desperately trying to dig my way out."

Greaves signaled with her eyes, and Park finally reached out and took the envelope. He said, "Maybe all you have to do is stop digging."

I wanted to say something clever, but for once, I was at a loss.

"What's inside this envelope?" he asked.

"Only one way to find out. Open it."

Park said, "Or you could just cut the theatrics and tell us."

"Photos of Baker and Cleary. The guys who hired me," I said. "I know I was supposed to text it over. I've been busy. I'm assuming Greaves already told you that Baker's dead?"

Park nodded. He opened the envelope and took out a sheet of paper. It was a color printout of one of the photographs Mimi had taken for me at the Market House.

He shook his head and then handed it to Greaves.

I was about to launch into my whole spiel, telling them what I'd learned about Baker's real identity, but I stopped as soon as I saw Greaves's eyes go wide and her face turn white.

She said, "Motherfu . . ."

"I take it you know him?"

She didn't answer, so I went on.

"No clue what the Russian connection is," I said, thinking of the cigarettes and the Snickers wrappers printed in Cyrillic. "He was born in a small town in Oklahoma, three sports in high school, and then straight into the Army. From there—"

Greaves spoke sharply. "What the hell are you talking about?"

"What?" Obviously, I was missing something.

Greaves pointed to the white dude. Cleary.

She said, "*He* was born in Russia, not Oklahoma." She handed the paper back to Park, leaned back against the bench, and looked at the sky. "I've got to make a phone call."

She stood up and waved her finger in a circle in the air. Ten seconds later two agents were standing on either side of me.

"Watch him," she said to the two agents. Then to me, she said, "Duke, you better listen carefully. I'm going to step away to make a call for a few minutes. You're going to sit down on this bench. Don't try to pull anything funny. If you run, we could chase you down, but we won't."

That sounded fine to me.

Then she looked at Park and her two agents again. "If he tries to run, don't bother chasing him. Just shoot him."

I didn't *think* she was entirely serious since she still wanted the cipher, but just in case, I decided sitting on the bench and waiting for her seemed like as fine an idea as any.

87

IT TURNED OUT THAT NEITHER of my two new babysitters had a sense of humor, and even Park wasn't feeling it, because he told me to shut up after a minute.

I sat on the bench, waiting.

I don't know what Meg was thinking, but I made a point not to look for her. Whatever was going down was heavier than I'd expected, and I didn't want to drag her in any more than she already was.

Greaves was gone at least fifteen minutes. When she came back, she told her two watchdogs to scram. She glanced at Park, and more gently than she had been with the other agents, encouraged him to take a walk as well.

She waited until it was just the two of us and then said, "Things have changed."

Stating the obvious.

I said, "No games. I'll hand over the cipher tomorrow. I'd give it to you right this second if I could. I'm sorry for screwing with you earlier, but the second that cipher leaves my hand . . ." The look Greaves gave me was cold and calculating, and it made me second-guess my gamble on leaving the cipher at Meg's. Nervously, I said, "The guy you twigged on was the guy who called himself Cleary, but the other guy, Baker, seemed like he was in charge."

"Doesn't matter," Greaves said. "Baker might have been in charge of the operation, but he was just a hired gun."

"He's a US national."

Greaves nodded. "I'm going to go with the technicality here, which is that technically, I don't *know* you killed him. But in the scheme of things, Baker was just a cog in the machine."

I thought of Paulie in her hospital bed and the implicit threat Baker had made against Ginny and said, "He wasn't just a cog in the machine to me."

The look of murder on my face gave Greaves pause, and then she said, "You know as well as I do that Baker was just doing a job. He's a clockwork soldier. Wind him up and point him in the right direction. Predictable. We don't care about the toy. We care about the toymaker."

"From my point of view, you seem to care a *lot* about the toy."

"The cipher? Yeah. That's not negotiable, Duke. I want that back."

I thought of it sitting on Meg's bookshelf. All this fuss over something smaller than a lemon. "What does it do?"

"You don't have to worry about it. All you need to know is that you shouldn't have stolen it, and you need to give it back."

I was fine with that. The sooner that thing was out of my hands, the better. I said, "Once you have it, my dad walks, you hold up your end of the bargain on Ginny, and then we're square. Sound like a deal?"

"No," Greaves said. "No deal." She shook the piece of paper with Baker's and Cleary's pictures on it at me. "You don't get it. There's a new deal on the table. You're going to do a job for me."

"Hell no."

"Hell yes, Duke. You do this job, and *everything* is back on the table. Everything, and then some. Your dad walks. I'm not talking time served. I'm talking a full pardon."

I raised my eyebrows. A pardon?

Greaves rolled her eyes. "Pick your jaw up off the floor. You want to know how big of a deal this is? It's *that* big of a deal. A full pardon for your dad, and you get what you asked for with Ginny: the best care the United States Treasury can buy. As for your aunt, I can make sure that the ATF, the FBI, *and* the IRS all erase the files they've got worked up on her. And you want the cherry on top? Not only do you avoid getting yourself charged with treason, that five hundred grand I offered is back on the table. Though I'm afraid, no, I wasn't joking about having to pay taxes on it."

I leaned forward over my knees, staring at the ground. "Taxes? So, it's an on-the-books job?"

Greaves laughed at that.

"Yeah," I said. "Didn't think so."

I straightened up and rubbed at my eyes. The coffee didn't seem to be doing me any favors. Across the way, Park and the two agents who Greaves had called in to babysit were sitting at a table. Watching me. I wondered if they were still operating under the orders to shoot me if I ran.

Not that there was anywhere to run.

"Can I think about it?"

88

"CAN YOU THINK ABOUT IT?" She looked me dead in the eyes and said, "There's nothing to think about. You've only got two options. Option one: do what I tell you. Option two: don't. But this is *not* a negotiation. This is an ultimatum. If you don't agree to my terms, I'll drop the bomb. Your aunt goes to jail, and your uncle gets to don a jumpsuit, too, as part of the package."

"But—"

She stepped on my objection. "Duke, you stepped in wet cement, and this is your only way to get out before it dries. If you say no, your dad goes to a supermax instead of Club Fed. The government seizes all the assets of everybody even remotely related to you. Your sister, Ginny, spends the rest of her life in the shittiest state-run institution I can find. Think bedsores for Ginny and grade-D ground beef for the residents who can chew their own food. Aunt Paulie gets RICO'd, and your uncle goes along for the ride. Those nice neighbors of yours who helped you get out of your apartment? The dad does a five-to-ten in a federal facility, and those two cute little girls get raised in foster care. If I can find your high school girlfriend, I'll have her arrested, too, just for fun. When I tell you that if you don't agree I'll drop the bomb, I mean full-on nuclear war. There's going to be a *lot* of collateral damage."

You know that feeling when the roller coaster goes over the drop? Yeah.

Except she wasn't done. "And as the icing on the cake, I guarantee you that no matter how hard *you* try to run, the United States government will hunt you down. It is not an understatement to say that there are some extremely important people who have a vested interest in what happens here."

Greaves continued, "I promise you, if you run, when you get caught—and you *will* get caught—nobody's going to read your Mirandas. What you'll get is a bag over your head and personalized attention from some extremely unpleasant people. You'll hand over the cipher just to stop the pain. But don't worry, because even though your family is going to be in jail, they won't miss your funeral."

"Because there won't be a funeral?"

"Correct. No funeral. Grantchester Ducaine will simply cease to exist. And that will make me sad, because I like you, Duke. In different circumstances, I'd probably enjoy your company. But in *these* circumstances, if you don't take the deal, I'll push the button. No joking. Nothing but the truth here, Duke. If you say no, I'll have you and everything you care about wiped off the face of the earth."

She raised her cup in a semblance of a toast. "Or you can take the righteous path and help your country out. If you do it my way, you get everything you want and then some."

"The CIA doesn't—"

She leaned in, grabbing my shirt and pulling me close. If we'd been somewhere private, it might have been an intimate moment. It was *not* an intimate moment. She whispered, "You think you're so smart, figuring out that even though I've got an office in their building, I don't work for the FBI. But do you really think that if I worked for the CIA, I'd use a phone number registered to Christians in Action? Please, Duke. I don't work for the CIA. The CIA works for *me*."

I'm good under pressure. I've very narrowly avoided arrest on multiple occasions, been around gunplay enough to think of it as an occupational hazard, and I've been shot more than once. I've robbed museums and banks and armored cars, and there was that one time in Switzerland when I jumped off a sixth-floor balcony. But it's been a while since I've been *that* scared.

She let go of my shirt and took a casual sip of her coffee. "Don't think I won't do it. I don't care about your aunt, and I don't care about your neighbors. I don't care about your sister, your father. I *like* you, Duke, but that's the *only* thing that's kept you alive so far. If I have to choose between a somewhat charming man-child and my country, you can bet every single dollar you've ever had that I'll choose my country."

I was out of witty things to say.

She considered me for a second and said, "I know you like to gamble, Duke. How's that worked out for you? This time, play the cards as they're dealt."

She turned on her heel and started to walk toward where Park and the other two agents were waiting for her.

I felt like I'd been gut-punched. Winded.

"Wait!" I called out.

She stopped, and then slowly turned. "Remember what you said to me earlier, Duke? This *isn't* a negotiation. You've got my number. If we aren't in business by midnight, it's mushroom clouds."

"No, I just . . ." She had me beat. We both knew it. "What's the job? What do you want me to steal?"

She drained her coffee and then casually chucked the cup into a garbage can ten feet away. Nothing but net, even though it was Park who supposedly played basketball in college.

She grinned, but it was tooth and claw, and I suddenly realized that the entire time I thought I'd been playing with her, it was only because she let me.

"What do I want you to steal?" she said. "Nothing. You aren't going to steal anything."

"You said that you need me to do a job."

"I do. But you aren't going to be stealing anything."

"Are you kidding?"

"Do I look like I'm kidding?"

She did not look like she was kidding. She looked like she was going to tear out my spleen, sprinkle a little salt on it, and eat it as a snack.

"Can you at least give me a hint?"

Slowly, she walked back to me. When she reached me, she put her hands on my shoulders and pulled me down a bit until her lips were right next to my ear.

It was a whisper: "No."

And with that, she left.

89

I SPENT CLOSE TO AN HOUR weaving in and out of campus buildings, taking blind turns, and ducking through doorways to make sure I wasn't being followed by any of Greaves's agents, and then did two passes with Meg watching and signaling I was clear before I met her at her truck.

Meg hadn't had any problems on her end: the only thing she'd had to do other than play spotter during my meeting was slap the GPS unit on Greaves's car.

I checked my phone to make sure the GPS unit was working, and saw the dot was parked in the lot for the FBI offices.

"So?" Meg asked when I put down my phone.

I ran through my side of it with her, including the midnight deadline to agree to Greaves's terms, though I didn't repeat Greaves's threat to put Ginny in the kind of institution that served up dog food and called it hamburger. The last thing I needed was for Meg to go headhunting.

When I finished, Meg said, "That's it? You asked for a hint, and she whispered no into your ear?"

"Yeah. I'm a little hung up on that detail too."

"Huh. So, she's not FBI, and she's not CIA?"

"Apparently not."

"NSA?"

"If I had to guess, I'd say it's some little organizational group that doesn't have a name or any real congressional oversight. One of those units that gets funded by the change in the couch cushions from the federal budget. You know, three thousand dollars for a toilet seat here, fifteen hundred dollars for a screwdriver there, and all of a sudden there's money for the kind of work that needs to get done but that doesn't look good when it's done on the record."

Meg drove with one hand on the wheel, nonchalant. Her other arm was on the windowsill, the wind blowing through the cabin and swirling her hair in the afternoon air. "And she really threatened to have you disappeared? She sounds intense."

"I think she was having fun right up until the minute I showed her the picture of Cleary. That changed the situation somehow. It was like she suddenly knew what everything meant."

"She's pretty," Meg said.

Even I wasn't dumb enough to take the bait on that. "Pretty intense."

"You sure slapping a GPS unit on her car was a good idea?"

"It seemed like a better idea *before* the meeting and all the threats."

"Second thoughts?"

I took her literally and thought about it. The idea had been to get Greaves to meet me, and with a little luck, have Meg tag the car. That part had gone like clockwork. It was the rest that was unsettled.

"No," I finally said. "Circumstances have changed, but the plan is still the same. The only real difference is that I need to know what I'm doing by midnight. Having you put the GPS tracker on her car was better than trying to tail her. She's not an amateur. Even if I didn't mind dragging you into this further than I already have, there's no way a pro like Greaves won't tip to it if we try an active follow just the two of us."

"I don't mean the GPS," Meg said. "I mean this whole thing in general. Planning to break into her house seems high risk, low reward to me. From what you've said, she doesn't seem like she's sloppy enough to leave anything useful lying around. Why don't you just give her the cipher and call it a day?"

"Because I have no idea if I can trust her to come through or not with my dad, and that cipher is the only real leverage I have," I said. "Besides, I'm tired of working for people I don't know."

I was sure Meg thought I was talking about Greaves, but I was thinking about Ginny. We'd made that mistake before in Paris.

And even knowing that I had a lead on Janus—thanks to Aunt Paulie, I knew that I had to go to Florida and look into a boat—I still didn't know who was ultimately responsible for burning us and destroying my family.

I wasn't going to make that mistake again.

We drove in silence the rest of the way until we got back to her sister's house.

Inside Meg's bungalow, she got some grapes out of the fridge while I grabbed the box from where I'd left it on her bookshelf.

Meg shoved a few grapes in her mouth and said, "So, what's next?"

I stuffed the ring box in my pocket and then shook my head.

She stared, and then, after a second, tilted her head. "You're ditching me, aren't you?"

"I have to finish this," I said, but I could hear it in my own voice. I was tired. Tired of all of it.

90

I SAID IT AGAIN, STRONGER, as if I could convince myself. "I have to finish this."

She bit her lip. Her face was somewhere between sadness and a smile. "You don't. Not really. You can just hand the thing over and walk away. You don't have to see this through," she said.

"I do," I said. "I owe it to Ginny. To my dad." I thought of my aunt in the hospital, of Uncle Charles sitting lovingly by her bedside, the whir and hum and click of the machines in the ICU. "I owe it to my family."

Meg thought for a second. "Do you ever ask yourself what your family owes you? Maybe it's time to walk away. Maybe it's time for you to have a life of your own." She didn't give me a chance to reply. "I know. I know what you're going to say. And I know what I'd say if somebody went after my sister or the kids, or if they went after my brother-in-law or my dad. But do you understand what I'm asking? When does it stop? Maybe now's the time."

"Maybe it stops when I find the son of a bitch who decided that it was better to chuck my sister off a sixth-floor balcony than to pay us what we were owed."

"Duke," she said, her voice so soft and full of sadness that it made me remember that I loved her, that she'd been friends with Ginny first, that nobody walked through life unscarred. "That's not what I mean, and you know it."

Neither of us said anything for a few minutes.

She was right. I did know what she meant. She meant, when would I allow myself to admit that I'd made a mistake, that there was nothing I could ever do to make it right? That I'd never be happy unless I was willing to let it go, to move forward with my own life.

And yet, she also knew that it was impossible. We were too similar for her not to understand. Where she mostly stayed on one side of the law, she came close enough to my side of things to understand that there was a certain kind of truth in violence.

My father made the deliberate decision to raise me to be a thief, but, intentional or not, he'd also raised me to be a weapon. Maybe if I hadn't shot that man when I was eleven, or maybe if my mother hadn't died, or maybe . . .

"Too many maybes," I said. "I'm sorry, but I have to go."

Meg gave me a pouty look and then almost instantly switched to something that could only be called a full smolder.

"Or, maybe," she said, "you could stay here. Wouldn't you rather stay here? With me?"

"Don't."

She let up. We both knew I wanted to say yes to her, that on any other day, I would have taken her up on the offer. We'd done it before, often enough to know that we were good at it and that it would be a fun way to spend the day. But I also knew that all she was offering was the day. A distraction. Nothing more.

Maybe someday Meg and I would take a real swing at an actual relationship, but it wasn't going to be today.

"Okay," she said. "Then I'm going with you. No reason you should do this alone. You can use backup."

I reached out and pushed a strand of hair behind her ear. "If I wanted backup, you'd be my first call. I know you'd go if I asked. Heck, you want to go even though I'm *not* asking. But I've got to ask this, Meg: Please let me do it on my own?"

"Are you sure?"

I could have told her it was because I knew Ginny would kill me if I dragged Meg further into this mess, or I could have pretended it was because I was a gentleman and had some anachronistic ideas about women, though I was pretty sure Meg knew where I stood on that.

I'd already picked my lie, though, and I stuck with it.

"It's safer as a solo affair."

Right now, Meg was off Greaves's radar. I wanted to keep it that way. In the past week, I'd flown to Europe, robbed a safe belonging to the CIA, stolen an item small enough to fit in my pocket but heavy enough to bring down the weight of the United States government, played Whac-A-Mole with Greaves in an attempt to stay one step ahead of her and the weight of said government, and in the process of trying to stay footloose and fancy free, had killed three people. And now I was about to try something as equally risky as all the rest.

I had told Meg it was a one-person job, but the truth was simple: I was afraid I was walking into something dangerous, and I couldn't handle the idea of losing one more person I loved.

"Duke—"

"Please, Meg."

She moved her hand to the same spot where I'd brushed her hair, and then reached out for me. "Okay, Duke." She pulled me in for a gentle kiss. "You know I love you, right?"

I kissed her back, equally gentle, riding the wave to shore. "But not in a permanent pack-my-bags-and-move-on-in kind of way," I said. I wasn't really sure if I meant it as a question or a statement, but I could hear the sadness in my own voice.

There was a cost to the kind of life I lived, and sometimes I felt it more keenly than others.

"I think," she said, her voice thick with her own sorrow, "to quote you from a minute or two ago, I'm probably safer as a solo affair right now. If I told you to pack up and move in, there'd be way too much baggage in my little bungalow." The sorrow was a warm sorrow, and that was almost enough for me to say screw it and take her up on her offer.

Instead, I kissed her one more time, and then walked out the door.

I WALKED FOR ABOUT TWENTY MINUTES, just trying to get my thoughts together, and then I called a cab.

I'd been raised to put the family first. As my dad liked to remind me and Ginny throughout our childhood, what we *wanted* took second place to what the family *needed*. But sometimes I wondered if that applied to him as well. Did he raise us the way he did because that's what he wanted or because it was what Ginny and I needed? How much of the way he raised us was because he knew our paths were inevitable, and how much of our paths being inevitable was because of how he raised us?

It felt like some sort of impenetrable Zen koan. I could wrestle with the question for the rest of my life. I might as well ask what it means to unfire a gun.

Which reminded me—while I was waiting for the cab, there was at least one problem I could solve. Having the cipher in my possession felt reassuring, but I still had to take care of the fact that I'd dumped my Smith & Wesson in the ocean after killing Baker. I needed to get a new pistol.

With the cash in my bag, that was a problem I could solve with a phone call.

The receptionist answered the phone with a cheery greeting. "Double Six Exotics. Take the drive of your dreams. This is Faisal speaking, can I help you?"

I didn't recognize the voice or the name. He was probably some-body who was looped in, but I didn't know that for sure. I said, "I need to speak to Noor."

"May I ask who is calling?"

"No, you may not."

My unwillingness to answer his question didn't seem to bother Faisal, which probably meant I could have told him who I was. Normally I would have, but right now, I wasn't taking anything for granted. He said, "Very well, sir. One minute, please," and soft cof-feehouse music kicked in as I was put on hold.

Noor's front was entirely legitimate. Double Six Exotics rented expensive luxury cars and supercars: you could get a Lamborghini Aventador for twenty-eight hundred a day, while a Porsche Panamera was a relative steal at three hundred bucks. Noor's cheapest cars were still close to five times what you'd pay for a tin can at the airport, but they had the full range. If you wanted a Bentley with a chauffeur for a week, that was fine, too, and if all you needed to do was impress a suitor for an afternoon by driving around in a Rolls-Royce Phantom with the top down, if you could afford the toll, Double Six had the wheels.

I wasn't looking for a car.

Noor's side business was in providing people like me with guns and any other kind of weapons or explosives that might be used in criminal enterprise. They only dealt in quality merchandise.

Noor came on the line with a voice that sounded as immacu-late and stylish as they always looked. I'd gotten tailoring tips from them in the past. "I'm sorry," Noor said, "but I don't recognize this number."

"But you would definitely recognize my ugly mug," I said. "I'm calling from a new number. And you ought to recognize my voice after all the business you've done with me and my family."

"A pleasure to hear from you. It has been a while, my friend. Nearly two years." A short pause, and then Noor's voice softened. "I was very sorry to hear about your sister's . . . accident. But with that, and your father's unavoidable detainment, I was under the impression that you were retired."

"I was."

I knew that Noor swept the phones in their office on a regular basis, but with a physical office with a legitimate business, it wasn't like they could cycle through burners. It was prudent to assume the line was tapped. Noor kept a very clean profile, but part of that was never saying anything dumb over the phone. If I asked directly about a gun, Noor would profess to have no idea what I was talking about and tell me I had called the wrong number.

Noor said, "And being retired no longer interests you? I am not surprised. You did not seem like you enjoyed playing golf that much. You certainly weren't very good at it."

"Hardy har. You're hilarious." They were. Kind of. We'd played golf together a few times. Noor was a scratch golfer, and even spotting me a stroke a hole, I ended up losing money.

"No," I said, "I'm still retired, but I had a sudden spot of unexpected business pop up that I have to take care of. Unavoidable and urgent. I need a car right away."

"Do you have time to come in and talk about your rental needs in person?"

"That's not going to work with my schedule," I said. "I'll need the vehicle brought to me."

Noor was quiet, then said, "That service requires an additional fee."

"I can't get out of the office. I'll pay the delivery fee. I'm not sure where I'll want to meet your driver, but it's got to be today. I can't put off my meeting."

"I'm sorry to have to ask, but I've heard some rumors that you've had some investment trouble and might be overextended. I don't mean to be indelicate, but are you sure you can afford our services? There are other rental car agencies in Los Angeles that are more affordable."

In the past, I'd had an account going with Noor. But that had been when I was working regularly. Word of my gambling problems must have gotten around. Noor was telling me as delicately as possible that they weren't willing to work on credit and they expected cash.

I said, "The rumors of my financial decline might be exaggerated. I was having a bit of a cash flow problem for a while, but I've moved some investments around and I'm fluid enough to afford a quality car. And I know if I work with you, I'll get the vehicle I'm promised without any hassle."

A pause. I could almost hear Noor thinking. "Given that you've said you are in a hurry and can't come directly to our office, is there a particular reason why you aren't just using a vehicle from the company fleet?" Noor asked.

In other words, if this was for an upcoming job down the pike, Noor would understand why I was calling, but given that I had an immediate need for a gun, why wasn't I using one I could get from Paulie or that I likely had stashed somewhere on my own?

It was a fair question. Basically, Noor wanted to know exactly how hot I was and needed assurance that nothing would blow back on them.

I had to think how to answer that one. Noor must not have heard about Paulie being in the hospital yet. They'd hear soon enough. "It's complicated, Noor," I said. "I don't have access to the company cars right now, and it's too difficult for me to get back to the office in time. But you know I'm a safe driver. No accidents. There won't be any hassle with insurance adjusters. I give you my word on that."

Noor processed that and then said, "Well, given our long-standing relationship, what kind of a vehicle are you looking for?"

I said, "I'm not price sensitive, but I'm not looking for anything complicated. The only thing that really matters is that, like I said, I need a good car, I need it today, and I need you to have somebody bring it to me where and when I ask. That's it."

I heard Noor click their tongue. Like the cars you could rent from Double Six Exotics, the weapons could get exotic too. "Will you be driving long distances, or do you just need a vehicle for around town?"

"Around town," I said. "Something reliable and fast. I'd rather have a sedan than an SUV. Something small that's easy to park. And speaking of parking, if you have a lot where I can keep it secure when I'm not driving, that would be swell."

Around town meant I was looking for a pistol instead of a long gun. Reliable and fast meant an automatic chambered in a common caliber. An easy-to-park sedan instead of an SUV meant I wanted a pistol that I could carry concealed. And finally, the secure lot meant I wanted a holster to go with it.

"Do you have a particular make or model in mind?" Noor asked.

"Noor, at this point, I don't care. I just need a car. If it's clean, drives straight, starts when I turn the key, and you can deliver it to me on deadline, as long as it's high quality, I'll take whatever you've got on the lot, and I'll pay whatever you think is fair."

Noor laughed. "Everything I carry is high quality, but there is no key to turn, my friend. Almost all of our vehicles are push-button start."

I didn't know what *that* was supposed to be code for, but I'd worked with Noor long enough to trust them. They'd deliver.

"One more thing," I said. "I'm going to start my trip as soon as I get the car. I'm not going to have time for a test drive. Make sure the car is tuned up, pristine, and full of gas." I was asking Noor to make sure the pistol was test-fired, cleaned, and loaded.

"Of course." They sounded insulted.

"Sorry. I know I didn't have to ask. Either way, though, I appreciate it."

Noor gave me a different number to set up delivery once I knew when and where.

I hung up feeling relieved. Even with Baker out of the game, there were still enough moving pieces that I wanted a gun. There were other ways to get a gun, but since I had cash to spare, going through Noor was the easiest, and guaranteed I'd end up with something good.

I closed my eyes for a few minutes, standing there in the California sunshine, until I heard the cab pull to a stop in front of me.

92

I HAD A LOT OF TIME TO KILL, so I had the cabbie take me to Beverly Hills. I browsed a few stores, but I hadn't gotten *that* much cash in Zurich. On a lark, I joined one of the celebrity home tours. It was fun playing tourist for a few hours, and between that, a movie, and then some time in a bookstore, I whittled the rest of the day away.

Around eight o'clock, I found a Thai restaurant and then arranged Noor's delivery.

While I was waiting for food—and the gun Noor had promised—I checked the GPS unit Meg had stuck on Greaves's car. I'd been checking it periodically all day, and I was feeling extremely frustrated: after meeting me on the UCLA campus, she'd driven back to the FBI building on Wilshire and the car hadn't moved since. Either Greaves was working late or . . .

Greaves picked up on the first ring, and without a greeting or a preamble said, "You got it?"

"Do you have the money?"

"What? With me at home?" she said.

"You're not at the office still?"

"I don't work *all* the time," she said. "I'm sitting on my couch, eating a microwave burrito, and watching television. But even if I was at my office, it's not like I'm going to hand over cash in a briefcase. Give me the cipher, do the job, then you get paid. Direct deposit." She paused and I thought I heard her take a sip of something. "Is that it? Because my burrito is getting cold. If you want to talk, come see me. With the cipher."

"I'll be in touch," I said.

"You better be. I wasn't joking about the midnight deadline to let me know where you stand," Greaves said, and she ended the call before I had a chance to do it myself.

As I put my phone away, I thought about what her being at home meant for my plans. I wanted to check up on her—I was tired of being in the dark—but with Greaves at home and the GPS unit still at the FBI building on Wilshire, I didn't have any real lead on where to find Greaves during her off-hours. No way to get more information on who she *really* was.

On the other hand, I realized, her being at home meant I knew her office was empty.

The waiter came over and slid a platter of pad see ew with chicken in front of me. It wasn't the most imaginative thing I could order, but I was in need of comfort food. I ladled some hot sauce over the noodles and thought about what it meant that Greaves's office was empty.

I was starting to have a very, very dumb idea.

93

I FINISHED EATING, CHECKED THE TIME, left cash for the bill and tip, grabbed my bag, and went to the bathroom. I did my business and then washed my hands. The door opened, and a young man came in carrying a FedEx box. He did a quick check to make sure it was just the two of us.

I broke the ice. "Punctual. I'm assuming you're Faisal?"

He grinned at me. "Yeah. I was the one who answered when you called earlier. I know who you are already."

"Is that a good thing?"

Faisal chuckled. "Good, bad, who knows? But it's a thing." He had an easy manner, and I instantly liked him. He stepped in front of the door to block it with his body. It would be a quick transaction, but we still didn't want anybody walking in.

I handed him a stack of cash and he handed me a FedEx box.

"Neither sleet nor snow," he said.

I looked at him. "That's the post office."

He grinned again, pocketed the money, and left.

I went inside one of the stalls, locked the door, and opened the box. It was a Kimber Micro in stainless with a rosewood handle. Noor had included an extra magazine in the box, and the holster had a pouch for the spare magazine. I did a quick field strip using the FedEx box as my table, checked to make sure the magazines were properly loaded, and put everything into my bag. Then I left the stall, chucked the FedEx box in the trash, and walked out of the restaurant. I was ready to take a big gamble.

IT WAS MY LUCKY NIGHT: a cab was dropping off a couple outside the Thai place. I snagged a ride to the In-N-Out Burger in Westwood Village.

Westwood Village bordered the UCLA campus, where I'd met Greaves earlier in the day. The In-N-Out Burger was less than a mile from the Los Angeles branch office of the Federal Bureau of Investigation.

Which I planned to break into.

HERE'S THE EASIEST WAY to get into a secure building: bribe a member of the cleaning crew to give you their ID card. A custodian's uniform and a garbage trolley make you close to invisible, and the cleaning crew usually has access to everywhere in the building. Even the top secret muckety-mucks need their trash cans emptied.

I had close to forty grand in the bag I was carrying, so anywhere else, it would have been a cinch. The problem was that I was sure the janitorial staff working an FBI building had been backgrounded. With a little bit of time, I knew I could find a mark; there's always somebody with a drug problem or alimony payments, and even if not, an inch-thick stack of bills makes almost anybody on an hourly wage go weak at the knees. Except I didn't have time to work the angles. I needed to get in tonight.

Which meant I had to find a very specific kind of bar.

I worked my way toward Wilshire Boulevard, checking out seven bars before hitting the jackpot on the eighth, a sports bar and grill. I didn't even have to go inside to know I'd found it: despite being less than a half mile from the FBI building, the parking lot was lousy with government vehicles.

Inside, it was about what I expected. All cop bars are the same, and this bar was just the FBI version of a cop bar. Given the proximity to the UCLA campus, there were still more students and civilians than federal agents, but despite the crowd, the federal agents were easy to pick out.

I bellied up to the bar, sliding between a pair of young women who were both on their phones and an old, fat guy nursing something dark poured over ice. I knew there'd be a go-to bar for the FBI agents somewhere near their building, but I'd gotten twice lucky: once in how quickly I found it, and the second time in that it was busy.

The FBI agents were mostly congregated off to one side. A dozen men and women in business attire, and an equal number dressed closer to the smart casual look I was rocking. A few still had their ID badges on display, and it was about fifty-fifty in terms of carrying a piece.

And third time lucky: one of the male agents who was dressed business casual instead of in a suit, a guy wearing thick-framed black glasses, had similar facial features and skin tone to me. His hair was uniformly dark without any of my sun-bleached highlights. He was also both a little taller and softer looking than I was, but I thought with a baseball cap, I could make it work.

I swapped a ten with the bartender for a beer and told him to keep the change, and then I pulled out my phone. I didn't need my phone for anything, but a guy staring at his phone is less suspicious than a guy staring at a cluster of FBI agents.

I mindlessly thumbed my screen, occasionally looking up as I took sips of my beer. My mark was drinking from a bottle of beer that even I thought was absolute piss-water. All I had to do was be patient.

Finally, after about forty minutes, he got up and headed back toward the toilets.

I timed it perfectly, bumping into him as he came back out.

"Oh, shit," I said as I reached out to steady him. "Sorry about that."

He gave me an annoyed look, but nothing else. Which was fine with me. I didn't particularly want to get into a stare-down with him.

I went in, emptied my bladder, washed my hands, and then, when I came out of the bathroom, ducked out the back door.

Only when I was walking away did I take a look at the ID card I'd dipped from the guy's pocket.

96

I RETRACED MY STEPS to the In-N-Out Burger and ordered a Double-Double combo. Not that I was hungry after the Thai food, but I had a plan.

After In-N-Out, I made a quick stop at CVS. I found a pair of low-strength reading glasses with blocky black frames that looked pretty close to what the agent had been wearing in the bar, and then went to work hunting through the makeup section. It only took me a few minutes to find what I needed there, but for some reason, I'd picked the only CVS in Los Angeles that wasn't selling Lakers gear.

Fortunately for me, when I left the drugstore, there were two teenagers sitting on the curb and one of them was wearing a ball cap.

"Want to sell me your hat?" I asked.

The kid touched the brim of his baseball cap like he was just checking to make sure he was actually wearing one.

"I'll give you forty bucks for it," I said. It was a Dodgers cap, which I wasn't exactly thrilled about. I'd been down on the Dodgers since I'd lost close to five thousand dollars on them early in the season, but I'd had some luck with betting on the Lakers.

The kid shook me down for sixty dollars, but I didn't want to mess around trying to find a hat somewhere else. If it weren't for my gambling problem, I would have been perfectly happy to wear a Dodgers cap. I was going to have to swallow my pride.

Two blocks from the FBI building, I stepped into an alley and pulled out my phone. I flipped the camera so I could use it as a mirror and got to work with the makeup.

The easiest way to keep your identity secret when working a job is simply to wear a mask that fully covers your face. Which would have been fine, if I wasn't planning to go through the front door. Even though I doubted anybody in the lobby was expecting somebody to be crazy enough to try to sneak into the FBI's office, wearing a mask that covered my entire face was going to tip off even the laziest security guard.

Fortunately, all I needed to do was to touch myself up enough that I could pass for the picture on the ID card I'd swiped. I worked around my eyes a bit to make them seem closer together, darkened my eyebrows a touch, and then smoothed out my forehead. I looked at the picture on the ID card and then at my face on the screen of my phone. It wouldn't fool the guy's mother, but with the glasses and the hat giving me a bit of cover, I'd pass unless I really got the shakedown.

The final touch was a little face hacking. I didn't know for sure if the FBI was using a facial recognition system on their security cameras, but it didn't hurt to be prepared. I couldn't go with a full dazzle—extremely quirky makeup and jewelry applied to break up my facial symmetry and fool a computer—because that would be as obvious as just wearing a mask, but with a few carefully placed dots in a color that was close enough to my skin tone that they wouldn't be noticeable to a person unless they were attentive and I was standing under bright lights, I could come close enough to blinding the cameras that I wasn't worried.

97

THERE WERE THREE SECURITY GUARDS working the entrance. One on the computer checking ID cards, one on the metal detector, and one on the X-ray machine.

I tapped the stolen ID on the reader and kept moving. If I actually worked here, I'd be used to breezing in and out. The guard, a woman in her late fifties, flicked her eyes at me just enough to confirm that I matched the picture on her screen.

I did not, of course, match the picture, but with the baseball cap, the makeup, the glasses, and my body language, it was enough to convince her that I was the person I was pretending to be. If you act like you belong, you do.

I put the bag from In-N-Out Burger on the conveyer belt and watched my Double-Double and fries crawl into the machine's guts. The guy working the X-ray smiled at me and said, "You get any for us?"

I laughed. "Sorry, man." I put my soda on the top of the X-ray machine and took one of the small plastic bins they had for keys and wallets, took out the metal ring box holding the cipher from my pocket, dropped it in the bin, added my phone, and pushed the bin inside the machine as well. Then I walked through the metal detector.

The guard on the metal detector watched the lights at the top of the device, and when there was no warning signal or beep, he gave me a nod.

I stepped back over to the other side of the X-ray machine, grabbed my soda from where it was resting on top, and then took the bag of fast food and the bin with the cipher and my phone out as they came trundling along the belt.

I took a sip of the soda and headed toward the elevator bank.

I was in.

98

I DECIDED THAT I'D START with the third floor. After all, when I'd spoken to Greaves earlier in the day, jokingly offering to bring the cipher to her at work, that's where she said her office was.

I wasn't exactly in a rush now that I was past security, but I didn't want to linger either. The thing that was making me the most nervous was not getting caught, but rather that I'd put my pistol in the bag with my cash and stashed it in some bushes a block away from the building. It was relatively well hidden, but getting another pistol quickly would be a hassle, and it was a lot of cash. I was not going to be happy if it was gone when I got back. I probably could have gotten the pistol into the building—agents carried service pistols after all—but when I'd dipped the guy's pocket at the bar, I had been pretty sure he wasn't carrying a weapon, and I didn't want to try to guess the protocol for bringing one in. The cash was a totally different matter. Bringing stacks of twenties in with me would have raised some eyebrows at the front desk no matter how I did it.

The third-floor elevators let me out in front of a big, open bullpen. The lights were on, but there was nobody sitting at any of the desks. I would have bet there was activity in pockets around the building, but a quiet floor was fine with me. I took off my decoy eyeglasses and put them in my pocket.

I had my choice of going either right or left from the bullpen, so I went left. No reason really. I just felt like it. Most of the doors I passed had name plates on them or had signs indicating specific duties. The third floor seemed like it was mostly housing the white-collar crime branch. I had met enough feds to know that the white-collar crime agents worked just as hard as the agents in other branches, but they worked more regular hours. The violent crime and RICO guys were more likely to be in the office at odd hours.

At the middle of the hallway, I came across a restroom. I made a quick check to make sure there wasn't anybody in the stalls, and then I put my In-N-Out take-out bag on the counter. With my free hand, I took the lid off my cup of soda.

I stopped, gave my hands a good wash, and then dipped into the soda and pulled out the set of picks that were swimming under the bubbles. I gave the picks and my fingers a rinse, used a paper towel to dry off, and went back out in the hallway.

I had gone down two of the hallways when I saw the door with a sign that read LIAISON OFFICE. Perfectly benign, perfectly boring, and the only door in the entire floor that had a keyed lock rather than something you could open with your ID card. And it wasn't just a keyed lock: it was a high-security, pick-resistant, drill-resistant, bump-resistant lock. I recognized the brand and the lock itself. It was something that I installed for customers when they wanted something that was really and truly going to keep out thieves.

Not a big deal, but it was annoying.

If it had been a normal office lock, I could have just raked it. You can use a standard pick for raking, but I had a Bogota rake and a couple of different other homemade rakes with me, and it's what I would have normally done. Raking is sloppy and amateurish, but it's also extremely quick if you know what rake to use: it's the lockpicking equivalent of brute force. You're just sort of smashing the pins and jiggling until everything lines up. With this lock, however, I was going to have to do single-pin picking.

The lock was rated for thirty minutes. In other words, a decent criminal was going to have to spend at least half an hour working it if they wanted in.

Needless to say, it did not take me thirty minutes.

Once it was unlocked, I took a few breaths and braced myself. The two most dangerous parts of what I was doing were getting past the security guards in the lobby and right now, opening what I thought was the door to Greaves's office. I was going in cold; I was simply hoping Greaves didn't have an additional alarm system. If she did, security officers were going to be thundering in here in no time at all if I couldn't disable it quickly.

I opened the door and stepped in. The room was a simple reception area: a couch, a coffee table, a desk with a computer and a lamp. The lamp was on, giving enough light for me to see that there wasn't a keypad on the wall, no blinking lights, no obvious motion sensors. It didn't mean I was home free, but it meant I could take a breath.

Except that the only door in the room—what I assumed was the door to Greaves's office—had a digital keypad on it.

Pain in the ass.

This was the problem with not having a real plan.

I looked at the keypad. If it could be picked, I could open it, but digital required the right tools. If I'd known I was going to be breaking into Greaves's office, if I'd had more time, I could have done it properly, but no. Here I was, in the Los Angeles district office of the Federal Bureau of Investigation, staring at an alphanumeric keypad with only a set of picks and a bag of rapidly hardening burgers and fries.

And ketchup.

Ketchup. I could use ketchup.

I reached in the bag from In-N-Out Burger and took out a package and some napkins. I opened the ketchup and spread a healthy smear across the keypad. Then I took a napkin and gently wiped the ketchup off. Then I took my phone, turned on the flashlight, and shone the light on the keypad from an angle.

Yahtzee.

Five of the nine numbers were clean, but four—the four that were most often touched, the four that had dirt and grease from fingertips, that had microscopic indents from being used to enter the code over and over and over again—still had hints of ketchup on them: three, four, six, and seven.

I could try all the different permutations—there weren't more than twenty-four ways to combine four numbers—but if there was an automatic keypad lockout after a certain number of failed attempts, usually three, it would be a hassle. Much easier to get it right the first time.

I thought for a second. 3, 4, 6, 7. What was the order? Did the numbers mean anything? Did they spell something?

No way.

She was extremely sharp. The kind of pro I liked working with and hated being matched against. No chance she was sloppy enough to use . . .

I gave it a try: 3, 7, 4, 6.

The lock whirred open and gave a friendly beep.

3, 7, 4, 6. Which, when matched up to an alphanumeric keypad like you found on a phone, spelled the name Erin. For Erin Greaves.

I had to laugh.

But when I stepped into her office, I stopped laughing, because the first thing I saw in the light that spilled over from the receptionists' lamp was a desk. The top of the desk was completely bare except for a single, sealed envelope. There was writing on the envelope.

Four numbers.

3, 8, 5, 3.

Duke.

99

I HAD THE CABBIE DROP ME OFF a quarter mile before my destination. The address Greaves had left in the envelope on her desk was in a purely residential section of Silver Lake. Single-family houses, mostly two-story places. Nice enough without being too fancy, at least by Los Angeles standards, and I didn't look out of place. Just another honest civilian out for a late evening stroll. You couldn't tell that I had a pistol holstered on the small of my back, some lockpicks in one pocket, and an apparently invaluable cipher and a lot of cash in the bag slung across my shoulder.

It would have been better if I'd had a dog to walk, but all I had to do was act like I belonged and I was functionally invisible. Better than skulking around and trying to hide in the shadows.

I'd walked about a block when my phone rang. The number showed Singapore.

I hesitated, and then I decided to answer it.

"How's my favorite hooligan? I trust you're staying out of trouble."

I smiled at the warmth in Helen's voice. "You know me," I said.

There was a short pause, and then Helen said, "I do know you, Duke. And that's not an answer." She sounded more businesslike, even from eight thousand miles away. "Did you call me just to chat, or is something wrong?"

"Just to chat." I knew she'd hear about what I'd gotten myself into eventually, but she was too far away to do anything, and it was too late to ask for advice. Maybe last night there was still a little bit of wiggle room, but I'd picked my line. The gun was cocked and loaded. There wasn't anything left for me to do but pull the trigger. Still, hearing her reminded me that I wasn't alone. "It's not really a great time for me to talk, though. I'm kind of in the middle of something. I've only got a couple of minutes."

"Me too, kiddo."

"Something interesting?"

"Something complicated," she said. "You'd like it." She gave a quick sketch of the job—it involved a casino magnate and his scorned lover—before saying, "And you?"

"Mine's complicated too." I was quiet for a second, and then I said, "I've got to get going, Helen, but I love you."

"Duke. What aren't you telling me?"

I shook my head, a sheepish grin on my face, not that she could see it. She'd known me for too long for me to fool her.

"You don't have to treat me like a kid, Helen. I'm good."

"Please. You can't tell me not to treat you like a child without sounding like a child, Duke. Besides which, I'm too old to pretend anything other than the truth. When I look at you, I see the man you are, but I also see the child you used to be. And," she said slyly, "the child you sometimes still are."

"Ouch."

"Do you need some sort of affirmation?" she said, laughing. "You know I'm proud of you. If I'd had children or grandchildren, I would have happily picked you to fill in one of the spots. As it is, I love you more than my nephew."

"Yeah, well," I said, "he's a spoiled prick, so you're setting the bar kind of low."

On the other side of the street, a couple pushed a sleeping baby in a stroller, leaning into each other and talking quietly. I wondered why they were out so late. Were they coming home from a party, or was this the only way to get the kid to sleep? Was this what it meant to be a parent?

"Listen," I said, "I've really got to go. But it was good to talk to you."

Helen said, "If you need me, I'll come. Anytime, anyplace."

"Thanks, but I'm good. It's nothing to worry about. I know what I'm doing," I said, lying through my teeth.

100

THE HOUSE WAS ON A CORNER LOT. A stand-alone, white two-story. A square stacked on a rectangle. Modern without being funky. Picture windows overlooking the reservoir. A long deck on the second story that had a few chairs. Nice, but not ostentatious. If I had to guess, I'd put at somewhere between two million and two point five. Middle of the road by Silver Lake standards, but if I'd still been under the impression that Greaves was FBI, seeing this house would have disabused me of the notion. Federal jobs came with good job security and a decent salary, but not like this.

The house was lit up, but there was no sign of life inside. I looked for the telltale blue light of the television. Nothing.

There was a low, decorative, rolling adobe-style wall around the property. A floodlight covered the driveway, but the yard was dark. I turned the corner, stepped into a pool of shadows, and then hopped the wall.

I waited a few minutes, crouching low.

No alarms, no lights. All good as far as I was concerned.

Except when I looked up, Greaves was standing on the deck, watching me.

"Took your time," she said. "Come on up."

101

GREAVES HANDED ME A CAN OF BEER.

"It's killing you, isn't it?" she asked. "Come on. Just ask."

I opened the can and took a sip. I didn't say anything.

I was sitting outside on the second-story deck. The city was laid out in lights below us. Greaves had a pair of yellow wire chairs on either side of a bistro table, and after handing me my beer, she sat down in the free chair.

"You're too proud to ask, aren't you?" I kept quiet, staring out into the night, but I saw her steal a glance. "Come on, Duke," she continued. "Do you really think I'd let you slap a GPS unit on my car if I didn't want you to?" She took a sip of her beer. "The whole thing was a setup. You thought you were calling the shots, but you were just making the calls I wanted you to make. I like your friend, by the way. She's good. Even with eyes on my car, we didn't catch her planting it until we went through the video frame by frame. She's got an interesting background."

"Leave her out of it," I snapped.

Greaves swiveled calmly to face me. I met her gaze. "That's up to you, Duke. It's almost midnight. Do you have the cipher?"

I reached into my bag and pulled out the ring box. I put it on the table but left my hand covering it. "Okay. I'll bite. How'd you know I'd go to your office? Was it some kind of a weird test to see if I could do it?"

She smirked. "I didn't know you'd break into my office. It wasn't a test. I knew you *could* do it; I just didn't know if you *would* do it. It was just a guess. We've got a good file on you. Seemed like the kind of thing you'd pull. Nobody is dumb enough to try to break into an FBI building, which made it perfect for you."

"People keep overestimating me and thinking I'm not dumb enough to do things, and yet here we are," I said. "But technically, I didn't break into the building. Just into your office. I *snuck* into the building." I'd made a point of dropping the ID card I'd borrowed onto the ground near the elevator bank in the lobby. The agent would get it returned to him—probably with a lecture about security protocols—and never know I'd lifted it unless Greaves made a point of telling him.

"As for how I knew you were in the yard? Credit goes to Park. After the little stunt you pulled with sneaking out of your apartment, I didn't want to let you out of our sight again."

God. It was hard to believe that I'd only skipped out of my apartment the day before.

Greaves continued, "I brought Park in because I needed an actual FBI agent for liaison purposes, and he was familiar with your family's . . . oeuvre."

"My family's *oeuvre*?" It was my turn to smirk.

"Yes. The Ducaines aren't exactly known as the smash-and-grab type." She pointed at my feet. "But Park has also been handy for other things. He tagged your shoe with a tracker when he frisked you at UCLA this afternoon."

I was both impressed and annoyed.

I took my hand off the metal box. "Here it is." Greaves reached for it, but I quickly covered it again. "What's it do?"

Greaves looked at me coolly, and then turned back to look out at the view. "Are you agreeing to my terms? You'll do the job?"

"Do I have a choice?"

She laughed. "I'm probably supposed to say something like, 'you always have a choice,' but no, not really. For what it's worth, though, your dad's out."

"What?"

"I had the Marshals Service pick him up earlier today. They've got him at a hotel in West Hollywood. Nice place. Way over the Marshals' usual budget, but I authorized it. I checked in with them about two hours ago, and he was busy eating room service and destroying the mini-fridge. The paperwork for his pardon is in place. That gets signed *after* you do the job, but I thought putting him in the hotel would be a sign of good faith. Speaking of which"—she nodded at the ring box—"is that the real deal?"

"What's it do?" I asked again.

She sighed and pinched the beer can between her fingers. The metal made a crinkling sound. "It breaks the bank."

102

SHE WALKED ME THROUGH IT.

Back in the day, when one bank owed another bank money, they used to exchange actual gold. It was unwieldy and slow, and of course, the physical transfer of gold was an open invitation to, well, people like me.

Then, early in the 1900s, banks moved to electronic ledgers. First through, no joke, the telegraph system, and then, eventually, through wire transfers. Nowadays, almost all banking is done through electronic transfers. Most of the money in existence doesn't actually exist. It's just a series of ones and zeroes floating around in the ether.

I knew the gist. I was thinking about the SWIFT job, from back in 2016. SWIFT stands for the Society for Worldwide Interbank Financial Telecommunication. It's exactly what it sounds like. Banks around the world use it to transfer funds from one bank to the other. Quicker and more secure than trying to run armored cars full of cash or gold.

But not *entirely* secure.

In 2016, somebody managed to get the codes for the central bank of Bangladesh. They moved about eighty million dollars from the Bangladesh Bank's main account at the Federal Reserve Bank of New York and laundered a big chunk of it through some casinos in Macau. As easy as it gets: press a button, the electrons fly, and suddenly you've got an extensive line of credit at a casino. Pull chips, cash them out, and you walk out the door with untraceable cash.

It was the kind of job that made me professionally jealous. A lot of people think it was the North Koreans, but I'd heard rumors that somebody I sort of knew might have been behind it, and he'd been off the radar since it happened. As far as I knew it was a trail gone cold. The perfect crime.

I told as much to Greaves, but she shook her head. "That's nothing," she said.

"I don't know," I said. "Eighty million dollars seems like something to me."

"It was almost certainly, at least partially, an inside job. All they had to do was get the credential from somebody inside the bank and then move the money faster than anybody could respond."

"Still. Eighty million dollars is a lot."

"In the scheme of things, eighty million dollars is a rounding error," Greaves said.

"Some rounding error."

"Duke, SWIFT is *an* electronic system for moving money." She tapped the cipher. "When I say this thing breaks the bank, I mean *the* bank. SWIFT moves a lot of money, but at the end of the day, it's retail compared to the Fedwire."

"Fedwire?"

"It's an electronic settlement system. Even if you didn't know about the Bangladesh robbery, SWIFT occasionally makes the news because the Department of Homeland Security tracks and blocks money going to terrorist organizations. But there are other big electronic settlement systems like SWIFT. China has its own version for the renminbi, and the Eurozone has TARGET2. But that only moves a couple billion dollars a day."

"Sorry. It *only* moves a couple billion dollars a day."

"Chump change compared to Fedwire. The Fedwire is run by the Federal Reserve. In any given month, somewhere between fifty and ninety *trillion* dollars moves through the Fedwire."

Trillion. With a *T*.

103

YOU'VE PROBABLY HEARD ABOUT THE PROBLEM drug cartels have with cash.

Selling illegal drugs is, not surprisingly, a cash business, and on the street level, it's done ten and twenty dollars at a time. Go back to my opportunity to stand in front of the cabinet full of cash in the warehouse in Switzerland, and you'll see the problem.

Cash is bulky. It takes up space and it's heavy. Serious drug lords don't count their money. They weigh it.

But the problem is, when you've got a literal ton of cash sitting around, it's hard to do anything with it. You want to launder a couple of million dollars over the period of a few years, you can open a strip club, or if you want to go for the laugh, an actual laundromat, or any other cash-heavy business. But when you've got a couple of billion dollars, you need to have your own banks.

I didn't know how the hell you were supposed to wash trillions.

I looked at the box on the table. "Yeah. Fine. Stealing a trillion dollars makes stealing eighty million dollars through SWIFT look like a small-time job."

Greaves put her beer on the table. "You still don't get it. This isn't about stealing money. This thing"—she tapped the ring box with her finger—"isn't just some electronic key."

"Isn't it a cipher?"

She giggled. An honest-to-god, playful, amused giggle. "Duke, what on earth do you think a cipher is?"

I started to answer and then stopped. I'd been working under the assumption that the box contained some sort of code breaker.

"You know I'm not with the FBI. I'm not with the CIA either. If this was only about spying, I'd let them play their little games." She stood up, picked up her beer, and finished it.

I stared at her. "Greaves, who the hell do you work for? It's not the FBI, and it's evidently not the CIA or DHS or any other alphabet soup agency. So who is it?"

She reached over, picked up my can, and gave it an exploratory shake. "I'm getting another beer. You want one?"

"I want you to answer the question."

"I work for the United States of America."

"That's not an answer."

She sighed. "Do you know what it means when I say that I'm category one Yankee White?"

It took me a second, but then I nodded. "Yankee White" was slang for the background check you had to go through if you were working with the president or the vice president of the United States of America. Category three was for the huddled masses in the president's orbit: soldiers in the military bands who played "Hail, Columbia" or "Hail to the Chief," honor guards, that sort. Category two was for closer contact: the staff at Camp David, DoD personnel assigned to the veep, parts of the White House staff and medical units.

Category one was . . . a category one Yankee White clearance almost certainly meant that Greaves was reporting directly to the president of the United States of America.

"How close are you?"

"Remember when I stepped away to make a phone call at UCLA?" I nodded, and she shrugged. "Who do you think I was talking to? Didn't you wonder how I could promise a full pardon?"

104

"YEAH," I SAID, "I'LL TAKE ANOTHER BEER."

She went inside and I looked out over the city. I could hear a helicopter flying somewhere nearby but didn't have eyes on it. Otherwise, it was peaceful. Quiet. I'd always wanted a house on one of the hills, earthquakes be damned. A place where I could sit out on my porch and watch the city. If I hadn't started gambling, I would have been able to afford one.

I wondered if Greaves owned this place. When she came back out, carrying two beers, I asked her.

"I wish. I think it was an asset forfeiture for some drug thing. I'm just borrowing it. Given what I do, though, it probably wouldn't be that hard to figure out how to steal enough to afford it," she said. "If I was so inclined. Which I'm not. Only one of us is a thief." She handed me one of the cans and then popped the top on her own beer. "Cheers."

We clinked cans.

I said, "Why are you here?"

She looked out at the view and then sighed. "I like Los Angeles. I'm an East Coast girl originally, but I like it out here."

"That's not what I mean."

"I know," she said. "I went to college on a track scholarship. It was only a partial, but it was enough. Do you know what my major was?"

"Criminology?"

"International political economy and business."

"Double major?"

She hesitated. "No. International political economy and business was the full name of my major. The *and* is part of the title."

"That got you a gig working for the president?"

As she put it, during the Cold War, the CIA and Department of Defense were always recruiting people who could speak Russian. Then 9/11 happened. As the Cold War morphed into the War on Terror, the hot recruits were the kids who could speak Arabic. But after the stock market wobbled in 2008 and almost took down the entire world economy, some smart people realized that maybe there were other threats than a couple of psychopaths with an airplane, and there was suddenly a new focus.

Greaves might as well have been made for the job. Her mother had been an analyst for the Company, and her father had been a lawyer who specialized in forensic accounting. With that background, Greaves would already have been catnip for the agency even if she hadn't been a star athlete and a straight-A student. All they had to do was teach her how to fire a gun.

She worked the counterterror beat, spending her time tracking down money and trying to stay a step ahead of the small-cell terror organizations that were hoping to pull off another 9/11.

But then, like she said, the people who realized there were other ways to wage war than with tanks and terror realized she was better suited for more specialized work outside of the normal channels.

"Technically, I work for the Treasury."

"But not exactly."

"Not exactly," she agreed. "I'm kind of a one-man band. With an audience of one. I take care of whatever needs to be done."

Yankee White.

She looked at the cipher. I looked at the cipher. She looked up at me. I said, "What do you mean that this thing breaks the bank? Like it could take down the Fedwire?"

"Only temporarily. Enough time to cause complete chaos."

"What's the point of that, other than chaos for chaos' sake?"

"To tank the markets. Short version is that this cipher wasn't designed to shut down the Fedwire permanently. It can take down *any* financial transfer system, at least for a few days. The code stuff is way beyond what I understand, but it works on the same framework."

"And this thing was in a CIA safe in Germany because . . . ?"

She considered me, and then said, "It was staged there for future use. We were going to deploy it to send a message to the Russians. They've got their own system that's similar to SWIFT, called SPFS. Our president was going to call their president and make it clear that Russia needs to stop meddling in our elections, and then, coincidently, the SPFS would go down for twenty-four hours, or whatever amount of time we wanted. Make their banking system stop working long enough to throw them into a panic. A shot across the bow kind of thing."

We were quiet for a minute. I was working it through in my head. The Snickers bar with the Cyrillic on it. Baker acting like how much he paid me didn't matter, which maybe it didn't, if we were talking the banking systems for entire economies.

Except there was something that didn't square.

"Baker was still promising me he could get my dad out of jail. That doesn't make any sense. If he was hired by the Russians, how could—"

"He wasn't hired by the Russians," Greaves said. "He was hired by *a* Russian. A Russian who can get your dad out of jail. Except, the man who hired him is not really Russian. He's an American."

"I'm not following. I mean, I think I have a handle on what this thing does, but you've lost me. An American who is Russian but who isn't a Russian? If it's a riddle, I'm not getting it. Tell it to me like I'm a moron," I said.

I had to listen to her laugh for quite a while after that comment. I'd set it up on a tee for her.

"Let me ask you a question. Why do you think you were hired in the first place?"

It was, I thought, exactly the question you ask a moron: I'd been hired to break into a safe. An American Castle Galaxy Nine. The kind of safe that was next to impossible to break into. Not impossible, but close.

Turns out I *was* a moron, because Greaves made the game show "wrong answer" sound.

She reminded me that I hadn't been hired to do the *next* to impossible. I'd been hired to do the *impossible*: break into the American Castle Galaxy Nine without anybody ever knowing I was there.

The distinction was important.

If it was *the* Russians rather than *a* Russian, they wouldn't have worried so much about discretion. Sure, you don't really want to tip off the CIA if you can avoid it, but what's the president going to do? Complain to the Russians that they stole a device that we fully intended to use against them?

"It matters because the person who hired you is a private citizen."

She didn't mean Baker. She meant the man who had hired Baker.

The "tell it to me like I'm a moron" version was that when I showed her the picture of Baker and Cleary, she'd recognized the man I'd known as Cleary. Except his name was Grigory Lebedev. But Cleary's real name didn't matter. What mattered was who Cleary worked for: Pyotr Volkov.

She asked me if I knew who Volkov was.

I did.

It was hard not to.

105

PYOTR VOLKOV.

You couldn't live in Los Angeles and not know who he was. He owned a seven-acre estate in Bel-Air valued at somewhere in the neighborhood of $150 million. He was a minority owner in almost every sports franchise in town, and on the board of, well, everything. A few years ago, he'd announced a series of $25 million donations to *forty* different local cultural institutions, a billion dollars in all in the space of one day. Plus, I realized, he was the "rich dude" who Meg said had loaned his collection of Georgia O'Keeffe paintings to the Getty. And that was just what he'd done in LA.

American mother, Russian father. His parents divorced when he was an infant, and his father kept him in Russia. The official story is that Volkov was some sort of a financial wunderkind. He came to the United States for college, but dropped out of USC his freshman year, starting a venture capital firm at nineteen. By twenty-five, he had stakes in nearly a dozen unicorns. By thirty, he was a billionaire many times over, earning himself a spot on those "Power 100" lists that run in magazines like *Fortune*, *Fast Company*, and *Entrepreneur*.

He spent the next decade working his way up the list of richest men in the world, until he was securely in the top fifty. It was at that point when Volkov got interested in politics.

He was a behind-the-scenes player. For a guy with as much money as Volkov, he kept a low profile. In certain circles, he was very well known as a serious art collector with an eye to match his checkbook, but he often turned that same eye and checkbook to politics.

If you were an aspiring politician and landed on Volkov's radar, a *lot* of dark money got funneled toward your campaign. An avalanche of money. And Volkov demanded a return on his investments.

Best estimates were that during the last presidential election, he'd put a billion five in the general fray, and another billion five behind his candidate.

Who was currently the sitting president of the United States of America.

That was all public knowledge. I was sure there were things that weren't part of the public knowledge too.

Volkov was most definitely the kind of guy who could arrange to have my father sprung early if that was what he wanted. When you're a kingmaker, the king tends to be willing to do you favors.

"Yeah," I said. "I know who Volkov is."

Greaves twisted her lips. It made her look both cynical and concerned at the same time. "If you know who Volkov is, then you can see why the situation has become a bit complicated."

106

A *BIT* COMPLICATED? A *bit* complicated was introducing your girl-friend to your ex, or whatever the hell it was I had going on with Meg.

Volkov wasn't a *bit* complicated. This was getting a tow on a surf-board from a Jet Ski into a monster eighty-foot wave. Ride it wrong and you didn't come up again.

107

AS GREAVES EXPLAINED IT, Volkov's involvement put her in an impossible situation.

You can't just accuse one of the richest men in the world—Russian or not, he was also born an American citizen and was one of the biggest political players in the country—of what was, essentially, treason of the highest order. Not without iron-clad proof.

I was sure that all of the money that had gone to fund Baker and his team was perfectly clean. When you were as rich as Volkov, moving money around so it couldn't be traced wasn't that different from breathing. And even though Grigory Lebedev—Cleary—was, as Greaves put it, "a known associate," there wasn't anything to tie Lebedev to the theft.

The only proof Greaves had was a partial picture of my face and my word that I'd been tricked into pulling the job.

She wanted to take Volkov down—the level of influence he had over the president had become a security threat—but she needed more than just an accusation.

"He's dirty, but if you have enough money, you're untouchable," I said.

"Essentially. There have been rumors for years that Volkov might have owed his early start to some of his father's old friends back in Mother Russia, but nothing that can be substantiated. And there have been some suspicious accidents and deaths with his business adversaries, kidnappings, too, real ruthless stuff, but again, everything has enough plausible separation from him that he scans as clean. And he donates enough money—to both sides of the aisle—that nobody has been willing to look too closely."

"I don't get it, though. Why on earth would he do something like this. Sure, it's hard to trace it back to him, but why steal this thing? Why tank the markets?"

"Because he made a bad bet."

Now that was something I was familiar with.

Apparently, Volkov had spent the better part of the last year making bigger and bigger bets against the financial markets. Between his hedge fund and his personal fortune, he'd shorted the market nearly a hundred billion dollars.

I wasn't really the sort of person who followed the stock market. Even when I'd been flush, my money had mostly been in cash and glitzy things, but as Greaves explained it, basically, Volkov had sold stock he didn't own in the belief that the market was going to dip.

"Why?" I asked.

"Why, what?"

"Why'd he think the market was going to dip?"

"How'd the people who shorted the market know back in 2008? I don't know, but his numbers told him the market was going to dip big."

When that happened, he could buy back stock to cover his position and make a killing off the difference. The problem was that the stock market had refused to go down, and that meant Volkov had to keep making bigger and bigger moves to cover his marker.

Or, as I liked to call it, he'd been chasing the bet.

Always a dumb idea. Which was one of the reasons I'd ended up in so much trouble in the first place. The idea being that if you lose five grand on a game, you bet twice as much the next time, so you can get even. But at some point, if you hit a bad streak, you might chase yourself into "too bad about your thumbs" territory.

That's what Volkov had done, except that instead of losing tens of thousands of dollars on baseball and basketball and football, he'd lost tens of billions of dollars on the stock market.

Either way, it was just a bet gone bad.

And then, somehow, he'd heard about the cipher.

"Somehow?"

Greaves considered, and then she said, "Through the Russians. And no, I can't tell you how the Russians found out about it, but I can tell you that they decided to use Volkov to put a layer between them and us. Indirectness is the same as plausible deniability."

And for Volkov, the cipher was an elegant solution to his problems: take down the Fedwire for a couple of days and watch the chaos tank the markets. If you knew when it was coming—and he would, since he'd be the one with the cipher—he could turn a losing bet into maybe the biggest payday of all time. Instead of facing dissolution, Volkov could move himself to the top of the ranks of billionaires.

It was like paying a boxer to take a dive. Except instead of the mob, it was the Dow and the S&P.

And all he had to do to make it happen was trick a down-on-his-luck safecracker into flying to Europe and opening a safe.

"What happens now?" I asked. "I mean, if Volkov doesn't have the cipher, and can't drop the markets, he's screwed, right?"

Greaves stood up. It had cooled down while we were sitting on her deck. It was close to eleven o'clock, and the lights below us had steadily been winking off. "I can't imagine somebody like Volkov is just going to throw in the towel," she said. "Billionaires are like cockroaches. They always survive."

"Billionaires are the worst."

"You have no idea. The shit they get away with. But Volkov is in a different league. There are the normal billionaires, you know, the tech moguls and the hedge fund guys, who are just the regular kind of evil, and then there are the guys like Volkov."

I gave her a tight-lipped smile. "What, like he's some kind of supervillain?"

"No," she said. "But he's more than *just* a psychopath."

108

GREAVES SAID THERE WASN'T ANY hard proof to the story. Nothing actionable, or at least nothing that could be used to prosecute him, but it's clear that it was true. This was early in Volkov's career. When he was "only" worth a couple hundred million dollars.

He'd gone in on some sort of a real estate financing thing. Greaves tried to explain it to me, but it involved exotic financial instruments and tax dodges that I didn't understand, but the short version is that in order for Volkov to make a nearly 300 percent profit and push him into the three-comma club, he had to put everything in the hands of his business partner for a short period of time.

And his business partner, another Russian, somebody who was already a billionaire and who fancied himself a much bigger fish than Volkov, decided he didn't want to give the money back. He told Volkov that he had a large family—eight adult children, some with children of their own—and too many mouths to feed. The deal wasn't, strictly speaking, legal, so who was Volkov going to complain to?

According to Greaves, the Russian holed up in a dacha—a holiday estate—on the Black Sea. He surrounded himself with a private army and started counting his profits. Volkov was a relative weakling at the time, hurting from the financial spanking the Russian had given him. The Russian figured Volkov couldn't touch him if he stayed in his dacha with guards everywhere. But the Russian made the mistake of thinking Volkov would skulk away like a kicked dog. And it was just the Russian in the dacha. His kids and grandchildren were out there living their lives.

About a month after he screwed Volkov, the Russian started getting packages. The first one was a hand. Small. From a child of no more than five or six. One of the Russian's grandchildren. The second package was a foot from one of his daughters. The third package contained the ears of his oldest son.

The Russian was a hard man. Former FSB and no stranger to fighting in the gutters. He wasn't the kind of man to retreat, and now he wanted something more than Volkov's money. He wanted revenge. According to Greaves, the Russian called in his best soldiers for a war council, to look for Volkov's weak spots.

"Except," Greaves said, "Volkov wasn't interested in waiting. While this guy is holed up with his war council, he gets a delivery. Another package, the fourth one from Volkov. But this one was bigger. He opens it up, and there's a note inside from Volkov that says, 'I'd like to introduce you to my wife.'"

"Just a note saying 'I'd like to introduce you to my wife'?"

Greaves actually laughed at me. "Of course not," she said. "There was also a woman's severed head."

I blinked. "What the . . . ?"

"Oh, you have no idea," Greaves said. "It was Volkov's way of telling the Russian that there was nothing he could do to hurt Volkov. That if he thought Volkov had a weak spot, he was wrong. The message was, basically, if Volkov was willing to cut off his own wife's head, well, how far was he willing to go?"

"You're telling me that Volkov sent *his own* wife's head to the Russian as some sort of message?"

"No," Greaves said. "That's the thing that scares me about Volkov. It *wasn't* his wife's head."

"What are you talking about?"

Greaves took a drink of beer. "It's why I said he's more than *just* a psychopath. I mean, sure, if you cut off a kindergartner's hand and send it to a business rival, you're a psychopath. But being a psychopath isn't necessarily some rare exception when it comes to the super rich. You've got to be willing to hurt people with no regard to right and wrong to build and hoard that kind of money. Hell, it's almost a requirement. Off the top of my head, I can think of at least four billionaires, who, if they cut off their spouse's head, I'd be like, 'yeah, figures.' But that's the thing with Volkov. He's never been married."

"That doesn't make any sense. It was his wife's head, wasn't it?"

"He's never had a wife, or a serious girlfriend. Or boyfriend or husband, for that matter. I've put a lot of effort into finding his vulnerabilities, and he doesn't seem interested in sex, let alone romantic relationships, at all."

"But . . . whose head was it?"

Greaves sighed. "We don't know."

"That's . . ."

"Yeah. But the point is that Volkov thinks outside the box." She grimaced. "Sorry. The pun was unintentional." She tapped a finger on her can of beer. "All I meant is what I said: he might be a psychopath, but he's not *just* a psychopath. There's something . . . different about him. Just when I think I've got a handle on him, he zigs when I expect him to zag. The only thing that stays consistent is that he's a scorched-earth kind of guy."

"No kidding."

"Anyway, after that, Volkov's erstwhile partner signed back the money plus a substantial penalty. Then, about eight months later, the Russian's private jet went down."

I said, "And he just got away with it?"

Greaves gave a harsh laugh. "You think billionaires have to play by the same rules as normal people?"

109

SHE WAVED HER HAND AROUND, encompassing the house and the lawn. "I like getting to use a place like this while I'm on the job, but I make a civil service salary. I'm not complaining. I believe in America. I know it sounds cheesy, but I mean it when I say it's a privilege to serve my country. But yeah, it's infuriating to see snakes like him getting away with whatever he wants. I'm sure he paid less in taxes in the last decade than I paid last year. Your dad's in jail for making a careless error while trying to steal something, but the only difference between most billionaires and your dad is the scale."

"Don't compare my dad to a monster like that," I said.

She stared at me evenly. "No? Fine," she said, "but trust me when I say that even without being a psychopath, Volkov deserves to be in jail."

"So arrest him."

"Get real, Duke. For what? Unless Volkov is literally holding the cipher, there isn't any way he's going to take heat. If it's in his possession, that's a different story. But anything short of that, there's nothing we can do. He's not stupid. He keeps everything at arm's length. He uses cutouts and brokers and hasn't gotten his own hands dirty in a very long time. He was untouchable even before he started dumping money into politics, but now, I'm under direct orders to leave him alone unless I am a hundred percent sure—and I mean a hundred percent sure—we can grab him with the cipher in a place where only he could have access to it. It pisses me off, but that's the way of the world."

I finished my last sip of beer. I said, "What, now I screwed up by not just handing over the cipher to Baker? Now you *want* Volkov to have it? Why don't you just hand it over, and *then* you can arrest him. Are you playing some kind of game?"

"Of course I'm playing a game, Duke. Obviously, I can't give Volkov the cipher. He'll smell a trap. He's not going to stand there with it and wait for the FBI to close in. Besides which, like I said, I'm under direct orders not to go after him."

"He just gets to walk?" I was furious. I was thinking about Paulie lying in the hospital.

"You don't get it, Duke. He's not just some random rich dude. He basically bought the last election. And he'll buy the next election too. Nailing him holding the cipher puts him on a leash, not in a prison cell."

I folded my arms in annoyance. "Better than nothing."

"We agree."

"We?"

"You're not listening. *I'm* under direct orders. Unless I can be a hundred percent sure the cipher is in a place where the only person who could have had access is Volkov, *I* can't do anything. But like I said this afternoon, if *you* want to get what's owed, *you've* got a job to do. And midnight approaches. In or out?"

I looked up at Greaves. She was staring down at me with an expectant look on her face, waiting for me to figure it out.

Oh. Crud.

"When does it have to be done?" I said.

"Tonight. Hence the midnight deadline. He's on his yacht. Anchor's up in the morning and once they're in international waters, there isn't a lot we can do."

"Tonight? You have got to be kidding me."

She walked over to the patio door and opened it up. "Time to choose, Duke. Play ball or *be* the ball."

TOTAL DENIABILITY.

Greaves was clear about that.

My father was a convicted thief, and even though I had a clean sheet, I was a suspect in more than a dozen high-profile heists around the globe. If I got caught, I was going to get thrown to the wolves. Complete disavowal. Greaves needed Volkov taken down, but the United States government was going to have no knowledge of my activities, would offer no official support. I was officially disposable.

Unofficially, of course, the deal was the deal: a pardon for my dad, Ginny's bills paid, Paulie going scot-free, and a payday for me. No matter what happened, my family would benefit, but I was only going to get to spend that money if I was still alive at the end of this.

Because, after the story Greaves told me, I was under no illusion what was going to happen to me if Volkov's men found me in the middle of trying to plant the cipher somewhere that only Volkov could have put it. At least if it was just a random gun for hire, I'd probably take a quick bullet. If it was Cleary who caught me, I was pretty sure he'd take his time to pay me back for the stun gun episode in Switzerland. Plus, the whole thing where I stomped on his nuts.

I was going to have to trust Greaves that she'd follow through on her end, one way or another, no matter what happened. And I did trust her: I'd taken my pistol and picks but left the bag and my forty thousand dollars with her. I trusted her as much as you can ever trust anybody holding her position.

Not like I had a choice.

CALLING IT A YACHT was like calling Michael Jordan a basketball player. I didn't know how you defined a yacht versus a superyacht versus a megayacht, but the way I looked at it, if your boat had a helipad, it was in big-boy territory.

Proper blueprints would have been nice, but Greaves had given me the brief: one hundred and ten meters long, or slightly longer than a football field. It had fourteen staterooms, a pool, a gym, a sauna, and yeah, a helipad. Custom designed for Volkov with a price tag reportedly in the three hundred million range. It was sleek and almost futuristic looking. The sort of thing owned by the bad guy in a James Bond movie.

Even when a job was dialed in tight, things could still go wrong; I wasn't thrilled to be going in blind on an hour's notice.

Normally, a job like this would take months of planning. I'd pull together a crew, even if it was a small crew, get blueprints, work on getting somebody on the inside. I'd have the entire boat wired front to back. Or, rather, bow to stern. I'd know the schematics of the security system and have a count on the armed guards.

From the beach, the boat looked like a floating palace. It was lit up, and I could hear the thump, thump, thump of dance music drifting across the water. It was anchored several hundred feet offshore, but I could see figures moving on the deck. Volkov was throwing himself a going-away party.

It was a shame that Greaves had to work—through me—in the shadows, because, in my opinion, this was exactly the kind of situation where modern warfare worked to your favor. A couple of Seahawk helicopters, a barrage of Hellfire missiles, and this could all be taken care of lickety-split. Though there'd be a heck of a lot of civilians—maybe some of the guests deserved it, but the crew was full of working stiffs—getting blown up for something that wasn't their fault.

Oh well. Work with what you have.

At least where I was standing, it was dark. I was blessed with a quarter moon and a cloudy sky. Unfortunately, there was a solid swell in the water. Good for an amateur surfer like me, with waves coming in at maybe two or three feet, but flat water would have been easier for swimming.

I stripped naked and added my clothes and shoes to the drybag Greaves had provided. At least she'd given me that much. But other than that, I was on my own.

Like she'd said, total deniability.

I swore as I headed into the water. What had been pleasantly cool in the morning sun was plain old cold at one o'clock in the morning. I looped my arm through the clip of the drybag and started a slow, gentle breaststroke, keeping my head above the waves so I could track my progress.

I wasn't in a hurry. It was more important to stay quiet and stay unnoticed than to move quickly. I figured Volkov's security detail was probably on high alert. It had been more than twenty-four hours since I'd taken out Baker and the two others. Maybe their boss was partying, but they were being paid to keep an eye out. Plus, it wouldn't surprise me if some of Volkov's party guests traveled with their own security. Rich people sure liked their bodyguards.

As I got closer, I had to swim past a few smaller boats anchored near Volkov's. Smaller being relative. They were big enough that they rolled gently in the waves instead of bouncing up and down.

I was still about a hundred feet out, creeping along, when a box of light outlined itself on the side of the yacht. It quickly went from an outline to an entire square. I realized it was, essentially, a garage—a storage space built into the yacht where Volkov could store toys and keep the boat he used to shuttle from shore to the yacht and back. It was hard to get a sense of scale, but it was a huge door, and the speedboat that came puttering out was probably thirty feet long.

Freakin' billionaires. A boat with a boat inside it.

The speedboat moved away from me at a forty-five-degree angle. I couldn't get a good look at it, but it seemed to only be carrying a couple of passengers. I watched it head toward one of the anchored boats nearby and figured it was just some partygoers calling it a night.

But the garage door stayed open, nice and inviting.

112

I APPROACHED THE OPENING in the side of the yacht cautiously. It was lit up inside. I expected there to be somebody on duty, maybe even an armed guard, and I wasn't sure what I'd do if that was the case. I was winging it, but my original plan had been to try to climb up somewhere unseen.

This seemed a whole lot easier. Except that as I got closer, it was clear that there was nobody inside the garage.

Maybe that was why it was still open? The speedboat that just left was probably making a quick round trip. I had a hunch that the pilot of the speedboat didn't have a clicker attached to the sun visor like he was driving a minivan and Volkov's megayacht was a suburban house with an attached garage. Which meant that if I wanted to use this as a way to get in, I had to hustle.

The inside of the garage was roughly the same size as, well, a deep four-car garage. There was an empty spot that the speedboat had just vacated, and then many playthings: four Jet Skis, an inflatable water trampoline, water skis, wakeboards, a couple of paddleboards, you name it. It was basically a giant toy chest.

I pulled myself out of the water and helped myself to one of the neatly stacked and folded white towels on a chrome rack that was next to a wicker basket with a few used towels inside.

Even though I was in a hurry, I took a second to appreciate how soft and plush the towel was. How much did a towel like this cost?

Then, realizing I was standing in the middle of a well-lit space wearing nothing but my altogethers, I got dressed. Once that was done, there were only five things left in the drybag: the cipher, still inside the ring box, which Greaves had let me take with a wink and a nod, a burner phone, a grand in cash rolled up and secured with a rubber band, my lockpicks, and my pistol. I had not bothered telling Greaves I had a pistol on my person. I wasn't planning on using it. The whole point of what I was doing was to get in and get out unnoticed and then call the calvary in the form of Greaves and the FBI. But that didn't mean I was willing to go into the lion's den unarmed.

I clipped the holster against the small of my back, where my shirt covered it, and stuffed the ring box in one pocket, the picks, phone, and cash in the other.

There was a map and directory on the wall near the towels. It made me want to laugh. Greaves's briefing had given me a reasonable sense of the layout, but Volkov's ship was large enough that you could get lost in it without a map. I oriented myself and memorized the map. It wasn't as detailed as I would have liked, but it had "guest quarters," "crew," and mechanicals marked. More importantly, it had two "private" areas, one floor above the other, neatly delineated. Promising.

I snuck a peek out the door of the boat garage and thought I spied the speedboat on its way back. Time to move.

I lifted up some of the dirty towels in the wicker basket and shoved the drybag underneath, then dropped my used towel on top.

I opened the door and almost stepped directly into a bulky young man wearing a black suit. He had a corded earpiece and even though his suit coat was well cut, I could see the telltale bulge of a gun in a shoulder holster. He had a stone-faced look and didn't speak.

"Well," I said, mustering up all the impatience and entitlement I could into my voice. "Are you going to help me get back to my stateroom or are you just going to stand there being useless?"

113

MUCH TO MY DELIGHT, IT WORKED.

He stammered an apology and then led me up a set of stairs and turned down a long corridor full of closed doors. I noticed that there was another copy of the map and directory for the yacht hung on the wall. Not essential, but helpful.

I doubled down on my attitude. "Oh, for God's sake. I can take it from here."

The guard hesitated, and then said, "I can take you to your room, sir. It's not a problem."

I tried to remember every time I'd seen a rich person be an asshole and funnel it into the next thing I said: "I've got it. Now piss off."

He left in a hurry.

Which left me standing in the middle of a long corridor full of closed doors.

Time to earn that five hundred grand Greaves had promised me.

I decided I needed some better camouflage than a bad attitude, so I pulled my lockpicks out and got to work. The yacht might have been a state-of-the-art billionaire's playground, but a drunk armadillo could have picked the locks on the staterooms. I barely breathed on the door before it opened. There was a two-thirds empty champagne bottle among the detritus of room service, and I grabbed it, figuring the guard I'd run into wouldn't be the only one.

I needed to find Volkov's office.

That was the deal. I had to put the cipher somewhere that made it impossible for Volkov to claim innocence. I couldn't just dump it in some poor guest's stateroom and call it a day. Greaves had wanted me to put it inside Volkov's personal stateroom, but I convinced her that his office was the better bet. I told Greaves that Volkov would almost certainly have a safe in his office, and it would almost certainly be one that only he had access to. I'd open the safe, put the cipher back in, lock the safe back up, and ghost. No worries about a maid stumbling across it or one of his guards finding it before Greaves had a chance to raid the yacht with the FBI in . . .

I looked at my watch. In about four hours.

I planned to be long gone before then.

I stepped out of the room, and as soon as I closed the door behind me, a man and woman entered the hall. The man was in his early thirties, wearing shorts, flip-flops, and a T-shirt. He was also wearing what I recognized as a Patek Philippe watch. Frankly, I thought my Dan Henry Diver watch looked better than what was on this chump's wrist, but my watch was also roughly eighty grand cheaper than his, so what did I know?

He had a big, dumb, goofy grin on his face, and walked with the loping stagger and enthusiasm of somebody who was drunk. Or, I thought, noticing the slight hint of white on his nostrils, a man who was coked out of his mind.

I hoisted the champagne bottle and said, "Who needs a glass?"

The man barely acknowledged me. His attention was on his companion: she was nineteen, twenty tops, and surgically enhanced in all the places that would make the guy she was walking with keep grinning for the rest of the night. I had very little question that she was in it for the money, but I also didn't care. It meant she was all business, and neither one of them seemed interested in what I was doing.

As they passed, I thought about the guy's outfit.

No wonder they hadn't given me a second look and the guard hadn't twigged. There had been a part of me that worried that, given the way the yacht looked, the party would be full of swanky men in tuxedos and women in ball gowns, but I'd forgotten the democratizing effect of the way internet billionaires dressed. The more money you had, the less you had to try. In my outfit, I almost looked formal.

The couple—or, rather, the rich guy and the escort—disappeared into a room three doors down.

I walked to the end of the corridor and headed up a flight of stairs.

114

THE STAIRS TOOK ME UP to a small, split corridor.

To the left, it was an open run. I could hear the thump of the music drifting from that direction, though there was nobody in sight. The room to my right was the first of the two areas marked "private" on the map. The other was directly below, but I'd had easier access to this one from the guest quarters.

I tried the handle to the frosted glass door.

Locked.

Fifteen seconds later, it wasn't.

It opened into a large living room with a two-story ceiling and a funky, modern chandelier. There were two matched, mirror-image couches, rolling like question marks that were about to mate. They didn't look particularly comfortable to sit on, and both were pure white. Neither one seemed as if it had ever been used. Either that, or his cleaning crew had bought out the stain remover at the local grocery store.

But at the back of the room, there was a heavy wooden door. It was the first door I'd seen that had what looked like a real lock on it. I was pretty sure I'd hit pay dirt: as far as I was concerned, the lock practically screamed "this room is important!"

Not that it took me very long to pick the lock.

Bingo. I'd found Volkov's office.

115

COMPARED TO ALMOST EVERYTHING ELSE on the boat, the office was modest. Which meant that it was still big enough to have a work area and a sitting area. Alas, there was no giant safe sitting out in the open.

In the work area, he had a wooden desk that was a single, smooth unbroken plank of gorgeous whirls and perfect shine. It was a type of wood I'd never seen before. Probably something exotic. Certainly expensive. It was about the size of a Ping-Pong table, and aside from a closed laptop, didn't have anything on it. The office chair was one of those aluminum Eames jobs that go for two or three grand, and for a moment I entertained the idea of trying to steal it. But only for a moment. On the "guest" side of the desk, he had a pair of equally expensive-looking side chairs.

First things first. I checked the desk. There were two drawers, both locked. Single pin locks that you could open with a paper clip if you didn't happen to have a full set of lockpicks and a lifetime of experience. But they were disappointments. One drawer held a few pens, a pocketknife, and a pair of headphones. There was also a six-by-nine kraft paper envelope with a button and string closure.

I unwound the string on the envelope and tipped the contents into my hand. Blackmail material: a thin stack of pornographic photographs, featuring a fat man on a tarp with two women who were . . . I had the immediate urge to wash my hands. I went to put the pictures back. And then I stopped and looked at the face of the man, and then looked at the rest of the pictures and had a better understanding of the lengths Volkov was willing to go to keep the president of the United States under his thumb beside simply pouring multiple billions into the election. No wonder Greaves wanted Volkov on a leash.

I considered filching the pictures, but I doubted they were the only copies. Better not to do anything that might alert Volkov to an intruder before Greaves sent in the uniforms. I put them back in the envelope, retied the string, replaced it in the drawer, and then wiped my hands on my pants.

The other drawer was empty except for a binder with blueprints of the interior layout of the yacht. Between Greaves's briefing and the directory on the walls, I'd been making my way, but this was better.

The seating area section of the office had an overstuffed leather couch and a pair of matching lounge chairs with ottomans. There was no rug, though, so that ruled out a floor safe. I suppose I could have just stuffed the cipher in the couch cushions and then jumped out the window, but I was pretty sure that wasn't what Greaves had in mind.

That left the obvious thing: the safe would be behind one of the paintings on the walls.

I started with the painting behind the desk. It was a decently sized oil painting, maybe forty inches by thirty inches. Big enough to hide a safe behind. I reached out, and then I stopped. It was a landscape. A sunset over water, with frenzied brushstrokes that had a familiar look. There was a signature in the bottom left corner.

Hot shit. It was a Renoir. I'd forgotten that Volkov not only appreciated art, but he could also afford to buy what he wanted.

I moved my hand back to the corner of the painting, and then hesitated again. Even if it wasn't one of Renoir's more famous pieces, a real Renoir was worth serious money. Which meant it might have an alarm.

I USED THE LIGHT ON MY BURNER PHONE to look carefully at the sides of the frame of the painting. It wasn't hanging free; there was a hinge. Which meant there was a safe behind it.

I spent several minutes examining the Renoir, running a few diagnostics with an app on my phone. If I'd had time to plan and my whole toolkit with me, I could handle anything, but I didn't have that luxury. I had to improvise.

Finally, after I had checked every way I could with limited resources, I sighed. Good enough. As near as I could tell, it didn't have an alarm. I reached out and swung the painting out from the wall.

A safe. With an optical handprint scanner as the only access.

There were fifty ways I could think of to get in a safe with an optical handprint scanner, but all of them required more than my good looks, a set of lockpicks, and a roll of twenty-dollar bills. I was utterly and completely screwed. I couldn't open that safe in the timeframe Greaves needed me to. The safe had no keypad, no dial, no way to open it unless I had Volkov's hand.

Or, I realized, examining the optical scanner more closely, a picture of his hand. If I could get a clear shot of Volkov's palm with the burner cell phone I was carrying, and then, with photo editing software I could download for less than five dollars, if I manipulated it right, I could just hold the phone up to the optical reader.

Holy crow. Make that fifty-one ways to get into that safe. I turned back to the desk and pulled out the binder with the blueprints.

FULL-SIZED ARCHITECTURAL DRAWINGS would have been nice, but the binder contained a fold-out overall plan for the full yacht, as well as floor plans, section plans, and room plans, complete with elevations. Those ran close to a hundred pages, with another three hundred pages of schematics and details. Fortunately, the binder was well organized, and because of Greaves's briefing and the maps and directory I'd already seen, I was able to work through it quickly and find Volkov's bedroom suite. As I'd assumed, it was in the other area marked "private," directly below the office I was sitting in.

The paper in the binder was US-letter-sized, even though all the work was in metric. The drawings for the bedroom suite were on a 1:100 scale, which meant that every centimeter represented one meter in real life. The suite was enormous, both grand and simple at the same time: a sleeping area, a walk-in closet, a bathroom, and a fourth room designated as "the lounge." The sleeping area was drawn with a king-sized bed, a full sitting area, and a small breakfast nook. One end of the bedroom connected to the attached full bath and walk-in closet. The other side of the bedroom connected to the lounge, which was another private sitting and dining area for Volkov or whomever his companion was for the night.

For some reason, the only way to access the bedroom was through the lounge, but that didn't seem like a huge obstacle.

If I could get into the bedroom and hide in the closet until he came back and went to sleep, I might just be able to sneak the picture of his hand, get back to the office, open the safe, stash the cipher, and collect my reward.

But there was a problem: the security office was across the hall from Volkov's suite. If he called for help, it was going to get there quick. Equally important, it meant trying to simply bluff my way into Volkov's suite was going to be a problem. It was one thing to convince a security guard that I needed a refill on champagne while I was wandering around public areas, but it was an entirely different level of stupidity to try to convince a guard that Volkov was expecting a late-night bedroom visit from me.

Continuing my path of bluffing my way through the hallways seemed . . . unwise.

I flipped through the schematics until I got to the mechanical systems, hoping I'd find alternative access, when I stopped. There was something niggling at me, but I couldn't figure out what it was. Something I'd just flipped past and ignored.

Carefully, I worked backward, page by page, until I saw it.

His bedroom was also a saferoom.

The bedroom was a box made of thick steel. The floor was made with the same material as most of the rest of the interior of the boat—as far as I could tell, fiberglass—but the walls and ceiling were reinforced steel, with a door to match. A punch of the "panic" button and the door was locked from the inside with no external access to the locking mechanism. Sure, I could get in with a thermal lance or some high explosives, but once it was locked, there was no way I was opening it without making a ridiculous ruckus. Even the windows were made of ballistic glass thick enough to stop anything short of a rocket launcher, and even then, I wasn't sure if a bazooka could punch through. I could probably cut my way in from below, but there were crew quarters underneath Volkov's suite, so even if I did have access to a drill or grinder and a reciprocating saw, it wasn't likely that I'd go unnoticed.

I did *not* want Volkov ensconced in his bedroom without me, because once he was locked in there, I wasn't getting in quietly.

Cool, cool.

All I had to do, then, was figure out how to get into his bedroom without passing the security office directly across the hall, and then get into his bedroom and hide, get a photo of his hand, and then leave and make my way back up to the office without anybody noticing. Anything's possible, right?

I put down the binder and thought for a second. And then I looked again at the layout of the boat to make sure before heading outside onto the office's terrace. I stepped up on the lower rail so I could lean over and look down.

As the plans had indicated, directly below, there was a matching terrace off the lounge area of Volkov's suite.

When I'd opened the Galaxy Nine in Berlin, I'd hummed a few bars of "Ode to Joy." Like I said, it has been every safecracker's anthem since *Die Hard* was released. But as much as I'd been on the side of Hans Gruber in that movie, at this exact second I was thinking John McClane: yippee ki-yay.

Time to saddle up and play the cowboy.

118

I WOULD HAVE LET GREAVES keep a hundred grand of the five hundred she'd promised in exchange for a calm ocean. The waves had picked up a little, and even with the size of Volkov's yacht, which I was sure had stabilizers, I could feel a slight roll.

The terrace off the office was about two feet deep. It was designed more as an extension of the room than as its own space.

The waves hit with a gentle rhythm, but above them, there was still music coming off the upper deck, and here and there I could hear the peals of laughter and the general sound of merriment. Judging by the guy with the white-tinged nose I'd come across earlier, it was some sort of party.

Light spilled out into the night, but as far as I could tell, Volkov's suite was dark below me.

I climbed over the railing, turned myself around, and then gently lowered myself. I swung for a few seconds, kicking into space, hanging there and thinking I'd just screwed myself, when I felt my toe come in contact with the railing off Volkov's balcony.

It was precarious at best.

I was going to have to gamble, but all I could think about was a football doinking off the field goalpost. Was this going to be one of those kinds of gambles?

I waited for the boat to roll out with the waves, and then, as it rolled back in, I let go.

You know the old saying about win some, lose some?

This was a win-some kind of day.

I landed as lightly as I could. Even with the sound of the party covering my movements, it didn't hurt to be careful. I figured Volkov was probably still upstairs playing the gracious host, but it would be just my luck to get lucky on the balcony and unlucky in terms of having a guard on duty in the lounge outside his bedroom.

Once I was settled, I was pleased to see that the doors to the lounge were already open. I didn't even have to fuss around with trying to unlock them or jimmy them open. It was as if Volkov had rolled out the welcome mat.

I took a step inside. There was nobody waiting.

The lounge was dark except for a dim lamp in the corner that cast as much shadow as light. There was a couch, a coffee table, and a pair of Eames loungers with ottomans. A pair of what I assumed were authentic Gauguin paintings hung on the wall by the lamp, but I wasn't here for the art. I was here for Volkov.

The door to the bedroom was closed. It either had a tight seal that didn't leak light, or it was also dark. Maybe I'd get lucky and find Volkov already inside, sleeping. Then all I'd have to do is take a picture of his hand and . . . well, I'd work out the rest once I had the picture. How hard could it be?

The thought made me want to laugh, except I didn't laugh, because as I was about to head into his bedroom, I noticed another piece of art hanging on the wall of Volkov's lounge.

IT WAS A SMALL PAINTING. Modest. There was nothing extravagant about it, except that it was, unquestionably, exceptionally beautiful. It was an oil painting. A portrait. A young girl from the 1880s, a dancer, with her back to the viewer, her head turned a quarter turn, just enough to get a glimpse of her profile. I didn't have to look for the signature to know it was a Degas. And I didn't need a little museum card to tell me the title of the painting: *Fille sur le point de danser.* Or, in English, *Girl About to Dance.*

I knew the painting because it was the one Ginny and I had stolen together in Paris.

And then they'd thrown her off the balcony and shot me in the chest.

EVERYTHING ABOUT THE DEGAS JOB had been elegant, right up until the end. Meticulously planned and executed. Ginny thought of everything that could go wrong, and then, on the day we pulled it, nothing did go wrong. It was the closest thing to a perfect heist that I'd ever been involved with.

Except, the one thing that Ginny hadn't planned on—not that I saw it coming either—was the person who hired us deciding that once the painting was out of our hands, it was cheaper to kill us than to pay us.

I could still hear the sound of her body landing on the van parked in the street below.

I'd spent the better part of the last two years trying to atone for that. But I'd never been able to find out who had commissioned the job in the first place. Who had decided not to pay up for the painting we'd acquired for them. I'd never been able to figure out who had made the decision that ended up with my dad in prison, my sister— perhaps permanently—in a coma, and me on the warpath.

I'd killed the driver and the crew working my way up the string, and I'd tracked down the man who'd shot me, but then I'd hit a dead end when he'd suffocated. I hadn't given up looking, but until Aunt Paulie gave me the envelope with Ginny's name on it, I wasn't sure what the next step was or how to find Janus.

Now I knew how to find Janus.

But even Aunt Paulie hadn't been able to come up with the only other name that truly mattered: the person who got Janus to set the job up in the first place. I wondered how long she'd been holding on to the lead about Janus. She must have known that once I had it, I would work through anybody in my way, grinding through bodies until they gave me Janus, and then working Janus until he gave me the person who had hired us, who had sold us out. It was the only way to make things right.

No, that wasn't really true. I'd never be able to make things right. But that didn't mean I was willing to just let it go. I understood why Paulie hadn't just given the information to me earlier; revenge isn't healthy. I'd gone after the men I could find on my own, and what I'd done to them would always be part of me, a permanent darkness on my soul. Paulie knew that, and I think as much as she loved Ginny and wanted revenge herself, she'd been trying to protect me too.

But maybe she'd finally realized that it was way too late to protect me, that my entire life had led me to this, and that the only chance I'd have at finding anything close to peace was to wipe the slate clean.

Sometimes the only thing that cleans is blood.

And here it was, right in front of me. The painting was unmistakable. It was ethereal and muscular at the same time. The girl was bold and full of life, hovering in the indefinable space between poise and action.

I could understand why Volkov had wanted it.

I wondered if he had seen it and just believed that it was something that should belong to him. If the previous owner had made the mistake of showing it to him, and Volkov had decided that he would simply take it. People like Volkov lived their lives thinking that they deserved everything. People like Volkov thought they could take anything they wanted.

I doubted he ever spent a minute thinking about what he'd taken away from me.

I doubted he ever spent a minute thinking the debt would come due.

121

MY WHOLE BODY FELT LIKE IT WAS VIBRATING.

I had to catch my breath.

I bent over, with my hands on my knees, shaking, gasping.

And I knew.

I knew what I was going to do.

Greaves might have wanted Volkov on a leash, but I didn't care what she wanted anymore.

If Volkov was sleeping, I was going to shoot him in the head. And if he was awake, I was going to shoot him in the head. And if he wasn't in his bedroom, I was going to wait inside, and when he came in, I was going to shoot him in the head.

Not a particularly complicated plan, but I didn't care. I was going to end him.

Greaves had given me marching orders, but I knew the truth: she wanted Volkov gone, and on a leash or dead, either way the job would be done. She had to play by certain rules—as bent as they were—but I was under no such constraints. Which was the entire reason she'd been willing to make a deal with me. I was a known criminal. Whatever I did was extracurricular and completely deniable. Greaves needed Volkov neutralized, and a federal raid uncovering the cipher in his personal safe was one way to accomplish that end, but she was going to have to accept that a bullet bouncing around Volkov's brainpan was also a win.

I was thinking about revenge, staring at the door from the lounge into Volkov's bedroom, getting myself ready for action, when I felt something move behind me.

Maybe it was the push of air of the door to the lounge opening from the hallway, or maybe I heard something almost imperceptible, but either way, I spun, just in time to see the person who had come into the lounge close the door behind him. He turned to face me, and we saw each other at the same time.

I was just as surprised as he was.

It was Cleary.

122

NEITHER ONE OF US HESITATED.

He reached for the pistol in his shoulder holster as I sprinted across the room. I barreled into him, catching him in the chest with my shoulder.

We tumbled over one of the Eames chairs. His pistol flew out of his hand and skittered under the couch, out of reach. Cleary didn't even try to go for it: instead, he caught me with a hard elbow in my thigh that made me grunt.

I kicked out, trying to create space, and I caught him just above his ear with the edge of my foot. It was glancing, but it gave me a chance to roll sideways and avoid another one of his brutal elbows.

Cleary popped to his feet a half second before I did. He snaked his hand into a pocket as I reached behind me.

I got my fingers on the Kimber Micro in the holster against the small of my back. As I touched the pistol's rosewood handle, Cleary pulled his hand from his pocket. He was holding a knife. He snapped it open with a quick flick, revealing a wicked five-inch blade.

He leapt over the coffee table as I cleared my holster. Cleary gave a broad swipe with his blade. I blocked it with my free arm and felt an icy tug at my forearm as Cleary's blade sliced through the flesh.

At the same time, I tried to get the pistol on him, but Cleary caught the wrist of my gun hand. He brought the knife back, trying to take another swipe, but I managed to catch *his* wrist.

We were locked like that, grunting, pushing, stumbling. Both of us in a desperate dance, trying to stop the other from bringing our weapons to bear.

As we turn and spun, I caught my heel on the corner of the rug at the exact instant Cleary tried to throw a headbutt into my face. As I stumbled, his forehead smashed into my shoulder. He must have hit a nerve, because a sharp, lightning sting surged through my arm, and I lost the pistol.

The Kimber Micro hit the rug, bounced, and stopped at my feet. My other hand was slippery from the blood leaking out of the cut Cleary had opened, and I wasn't sure how much longer I could keep a grip on his wrist. I had to make a move.

Even though going for the gun would have meant letting go of the knife—a quick way to kill myself—I feinted as if I was ducking.

Cleary sent a brutal knee. If I'd actually been going for the gun, it would have caught me in the head, either knocking me out cold, or, at the very least, slowing me down enough so he could finish me off.

Instead, I twisted my free hand under the crook of his knee and lifted.

I tipped him back and then plowed into him. The two of us crashed down through the coffee table, wood splintering and cracking. As we landed, I whipped two quick crosses into his jaw with my free hand before he got his arm up to block me.

And then Cleary stopped trying to block me and started grasping above his head, under the couch, where his pistol was within reach.

I rolled and pulled—still clutching tightly to the wrist holding the knife—so I could pull him away from the pistol.

And in doing so, I was suddenly within distance of my own gun.

But now, Cleary was on top of me. I still had a grip on his wrist, but he was bearing down. And then he clamped down on my throat with his other hand.

I strained toward the Kimber. My fingers barely skimmed the edge of the stainless-steel pistol's handle.

I could hear my breath cut out raggedly. Cleary could hear it as well. He smiled down at me, opened his mouth to speak, and—

And I bucked, just enough to shift his weight and move the inch I needed.

I wrapped my hand around the pistol.

In one quick motion, I shot Cleary in the chest.

Three times. Point-blank range.

I rolled him off me, and in the echoing silence that followed the bang, bang, bang of the gunshots, I heard another sound that made my heart sink: the thunk of a bolt being thrown.

Volkov was inside his bedroom.

And at the sound of gunshots, he'd hit the panic button.

He was locked in.

123

I KNEW I HAD SECONDS, AT MOST.

Not enough time to enjoy the fact that I'd killed a man who was very much an asshole and deserved each of those three bullets.

Maybe Volkov's bedroom was soundproofed enough that he hadn't heard me and Cleary fighting, but gunshots were hard to ignore. With one push of a button, Volkov was now locked inside an impenetrable saferoom.

And with the security office across the hall—I had to assume at least four armed guards on the ship, and maybe as many as ten—it seemed very likely that I was going to be swarmed by well-trained men with guns in short order.

Which meant the only thing I could do was to act before they did.

I climbed to my feet, a bit more unsteady than I would have liked, and hustled to the door, opening it, and sliding out into the hallway just as the door to the security office opened.

The man who opened it was carrying a short-barreled shotgun designed for close-quarters combat. Ideal for a boat, with tight corridors and sharp corners. But not very helpful when pointed at the ground at the same time you come face-to-face with somebody pointing a pistol at, well, your face.

He froze, and then carefully dropped the shotgun to the ground and raised his hands, which was what I was hoping for. I reached inside his jacket and removed his pistol. My hand was covered in blood, either mine or Cleary's, I wasn't sure.

"Go," I said, nodding at the office behind him. "In the chair. Keep your hands up."

I used my foot to nudge the shotgun all the way inside the security office, closed the door, and locked it, all without taking my eyes off him. He was wearing a suit, and had a corded earpiece, same as the other guards I'd encountered, but he also had a pair of cuffs in a leather holder attached to his waistband.

"Take out the cuffs," I said, "and cuff yourself to the counter there. I'm not here for you."

He didn't move.

"Do it now," I said, "or I'm going to shoot you."

"I heard three gunshots," he said in Russian-accented English. "Who is dead?"

"Look," I said, "I don't want to shoot you. But I will."

He stood straight, no trace of fear in his voice. I aimed the pistol at his leg. He didn't even flinch.

"Who did you kill?" he asked.

"The cuffs."

"Who did you kill?" he said again. "One of mine?"

"I knew him as Cleary," I said.

His face stayed blank, then he said, "Describe him."

I did, and after a few seconds, something shifted in him, a sort of loosening, and he nodded. "All right," he said. He sat down in the chair and then cuffed himself to one of the table supports like I'd asked.

As he worked the cuffs, I noticed something on the inside of his wrist, a quarter-sized tattoo peeking out from under the sleeve of his dress shirt. The head of a wolf surrounded by four angled lines. He shuffled his sleeve down hurriedly, like it was something I shouldn't have seen. There was something familiar about it that I couldn't quite place.

The whole thing, from when I finished off Cleary the way he so richly deserved, to having this man cuffed in the security office, took maybe a minute.

Which was still too long.

With the man cuffed, I was able to take my eyes off him long enough to look around the room. There wasn't much to it. A desk, a couple of chairs, and what I assumed was a weapons locker. It was small, as befitting a group of people who didn't normally get the kind of respect they deserved. There was a single video monitor, split into eight boxes, all showing the exterior of the boat. It didn't seem to be cycling through to show any other views.

"No cameras inside the boat," I said. "Why aren't there any inside?"

He considered and must have decided that talking was a good way to stall for time until one of his compatriots came to rescue him, because he said, "What happens on the ship stays on the ship."

Which made a kind of sense. Rich people like their privacy.

He continued, nodding at the monitor. "The exterior view is insurance. If somebody gets on board who isn't supposed to," he said, glaring at me, "we deal with them."

"Fair enough," I said. I looked at the corded earpiece. "Is everybody wearing earpieces? I mean the security team."

"Why?"

"Because I want to make sure nobody gets hurt who doesn't have to."

He scoffed. "Yes. All of *my* men have earpieces."

All *his* men? Something about the way he stepped on the word made me think. Because Cleary wasn't wearing an earpiece, that meant he wasn't one of *his* men. As soon as he realized that's who I'd shot, he suddenly became compliant, as if his team was more important to him than the job itself. And then there was the tattoo, the one he hadn't wanted me to see.

"Secure frequency?" I asked.

"Yes."

I nodded. "What's your name?"

"Konstantin." He enunciated.

"I'm going to reach inside your jacket and pull out your radio."

I did so, unplugged the cord to his earpiece, and then thumbed the mic. "Listen up," I said. "This is your uninvited guest. I've got Konstantin here cuffed and at gunpoint. Konstantin, tell them that you're unharmed." I held out the radio in front of Konstantin's face.

He gave me a withering glance. "I am unharmed."

I pulled the radio back and said, "I assume we'd all like to *keep* Konstantin unharmed, so I'm going to ask you to just hold off on the guns blazing thing for a little bit."

I let go of the microphone, and then after a short silence, it crackled to life.

"You are a walking corpse."

Another Russian-accented voice.

I turned and looked into Konstantin's dead eyes. And then I realized where I'd seen the tattoo before. It had been in a picture in a magazine. An article about human rights abuses by Russian private military companies in Africa. It was on the shoulder patch of a contractor for the Bruckner Group. And they were seriously bad news. They did the business that was too dirty even for the GRU and had been established by a weapons-grade hardcase named Ilya Balandin, who'd named them after Hitler's second-favorite composer. Charming. Maybe I should have put a bullet in Konstantin after all. But it was too late for that now. I'd committed to my line; I had to see it through.

"Look," I said, "I know you're all tough guys. Well trained. I'm guessing you're all mercenaries of some sort, am I right?"

Another crackle, and then a different voice—deeper, but still a Russian accent. "As he said, you are a dead man."

One Russian merc on a yacht docked off Los Angeles was bad luck. Two was a hell of coincidence. Three? Three meant it was time to play a hunch.

"You guys are Bruckner Group," I said authoritatively into the radio. "You're a long way from home." I thumbed the mic for the response.

Dead air.

Bingo.

I was sure working security for Volkov was a cushy job, one that paid well and didn't, my current escapade aside, require that much real exposure. In other words, easy and lucrative. And Konstantin hadn't *meant* to show me that tattoo. Which meant that he didn't want anyone to know who he worked for. If you were a merc, you only took this kind of gig because you were moonlighting.

"So," I said into the microphone, "if I can assume you're all Bruckner, I'm also going to assume you understand me when I say this." I paused. I was about to try something dumb.

Again.

124

IT WAS ALL I COULD DO to not literally cross my fingers.

I held the radio close to my mouth. "Here's the deal. I'm working under Yankee White, category one orders. Please acknowledge that you understand what it means when I say my orders are Yankee White, category one."

I let go of the microphone and waited.

And waited.

Five seconds. Ten seconds. If these guys were the kind of international operators I figured them for, they'd know what I meant. They certainly weren't going to take an order from the United States government, but they'd also know that Yankee White meant the United States was going to come at them like a steamroller.

Konstantin stared at me, his anger morphing into something that I wasn't entirely sure I recognized.

Finally, after what had to have been at least fifteen seconds but felt like fifteen minutes, the radio crackled again.

"Go on."

I wanted to give a sigh of relief, but instead, I gave Konstantin my most intimidating stare and thumbed the mic again.

"You boys have to make a choice, right now. We have business with your boss. And if you know what Yankee White means, then you understand that there are two options here. You can either evacuate the boat with all the passengers and crew and go back to whatever hole you crawled out of, so that I can finish up this business with your boss, or you can stick around and wait for the cavalry to come and take your chances."

I was watching Konstantin as I spoke. It was like having a staring contest with an enraged statue. I lifted my thumb from the mic button.

He shook his head. "We can take you easily."

I had one move left.

"Okay, fair point." I triggered the microphone again. "Listen to me. When my boys get here to bag Volkov, they are going to be coming in hot. If you try to take this all the way, there's going to be a lot of lead flying around. What are the chances you're all going to make it out of here?"

I nodded at Konstantin and continued. "In about a couple of minutes, the fire alarm is going to go off. Get the crew and the guests to their boats. Then get your boys and walk away and you *all* get out alive."

This was the gamble. Konstantin had been upset when he thought I'd taken out one of his guys. And given that he hardly seemed like the sentimental type, I guessed that if his crew came home from an unsanctioned weekend job on foreign soil minus even one warm body there would be questions. Balandin wasn't the sort of employer who'd let a misstep like that slide. But Balandin was also smart enough not to want his men to engage in direct military conflict with the United States. That wasn't ideal for business, and I was offering them a way out.

The radio crackled. "Let us speak to Konstantin."

"I'm going to uncuff him now."

I looked at Konstantin, and he nodded. I kept my pistol on him, and then uncuffed him. For the blink of an eye, I thought he was going to make a move, but then he just held out his hand for the radio.

He pressed the talk button and said, "Stand down. We are leaving."

I had to pretend that I hadn't been holding my breath.

Konstantin let go of the button and looked at me. "His bedroom is a steel box, once he hit that panic button . . ."

"I know. He's locked up nice and snug in his saferoom."

I almost smiled. There was a part of me that couldn't believe that they had fallen for it, except, I realized, I'd more or less told them the truth. Except for the part where I had backup. Now, I thought, all I had to do was figure out how to smoke Volkov out of his hole.

Konstantin held the radio to his mouth, hesitated, then lowered it. "*My* men will do what I tell them, but . . ."

It took me a second, but I got it. Now that things were slipping out of his control, he couldn't take the chance that anyone would talk—Volkov included. He and his men were going to walk out of here alive, but he needed to make sure nobody followed. "How many?"

"Two. The man you called Cleary, and another. So now only one."

"The other man, anything I need to know?"

"We don't exactly take tea with Volkov's creatures. Think what you want about what we do, but at the end of the day we are"—he searched for the right word in English—"*pragmatic*. This other man is something different. He will come for you."

"Noted," I said. "Now, you ready?"

"We will leave, but we will not forget this," Konstantin said.

I didn't answer. It was a problem for another day. I just gestured with the gun.

Konstantin stepped out into the hallway and pulled the fire alarm.

125

IT TOOK THE BRUCKNER CREW seven minutes to clear the entire boat.

Turns out they were efficient when it came to beating the retreat.

I used the time to take out the first aid kit and deal with the cut Cleary had opened on my forearm. It was fifty-fifty on if I needed stitches, but for now, butterfly bandages, gauze, and a generous dosing of medical tape would have to do.

For a couple of seconds, there was a small part of me that was paranoid that the Bruckner guys had stayed behind to set an ambush.

No, they were gone.

But not the other guy.

If he was anything like Cleary, I didn't want to let him get the drop on me.

I jumped out of the office and into the hallway, pistol out, spinning quickly to cover all the angles, and . . . nobody was there.

Big ship. I was going to run into him sooner or later, but with the size of Volkov's yacht, there was a chance it would be later.

The fire alarm was obnoxiously loud in the corridor, so I popped through the door into the lounge outside Volkov's bedroom.

I ignored Cleary's motionless body on the floor and stared at Volkov's door.

I was so busy trying to get rid of the security team, crew, and guests after I shot Cleary, that I had not thought ahead to actually *getting into* Volkov's room.

I had to hurry.

And I had hurry around the ship with Volkov's lone remaining hired gun trying to finish me off.

I didn't have explosives, and I didn't have any of the tools I would normally have had with me if I knew I needed to get into a hardened steel box. There was almost certainly a well-equipped workshop somewhere on the yacht, but it would be designed for repair work, not to break into a saferoom. I supposed I could get in through the floor of Volkov's room—or the ceiling of the room below him—but I couldn't figure out how to do that quickly without explosives.

There was a weapons locker in the security office, but even though it was well stocked for a civilian vessel—there were smoke bombs, flash-bang grenades, tactical shotguns, assault rifles, pistols, and a couple of waterproof duffel bags stuffed with odds and ends—there was no demolition equipment.

And it wasn't like I could call Noor and put a special order in for something exotic to be delivered in the next half hour. I mean, with advance notice, Noor could get me pretty much whatever I needed, but this wasn't that kind of situation.

I was limited by what was on the yacht, and even if I had all the time in the world to search, I was pretty sure I wasn't going to stumble across a supply of C4 or a bucket full of . . . unless I figured out some kind of homemade . . .

I had an idea.

I was going to have to gamble that Volkov wouldn't try to slip out of the saferoom while I did my work. The fire alarm was still blaring, and it had been less than ten minutes since I'd shot Cleary; Volkov would do the smart thing, stay inside his impenetrable box until somebody assured him the threat was gone. As long as I could avoid the other guy, I didn't have to worry while I was scavenging.

I stepped into the corridor.

And I almost got my head blown off.

126

I HEARD THE WHINE OF THE BULLET zip past my ear as I jerked back. I ended up on my ass, back in the lounge, feeling very, very stupid.

I didn't have time for this. I knew the response from outside authorities would be slow, but it wouldn't be indefinitely slow.

I thought for a second about the hallway. In this part of the ship, it was straight and long, maybe fifty feet. I was closer to one end than the other, but I still had to get out the door and from there sprint about ten feet before I could get out of the line of fire. Two, three seconds of exposure.

But all that would do is trade my pinned-down position for a game of cat and mouse. There was no way I could carry out my plan and get to Volkov while his man was out here hunting me. Either the guy would get the drop on me, or I'd have to be so careful that I'd run out of time.

I had to take care of this now.

All the doors in the hallway were flush, so there weren't any pockets to shelter in. There were some paintings hanging on the walls, and I was pretty sure there was a fire extinguisher hanging at either end—kind of ironic given that I had used the fire alarm as an excuse to clear the boat—but otherwise it was a shooting gallery. And the longer I stayed in here, in the lounge, the more likely it was that next time he wouldn't miss. He could stay protected by the corner at the end of the hallway, but there was no place for me to hide. And no way to distract him.

Unless . . .

I looked around the room.

Ugh.

Cleary's body was literally deadweight. Even after I'd killed him, he was still making my life difficult.

It took some effort, but I got him up and over one shoulder. I readied the pistol in my free hand and shuffled as close to the door to the hallway as I could get without exposing myself.

Three, two, one.

I dumped Cleary's body through the doorway. As soon as he cleared the threshold, I heard the man shoot.

While he tracked low, taking the bait and shooting at Cleary's body, I went high: I whipped smoothly around the doorframe, keeping as much of my body protected as possible. I aimed for the muzzle flash.

I missed with my first shot.

Which gave him time to recalibrate.

As I squeezed the trigger a second time, I felt the sting of debris from the bullet hitting the wall next to my head, but I kept my aim true.

It was a hell of a shot.

He fell with part of his body obscured by the corner, but he went down with a fierce adherence to gravity that told me everything I needed to know.

With the last man dead, it was down to me and Volkov.

127

I GAVE MYSELF TEN SECONDS to get it together. The hall echoed from the ringing alarm, lights blinking.

After the gunfight, I was absolutely sure Volkov wasn't going to venture out of his little hidey-hole while I was off rummaging around for the materials I needed. For good measure, however, I took Cleary's gun and fired a few shots into the wall of the lounge.

Still, even with Volkov tucked away, I didn't have unlimited time. I closed my eyes and recalled the schematics I'd looked at in Volkov's office, double-checked my memory against the map and directory on the wall, then I hustled down to the service area, in the bowels of the ship.

The door to the engine room was unlocked, and it gave way to a surprisingly cavernous space that had none of the luxury finishes I'd seen everywhere else.

First things first: I found the control for the automatic fire suppression system. It was an easy-to-find valve, helpfully labeled with instructions telling me to ensure the valve was turned fully clockwise to ensure "proper operation and maximum fire safety." I turned it counterclockwise.

The engine room, though large, was full of odds and ends. In my experience, most mechanically minded people were either pack rats, refusing to throw anything away in case it might turn out to be useful someday, or desperately neat and allergic to clutter. Fortunately for me, the engineer on board Volkov's yacht was the former.

Much to my delight, I found a large rubber bin full of rusty nails, screws, and rusted bits of metal of indeterminate age. The bin was about the size of a checked suitcase. It was heavy enough that I had to lift with my knees.

I was sweating and out of breath by the time I got it to the kitchen.

It was a small kitchen by the standards of industrial kitchens, but it was enormous for a kitchen on a yacht. There was a Hobart mixer in one corner, and I dumped in as much of the rusty scrap as would fit. I turned it on.

It made an ungodly racket.

While the mixer was running, I rummaged until I found a huge roll of aluminum foil. I was once again helped by the fact that this wasn't somebody's home, but a kitchen designed for catering.

I started tearing off strips of aluminum foil and dumped them into a food processor. I turned it on high, and as the blade whirred—and as the Hobart mixer thumped and jangled and groaned away, banging at the scrap metal—I kept feeding bits of aluminum foil into the processor. After a couple of minutes, I had a generous amount of aluminum dust.

Then I went over to the mixer and turned it off.

The fire alarm sounded like the sweet singing of angels after the racket of seventy pounds of scrap metal roiling in an industrial mixer.

I pulled all the solid pieces of metal scrap from the mixer's bowl and looked at what was left: a pile of powdered rust. There wasn't as much as I'd hoped. I figured, packed tight, it would be about the size of a standard household brick. But it would have to do.

I grabbed an eight-quart polycarbonate food storage bin holding some peppers and dumped it out on the floor. It took me another minute to find a scale. I put the storage bin on top of the scale and pushed the tare button to zero out the weight.

Using a spatula and a frying pan, I reached into the Hobart mixing bowl and started scooping the powdered rust into the polycarbonate bin. Once I'd gotten all the rust out of the mixer, I looked at the scale. A whisker more than two and a half kilos of rust, which was better than I'd been expecting based on the volume.

Though, if I was being honest, I didn't really know how much I'd need. This was a wing and a prayer territory.

With two and a half kilos of rust, the math on the aluminum was easy. I needed one part aluminum to four parts of rust. I hit tare on the scale again, then poured the aluminum dust from the food processor in until I'd added a bit more than six hundred grams of aluminum dust to the rust, for a grand total of nearly three-and-a-quarter kilograms.

Next, I took a wooden spoon and mixed the rust and aluminum together inside the polycarbonate bin. Then I scoured through the fridge and pantry for a couple other ingredients that would amp everything up, took a wild guess at what would work to bring it all together into a moldable kind of putty, and stirred the whole kit and caboodle for another minute or two. It ended up more like a kind of dough than a putty, but I was pretty sure it would work.

Finally, I grabbed a butane kitchen torch—the kind a chef uses to make the crust on a crème brûlée or put a sear on something—and headed back upstairs to Volkov's office.

I checked my watch. It took me about half an hour from shooting Cleary to getting back to Volkov's office with my polycarbonate bin full of rust and aluminum. With any luck, I still had some time left.

I looked at the ship's plans in the binder again, and then carefully paced it off until I was sure I was right on top of Volkov's bedroom.

Then I gently molded my "dough" of powdered aluminum and rust into a thick rope and formed it on the floor into a circle a bit bigger than a manhole cover.

And then I fired up the butane torch.

IRON OXIDE IS JUST the fancy name for rust.

Four parts of iron oxide dust mixed with one part aluminum dust gives you thermite.

Thermite is wonderful. It burns at a temperature of around four thousand degrees.

And it will turn steel into a molten mess.

But thermite is also dangerous as hell. If you get it on your skin, it will burn through to the bone, and then it will keep burning. And once you've got thermite lit, it's almost impossible to put out. It will burn underwater. It will burn until it's done burning.

Thermite is stable because it takes great heat to ignite. In a lab, you'd probably use magnesium. But if you don't have a lab—for instance, if you're stuck on a yacht and in a hurry—a professional butane kitchen torch will do the job.

I MADE A QUICK TRIP down to the security office and rummaged through the weapons locker, grabbing a few items I'd seen earlier, before heading back up. Next, I filled the polycarbonate kitchen bin I'd been using to carry the thermite with cold water. Finally, I grabbed a fire hose and tied it off securely, testing to make sure it wouldn't come undone once I put my weight on it.

And then, I fired up the butane torch and lit the thermite.

It took a few seconds for the thermite to ignite, but once it did, it went fast, in a dazzling sparkle of light and heat.

At least I didn't have to worry about setting off the smoke alarm since it was already going off.

More quickly than I would have expected, the thermite ring burned through the floor of the office and then through the steel of the saferoom. It fell through to the floor of Volkov's bedroom in a sort of pinched-off oval, still burning bright. The edge of the hole dripped liquid steel in a brilliant red rain. The saferoom must have had its own ventilation system, because the smoke from the burning thermite moved swiftly sideways, as if pulled by an invisible hand. And, as I watched, curious to see how long the thermite would burn— thermite burned fiercely and quickly, but I'd also prepared a ludicrous amount—it cut a hole in the floor of Volkov's bedroom too.

Which was something I hadn't thought through. If there had been anybody below, they would have been immolated. As far as I could tell, there was still a small amount of thermite burning on the floor below Volkov's bedroom, two floors below me, and the molten steel that had melted from the ceiling of his saferoom glowed with a dangerous beauty. It was mesmerizing.

My curiosity almost got me killed: there was the blam of a gunshot and the whing of the bullet's ricochet.

I jerked my head back out of view.

Evidently, Volkov had a pistol.

Making sure to stay out of view from below, I carefully poured the cold water from the polycarbonate bin around the edge of the hole I'd burned in the ceiling of Volkov's steel box. The water sizzled, turning to steam at first, before the metal cooled enough to touch.

"Hey," I yelled down. "I don't suppose you want to just come out with your hands up?"

I was answered with another gunshot.

Between that and the fire alarm, I figured I was going to have ringing ears for a week. Which was still better than what Volkov was about to experience.

I pulled out the flash-bang grenade that I'd snagged from the weapons locker, removed the pin, dropped it through the hole, and then mashed my hands over my ears and squished my eyes shut.

130

I USED THE TIED-OFF FIRE HOSE AS A ROPE, climbing down into Volkov's bedroom. I had to be careful, because aside from the hole in the floor courtesy of the thermite that had fallen through the ceiling, there was a puddle of melted steel still smoking on the carpet. I touched down, tiptoeing around the hole and red-hot steel. A plume of smoke came from the deck below Volkov's bedroom.

The flash-bang grenade had done its job: Volkov was on his knees, rocking back and forth, with one hand rubbing his eyes and using a finger on the other hand to dig into his ear. His pistol was on the ground beside him.

I took the pistol and chucked it through the hole in the floor.

The ventilation system in the saferoom seemed to be keeping up with the smoke, but as I looked down through the hole, I realized that maybe dropping the pistol down there hadn't been the smartest idea. Whether it was the last gasp of burning thermite, or the molten steel, something had started a fire below us.

But that wasn't my present concern. I walked over to Volkov and nudged him in the forehead with my pistol. He managed to open his eyes, and I took a few steps back, careful not to accidentally and idiotically fall through the hole in the floor.

Volkov didn't startle at the sight of a man pointing a gun at him. His eyes were watering, and his voice was too loud—an aftereffect of the flash-bang—but he simply looked at me, took in the situation, including the smoke wafting up from the hole in the floor, and said, "What do you want?"

What I wanted to do was squeeze the trigger.

But I didn't.

Instead, I said, "Do you know who I am?"

"Should I?"

Against my own will, I was impressed. He was incredibly calm. I might as well have been one of his maids asking if he needed more towels.

"The painting in the lounge." I motioned to the locked door of his bedroom. "The Degas."

Volkov rubbed his eyes again. Then he said, "I take it that you are one of the thieves who helped procure it for me. Is that correct?"

He was quick.

I nodded, and he continued, "Then, am I to assume that you are here because you are still upset that you did not get paid for your services?" He was either starting to recover from the flash-bang or he was a very good actor, because he gave a dismissive wave. "Fine. We can settle this now. I have several million dollars in cash on board. What you were owed, and then some. Or, if you prefer, I can simply wire it to you."

I scoffed.

He eyed me. "No? Am I wrong? You aren't one of the people I hired? I cannot think of any other reason why you would care about the Degas. It has meaning to me, but . . . Well, did I hire you or not?"

"Actually, you've hired me twice." I reached into my pocket with my free hand, dug out the ring box, and opened it to show him the cipher. "Do you know what this is?"

He tilted his head, squinting. He was having trouble focusing, and at first, he didn't understand. And then he did.

He lit up with greed.

"Ah. I'm prepared to pay quite a bit more for that item in your hand. How does . . . thirty million dollars sound?"

"Thirty million?" I held it out, over the hole in the floor. Down below, I could see the flicker of actual flames cutting through the rising smoke. In the saferoom, there was the first hint of a haze. "Nah. Thirty million isn't enough. Maybe I'll just let it burn."

The heat coming off the thermite, even at the height of my hand, was enough that I pulled it away.

"Forty million."

"See, here's the thing. You've hired me two times, and two times you decided that it made more sense to just have me killed than to pay me."

He shrugged. "You don't become as rich as I am by paying full price if you can avoid it. I assure you, it was not meant as an insult. It was simply a business decision. Why would I pay any tradesman full price?"

I could feel the ache in my jaw as I clenched my teeth. It was all I could do not to shoot him and end it here and now, damn the consequences. But I wanted answers. I wanted to know why this man had ruined my life. I snapped the ring box shut.

"Why?" I asked.

His face stayed blank. "Why, what?"

There was a hissing sound from below. I risked taking my eyes off Volkov for another glance. Whatever was below us sure seemed flammable.

I gave my full attention to Volkov. Which was difficult knowing that the boat underneath me was on fire, but still, I had priorities.

"Why did you think there wouldn't be any consequences? What made you decide it was okay to just try to kill me instead of following through on the deal? Why did you think you could just get away with that?"

Volkov considered me, and then he did something unexpected: he laughed.

131

IT WAS A DRY LAUGH, that then turned into a cough. The ventilation system in the saferoom was starting to struggle to keep up with the smoke.

After a few seconds, he said, "Before I answer, I must ask *you* a question. What about you?"

I was taken aback. "What about me? What do you mean, what about me?"

Volkov said, "You are so aggrieved. So *righteous*. You are a *thief*. As if I did something you would not have done, as if there is morality in your life where there is none in mine."

"I—"

He waved his hand, cutting me off. "How is what you do any different than what I have done? I have *betrayed* you? You, a thief, lecturing me on what is right and wrong?"

I hesitated. "We had a deal," I said.

He laughed again, shorter, rougher, but with true amusement. And scorn. He was dripping with it.

"I did nothing that you would not have done if the situation was reversed. You are so sure that you are right, and I am wrong. You are a thief; I am a billionaire. The only difference is scale. We are the same, you and me. The same."

I could feel the weight of the pistol in one hand, the lightness of the cipher in the ring box in the other. "Bullshit."

Volkov put his hands flat on the floor and leaned forward. "We both take what we want. There is no difference. None. I offer you money. Take it and let me go," he said, gesturing at the door. "You want money, now take the money."

"We're not the same," I said. But then, suddenly, I wasn't so sure. Greaves had said something similar, that there was no real difference between my dad and Volkov, that they both belonged in prison. Except it wasn't true. It couldn't be. The man in front of me was the reason why Ginny was in a coma.

"We're not the same," I said again.

Volkov smirked and then wagged a finger at me. "You point a gun at me, but that is not why you are here. You are here because of that," he said. He pointed at the ring box. "Did you come by it honestly? No. It was something you wanted, and so you took it."

We both startled at the sudden *bang* from below. It was the pistol I'd taken from him and dropped through the hole. The fire was igniting the bullets.

A sign that I'd overstayed my welcome. But I wasn't done with Volkov yet.

Another bullet went off, but I ignored it, as did Volkov. I stuffed the ring box back into my pocket, and took a step forward, keeping my own pistol level. "It was a job," I said. "Tell me why I shouldn't just shoot you now?"

"If you shoot me, you will have nothing. Is that what you want?"

Perhaps my face answered his question in a way he didn't like, because his tone changed, smoothed out. "As I said, no offense was intended," he continued. "What happened was unfortunate, but it was, as I have mentioned, simply a business decision. Take the money I'm offering in exchange for what you hold in your hand," he said, gesturing toward the ring box. "And then we shall both live, as they say, happily ever after."

He looked past me, and I looked as well. The smoke coming through the hole in the floor had thickened, and I realized there was a layer of it pushing against the ceiling of the saferoom. Even with the ventilation system and the hole the thermite had punched through the ceiling to let me into the saferoom, it wouldn't be long before we were overwhelmed. With the fire suppression system turned off, the fire below must have been spreading. Growing.

I wasn't sure how much time we had left.

I thought about Greaves's story about Volkov. Cutting off and mailing body parts from the children and grandchildren of a competitor—plus, apparently, some random woman's head—was a "business decision." And he didn't seem to have any compunction about blackmailing a sitting president either. I didn't have a lot of faith that if I agreed to take his money, my "ever after" would last more than a few weeks.

"Shall I tell you a story?" he asked.

"By all means," I said. If he wasn't going to act as if time was a factor, why should I?

"Recently, a man came to me complaining that I owed him something. Perhaps I did, perhaps I did not, it doesn't matter. But I wanted to be fair. I am a fair man," he said earnestly, as if it mattered if I believed him. "I offered him a sum. Not as much as I am willing to offer you, but it was a substantial amount."

"How much are you offering me?"

"Perhaps fifty million dollars would serve as an appropriate apology."

"You think that's my price? You think fifty million dollars, and all is forgiven?"

Volkov considered. "It is less than I offered to this other man. He said no to the money I offered him."

"Let me guess," I said. "You had him killed."

"No," Volkov said. "Not him. But he had three children. And after he said no, after he disrespected me, I brought him to a building where . . . how do you say? A room for killing cows?" Volkov shook his head. "It does not matter. But I had caused the man's three children to be brought there and tied up, and I showed this ungrateful man his children and my pistol. I told him the pistol had three bullets in it, and if he chose one of his children, I would only use one bullet. But if he chose none, I would use all three bullets. And then I gave him five minutes to decide, one child or all of them."

He finished, and then it was *my* turn to burst out laughing.

"What, I'm supposed to just roll over and show you my soft belly now?" I said, still chuckling. "Please, *please* tell me that story doesn't work on people," I said.

A hummingbird smile flitted across Volkov's face. "You'd be surprised," he said. "Once you cultivate a certain reputation, people believe anything."

"How about the truth?" I said.

132

VOLKOV CONSIDERED ME. "The truth? No. I did not make that man choose between one child or all three. But does the truth matter when I am willing to offer you fifty million dollars? Fifty million dollars is quite an apology. But then again, you seem quite . . . I am not sure how you managed to overcome my guards and . . ." He trailed off again, glancing first at the hole in the ceiling and then at the hole in the floor. He waved away some of the smoke in front of his face and coughed. "Well," he continued, "you are a resourceful gentleman."

Another one of his bullets exploded in the fire below, and then a second. Volkov flinched at both, and for the first time, I could see the hesitation, the uncertainty on his face.

"All of this," he said, "over a painting."

"Why?" I asked.

I turned and strode to the bedroom door. I unlocked it, keeping an eye on Volkov, and threw it open. We both had a clear view through the doorway and to the wall where the Degas hung. I pointed.

"Why *this* painting? Why hire us to steal it when you could have easily bought whatever you wanted?"

Volkov gave me what could only be defined as a polite smile, as if I was a child he was humoring, as opposed to a man pointing a gun at him. "But I *did* buy what I wanted. I bought your services so that I could acquire this painting." He stared at it, squinting, lost in thought just for a tick, before continuing. "Not legally, perhaps, but I wanted *this* painting. Why should I not have what I want? Exactly what I want."

I didn't say anything. Because it was true. He could have *anything* he wanted. Forget the Degas hanging in the lounge, or the other paintings in his office. Forget the yacht and his vacation homes and his private jet. He'd spent billions of dollars on the last election. He as good as owned the president. He was the kind of man who could change the laws. No wonder he didn't think they applied to him.

Volkov closed his eyes. It wasn't fear. He wasn't closing his eyes in the face of my pistol. He didn't seem to care that a gentle squeeze—the trigger was weighted for less than five pounds—would turn his skull into a dark, wet, empty cavern.

He said, "I look at that painting, and I think of my mother."

"Your mother?" I took a step forward. The smoke caught in my throat, and I had to cough to clear it. I said, "You had us steal that painting because of your mother?"

Even with the wail of the fire alarm, I could hear the crackling of the fire below.

Volkov sighed. "She was not a happy person. She was warm, at least that is how I remember her, and she loved me, but she was not happy. She died before I was old enough to know her well, but even as a child I could tell that she was unhappy."

He was quiet for a second, even as noises surrounding us started to seem louder. I could hear something popping below, the growl of the fire, the groan of metal expanding. But Volkov was apparently oblivious to whatever external noises there were, because he said, "It was as if the blinds were always drawn in whatever room she inhabited. But she was a ballet dancer. She was from Nebraska, but still, she was a ballet dancer. With the Boston Ballet. From Nebraska to Boston. Boston, of all places. Did you know she was a dancer?"

He didn't wait for me to answer. He waved his hand languidly, gesturing at the Degas hanging in the other room. He was still on his knees, but there was something almost dignified about him. "She was not the principal dancer," he said. "Nothing more than a member of the company, really, but I remember visiting her backstage before she performed. I was young. Very young. But in those minutes before she went onstage, it was as if somebody raised the blinds. She was filled with light. As she prepared herself to dance, my mother became a different person entirely, as if . . ."

He coughed and then pinched the bridge of his nose. Under my feet, I felt something shift, move. I wondered how far the fire had spread. And I suddenly recalled the layout of the boat I'd studied in the binder in Volkov's office. At some point, the fire would reach . . .

I was running out of time.

But Volkov seemed to think he had all the time in the world. I wondered what he thought was going to happen. If he expected his men, or the police, or *somebody* to come bursting in to save him. He'd lived for so long with so much money and power that maybe he couldn't conceive of me holding his life in my hands.

He opened his eyes, and he pointed through the door. "The painting reminds me of that moment, the moment between preparing and doing." He lowered his arm. "But that was a long, long time ago."

He stopped talking and just stared at me, and I was shocked: he had tears welling up in his eyes.

"As I said, that was the past. None of it matters now, does it?" he said. "You will kill me, or you will not kill me. In enough time, time soon enough, you will be dead, I will be dead. That is inevitable. But the painting . . ." He closed his eyes in a long, slow blink, raising one hand up and pointing lazily through the door again, almost as if his hand was a gun. "We will be gone, but the painting will remain. That is the power of art, perhaps, because I cannot explain . . ." He trailed off, sorrow filling his voice, sorrow filling the silence.

For an instant—but just an instant—I let the gun waver. I felt almost sorry for him.

And then he spoke again, finishing his thought. "This painting, it reminds me of my mother. It reminds me of what I have lost. Of what can never be recovered."

I didn't say it out loud. I didn't tell him that the painting didn't remind me of what I'd lost, of what could never be recovered.

No, it reminded me of what *he had taken from me.*

"So," Volkov said. "Let us make a deal. How much money do you want? How much will it cost me to fix this?"

I closed the gap between us, cutting through the smoke with a sudden viciousness. I clubbed him with the pistol, knocking him out.

133

I HIT HIM AGAIN, HARD. And then again. And again.

Too many times.

How much would it have cost Volkov to fix this? There was no amount of money he could have offered me that was worth my sister, no dollar amount that could have bought back even a single day that had disappeared.

I dropped the bloody pistol next to his body and walked from his bedroom into the lounge.

134

THE SHIP WAS NOTICEABLY LISTING as I strode into the lounge.

The automatic fire suppression system would have put out the blaze, and if there was a crew on board, they could have closed doors to seal the fire off from oxygen. But I was the only living being on board, and I'd made sure to turn off the fire suppression system.

It was only a question of time now.

I stared at the Degas and thought about what Volkov said, that the two of us were not so dissimilar: we were both men who took what we wanted. And Greaves had said a similar thing about my father. I wanted to say they were both wrong, that they didn't know what they were talking about, but I wasn't sure it was true. Was it enough that I lived by a certain kind of code, that I believed in honor between thieves?

I knew what my dad would say, and what Ginny would have said if I could ask her, but I didn't know my own answer. Not anymore.

But there were two things I knew for sure: the first was that Volkov was dead and gone while I was still breathing. And the second was that I was too damned tired to think about the question anymore. It was time to go.

I pulled the cipher out of my pocket and bounced it in the palm of my hand.

I was just about to throw it into the bedroom to burn with Volkov's body when I had second thoughts. I stepped out into the hallway. Thick, dark smoke crawled across the ceiling. I had to duck down slightly to get clean air.

I went into the security office across the hall from Volkov's suite and pulled two of the waterproof duffel bags from the weapons locker. I dumped their contents on the ground, and then went back into the lounge. As I did, the boat shuddered, and the floor seemed to drop a few inches, making me stagger.

I caught my balance, and then searched quickly for Cleary's knife. There was still blood on the blade from where he'd tagged me.

I yanked the Degas off the wall and put it down flat on the carpet. I used the knife to pry off the frame and remove the canvas. Then I rolled it up and put the painting inside one of the duffels. I dropped the cipher inside with it, closed it up, and then stuffed that duffel inside of the second one. I was hoping the duffel bags were as waterproof as advertised.

The terrace door was still open, and as I stepped out onto the balcony, the boat shifted again. I stumbled into the railing and dropped the duffel bag at my feet.

I took the burner phone from my pocket and texted HE'S DEAD to the number Greaves had given me. Then, without waiting for a response, I chucked the phone into the ocean. I didn't see or hear it splash. All I had left in my pockets were my lockpicks and the roll of cash I'd brought.

I pulled off my shoes and threw those in one by one. Then, I picked up the double-bagged Degas and dropped it overboard. It fell lightly, and then bobbed on the surface of the water, the air trapped inside the duffel bag keeping it afloat.

Finally, I climbed up over the railing and dove in.

135

I SURFACED.

Breathing in the night air made me feel like a new man.

I took a second to orient myself and find the duffel bag, and then I looped one of the handles over my shoulder and started swimming.

After a hundred yards or so, I looked back. The yacht was sitting cockeyed. It was leaning at least fifteen degrees starboard, and I thought the stern was higher than it should have been relative to the bow. I could see a flickering lick of fire coming out one of the balconies on the side of the ship.

I wanted to put some distance between myself and the burning yacht, but I thought I heard sirens. I couldn't tell if they were coming from Coast Guard ships running across the water or if they were from the shore, so I swam parallel to the shoreline.

I had probably swum close to a quarter mile when it finally happened: the fire inside the yacht reached the fuel tank.

The diesel ignited with a whoomp that flew across the surface of the ocean and stole my breath.

I turned to look. The yacht was engulfed in flames, a fireball reaching two hundred yards into the sky. I could see a dark chasm in the middle of the ship, and then, with a groan that could have been heard in Pasadena, the ship seemed to fold together. The bow and the stern both lifted at the same time, the middle pulling downward. And then, in less than ten seconds, the yacht slipped beneath the sea, leaving only a floating slick of burning diesel on the surface.

It was a beautiful sight to behold.

I SWAM PARALLEL TO THE BEACH for another ten minutes—far enough that I figured I'd be able to avoid any first responders—before heading toward land. When I got to shore, I walked up the sand and then found a car I could steal.

I dumped the car around the corner from a bar in Pasadena, and then, when the passing cabbie who stopped for me looked askance at a barefoot guy in damp clothes holding a duffel bag, I offered to pay in advance, peeling three hundred dollars off my roll of cash.

Greaves had gotten my message. By the time I got to my apartment, she'd called off the dogs. Unless she'd significantly upgraded her surveillance operations, I was no longer under observation.

The first thing I did once I was inside my apartment was text Uncle Charles and then Meg with the word SAFE from my phone. Then I shoved the duffel bag under my bed, stripped down, and dropped onto the mattress.

It was nearly four in the morning.

I was exhausted, but for the first time in a long time, I didn't feel like I was weighed down.

I fell asleep immediately.

I WOKE UP TO KNOCKING AT MY DOOR.

Instinctively, I reached behind my nightstand, where I had a perfectly legal, registered SIG Sauer.

Except, if it was somebody who needed to be greeted with a pistol, I was doubtful that they'd knock.

I got out of bed, grabbed a pair of shorts and a T-shirt, and padded over to the door. I glanced at my wrist as I did. I'd slept for twelve hours.

I looked through the peephole. It was Taneesha.

I opened the door. "What's up?"

"Were you sleeping, Duke? It's the middle of the afternoon."

"Sorry, kid," I said. "I was out late."

She leaned over and picked a bag up off the floor.

It was the bag I'd left with Greaves. "I'm supposed to give you this," she said.

I took it, opened it, looked inside at all the lovely cash that was still in there, and did a little jig.

"This too," Taneesha said. She thrust out a sealed, padded envelope with my name written on it in neat block print.

"What's in it?"

By her reaction, I'd clearly asked the dumbest question of all time. "How am I supposed to know. It's got *your* name on it. I just dropped Maya at a friend's place and was walking back, and some lady stopped me and told me to give you that bag and envelope."

I took the envelope. There was something small and hard inside it. "Okay. Thanks."

"Duke?"

"Yeah?"

"Is everything . . . ? You know?"

I considered it. "Yeah. I know. And yeah, I think so."

She nodded. "Dad's making pizza for dinner tonight if you want to join us."

"Love to, but I've got a few things to take care of. Rain check?"

She agreed and I started to close the door, but then I stopped. I remembered what I'd thought of the night before, when I had been about to chuck the cipher into the ocean.

"Hey, Taneesha?" She stopped walking and turned around. "If I give you something for your computer, can you tell me what you think? It's important."

I left her in the doorway and then went into my bedroom. I pulled the duffel bag out from under my bed and opened it up. The duffel I'd stuffed inside was bone dry. I opened that as well, ignored the rolled canvas, and took out the ring box.

Then I opened the ring box.

It was . . . unimpressive. It was a simple USB drive. One of the micro-sized ones. No wonder it was in the ring box: otherwise, it would have gotten lost immediately.

I took the USB and brought it to Taneesha.

"What is it?" she said. "Other than the obvious."

"Got me," I lied. "Just, can you take a look at it and tell me what you can figure out? Do me a favor and keep it close, though. Probably not a good idea to let anybody else know you have this. And it might be full of viruses and stuff, so sandbox it well."

She assured me with all the utmost seriousness of a thirteen-year-old on a mission that she'd get to it after dinner.

138

I WENT BACK INTO MY BEDROOM and looked at the duffel bag holding the painting. Then I closed it up again and stuffed it back under my bed. In the unlikely event anybody broke into my apartment, they'd look for valuables in one of the safes. Under my bed seemed as secure of a place as any other I could think of.

I took a quick shower, rinsing off the salt water from the night before, and then I called Greaves's number.

Disconnected.

I bounced the envelope in my hand, and then, finally, I opened it. There were two things inside.

The first was a simple piece of cardstock with one single phrase written on it: "Not very subtle, but a deal's a deal."

Which made me laugh.

Because, yeah, I'd sunk a yacht off the coast of Los Angeles with one of the richest men in the world on board. That would probably make the news. Greaves was correct: it was not subtle.

The second was a car key fob. It had a sticky note attached to it, with a bonus scrawled across the paper.

I wondered if the bonus was despite or because of my lack of subtlety.

I grabbed my wallet, stuffed it with some cash from the bag Taneesha had just dropped off, and then went outside with the key fob. The truck it belonged to was parked three spaces down. A brand-new, full-sized, top-of-the-line pickup with an off-road package. There was even a surfboard rack already installed.

I started it up, figured out how to connect my phone, and then dialed Uncle Charles.

He picked up on the first ring.

"Duke? I got your voicemail, and then your text message, which, thanks, but I'm glad you called back," he said.

"How is she?"

"Your aunt? Oh, she's fine. Pissed off, but fine. The ventilator's out and doctors just upgraded her condition. They think another week or so in the hospital, and then a couple of weeks in a rehab facility, and then she'll be home. You know her. It would take a lot more than that to kill her. But your dad . . ."

I was holding my breath.

And then Charles said, "He's right here. Let me put him on."

A rustle, and then, "You know I spent the night in a hotel in West Hollywood getting babysat by the Marshals Service?" Even through the truck's speakers, I could hear the warmth in my dad's voice.

I couldn't help but grin as I said, "I hear you did a number on the mini-fridge."

"That's nothing compared to the room service bill," he said. His voice turned serious. "You okay?"

"Close enough to be within the margin of error," I said. "You?"

He didn't say anything for a few seconds, and then he cleared his throat. "Duke?"

"Yeah?"

"I know we've got plenty to talk about," he said, "but you did good, kid."

He paused again, and then he said it once more, as if he wanted to make sure I heard him clearly: "You did good."

139

WE CHATTED FOR A FEW MORE MINUTES, but both of us knew we couldn't talk freely on the phone. That was fine. I'd see him soon. But in the meantime, there was somebody else I needed to see.

I sat in my new truck in the parking lot for nearly an hour before I worked up the courage to go inside.

The attendant at the front desk greeted me with a big smile. "Hello, Duke. We haven't seen you in, gosh, has it been a full week? I was beginning to get worried about you. It's unlike you to go so long without coming to see your sister."

"All good," I said. Because it was as close to all good as it could ever be. "I was out of town for some business. Thanks."

I began to walk toward Ginny's room, but the attendant stopped me. "Oh, Duke, there's a note here that you're supposed to sign something when you came in. Do you mind?"

She pulled out a file folder and slid it over to me. "I've never seen an insurance policy with terms this generous." She winked conspiratorially. "Good for you. Those insurance companies are leeches. I say, if they're willing to pay, milk 'em."

Inside was a form indicating that we were switching Ginny's payment over to the "Clockwork Insurance Agency." Greaves sending a wink with the acronym.

I signed it, and then had a thought. I pulled out my phone. I logged in to my banking app. The previous week, when I'd opened the safe during the estate job, I'd had thirty-eight dollars in my account.

Now it was showing $500,038.

I thought of Volkov being so blasé about double-crossing me.

Greaves was a smart lady. A deal is a deal. Pay what you owe.

140

THE PHYSICAL THERAPIST WAS just finishing up when I got to Ginny's room.

I had no idea how much Paulie had been spending on Ginny's care, but she'd decided early on that cost was no obstacle; the best medical care that money can buy might not be able to get Ginny out of a coma, but it could keep her in as good of shape as possible. The physical therapist showed me a new gadget that she unwrapped from Ginny's arms. Electrical stimulation that was supposed to mimic muscle movement, so she wouldn't be crippled if—when—she woke up. Just one of dozens of things that Paulie had been paying for.

I felt good knowing that I'd taken those expenses off Paulie's plate. They were my responsibility, and I'd taken care of it. It wouldn't change Ginny's prognosis, but it was *my* burden to shoulder.

I waited for the physical therapist to finish packing up and leave, and then closed the door to the room.

I pulled a chair close and took Ginny's hand. She looked like she might wake up at any second. Except she didn't.

I don't know what I would have said if she did. I'm sorry? That didn't feel like that could cover everything that I needed to say. I wasn't sure what else there was to say, but "I'm sorry" didn't even come close to telling her how I felt. How tired I was of screwing up.

Instead, I told her everything that happened from the second Baker and Cleary approached me at the Market House. I told her about killing Volkov, and about Greaves following through on her deal. I told her all of it, including that Paulie was in the hospital, that

Dad was out of jail, that I had a lead on Janus, and that I had the Degas hidden in a duffel bag stuffed under my bed.

And I told her that I missed her.

And when I finished, nothing had changed. I was still alone.

I don't know what I'd expected. If I'd hoped for some sort of miracle. For something. Anything. But her eyes were still closed, and she hadn't given any indication that she'd heard or understood anything I'd told her.

I looked over at the picture of the two of us on her dresser. Curaçao. We were so young back then, but I wondered if my mother had known. If she'd had some sense of what was coming when she told me that Ginny and I had to watch out for each other.

There wasn't anything else for me to say, so I sat there quietly for a while, holding Ginny's hand, thinking about how there were some debts I would never be able to pay.

CODA

"DO YOU MIND IF I JOIN YOU?"

Greaves looked up from the papers she'd been reading, squinting. The sun was still rising, and I had it at my back. When she registered who it was, she showed honest surprise.

She wasn't expecting me.

It had been six weeks since I'd killed Volkov. I'd spent four of them in Hawaii with my dad in a rented condo near the beach. It was relaxing. We surfed and swam as my arm healed. Dad made me watch some old movies with him, and we mostly just decompressed and ate shrimp tacos. Meg came out for two of the four weeks, which made Dad even happier. I think he liked her more than he liked me.

Meg slept in her own room the whole time—we were in an "off again" phase—but the extra company was still nice. Beyond the first couple of days, I didn't even check the news to see if there was any new information discovered in the mysterious fire and subsequent sinking of Volkov's yacht with the billionaire still on board.

And then, when we got back home, I set about the business of tracking down Greaves. I checked the house in Silver Lake, of course, but a family in witness protection was living there. I hit a series of dead ends until I thought of something.

Greaves had told me that she majored in international political economy and business, and when I asked her if that had been a double major, she'd hesitated. There'd been something there. And then it took me a couple of days to dig up the memory of where she said she'd gone to college: Georgetown.

Every liar accidentally tells the truth sometimes.

Her last name wasn't Greaves—though I kept thinking of her as Greaves—but her first name was Erin, and she *had* gone to Georgetown. And she had run track. That was true too. And one of her majors was international political economy and business, but she'd lied about not having a double major. Maybe one of the reasons she'd done such a good job of playing me for the fool was because her other major had been theater.

She was a damn fine actress.

A little razzle-dazzle, some smiles, feigned surprise and outrage, a ticking clock, money, threats, promises. I'd fallen for the whole performance even though she *literally* told me all the shots I thought I was calling were pinned up by her. She could have won an Oscar.

Greaves was sitting outdoors at a café. We were in South Beach, Miami. The café was across the street from the beach. I wondered if she liked being near the ocean, or if she was just here for work.

The café was empty inside, and only three of the other dozen tables on the patio were occupied. A genteel old lady in a teal dress reading a book, a young couple who were both so attractive that they were hard to look at, and a middle-aged man staring listlessly at his laptop.

"Of course," she said. "Sit." She slid her right hand off the table and onto her lap, where I couldn't see it.

"It's not that kind of a visit," I said.

"We'll see."

"I just need you to answer a question," I said.

"Shoot."

I gave her the stink eye.

"Sorry," she said. "*I* thought it was funny."

It was. A little. I really did like her. Under different circumstances, I might have asked her to get a drink. But right now, I wanted her to solve something for me: "Was the entire thing a setup?"

"*That's* your question? I thought you were going to ask me how I figured out Volkov was the one who'd hired you to steal the Degas."

I thought warmly about the painting. It was still tucked under my bed.

But Greaves didn't have to know about that, so I said, "I already know the answer to that. You were the go-between for Volkov and Janus on the original job. Even if I had gotten to Janus, he couldn't have connected me directly to Volkov. You set everything in motion." I waited a second, and then I said, "Pick up your jaw."

"How did . . ."

"Now," I said, "answer my question."

Honestly, it was Meg who put two and two together. We'd gone through it time after time, and we only had two questions left: How had Greaves connected the dots, and how had Volkov found out about the cipher? Meg was the one who pointed out that the reason why I'd never been able to find out who had originally hired us to steal the Degas was because there was a firewall somewhere along the way. And it couldn't just have been Janus. Volkov was too rich and too famous. If Janus had been working directly with Volkov, he would have told *somebody*. Greaves was the cutout. And that person was the *only* person in a position to know. The cutout and Greaves had to be one and the same.

Greaves shifted and then seemed to come to a decision. I could see the muscles on the arm that was angled under the table tighten up.

"That's not a good idea," I said.

"Why? I can see both your hands. I shoot you, I'm gone before the cops even get near here."

I said, "Two reasons. The first is, there's no reason to shoot me. I'm not here for revenge. We took the Degas job knowing what it was. Volkov was the one who screwed us. Not you. And I'm betting you only set it up in the first place because you were looking for leverage on him." She squinted a little. A small nod.

I continued, "And I'm not here because I'm upset that you tricked me into doing your dirty work by killing Volkov for you."

She opened her mouth, and I said, "Ah, ah, ah. Don't bother. You said it yourself. Volkov was untouchable. He basically decided who got to win the last election. That's a lot of power for one man to have. There wasn't anything your boss could do about him. Even if he did have the cipher in his grubby little hands, you'd have to let him go. If Volkov went down, he'd sink the whole ship. And if he didn't go down, well, what if Volkov decided to back another horse? I'm sure your orders weren't anything overt. A wink and a nod and a nudge all the way down the line. I can't imagine your boss came right out and said Volkov was a problem that needed to be solved permanently. Because that's what you *really* are, right? A problem solver."

I saw the waitress walking our way and I waved her off. I wasn't planning on staying.

"You like to muddy the waters so much that it's impossible to see clearly. You're not CIA or FBI, and you're not just Yankee White or any of that bullshit. That stuff you fed me about economic terrorism was all just more crap. You're one hell of an actor, but your job wasn't watching the banks. Your job is dealing with problems like Volkov. You're just a straight-up fixer. And I was the fix."

She narrowed her eyes. "And what's the second reason?"

"What?"

"You're not here to kill me. Fine. Because you're right. I didn't have anything to do with screwing you and your sister over. I found out about it after it happened. Once I connected Volkov with Janus, Volkov ran Janus through Cleary, and I was out of the equation. I couldn't tell you where Janus is now even if I wanted to."

I didn't need her help with Janus, not with the information Paulie had given me, but the part about Cleary was new information. It made me feel even better about killing Cleary, though there was a part of me that wished he was still alive so I could kill him a second time.

Greaves continued, "But it was stupid of Volkov. He should have just paid you what you were owed. The thing is *I* paid you, and still, here you are, bothering me. My life would be a lot easier if you were just gone. So, Duke, if the first reason not to shoot you is because you aren't here to get revenge, what's the second reason I shouldn't shoot you?"

"Oh. That. Yeah, because I didn't come alone."

Greaves took a quick scan. There was nobody within fifty yards except for the other patrons of the restaurant. The old lady in the teal dress was apparently engrossed in her book, the gorgeous couple were engrossed in each other, and the middle-aged man with the laptop had his back to us.

"I don't believe you."

"You're going to have to trust me on that," I said. "Now, can we get back to the reason why I'm here?"

Greaves took another look: the middle-aged guy, the two beautiful people . . . and the older woman.

Who was my mentor, Helen MacDonald.

Helen had told me on the phone that if I needed her, she'd come, anytime, anyplace. And she had.

Helen put her book down. She moved the tablecloth discreetly, letting Greaves see the cold metal of the pistol pointed her way.

"I assure you," I said, "despite her age, Helen is an excellent shot. And she thinks of me like a grandson. She loves me more than her own nephew," I said, loudly enough that Helen could hear.

I added, "She won't hesitate to shoot you, if necessary, but if I'd come here to kill you, you'd be dead already. Now, why don't you put

your gun away and answer my question. Was the whole thing—all
of it—a setup?"

Helen lifted her book up again and went back to pretending to
read. Her pistol didn't waver. I was going to have to write her a very
nice thank-you note tomorrow.

Greaves had nerves of steel, because she slowly put her gun away
and then gave me her full attention, acting as if Helen wasn't even
there.

"No," Greaves said. "Not the first job. Like you said, I'm a fixer,
and Volkov was my job. He didn't know it was me; I was a cutout.
Sure, Volkov ran it through Cleary, but I played Janus, suggesting
you and your sister for the Degas thing. That's why Janus reached out
when he did . . . But *that* job wasn't a setup. I didn't expect Volkov to
burn you. I wasn't even thinking about you or your sister at the time.
You called it. All I wanted was to get some leverage on Volkov, but
even with me in the middle of the process, knowing almost every bit
of it, I couldn't get anything to stick on him.

"But the rest? Yeah. It was a setup. But it was messy. A lot of
improvising. The target was supposed to be the Russian security
services, but when you make a spiderweb, you can't always choose
what fly you catch." She looked away from me, blinked twice, looked
back. "When Volkov got involved, I saw an opportunity. The CIA
site was designed to be breached, and the rest of it, the safe, the
cipher, all deliberately leaked, all leaked to the Russians, and from
them to Volkov, pointing him in the only direction he could go,
which was to hire you. He needed the cipher to solve his problems,
and he needed you to crack the safe. I stacked the deck. I had the
ten, the jack, the queen, and the king. It was a big gamble, but all I
needed was my ace."

"Me."

"You were more of a wild card. And I had a hell of a time getting you to do what I wanted."

"Sorry."

"Are you?"

"Not really," I said. "Parts of it were fun."

A half smile. "Just because I manipulated you doesn't mean you can't enjoy what you do. I might have stacked the deck, but it was still a real game."

"Weren't you the one who told me to play the cards as they were dealt?"

Greaves shook her head. "Because *I* shuffled. It was a stacked deck, and when I couldn't stack it, I dealt from the bottom. You said it: I'm a problem solver. And Volkov was a problem that *I* couldn't fix."

"You're something special," I said.

"Yeah. I know," she muttered quietly, her voice full of sadness. She said, "Can I ask *you* a question now?"

"How did I get from there to here?"

She nodded.

I said, "I should have figured it out the second you let me walk out of the airport. You sold me so hard on the cipher being important that I was running all over the place, and it was the only thing I could see. I got distracted by the shiny thing right in front of me and didn't look at the details. But I figured it out when you let me take it to Volkov. If the cipher could really do what you said, you never would have taken the risk of letting him get his hands on it."

I didn't bother telling her that none of it came clear until I was already in Hawaii, relaxing on the beach, until I worked through it with my dad and Meg. And I didn't tell her I still had the USB drive. That Taneesha had dug into it and told me that the code on it was worthless once you broke it apart. The cipher was nothing more than beautiful gibberish.

I stood up.

"Duke," she said. Her voice was quiet, and even though she'd fooled me six ways to Sunday, the note of regret sounded genuine. "I'm sorry for playing you. But it worked out okay, didn't it? Paulie's out of the hospital. Your dad has a pardon. You've got a full bank account. Everybody gets to walk away happy, right?"

"Not Ginny," I said. "She doesn't get to walk away."

Greaves flinched.

I crossed the street and didn't look back.

Once I was on the beach, I took my shoes off and started walking down the sand, keeping the sun at my back.

I thought about what Greaves had said.

I wasn't wrong about Ginny, but maybe Greaves wasn't wrong either.

Volkov was dead, and for that, good riddance. Paulie would be doing physical therapy for a few more months, but she was back home. This morning, my dad was supposed to have breakfast with her and Uncle Charles instead of eating prison food for the foreseeable future. Ginny was being taken care of, and as for me?

I looked down at my thumbs and thought about Rick's confusion over whether or not he was supposed to rip them off or just break them.

Well, I suppose, as for me, I had the answers I wanted.

I was going to keep the Degas hidden under my bed for the time being, but I had plans for it.

Meanwhile, I had money in the bank. Sure, I was going to have to pay taxes, but it was enough to last for a long while. And I had a brand-new truck.

I was done with betting on sports. I had possibilities. I had choices.

I also had a lead on Janus.

And if nothing else, the forecast back home was calling for a straight week of good surf, and I didn't have a job to go to.

I didn't know if I was happy or not, but it was close enough.

THE END

ACKNOWLEDGMENTS

If it weren't for Bill Clegg, this book wouldn't exist.

Thank you to the entire crew at the Clegg Agency: Marion Duvert, Simon Toop, Julia Harrison, MC Connors, and Rebecca Pittel.

Thank you to Anna DeRoy at WME. No relation, but you're as kick-ass as Aunt Paulie.

One of the things you learn when you sell a book, is that it takes a lot of work to get a manuscript ready for publication. At Union Square & Co., thank you to Claire Wachtel, Barbara Berger, Alison Skrabek, Igor Satanovsky, Kevin Ullrich, Juliana Nador, and Sandy Noman, as well as Tim Green and Hayley Jozwiak.

And to my friends and family, old and new, you know who you are. All my love.